MYSTERY!

EX LIBRIS

The Other
Woman

The Other Woman

Jill McGown

St. Martin's Press
New York

ISBN 0-312-08868-X

First published in Great Britain by Macmillan London Limited.
First U.S. Edition: March 1993

The Other Woman

One

Melissa Whitworth shook hands and said thank you to the woman who had just told her that she was having an affair with her husband.

The powerful floodlights lent the late October sky an intense ice-blue glow; the trees that ringed the sports ground were thrown into relief, black against the almost ethereal light, still and silent.

The scattering of vehicles belonging to Stansfield Town's hardy, ever-optimistic, but limited support, were parked behind the still unfinished leisure complex in a small tarmacked area hidden from the main road by high, mist-enshrouded hedges. In the privacy of her car, Melissa blinked away tears. She was two weeks short of her thirty-third birthday; she checked herself in the mirror to see how she compared.

Her thin, oblong face was devoid of make-up save for what remained of the lipstick she had hurriedly applied before making her rendezvous; the cheeks were slightly pink, but only from the same anger that had prompted the tears. Her short brown hair was brushed back from her brow in a style that could withstand wind and weather and the office central heating. The woman she had just left was a make-up manufacturer's dream come true, a hairdresser's nest-egg incarnate, and ten years her junior.

Of course, she hadn't known that she was talking to her lover's wife; she had just been giving an interview to a local journalist. Melissa had always used a professional name, and the girl had no reason to suppose that she knew Simon from a hole in the ground. Melissa took the tape from her bag, and wrote the interviewee's name on the label, as she had done with all the others.

Sharon Smith. It had intrigued Melissa when Sharon had replied to the ad that she had placed in the personal column, asking:

Are you the Other Woman? This newspaper is doing a series of articles on marriage and morals, and would like to hear from women whose men belong to someone else. Your contribution would be held in the strictest confidence, and nothing will appear in print which could in any way identify you or your partner.

7

It had been Melissa's idea. Why should the woman's page – recently retitled 'Life' – always be about fashion and cookery, she had asked. Women had other things on their minds at times. At first, the editor had hummed and hawed, uncertain about it on several fronts. It might be seen to be encouraging immorality; it *would* encourage all sorts of nuts to contact them (it had); it was a little risqué for a local paper – more your Sunday stuff, or a TV special – Melissa had worked for too long on women's magazines, if you asked him; anonymity would have to be paramount – the paper might cover a large area, but in his opinion no area was too large for brawling women; it would have to be made absolutely clear that the paper was in no way condoning or condemning, merely examining the social manners and mores of the nineties . . . and so on, until he had talked himself into it.

The ad had appeared six weeks ago; to start with *only* the nuts had replied, but eventually a trickle of genuine replies had redeemed Melissa's reputation in her editor's eyes. By the time Sharon had responded, Melissa had been working on the wording for the next one: *Are you the Wronged Wife?* But her interview with Sharon had driven all thoughts of the series from her mind.

Sharon Smith. Melissa should, perhaps, have declared her interest, so to speak; Sharon might not know who she was, but she knew of Sharon. Simon had mentioned her, naturally, for she was his secretary, in the time-honoured fashion. But the universal enjoyment of a bit of gossip on which she was counting for the success of her series had made Melissa decide to see her. She was not, after all, a judge; she was more in the position of a priest. She would hear Sharon's confession, and if it was raunchy enough, bizarre enough, or touching enough, it would appear in the paper in heavy disguise; if not, it wouldn't. She would never have told Simon or anyone else.

But, as things turned out, Simon didn't need to be told. Melissa pushed the tape into the cassette recorder again out of a masochistic desire to hear her say it again, and listened to the woman whose unsuspected influence over Simon explained so many of the things which had worried and bewildered her over the past few months.

To start with it had just been another interview, different only in that Sharon did not present herself, as the others had, as the helpless victim of a doomed love; in answer to Melissa's standard query as to why a married man, she had spoken with a refreshing candour about the situation.

'*I give him what he needs, he gives me what I want.*'

'*And what is it that he needs?*'

8

'*The excitement. He says his life's always been too safe. Too tame. It adds spice if you risk being caught.*'

'*Don't* you *worry about being caught?*'

'*Me? Why should I? I'm not answerable to anyone.*'

'*But his risk is real?*'

Her own voice, still just interested because it was her job to be interested.

'*Oh, yes. He doesn't want to lose what he's got. It's a bit like kids playing chicken. You have to be running a real risk. And you have to wait longer and longer each time before you run across the road. It's like a drug, really.*'

'*So . . . what's in it for you? What is it that you want?*'

'*Him.*'

Sharon had smiled then. Melissa could see that smile again.

'*But he wants to hang on to his marriage?*'

Melissa heard her own voice, so confident and glib, asking the right question at the right time, looking for the offbeat, the interesting answer, the piquant situation that would make a good column.

'*Oh, that's all right. I prefer married men. Single men think they own you.*'

The silence was Melissa's now, hissing from the tape, as she had formulated her next question.

'*Love doesn't come into it, then?*'

'*He says he loves me.*'

'*And how do you feel about him?*'

Not a breath of wind stirred the still leaf-laden branches of the trees as the fog began to collect and gather and weave its way through the harvested fields with their regimented bales of corn, round the hedgerows, heavy with berries, rising up from the earth and the grass and the wide flat streets on the outskirts of Stansfield, insinuating itself through the semi-constructed buildings of the sports and leisure centre, to where Melissa sat reliving the moment, as though this time it might not happen.

'*I want him. And he needs me. He does have a problem with that. He wishes he didn't need me. I think sometimes he hates me.*'

'*Do you mean that? Sometimes he* hates *you?*'

'*Hates the need, anyway.*'

Melissa could see again the thoughtful look, then the brisk nod.

'*Hates me. Yes, sometimes. And himself. I don't know which of us he hates more when he feels like that. He feels guilty, I suppose.*'

'*And that doesn't bother you?*'

She could see again Sharon's shrug.

'It gives him a high. And you come down off a high, don't you? That's when he feels guilty. But it doesn't last.'

The conversation had been taking place in Melissa's car; it was as though Sharon hadn't left, as though she were still sitting there beside her. Melissa had asked her next standard question then.

'Why did you reply to the advertisement?'

'I just wanted to talk about it to someone. That's the drawback with married men. I don't like the secrecy. Not being able to mention him to your friends, or have him at the house.'

'I wondered about that. When you agreed to this interview, you suggested that we meet here – does that mean you can't have privacy at home?'

Melissa listened to the silence which had followed her question as the fog curled up at the car windows, like some silent creature trying to come in.

'I live with my mother, and my sister.'

'So where do you go for privacy?'

'The office, usually.'

Melissa switched off the tape, the pain even sharper now than when Sharon had originally said it.

The office. Not his office, or my office. The office. The shared office. It explained everything that she had found so baffling and so hurtful about Simon's attitude to her lately, all the things that had started going so disastrously wrong between them. And she felt foolish that it had never occurred to her, not once, not even after Sharon had answered the ad.

Sharon had said that she didn't know who Simon hated more, her or himself. But Melissa knew where she stood. Especially now that she knew, having had time to get her breath back, exactly what Miss Smith had really done.

'Yes, well,' said Mac, acutely aware that his landlady was listening to every word. 'It can't be helped.'

Donna apologised again, and he ran an embarrassed hand through thick but greying hair. 'Yes, right,' he said. 'Well, fine. I mean – don't worry about it. See you.'

He hung up, his hand resting on the receiver. If she hadn't wanted to come, why hadn't she just said? Damn it, he'd only asked her out for the evening. Easy enough to say no thanks. Well, that was that. He had to go; it was work. He left just as his landlady came to enquire if everything was all right, and closed the door behind him, affecting not to have heard the question.

The dampness invaded his bones as he walked along the quiet side-street to the main road, but he checked his automatically raised arm as the taxi went past; he wanted to walk, despite the weather. The first woman he'd asked out for years, and she'd stood him up. Well – as good as. He'd forgotten how to ask a woman out, that was the problem. He should have taken her for a drink at lunch-time or something first. But damn it, it was only an invitation to the opening of the new leisure and sports centre – hardly a big seduction number. Anyway, lunch-hours weren't long enough to go anywhere decent, not when you didn't have a car.

Once, there had been a time when not having a car would have been like not having legs; he wouldn't have known how to get from A to B without one. But now he was getting used to it; he rather liked walking. Even in the fog. Perhaps especially in the fog, which folded itself round him, secret and dark, and he could simply disappear.

The hum of conversation in the executive box was soothingly pleasant when Mac finally popped his head round the door, trying to be unobtrusive. It didn't work.

'Mr McDonald! Glad you made it. I'd just about given up on you – thought the weather had put you off.' Parker snapped his fingers as the girl passed, and Mac was instantly offered hospitality. He took a soft drink, and tried to retire to a safe distance, but once again, it was not to be. He found himself being introduced to Lionel Evans, Parker's solicitor, without whose firm's tireless efforts there would apparently have been nothing to celebrate. There didn't seem to Mac to be much to celebrate anyway; most of the complex still had to be begun, never mind finished.

'This is Gil McDonald,' Parker was saying. 'We tried to get him to play for the All Stars tonight, but he decided the old legs weren't up to it.'

Evans nodded, unable to shake hands since he was holding both a drink and a plate of food, a stocky figure with what had once been muscle but which was, in early middle-age, running to fat. A frame more suited to the boxing ring than the legal office, it seemed to Mac. He knew a little about Evans; his family had had a practice in the old village of Stansfield since the turn of the century, and the office from which its business had always been conducted was now a listed building. They seemed an odd choice of firm for the brash Mr Parker, but Mac supposed that it lent his operation some credibility that it might just otherwise have lacked.

Parker had been talking for some time; Mac thought that he had better pay attention, but it soon became clear that the sales-pitch was not meant for his ears. *The Chronicle*, for which Mac was covering the opening, had already gone into premature (in Mac's opinion) raptures about Parker's plans, and could really be of no further use to him. Parker's soliloquy was for the ears of potential investors, who had been invited in force.

'Oh, yes,' Parker was saying. 'I got some funny looks when I said I was developing this site. But it's perfect. Central, easy access on A-roads – in a town that is beginning to thrive again, and right on the edge of real English countryside.'

Mac chewed and drank, and smiled and nodded. Parker was in his late thirties, a self-professed financial whizz-kid with a dubious past. His short, light-brown wavy hair was held in too-immaculate place with just a touch of hair gel; his skin was tanned, his teeth were white, his clothes had designer labels. If Evans looked like a boxer, which he had never been, Parker looked like a street-fighter, which he was, and sounded like nothing more than a market trader barking his wares. Most of his audience, however, were leaving, trying to beat the weather before it closed in.

'And Stansfield Town will be playing League football next season, with any luck,' Parker went on, with a nod over to the window overlooking the ground. 'Once they're in, the sky's the limit. I believe very strongly in our national sport.'

He did indeed, thought Mac. When he had bought the Stansfield Town ground, the planning permission to develop it as a sports and leisure complex had been contingent on maintaining facilities for the football club, against which proviso Parker had fought tooth and nail, but lost.

The result was borrowed surroundings which would hardly have disgraced a First Division club, never mind one struggling to break free of the sort of league that suddenly pops up on football coupons at Cup Final time. The building they were in was so newly finished that he felt he had to be careful not to touch the paint. It was also the only entirely complete building on the site.

'I'm doing some homework on tennis,' Parker said. 'A clay court or two would cost money, but if I could swing it, we could quite possibly get sponsorship for a pre-French open tourna—' He broke off as a telephone rang, which was just as well, as Mac felt that even the most gullible of people with more money than sense would not have swallowed that one. One of his few remaining guests apologised in the smug way that portable telephone users do, and answered it.

'See that?' said Parker, nodding out of the window towards the floodlit pitch. 'That's an all-weather running track round that pitch. Athletics is big business these days. Not to mention doing laps for the sake of your health.'

Mac fancied his voice had risen a decibel or two so that the merchant banker's friend on the other end of the line could hear what a good deal he was offering. But his unsubtle methods worked; he had already persuaded a great many people and businesses to invest millions in his much-touted dream of the future.

'And that . . . ' He nodded over to the dark bulk of the other, semi-constructed building. 'That is going to be a leisure centre with every facility you can think of, and more. When that's open, they'll be queuing up to get in. Bars and restaurants – a gymnasium, indoor tennis courts, basketball, squash – maybe even a shopping complex in time – you name it, I've got plans for it.'

'Yes,' said Lionel, his voice equally carrying. 'Simon showed me them. Very impressive.' He turned to Mac. 'Simon Whitworth,' he said. 'My partner – he really looks after Mr Parker's business. I'm here for the beer, as they say.'

Mac smiled politely, and thought he had better move around before he actually fell asleep in the smoky atmosphere. He wandered over to the windows, which slid back to enable the executives to wander out into the elements and actually watch the football. He stepped through the open window, where the night air damply kept the temperature at a tolerable level in the room, and looked at the misty figures as they ran through churned-up mud, heard the shouts of the players, and the thud of the ball, watched moisture bead the rail round the balcony. If play moved to the far side of the pitch, he couldn't see it at all. He didn't want to see it anyway.

He went back inside, and wondered how soon he could escape. Parker was seeing some of his guests off; Evans was tucking into the buffet. Mac positioned himself in a darkened corner where air from the window could be breathed, and waited until he was pretty sure that no one was aware of his presence, then slipped away.

Parker returned, and Lionel Evans found himself being led to the open window. Together they went out on to the balcony, and the window was very firmly closed.

Lionel sighed inwardly. It was Simon who ostensibly looked after Parker's dealings in the town; Parker's business had been the sole reason for Lionel's having taken on a partner. Parker really shouldn't be seen conspiring in corners with him.

Simon had declined the invitation to the opening, and had worked late as usual. Lionel had left him dictating to Sharon, who was pleased to have the overtime, he supposed, though he would have thought that a girl of her age should have better things to do on a Friday night. Lionel had received a last-minute invitation, and was there because it had seemed like a pleasant way to spend an evening; he should have known that there was no such thing as a free lunch.

13

'You know Sharon came here to speak to me?' Parker asked.

Lionel frowned. 'Sharon?' he repeated, uncomprehendingly, feeling the vulnerable way one does when one's thoughts are apparently read.

'Sharon,' repeated Parker. 'Your secretary.'

'I know who she is,' said Lionel, testily. It had been Parker who had recommended Sharon when Lionel's previous secretary left. Why should a visit to her old boss be newsworthy?

'She told me something that you ought to hear,' said Parker.

The young man came into the office. 'You wanted me, sir?' he asked, his round, almost child-like face belying the commendation for bravery that he had received. His fair hair was curly, and cut short, adding to the impression.

Chief Inspector Lloyd looked up from the report he was reading, and nodded briefly. 'Interested in conservation, are you, Detective Sergeant Finch?' he asked, employing what Judy called his RSC Welsh.

'Yes, sir,' replied Finch, a little uncertainly.

Lloyd wished he hadn't thought of Judy. 'Sit down,' he said, with an extravagant sigh.

Judy Hill had been a previous sergeant of his; she was a detective inspector in B Division now, based at Malworth. She was also the woman with whom he shared his life and with whom he had shared his flat until six weeks and three days ago.

Finch swallowed a little, and sat down gingerly, rather as though he thought the chair might have a whoopee cushion on it.

'Preservation of endangered species?' he asked the youth. Detective sergeant, indeed. In his day you had to have had some service before they went about promoting you.

'Sir,' said Finch, his voice deeply suspicious.

'Mm,' said Lloyd. 'I saw the catalogue.'

'Sorry, sir,' said Finch. 'I didn't think anyone would mind me bringing it in.'

'My,' said Lloyd. He didn't mind what he brought in, even if it was a Christmas catalogue in October. He minded the language being misused.

'Sorry?'

'*My* bringing it in, Finch.'

The young man frowned. 'You, sir?' he said, then coloured. 'Oh – I didn't realise. I'll take mine away.'

Lloyd unnecessarily smoothed down what was left of his dark, short hair, a gesture that those who knew him recognised only too well. 'No,' he said, with dangerously exaggerated patience, 'I

14

was—' He broke off. 'Forget it,' he said wearily. 'In fact – let me see the catalogue some time – I'll buy something from it. I'm very interested in endangered species.'

Finch looked puzzled. 'But if you've already got a catalogue—' Lloyd jumped to his feet and leant over the desk. '*I don't have a catalogue, Finch!*' he shouted, making the sergeant jump. 'All right?'

'Sir.'

Lloyd sat down again. 'Endangered species,' he said, his tone well-modulated once more. 'There's a little creature that I'm very fond of. Tiny little thing. Its tail's longer than its body.'

Finch looked a touch desperate. 'To be honest, sir, I don't know too much about animals. I just . . . ' He cleared his throat. 'I just think we should hang on to the ones we've got, that's all. Some sort of monkey, is it?'

Lloyd shook his head. 'It performs two distinct and very useful functions,' he said. 'And yet it's dying out.'

Finch nodded. 'Habitat being destroyed?' he suggested, hopefully.

'Oh, yes.' Lloyd stood up again, and walked over to the table on which he had piled baskets of files and street-maps and his in-tray, on the grounds that that way his desk looked tidier. He perched on the only available corner, and regarded Finch. 'Yes,' he said again. 'Its habitat's being destroyed all right. Being eroded further and further every day – every minute of every day.'

The sergeant looked round, as though he thought someone might rescue him.

'But that's not the worst of it,' continued Lloyd. 'Some well-meaning but ill-informed people pick them up and put them where they don't belong at all.'

'In zoos,' Finch volunteered.

Lloyd beamed. 'Yes,' he agreed, enthusiastically. 'In zoos – very often in zoos. And . . . ' He leant over to his desk, and picked up the open file on the rapes, two in Malworth and one in Stansfield, on which Finch had prepared a report for the incident room which had been set up in Malworth. He reached into his inside pocket for the glasses that he had discovered, much to his chagrin, that he needed for small print. He didn't need them for Finch's large, clear hand, but he had been given a new prop, and that had taken a lot of the sting out of losing his twenty-twenty vision. He took them out of their pouch, cleaning them carefully before putting them on and glancing at the report.

'In zoos,' he repeated, with a sad shake of the head. He took off his glasses again and looked at Finch. 'And cafés.'

15

Finch stared at him. 'Cafés, sir?' he repeated, his voice incredulous.

Lloyd's eyes widened. 'I don't know why you look so astonished,' he said. 'You're the one who puts them there.'

Finch's eyes held something very like alarm.

'I am very well aware, Finch,' said Lloyd, 'that you would infinitely prefer to be facing a crazed gunman, but this is part of your job too.' Lloyd was almost enjoying himself, despite his dark mood.

He glanced down at the file again. '. . . "anywhere that young people can be expected to gather, especially cafe's",' he quoted, holding his glasses a few inches from the page like a magnifying glass. 'It's called an apostrophe, Finch,' he said. 'And when you add an 's' to a word to make it plural, that is all you are doing. Even if the word ends in a vowel, though that does seem to be the bastard rule that has evolved amongst those who were never taught English grammar and punctuation. It is quite, quite wrong – believe me, Finch. It is wrong, and no amount of popular usage will ever make it right, because it conveys an entirely different meaning from the one that you are attempting to convey.'

'Sorry, sir.'

'And it can in no way substitute for an acute,' Lloyd continued. 'But that's another matter. For the moment, it's the rudiments of English punctuation with which I would like you to get to grips. I want you to find out exactly what functions the apostrophe performs for us, and I want you to use it correctly in your paperwork or not at all. I'd rather the poor thing died out altogether than it languished in words where it has no business to be. Off you go,' he concluded, without drawing a breath.

Finch stood up, and walked to the door, doubtless raising his eyes to heaven for the benefit of the cleaner who was carrying a vacuum cleaner along the corridor to the interview rooms, if the sympathetic smile she gave as she looked up at him was anything to go by.

And that was another thing, thought Lloyd sourly. They were all too bloody tall these days. He stared at the door as it closed, feeling disgruntled and just a touch guilty. Why had he picked on young Finch? They all did it. But Finch was on night-shift and therefore still there because he had to be, and not because he didn't want to go home. That was what had really annoyed him.

For the truth was that Detective Chief Inspector Lloyd's life was not, for the moment, as he would choose it to be. He finished reading Finch's report, put the top on his pen, closed the file, stretched, yawned, and looked with a lacklustre eye at the clock.

16

He frowned as he heard the commotion outside his door, and went out into the corridor in time to see a bruised and bloody constable manhandle a man towards the cells. Perhaps his clock had stopped; he looked at his watch. No, it was just eight fifteen.

'What's this?' he asked the desk sergeant. 'Isn't it a bit early for the Friday night round-up?'

Sergeant Woodford looked up from what he was writing. 'Crowd trouble at the match,' he said, his face totally expressionless. 'We've another one already down there.'

'You arrested the entire crowd?' He liked getting Jack Woodford going. He was a staunch supporter.

The sergeant would not take the bait. 'Near enough,' he said. 'But you know who that *is*, do you?' he asked, jerking his head towards the disappearing miscreant.

Lloyd didn't, and didn't particularly want to know. 'I thought this was a friendly,' he said, not above making very old jokes when the occasion presented itself. 'Who's winning?' he asked.

'The match was abandoned on account of the fog.'

Lloyd groaned. 'Oh, God, it's not foggy, is it? Tell me it's not.'

'A pea-souper. Haven't seen one like it since the fifties.'

'Don't tell me – Stansfield were on the brink of clawing back the three-goal deficit when the ref abandoned the match, and both supporters staged a pitch invasion.'

'No,' he laughed. 'There were no goals – and there were two hundred odd there, I'll have you know. But it wasn't the passion of the game this time, Lloyd. It was an older passion even than that.' He shook his head sadly. 'All over some woman,' he said, a mock-warning in his voice. He was retiring later in the year, and had had a whole ten years more experience of life on this earth than Lloyd had had. This, he seemed to believe, conferred on him great wisdom. 'More trouble than they're worth, if you ask me.'

'Don't I know it?' said Lloyd with feeling. 'Is she the one in the cells?'

'No – she was long gone. Just left the fellas fighting over her.'

Lloyd grinned. 'Are you charging them?' he asked.

'Not Barnes, I shouldn't think. They can hit each other if they want to as far as I'm concerned. Let him cool his heels and send him home. But Rambo there' – he pointed in the direction that the constable and his prisoner had just walked – 'that's Jake Parker.'

Lloyd's eyebrows shot up. 'The bloke who bought the ground?' he said. 'What is he – some sort of hooligan-in-residence?'

'Don't ask me. But he's going to get done for assaulting a police officer if I've got any say in the matter.'

'Why on earth was he hitting policemen?'

17

'He says he didn't know it was a policeman.'

Lloyd still looked wonderingly at Woodford. 'Why was he hitting anyone?' he asked.

'From what I can gather, he was the one who was chatting up this girl – the other bloke objected, and the next thing the fists were flying. Or perhaps it was the other way round. No one seems too sure.' He reached across to answer the phone as he spoke. 'And Parker's head flew into our lad's face,' he added. 'Money. They think they can do what they like and get away with it, people like him. Stansfield Police,' he said into the receiver, then held his hand over the mouthpiece. 'He didn't even go to public school,' he said, with a grin. 'Or you'd understand the attitude.'

Lloyd laughed. 'Have a nice night. I'm off.'

'Hang on!' called Jack. 'It's for you.'

'I've gone,' said Lloyd, in a stage whisper.

'It's Judy,' said Jack, smugly. Jack, who had known Lloyd since he was fourteen years old, was now the only person at the station who knew for a fact, rather than for a rumour, what was what in the Lloyd-Hill saga.

Lloyd took the receiver. 'Hello, stranger,' he said.

She sighed. 'Don't be like that. Are you thinking of coming home at all tonight?'

Lloyd beamed. 'Are you at my flat? Have you eaten?'

'Yes and no.'

'Good. Then don't.'

'I want my solicitor,' said Jake.

Detective Sergeant Finch sighed, and looked at his watch. 'I take it you have someone in mind?' he said.

'Whitworth. Simon Whitworth.' Jake gave him the number, and the sergeant looked at his watch again. 'He'll come,' said Jake. 'My business is worth too much to him not to come.'

'I'm not sure why you want a solicitor,' said Finch, getting up. 'You can walk out of here on police bail.'

Jake shook his head. 'I'm not being done for assaulting a police officer,' he said. 'It doesn't look good.'

Finch shrugged. 'But he is a police officer, and you assaulted him,' he said.

Jake looked up at him. God, he looked about twelve. Did that mean that he was getting old, at thirty-eight? He wondered how old Detective Sergeant Finch was. 'I didn't know it was a cop,' he said. 'I was grabbed from behind, and did what came naturally.'

'Head-butting people comes naturally to you, does it, Mr Parker?'

Jake smiled the smile that had got him out of scrapes when he was six, and still worked on occasion. Usually with women, but sometimes even with men. 'I never claimed to be a saint,' he said.

'The sergeant is quite adamant that you should be charged with assaulting a police officer,' said Finch.

Jake still smiled. 'I know. But I think my solicitor might talk him out of it – you get him.' He frowned. 'Why are you dealing with this?' he asked. 'It's not a CID thing.'

It was Finch who smiled this time. 'You know all about the set-up, then?'

'Spent more time behind bars than I have in wine bars, I can tell you that,' said Jake.

'I can believe it,' said Finch. 'Don't panic – we're just a bit short-handed. I volunteered.' He went off, presumably to phone Whitworth. Jake sighed, and looked round the cell.

He hoped Whitworth hurried up and got him out of here.

Twenty-five to nine, said the green analogue clock on the dashboard. Simon Whitworth pulled into the verge, his heart sinking when he saw the lit window, and brought the car to a halt. Melissa was home, and there would be questions. She had said that she would be working this evening. He could have been home earlier, but he had caught up on the work that really did need doing before he left the office, on the grounds that that diluted the lies. He should have gone to Parker's shindig at the club instead, and given himself an alibi.

He got out of the car, pointing the remote at it, and walked up the path, his thin face pinched with cold and tiredness and worry, his unbiddable hair falling over his forehead, being automatically pushed back. The sky was lit with the strange light projected by the new floodlights at the sports ground; it was just a mile away across the fields, and the fierce glow in the sky told them when a match was on. Tonight it was muted by the mist, and as he watched, the glow diminished, disappearing by swift degrees until the sky was black once more.

He unlocked the door, feeling wretched, wishing the lights hadn't gone out like that, like some sort of heavenly reproof. For God's sake, it was only the floodlights being switched off, he told himself angrily, but the darkness and the fog seemed to be claiming him. He could always say that he *had* been at the so-called opening, he supposed. But no – *The Chronicle* might be covering it, and she would find out that he'd lied. But working late was palling as excuses went, however true he tried to make it. The police station – he had been called to the police station, he would tell her. It was difficult to remember all the lies. Lying to Melissa, lying to Lionel. Lying to Sharon, even.

She *wasn't* in. Simon frowned, and went upstairs to check. The house was empty, but she must have been home for the light to be on. And she was a checker; they could never leave the house even for five minutes without her checking gases and lights and windows. On a night like this – what could have taken her out again in such a hurry?

The cat, perhaps. He had gone to the vet at lunch-time to be shorn of his tomhood – poor creature, curled up happily on the passenger seat of Melissa's car, quite unaware of what fate had in store for him. They had discovered Robeson's love of travelling by accident; as a kitten, determined to win round a less than enthusiastic Simon, Robeson had spent weeks following him with a dog-like devotion which had extended one day to getting into the car with him. Simon had felt the first and fatal stirrings of proprietorial pride at being thus honoured, and had taken the cat for an experimental drive. By the time they had returned, Robeson had smugly reeled in his catch, and Simon was his for ever.

They weren't due to pick him up until tomorrow, but perhaps they had done the operation sooner than expected. Or perhaps something had gone wrong, Simon thought, with a stab of alarm.

The phone interrupted this unhappy speculation.

'Mr Whitworth?'

'Speaking.'

'Sergeant Woodford, Stansfield. We've got a Mr Parker in the cells – he was involved in an incident at the football ground, and may be charged with assaulting a police officer. He's asked us to ring you.'

Simon listened to the dead-pan delivery with disbelief. 'Jake Parker?' he asked.

'The same. Sorry to drag you out.'

Simon, who might have been expected to be irritated at being called out on such a night, smiled broadly. 'I'll be there, Sergeant,' he said.

'So I can tell him you're on your way?' said Sergeant Woodford, with much relief.

'You can, Sergeant. I'll be there as soon as possible.'

The sergeant's relief was nothing compared to Simon's, as he backed the car out again, and plunged into the mist.

No lies. Just an economy of truth. God had sent him a real, live client. Jake Parker, involved in a punch-up during his opening party? In character, he was sure, but a funny night to show your real colours. Still, football seemed to do that to people.

God bless him, anyway.

Half an hour after her phone call to the station, Judy was being presented with food, and a catalogue of complaints about the standard of English education in schools.

'Are you going to spend all the time grumbling?' she asked, as she surveyed the many Chinese dishes at her disposal, and selected a spare rib dripping with syrup.

'I just wish one of them could spell, for God's sake. Is that asking too much? What do they teach them at school, that's what I'd like to know. Can't multiply or divide without a calculator.'

Judy smiled. 'Neither can you,' she said.

'That's different. I know *how*, even if it's not my forte. They don't. *And* they can't spell.' He stabbed at a prawn ball with his fork. 'Watch your sweater,' he advised.

Judy put a hand under the treacherous rib to catch any drips. It was really a little too warm in Lloyd's flat for the sweater, but he liked her in it. 'It's not new, you know,' she said.

'You still don't want to drip syrup on it.'

'Not the sweater! The problem.'

'Oh.'

'Just after I started in the job, I had to deal with the applications for licence extensions. They were supposed to be addressed to the chief superintendent, but one firm of solicitors always addressed them to the chief inspector.' She rescued some syrup that dribbled down her chin. 'Anyway, one day I was in their offices, and I asked the typist why she addressed them to the chief inspector. She said it was because she couldn't spell superintendent.'

Lloyd permitted himself a reluctant smile. 'At least she *knew* she couldn't spell superintendent,' he said.

Judy knew that it wasn't the prevailing standard of literacy that was really bothering him, but she kept up the pretence, listening to the moans about grammar and punctuation that she had heard a million times before, because the last thing she wanted was for him to get on to the real reason for his mild fit of depression.

That, she knew from experience, led to rows. Rows in which she was always the loser, always the guilty party. In the past, this had been true; she had been trying to string him along and keep her marriage going at the same time. But she could hardly be held responsible for a job where your bosses had the right to make you live where they wanted you to live.

But everything was always her fault. Lloyd was always right, always knew best. He had been analysing her and her motives for seventeen years, and she didn't suppose he was going to stop now. Every time they had a row – if you could call the one-sided harangues rows – she was told precisely what was wrong with her, and how that could all be remedied if she would just think about other people for a change. The fact that his words echoed uncomfortably closely those of her mother when she was in her teens, and Michael when their marriage finally hit the rocks, did nothing to make it easier to take.

So she would let him go on about people using commas instead of semicolons, because that was only an indirect criticism of her, and not one which gave her any sleepless nights.

'Are you listening to a single word I'm saying?' he demanded.

'No,' she said, with a grin, spooning fried rice on to her plate.

Fog hovered still and thick, flooding the football pitch like a phantom sea, blanketing the public playing fields beyond. Moisture beaded the mud-guard of the bike and the PVC of his gloves as Colin Drummond pushed up the visor and waited. Slowly, he drew off one glove, and without taking his eyes away from the car, he undid the strap and removed his helmet, running his bare hand through black, well-cut hair, his youthful, handsome face set and determined. He laid the helmet on the seat behind him, and slipped his hand into the glove again.

He had seen the fight, seen her walk away. He had watched her, and had gone to the bike and started it up, just as her back view became indistinguishable from the rest of the blotted-out landscape. His foot touching the ground now and then to keep the bike balanced, he had followed her as she walked down the hill. She may or may not have been aware of his presence; she didn't turn round.

He had been undecided as to his next move. In the event, it had been decided for him, as a car had come past, its outline fuzzily visible as it pulled away. But then it had seemed to stop, the rear lights which he had expected to vanish within a hundred yards inexplicably remaining as two red splashes in the mist. Except that it hadn't stopped; it had merely been moving at exactly the same pace as he had. Walking pace. Her pace.

He had frowned, increasing his speed slightly, to see what was going on. That was when he had seen the brake lights glare, then the door had opened and she had got in. The car had moved off, keeping to ten miles an hour as it had groped its way through the almost impenetrable fog, completing a tricky turn in the road to head back the way it had come. He knew its speed precisely, because he had followed, far enough back to be unnoticed.

Followed them right back to the football ground, deserted and in darkness. He had stopped, headlamp out, just at the entrance, as they drove to the farthest corner. He had wheeled the bike up on to the verge, behind the high hedge, as the car's engine was cut, and the headlights extinguished. They had been there for almost ten minutes now; away, they thought, from prying eyes.

But hidden by the hedge, silent, and all but invisible in his black leathers, Colin watched them.

TWO

Lionel sat staring at the television screen, not seeing. He felt sick, and afraid, and he had to work out what he was going to do.

He had never really known until now how important his life was to him. If anything, it had seemed pointless; a job he didn't much care for, a marriage that had evolved into a near master-servant relationship which was not of his making, whatever Melissa Whitworth thought. No children. No social life to speak of, unless you counted going to the pub.

Fridays used to be drinking after hours in Sid's back room and watching adult videos. They all knew that it was about as adult as comparing genitals behind the toilets at the mixed infants, but it passed the time, and they were good for a laugh. Frances had found out, of course, somehow. One of the wives had told her; one of the more broadminded wives.

They were only rented videos, for God's sake . . . they were just a bit of fun. Frances had never mentioned it, of course. She didn't have to. He had seen the look she had given him the following Friday night when he had got ready to go out. The same look as when she'd found that magazine – if she saw some of the stuff that people got hold of, she wouldn't . . .

So, he had stopped going out on Fridays, and had missed his little bit of excitement, though that had been more than made up for by what had happened since. Tonight, however, he had gone out – he had received a call when he got home, inviting him to the do at the football club. He had asked Frances to come with him, but she had refused. Which was, as things had turned out, just as well.

There were tears in his eyes. He had thought he hated his life, but he didn't. He didn't. It was important to him. He looked at his wife, who had been watching television when he had come in, and hadn't turned her head; neither of them had spoken. They had long ago abandoned conversation. But Frances was important to him, and he had to work out what to do now, if he wasn't to lose everything.

The phone rang; Lionel stiffened, and tried to marshall his wits.

'That's the phone, Lionel,' said his wife.

He looked at her. 'I know it's the phone, Frances,' he said, but still made no attempt to move.

'Would you like me to—?'

'I would not.'

'Aren't you going to answer it?'

She looked older than he did, though she was three years his junior: he still had a full head of curly brown hair; she had started going grey in her thirties.

'Yes!'

He wondered if she should try that hormone replacement business. He closed the door to the sitting-room, and picked up the phone, his heart beating hard.

'Lionel?'

His heart somersaulted with relief. 'Yes – is that Melissa?'

'Yes.'

He didn't often get a call from Melissa Whitworth. He always rather got the impression that she tried to avoid him. He had never been so glad to hear anyone's voice, because it wasn't the one he had been expecting.

'I . . . I was just wondering . . . is Simon working late again?'

He was having difficulty taking in the words. 'Sorry, Melissa? I didn't quite catch that.'

'Simon,' she said. 'I phoned the office, but there was no reply.'

'No, there wouldn't be,' Lionel said, unsure of what to say. 'Sharon closes the switchboard at five.'

'Doesn't he usually have a line through to his desk when he's working late?'

'*I* don't know!' he snapped, relief giving way to anger.

'Why does he have to work late so often anyway?' she asked. 'I never see him. It's after nine o'clock.'

Lionel had more than Melissa's sensibilities to worry about. 'I've no idea,' he said. 'Why don't you ask him?'

'I would if I ever saw him.'

The dialling tone hummed in his ear; he replaced the receiver, and stood for a moment in the hallway, trying to sort out what he was going to do.

Perhaps nothing was the wisest course.

Judy had tried to reason her way out of the inevitable row which she had failed to stave off, but it hadn't worked. She hardly participated in the rows; she would defend herself from the more outrageous accusations, but she couldn't find the words to combat his, and she wouldn't want to use them if she could. She didn't want to hurt him back.

And yet it seemed that she did, all the time, without trying. So he tried all the harder to hurt her, and it worked. She didn't know if what he said stung because it was unwarranted or because it was true. She didn't *want* to know; she just wanted him to stop.

This was the final phase, when the accusations would come in short bursts between the long silences, like a sniper just letting the enemy know he's there in case they've forgotten their predicament. One such came now.

'Don't be silly,' she said tiredly, in response to the old, old bottom-of-the-barrel suggestion that she really wanted Michael back. He knew that that wasn't true; once, it had hurt her, when she thought that he believed it. Now, she knew better.

'Then why haven't you done anything about divorcing him?' he demanded, as though they hadn't had the conversation forty times before.

'I have. You know I have.'

'Oh, sure. By mutual consent – it could all have been over and done with if you'd divorced him for adultery, and we wouldn't have to be living in two separate flats!'

She asked him what right she would have had to do that, since she had been committing adultery for two years before he had finally set up home with some girl from the office.

'You told me he had women all the time you were married,' Lloyd said, managing to make it sound as though she had lied about it for some reason.

She sighed. 'He did. I'll rephrase it. I was committing the kind of adultery that would stand up in court long before he was. You can hardly cite some woman in Brussels or an air-hostess he spent the night with in Frankfurt.' She even smiled; this was, she thought, the winding down process, when the argument would give way to near-banter and eventually to a sort of forced humour. 'Besides,' she said, 'I didn't care at the time, so I can hardly get all moral about it now, can I?'

'Then you could have let him divorce you.'

'I don't believe this,' she said, the exasperation almost manufactured these days. He was trying to exasperate her, so she would be exasperated. Acting. Lloyd did a lot of that; it must be rubbing off on her.

She was relaxed now; it was all over bar the making-up, which she didn't enjoy as much as they said you were supposed to. It was all part of the inevitable pattern of the rows, and the very predictability made her uneasy. But it was better than the row itself, and she welcomed the signs of a truce, so she played along. 'If I'd done that, he would have named you – and then where would we have been?'

'Where would *you* have been, you mean.'

She frowned, puzzled, but carried on, perhaps a touch grimly, with the point-counterpoint. 'No, I don't,' she said. 'You're the senior officer – you're the one who would have been held responsible.'

'But I'm not the one who's looking for promotion, am I?' he shouted. 'I'm not the one who's suddenly decided that I want to be chief constable!'

She hadn't predicted that.

The bank of fog reflected back her headlights, and Melissa, suddenly aware of how fast she was driving, braked hard, almost as though the wall of vapour was a solid obstruction. The car entered its yellow depths, and visibility was virtually non-existent. She signalled the right turn; ahead of her she could see pinpoints of light. Much sooner than she expected, the car was almost on top of her, and she realised that she had strayed on to the wrong side of the road. She wrenched her wheel to the left, swearing with shock.

She didn't see the motorcyclist at all until she was almost on top of him. She was still pulling left, cutting in front of him, and for a desperate moment, a crash seemed inevitable. The motorcyclist took the only option open to him and roared through the almost impossible gap to safety.

Melissa's hands shook on the wheel as she pulled the car up on the waste ground, and watched him go on his invisible unlit way into the layer of mist, apparently unconcerned that he had been an inch away from being a statistic.

Colin Drummond knew how narrowly he had escaped death. He had accelerated away from the danger in instinctive self-preservation, but he didn't reduce his speed now that the danger had passed; he wanted it; he needed it. And he still didn't put on his lights, because he didn't want to be seen.

He was roaring round the roundabout which guarded the entrance to the old village, revving hard as he straightened the bike, thundering past the old shops and offices. His hand gripped the handlebars tighter as he swung left at the junction, leaning over, his knee almost touching the ground, righting the bike and bombing through the opaque night, shattering the stillness of a community that had closed its doors on the hostile weather, weaving round the parked cars as he suddenly became aware of them, heading for the dual carriageway, and the open road.

There, he let the bike go at full throttle, and was joyously, thrillingly, gunning through the zero visibility as fast as its powerful engine would let him. Nothing could touch him, nothing could harm him.

He heard the siren, saw in his mirror the car come out of a lay-by, light flashing.

They'd have to catch him first.

'Have you told anyone you're here?' asked Simon.

Parker shook his head. 'Who needs to know?' he asked. 'I feel soft enough as it is. Just get me out of here. What time is it, anyway?'

'Just after twenty to ten.' Simon wasn't convinced that it was going to be that simple. Parker had needled him as soon as he had arrived, with his complaints about how long it had taken him to get there, rather as though his head-butting a policeman was somehow Simon's fault. And Sergeant Woodford had not seemed to be in a compromising mood; Simon's only hope was the duty inspector, who might persuade the sergeant not to charge Parker, if Simon could produce a good enough excuse.

'How on earth did you come to hit a policeman?'

'I didn't know he was a policeman! I just felt someone grab me, and I jerked my head back.'

'So it was accidental?' asked Simon, a little more hopeful than he had been.

Parker nodded. 'It was an accident,' he repeated. 'I had my back to him. It was pure reaction to being grabbed from behind.' He looked at Simon, the picture of injured innocence, with an incipient bruise forming round the left of his wide eyes.

He reminded Simon of a footballer trying to convince the referee that bringing his opponent down in the penalty area was simply not in his nature.

'How did you get involved in a fight on the terraces?' he asked. 'Why weren't you up in the box, hosting your party?'

'I saw Sharon – I was just having a word with her, that's all. Then this nutter comes and thumps me.'

'Sharon?' asked Simon sharply.

'Yeah. She used to work for me – didn't you know?'

Simon frowned. 'Yes,' he said. He knew that. What he hadn't known was that she was the girl that this fight had all been about. There were conflicting accounts of the incident; Parker said that she had been chatting up Barnes and that when he spoke to her,

Barnes took a swing at him; Barnes swore that she had simply asked him the time, and that the next thing he knew Parker was laying into him.

As far as Simon's professional involvement was concerned, how it all came about hardly mattered; Parker had injured a policeman in the ensuing fight, and that was why he was there. But now that he knew it was Sharon, the whole thing took on a different complexion.

He stood up. 'I'll have a word with the duty inspector,' he said.

'Good lad. Let's get out of here.'

Mac was lost. He didn't know the town well enough yet, and all his useful landmarks had been blotted out. His desire to walk had wilted a little, but taxis weren't forthcoming in this fog.

Before the total obscurity, his life had been a bit like the weather. Clear patches, when people knew who he was and wrote earnest articles about his downfall. They blamed everything from booze to birds to betting to brains, even; he should never have been a professional footballer, according to one. He was too clever to mix happily with people whose brains had a tendency to be in their feet. He should have used his A-levels and gone to university. No wonder he'd ended up pickling his brain; dying from lack of use, it was the only way it could be preserved, he'd said. Nice one, thought Mac the journalist.

But what did the stupid sod think he'd used? How did he suppose he had risen out of the pack? Oh, sure, there were some natural talents who could practically drag the ball towards them and whack it in the net, but he had never been like that. He had used his head to think, not to knock a football around.

By the time he was playing serious amateur football, he had worked out that his opponents very rarely planned ahead unless the move had been worked out in training so often that it had become second nature. And you could always use that to their disadvantage. It wasn't teamwork; if it didn't come off he got accused of laziness. But it had worked, more often than not, and then the glory had been all his, as he had gone from good to better, and begun to grab the headlines. Almost ten years right at the top, and all the goodies that that brought.

Money – what had seemed like an endless supply. People stopping him in the street for autographs; girls clamouring for him at the club-gates. Parties, nightclubs, TV shows, sharp suits and haircuts. Marrying a model who gave up her career to have his baby. The baby had been an attempt to save the marriage; it hadn't worked.

Going abroad; sneaking out to play the casinos and find girls. It was even better over there; women were as interested in football as men, and footballers were gods in some of these countries. The angel Gabriel must have felt like this when he came up with the best chat-up line of all time, Mac had thought on more than one occasion, but had had the sense not to say so to the good Catholic girl in his arms. Getting fined for missing training. So what? He could afford it, and he didn't need to train. He didn't follow set moves like a performing animal. He did what he was paid to do on the day, and that was what mattered.

Being brought back to England in a blaze of publicity, to rescue an ailing side, but the team had gone down anyway, and in its second season in the Second Division, the club had had a cash crisis. He'd gone on the market, and he'd waited confidently for a First Division team to make an offer, but none had come. His reputation was too bad, no one wanted to risk him now that he was in his thirties. He was over the hill. Too fond of the good life, too much of a liability. It had even been suggested that the club might never have gone down if it hadn't persevered with him.

He thrust his hands in the pockets of his overcoat as the chill dampness of the evening got to him again, and he realised that he had simply been walking, without any attempt to find his way. Now, he might as well be on the moon.

Snowy winter evenings sitting on the bench; wet, cold Saturday afternoons when he wasn't even sub. Watching the team, when he could be bothered, climbing its way back up. It had got back to the First Division after two seasons of not quite making it; his contract hadn't been renewed.

Management. He shuddered. Not for him, but he'd taken the opportunity when it had been offered, at Sandra's insistence. Sacked after the first season. Then it was days in the plural that he couldn't remember, and the next few years saw him spending what he had left and what he could earn from hazy chat show appearances. Then just womanising and boozing. Then just boozing, until he'd woken up in a hospital bed, two years ago, with no memory of how he had got there.

He walked further down the road, and came to a roundabout. He took the left turn, and walked down to where there appeared a T-junction, and suddenly, he realised where he was. He was in the old village, the part of Stansfield that had always been there, on which the new town had been foisted. If he went back up to the roundabout, and went straight over, up Byford Road, he would join the bypass. It was a long walk, but at least he'd know where he was going. Home, if his rented room in someone else's house could be called home.

He'd pulled himself up from as near the gutter as a man could get without slipping down the drain, and for what? So that he could see quite clearly, without the alcoholic haze to protect him, that no one remembered him except a few sports hacks, and no one wanted to know. Parker had got together a so-called all-star side to take on Stansfield for his opening, and had tried to persuade Mac to play for it, but only because *The Chronicle* had suggested it, not because he knew who Mac was. Football, he had declared in a less public moment, was something he'd never had much time for. Neither had Mac now.

He trudged back up the way he had just come, resenting the fates which had even made him turn left instead of right, thus making him retrace his steps. It was all he ever seemed to do. All he could do. Retrace his steps, retrace his life. He smiled a little reluctantly. Most people didn't have that sort of life to recall, he supposed.

He was not looking forward to the last stage of his walk. The bypass was something of a hazard for those on foot on a night like this, with only muddy grass verges instead of footpaths, and no visibility at all to speak of. But, he realised, he still thought of routes in terms of driving; he could make use of land denied to traffic. With any luck he could cut across the sports ground; there were gaps in the so-called security fencing through which youths could get into the matches for nothing.

He wouldn't voluntarily go to the matches, but he'd had to cover a couple when neither of the real sports reporters could find the time to go. Football wasn't top of his list of favourite things. It had taken a while for any of his normal drives to get back into working order; his appetite had returned first, and he began to enjoy food again. Then music's appeal had returned; he'd found his record collection being sold at an auction, and had withdrawn it from sale, though he couldn't afford anything to play it on. His enjoyment of words, dormant since his English essay-writing days, had come back to him, prompting the thought of writing for a newspaper. And finally, he had found one that wanted him.

It had had to be sport, of course. To start with. Which included football. Perhaps one day he'd be cheering Stansfield on as they rose out of their obscurity, but he doubted it. No one was cheering him on as he struggled out of his; he was having to do it by himself. He could take no pleasure in football.

Nor in women. But his eyes had begun to follow the girls at the paper as they came and went; they, of course, didn't even look at him. He was some middle-aged bloke with grey hair that came into the office now and then, old enough to be their father. He had felt frustrated, with all that new found energy and nothing to expend it on, but he hadn't wanted a woman's company, not at first. He had simply wanted the less complicated and more immediate pleasure of a woman's body, and had satisfied the need from time to time. But there was little pleasure to be had that way, and he had begun to want more. He had thought that tonight might be different, but he had been wrong.

Shoulders hunched, jacket collar turned up against the clouds of thickening fog in which he walked, he reflected on how he had meant to be spending the night, for Donna, if the boys on the sports desk were to be believed, was a dead cert.

And even she hadn't wanted to know.

Lloyd stopped speaking, wanting to make the words disappear again. He didn't look at Judy as she got up and went out into the hall; he knew he had done it again, and he didn't try to stop her leaving. The more precious his time with Judy became, the more he wasted it. Neither working nor living with her, he hardly saw her in view of their ridiculously unsociable hours.

But no hours at work had ever been as unsociable as the last one had been. He heard the door slam, and closed his eyes. He didn't know what made him say things like that, but he always did. And he couldn't stop. He would try to; he would try to calm down, to discuss their situation rationally. But when he opened his mouth, what came out was just another grievance. She was leaving before it got any worse, and he wouldn't try to stop her. Once, she wouldn't have gone, not wanting to leave before they'd made it up. Once, he would have asked her to stay. But they both knew now that all that happened was that his wounding tongue would run away with him.

Judy's divisional DCI had taken it into his head to advise her – or order her, depending on how you looked at it – to find accommodation in Malworth rather than Stansfield; there wasn't much to be done about that, given their less than official domestic set-up, so she had, with considerable misgiving, moved out of the flat and into one of her own in Malworth. It wasn't her fault – she could hardly have objected to the move on the grounds that she was living over the brush with Stansfield's DCI, a fact that she had failed to mention to her superiors.

So why was he blaming her? Why did he *do* this to her? He'd done it when she was living with Michael, and he was doing it again. There had to be a reason. He wanted to be with her more than he had ever wanted anything, and perhaps, he thought

32

bleakly, that was the problem. He couldn't be sure that she felt the same.

He heard her car finally agree to take her home, and moved the curtain aside a little, intending to watch the little green mini make its way out of the garage area. But all he saw was a blanket of thick fog, worse even than it had been.

Get home safe, he said silently. Whatever you do, get home safe.

Whitworth wasn't as useless as he looked, thought Jake, bailed to appear at Stansfield Magistrates' Court on a charge of disturbing the peace, for which he would be bound over. He hadn't even let the news about Sharon shake his professional composure, which said something for him. But now that he was running Jake back to his car, he obviously felt that the circumstances had altered, because the subject was broached.

'What really happened?' he asked.

'On my life, Simon, it was an accident,' said Jake, his hand cheekily on his heart, deliberately misunderstanding the question.

'Not that,' said Simon. 'With Sharon.'

'Oh, Sharon,' Jake said, glancing at Simon as the car crept along through dense fog. 'She was with this bloke, chatting him up. I just said hello and all hell broke loose.' He couldn't see Simon's face. He didn't suppose he believed him. Which was, he thought, probably fair enough.

He wasn't, after all, telling the truth.

Three

Driving gingerly through the outskirts of Malworth, Judy slowed down to a near stop as she came up to a tableau of police car and motorbike on the dual carriageway, and signalled right to overtake them. That must have been the siren that she had heard, she thought, a little puzzled that the incident still seemed to be in progress. It had to have been well over an hour ago now. The bike wasn't damaged, and neither was the rider.

She found herself, as she always did in these circumstances, feeling for the offender. She wondered if this was a basic flaw in her character – surely she should be sympathising with her colleagues, who had had to get out of their nice warm car to deal with him? But then, she thought with a sigh, there were apparently a great many flaws in her character.

She had left as Lloyd was getting into his stride. She had learned to do that, at least. Not to let the row get to a stage where Lloyd could and would do real damage. She had had to do one or two major repair jobs on her feelings in her time with Lloyd, and opening old wounds hurt more than first time round; he knew that, and when he was angry with her, he had no use for ethics. She had learned to live with that. The really worrying part was that she had believed they had put the promotion business behind them. Evidently not.

She shifted up a gear, and drove away from the hazy, street-lamp lit scene at the side of the road, deciding against seeing if her colleagues had a problem; quite frankly, she didn't give a damn whether they had or not.

Melissa was at the hotel, just one of the sudden crop of buildings which had sprung up on land once owned by the now defunct Mitchell Engineering works, whose existence had brought the new town into being, and which had now vanished. She had a male companion; this was not altogether unpleasant, she had decided, after a much-needed intake of alcohol.

She had arrived at the hotel, disturbed by her near-miss with the motorbike, and had sat sipping a calming whisky and soda in the long lounge and dining-room, regulation pink and grey, and quite empty. She had had two more drinks before another customer entered.

He had grey hair, and a face that she recognised, but to which she had been unable to put a name. 'I think the barman may have died,' she had said. 'I haven't seen him for half an hour.'

'Hello,' he had said, smiling, holding out his hand in greeting. 'It's Melissa Fletcher, isn't it?'

He had met her at *The Chronicle*; Fletcher was her pen-name. But she hadn't had the faintest idea who he was.

'Mac,' he had said, and she had remembered then. He wrote a column for the Saturday edition.

He was a lot older than Simon, but not as old as the grey hair would suggest. He had blue eyes; she hadn't noticed that when they had met before.

After some moments, the youth who looked too young to be serving behind a bar had almost sidled out, clearly finding two customers a bit on the hectic side.

Now, she was on her fourth drink. Mac drank soft drinks. They sat side by side on a wall seat, the huge leather bag in which she carried her tape-recorder and half the contents of her files between them, until Mac found its presence uncomfortable.

'I'll put it up here,' he said, picking it up and sliding it on to a shelf above his head. He hadn't expected the weight; the bag slipped a little, and as he righted it a loose tape slid out and fell to the floor. He stooped to pick it up, reading the label. 'Sharon Smith?' he asked.

She felt her cheeks go pink, and he looked at her when she didn't answer.

She snatched the tape from him. 'Just work,' she said, standing up and pushing it back into the bag. She sat down again, hoping she hadn't reacted too obviously.

Mac knelt one knee on the imitation pink velvet to push the bag further back, and his hand rested lightly on her shoulder as he righted himself again. 'There we are,' he said, sitting beside her. 'So – what brings you out on a night like this?'

Melissa took a fortifying sip before she spoke. 'I was working late,' she said.

'Winding down?' He looked at her drink.

'Something like that.'

He looked at her seriously. 'Take it from one who knows,' he said. 'Tiredness, whisky and cars don't mix very well.'

'I don't intend driving any more tonight,' she said.

He frowned, puzzled.

'I'm staying here,' she said.

'I see.' He made himself more comfortable, moving closer to her as he did. 'You . . . you don't live in Stansfield, then?'

She coloured slightly, and he noticed. 'Yes – but I don't fancy driving in this.'

He looked at her curiously. 'Won't anyone be missing you?' he asked.

Melissa felt the flush grow deeper. 'Why the third degree?' she snapped.

He held up his hands. 'Sorry.'

'So – what's your story? How come you're here?'

He smiled. 'I was covering the opening of the leisure centre,' he said. 'I left early, and got lost. Finally worked out how to get home, found myself passing a hostelry and came in.' He looked at the bitter lemon. 'I've broken most of my bad habits,' he said. 'But I still can't pass licensed premises.'

Melissa looked round at the empty tables and chairs, looking like a low-budget film set before the actors have arrived. 'It must be for the company,' she said, startling herself. It was, in its way, a joke. She wouldn't have thought that possible.

He smiled. 'The company's all right from where I'm sitting,' he said quietly, his eyes looking into hers.

'And is no one missing *you*?' she asked, her voice as low as his had been.

He shook his head. 'No one's missed me for years,' he said.

Melissa sipped her drink. 'Poor Mac,' she said.

He smiled. 'They did once,' he said. 'I don't blame them for giving up on me. I had.'

She glanced at the soft drink, and he nodded. 'You weren't a football fan in your teens, then?' he said.

She shook her head, smiling a little at last. 'You're an ex-footballer?' she asked.

'Ex-footballer, ex-husband, ex-alcoholic and ex-convict,' he said. 'Or so my ex-wife likes to describe me.'

'Ex-convict?'

He smiled. 'Oh, yes. After spending the best part of ten years in an alcoholic stupor, I finally crashed the car through a shop window. I got six months, and I'm still disqualified from driving.'

Over the next few drinks, Melissa got a rundown on the rest. He had used his time in prison to resurrect his brain; he had dried out, he had got himself straight. He hadn't looked at a betting slip or a woman or a glass of anything stronger than fruit juice since the day he'd come to in hospital with a nurse flitting past, two years ago.

His wife had left him early in their marriage for an accountant, taking their then three year old son with her.

'Do you see much of your son?'

She had hit a nerve. They lived in America now, and his son didn't know who his real father was; Sandra, Mac's ex-wife, had begged him to stay away. So far, he had. But maybe not for ever, he added. He'd soon be able to afford the fare.

She looked at him. 'Do you think you should tell him who you are?' she asked.

He shrugged. 'I don't know. Do you think I should?'

'Me?' she said, startled. She really didn't need anyone else's problems tonight. She had surprised herself by being able to make small talk, even, but she supposed that that was second nature now, after years of doing interviews.

'I'd like to know.'

She shook her head. 'But I've got nothing to do with it,' she protested.

'But you do all these articles on . . .' He shrugged again. 'I don't know – moral dilemmas. That's what this is, isn't it?'

Melissa smiled a little sadly. 'I'll say,' she said. Then she looked at him. 'You don't sound much like an ex-footballer,' she said.

His still-dark eyebrows rose very slightly. 'You mean I'm not supposed to know words like "moral dilemma"?'

She blushed, then rallied to her own defence. 'You pretend not to know them,' she said. 'You had to hedge it round with "I don't know" and "that's what this is, isn't it?"'

He smiled. 'That's a habit you get into if you think you're cleverer than everyone else and you don't want to admit it in case you get a hostile reaction,' he said.

'And were you cleverer than everyone else?' she asked, her voice gentler than the question, a trick she had perfected over the years.

He sat back. 'The blokes I played with,' he said, his forefinger on his thumb as he began to count them off. 'One of them's the manager of a First Division side and has been for the past eight years. One of them's the managing director of his own sporting goods business. One of them took a pub in the Cotswolds . . .' He let his hands drop. 'No,' he said. 'I wasn't.'

Her eyes held his.

'But you're clever,' he added.

'Am I?'

'You were a university lecturer, according to the sports desk,' he said.

She smiled. 'Yes,' she said. 'For about five minutes.'

'Why *The Chronicle*?' he asked. 'I would have thought that the ladies' page was slumming for someone like you.'

'It pays quite well,' she said. She didn't argue with his definition of her activities; one reason for the pseudonym was so that her more academic acquaintances didn't find out what she did for a living. 'And I enjoy it,' she said. She had enjoyed it. Until this evening.

His eyes went from hers to take in the rest of her. 'You're not anything like any of the other women I've known,' he said.

'Oh?'

'No. They all wore lip-gloss and had their hair dyed.'

'And because I don't, you want my advice on what you should do about your son?' she asked incredulously.

'I'd like to know what you think,' he said. 'That's all.'

She considered that. 'Does he know he has a real father somewhere?' she asked.

'Yes. They legally adopted him. I think he assumes he was in an orphanage.'

'How old is he now?'

'Fifteen.'

'Then it has to be between you and him,' she said. 'I'd be inclined to think that he has the right to know.'

'Yes,' said Mac. 'But would he want to know?'

Melissa thought. 'You could use a third party,' she said. 'A solicitor, or someone. He could write to him, letting him know that the possibility exists of meeting his real father. Then it would be up to him.'

Mac's brow cleared a little. 'I said you were clever,' he said. 'I never thought of that.'

'What did you do once you'd decided to walk the straight and narrow?' Melissa asked, changing the subject quickly before he could get round to asking her if she knew any solicitors.

'I signed on as unemployed,' he said. 'And I did anything they gave me, anything I could find myself. All over the country.' He smiled. 'It was a good way to see the place – maybe I should write a book about it.'

'What sort of jobs?'

'Labouring, gardening, washing windows, cars. I've been an ice-cream salesman, a courier – on a pushbike. I still don't have my licence back.'

'What brought you here?'

'You have to be somewhere,' said Mac. 'I thought there might be work on the building sites, but there wasn't. I got a job in a garage – I'm a sort of a salesman.'

Melissa sighed. Mac's work record sounded very like a hair shirt to her. 'How did the column come about?' she asked.

It turned out that the sports editor had taken his car in for its MOT, and had been startled to find an ex-international footballer in the showroom, when he had gone to drool over the new cars. Mac had persuaded him to let him put his name above a column.

'He was as startled as you to discover that not only could I write my name, but I could write the column too,' he said, teasing her.

It was being syndicated to a few local papers now, and some money was coming in. But he still worked for the garage.

He sat back again and looked at her. 'So why have I just told you my life story?' he asked.

She shrugged, and drained her glass, feeling pleasantly woozy and warm, despite everything. 'I don't wear lip-gloss,' she said. 'No,' she relented, smiling at his offended look. 'I suppose it's just talking to a stranger. It's easier.'

'You're not a stranger though, are you?' He leant over towards her, and tapped her knee lightly. 'You're adrift in an open boat too. I can tell.'

She made to stand, to go and get another round, but he caught her arm and gently pulled her back down, taking her empty glass.

'It's no answer, Melissa,' he said. 'Believe me.'

He released her, but there was a tension between them now that he had touched her. She hadn't led a particularly sheltered life prior to Simon, but she had never picked up a man in a bar before. She could pick Mac up; that much was obvious.

She had toyed with the idea when he had first arrived, and it had seemed crazy. She barely knew the man. By the time she had finished her drink it had seemed an attractive idea, and now that she had downed her fourth, all she knew was that he was right. She was adrift in an open boat, and he could rescue her. He could put his arms round her and haul her into safe harbour for the night.

She wanted that more than anything, and set about getting it with the same single-mindedness as she had done everything else since meeting Sharon Smith. It didn't take long; she did have another drink, despite Mac's advice, then excused herself and went to the ladies to look at herself in the mirror. Her head felt a little detached from the rest of her, she conceded, but otherwise she was all right.

He stood up as she came back.

'Bag,' she said, leaning across him to reach up to the shelf.

'Let me get it,' he said, but it was too late; she had caught the bag but lost her footing as she tried a too-complicated balancing manoeuvre for her displaced centre of gravity. She fell against him so that all three of them landed on the pink velvet; him, Melissa and the bag.

'Sorry,' she said, giggling just a little tipsily as she lay sprawled on top of him. She felt his physical reaction as she moved, and smiled at him, disentangling herself slowly, as much for her own benefit as his. 'Let's go,' she said.

He didn't need to be asked twice.

Frances had come up to bed while Lionel was in the bath; he had made as little noise as possible as he got into bed beside her, though she could have slept through an air-raid. He wasn't sure why he was taking such precautions anyway; if she did wake, there would still be no conversation, and no need to answer the questions that he could feel hanging over him. Questions that would be asked. Sooner or later.

Her heavy, rhythmic breathing filled the room, and he lay in the darkness, wide awake. He wasn't convinced that he would ever sleep again, but the worry and the fatiguing drive home had worn him out, and his eyelids grew heavy.

They shot open again as the dream which had instantly invaded his unconscious mind became unbearable.

Swaths of mist hung round the hedgerows as Simon Whitworth arrived home for the second time that evening. Melissa must be home this time; the light was on again. But of course, he remembered, he of the carefully contrived alibis had deliberately left it on, as it would have been if he had never been home. Which would, of course, be his story.

Their house was built at the top of a hill just on the town boundary, where built-up areas gave way to farmers' fields with sheep grazing, and tiny villages. It was a solitary listed cottage which stood on the bypass, and with which Melissa had fallen in love when they had moved to the area. The view was non-existent tonight, he thought, as he looked at the soft cloak in which the town had wrapped itself.

The front door opened directly into the living-room with the open staircase on the left; she wasn't home yet. There was an odd quality to the emptiness of the house; an abandoned feel. Simon felt like he had when the floodlights had gone out, and it was the house that was doing it to him. Without Melissa, without even Robeson, yelling for food and wrapping himself round his legs, it didn't have much to offer. Where *was* Melissa? Had something happened to her?

He put the kettle on for coffee, chiding himself for being fanciful. She had said she was doing a late interview. Why in the world should he feel as though her absence were somehow sinister?

He had had no idea that Sharon had any involvement with Jake Parker; perhaps they were just passing the time of day. But why would that make this other man react like that? If that was how it had happened. And no matter how you looked at it, Sharon was at the football match. Why? And why hadn't she told him? She had said she was meeting someone – why wouldn't she have said that that was where she was going?

He made tea, and wished that Melissa would come home. He was worried about her. He glanced at the clock, a pool of dread forming in the pit of his stomach. He had been so relieved once again to find the house empty; it had given him a chance to think about what was happening without Melissa asking all the time what was wrong. But it was such a dreadful night; she could have had an accident. He could imagine the scorn with which he would be greeted if he were to start ringing hospitals, but it was really very late now.

He pulled the telephone towards him, and dialled the number of the police station.

'Sergeant Woodford, please,' he asked when he got through.

'Who's calling?'

'Simon Whitworth.' His hand gripped the receiver as he waited for the call to be put through. If Melissa had had an accident, he'd—

'Woodford.'

'Ah . . . Sergeant Woodford. It's . . . er . . . it's Simon Whitworth here – I was in earlier to see Jake Parker?'

'Yes, Mr Whitworth.'

'Well . . . I hope this doesn't sound too hysterical, but my wife – she did say she would be working late, but it's almost half-past eleven now, and – that is, she works in Barton, you see. Well – she was interviewing someone, but I don't know where that would be – it could have been anywhere in the county, really.' He took a breath, aware that what he had just said probably hadn't made any sense at all. 'I wondered if you had had any accidents reported,' he said.

'I can check for you, Mr Whitworth,' he said, his voice entirely calm. 'One moment.'

Simon's foot tapped nervously on the floor as he waited once more, his ear cocked for the sound of a car engine that never came. Please Melissa, please. Don't have had an accident.

'The good news is that we have had no serious accidents reported,' Sergeant Woodford's reassuring voice said.

41

Her car could be in a ditch, unnoticed. She could be bleeding to death somewhere . . . Simon couldn't bear it.

'If you can tell me the make and number of your wife's car, we'll certainly keep an eye out for it,' he went on.

Simon supplied the information, wondering in a detached way if they did that for everyone, or just for people with whom they happened to have a professional connection. He had a good relationship with the police, unlike some of his colleagues; his practice tended towards property and divorce, and he really only got involved in the criminal courts with people who had got themselves into a scrape, like Parker, rather than the persistent offenders, whose solicitors were seen as an evil insisted on by the law.

'Try not to worry, Mr Whitworth. She may have stayed over in Barton, in view of the weather. It's like this all over the east of England, they tell me.'

'She would have phoned,' said Simon. But then, he hadn't been there, had he? He closed his eyes. Had he heard the phone ringing just as he got to the front door? It could have been. It could have been Melissa, trying to tell him where she was.

Please God let it have been Melissa, he thought, as he thanked the sergeant, and replaced the receiver.

Lloyd knew that he shouldn't have said the things he had, but he had been angry.

She made him angry, therefore it *was* partly her fault. He had known Judy since she was twenty years old, which was when he had fallen for her; fallen in love almost instantly with an open, friendly face, shining dark hair and honest brown eyes, almost before they had even spoken to one another. Once they had, he had discovered the quick intelligence which had almost been buried under a lack of belief in herself; he liked to think that he had had a hand in bringing it out.

But she still hated change, hated having to adjust to new situations, and he knew what would happen. She had been in her new flat for almost two months, and it was turning into home. Even though she didn't like it much. Even though she missed being with him. It was home, and the longer she lived there, the more used to it she would become, and it would be the devil's own job to make her leave the damn place again, once she had dug herself in there.

Despite that, Lloyd hadn't tried to put obstacles in her way – in fact, he had been a positive tower of strength; it wouldn't be forever, he had assured her. It wasn't as if they couldn't see each other. And it would only be until the divorce, when their relationship could at last come out of the closet in which it had been uneasily and inconveniently concealed for the last two years. Not particularly well concealed, come to that; bits of it had invariably got caught in the door, and were visible to anyone who cared to look.

But as far as the top brass were concerned, she had shared with another policewoman until the move to Malworth, and in amongst her usual dread of the new, he fancied he had seen a hint of relief in Judy's eyes that the deception was over. There would have been a hell of a stink if anyone had found out, so he could understand that, even though it had been her idea in the first place. He would never have suggested that she put herself in such an invidious position. It had been her idea, and then she had worried about it, all the time. He hadn't complained about that either – in fact, he told himself, he had been entirely understanding about the whole thing.

The trouble was that the more he glowed with righteous indignation at her treatment of him, the less he understood just what she was supposed to have done. He was faced with the unwelcome thought that he might be being unreasonable.

Never. He poured himself a whisky and picked up his book. Never.

They would probably be charging him with reckless driving. They had given him a speeding ticket. They had examined every inch of the bike by torchlight, trying to find something wrong with it. They'd have been lucky. Colin spent hours on the bike; it gleamed with health. They had breathalysed him, and had been really disappointed when they had found out he hadn't been drinking. His road tax, insurance and licence were all in order. He had been wearing his crash helmet.

They hadn't liked that. They had wanted to be able to take the bike away from him. And when the radio had confirmed that he was the owner of the bike, they had liked it even less.

They had kept him there for an hour and a half, and then had had to settle for the ticket. But they hadn't liked it.

'You're going to remember us,' one of them had said.

Back at home at last, Colin bathed his face, and looked at himself in the bathroom mirror. Thank God his parents were away, though with their usual perversity, they were coming back tomorrow, rather than adding the weekend to their holiday, like everyone else. Colin looked at his own eyes burning back at him, and threw up in the basin.

He felt suddenly and desperately tired; he collapsed into a chair, and fell into an almost immediate and almost unconscious sleep.

Jake Parker let himself into the large bungalow which he rented from people who had gone to the States on a twelve-month exchange. It was much too large for one person, but it had the right image. Stansfield didn't go in much for penthouse flats, which would have been rather more his style than the over-fussy architecture of the bungalow, not to mention its Laura Ashley interior. Still – it was all right for entertaining business acquaintances.

Bobbie liked it – not that she had been there that much. He preferred to keep her in the background – she didn't quite fit in with the image he was trying to project. She shared a flat with another girl in Malworth, and lived on presents and promises of great things to come.

And they would come. Nothing was going to stand in his way. He'd made damn sure that he could distance himself from the whole thing – not so Lionel. And if push came to shove, he would have no hesitation in dropping Lionel right in it.

He pulled off his tie, and poured himself a drink. He was tired, after his exertions; his eye hurt. He looked at it in the mirror over the bar, and held the glass up in a grim, silent toast.

Out in the lobby there was a cigarette machine; Mac had given that up too, but he stuffed coins in and pulled out the first packet he came to, tearing off the cellophane as he glanced into the lounge. He longed to be back in bed with her, but she had wanted him to leave, and he wasn't about to spoil things.

It had never been like that with any of the peroxide blondes with their tight skirts and sexy wiggles that more often than not were violations of the Trade Descriptions Act. Melissa wore old jeans and a shapeless sweater; that, he had discovered, was because she didn't need to look sexy. She just was.

The lads on the sports desk didn't know about her, did they? Melissa Fletcher, the one who hadn't had the faintest idea who he was when he had been introduced to her at the paper, who hadn't even remembered his name earlier on this evening, had just given him the best time he'd ever had.

He could have had anyone he wanted in the old days. And had. Models, film stars . . . falling at his feet, they'd been. But it was a funny old game, life. Stood up by Donna the dead-cert divorcee who was well past her sell-by date, only to be seduced by someone twelve years his junior who until now hadn't known he existed. Perhaps it had been his personal charisma all along, and nothing to do with the fame and the money. Or perhaps Melissa Fletcher was a pushover, which seemed a touch more likely. He'd have to tell the sports desk to update their files.

He wondered if she did this all the time. A couple of reps had appeared since he had gone upstairs with Melissa; if he hadn't bumped into her, it might have been one of them. Tough luck, lads, he thought. You don't know what you missed.

She was on the skinny side, and the tall side – Mac had a preference for ladies a couple of inches shorter than he was, and if anything, she was just a touch taller. Thinking about her made him want her again, despite the tendrils of ardour-damping fog wrapping themselves round him as he stepped out into the damp air. He could have gone on all night, and so could she. But she had asked him to leave.

The mist was patchy now; some spots were clear, and he could see the stars. But then he would find himself walking into its depths again. He drew out a cigarette, and put it between his lips, then automatically searched his pockets for non-existent matches. He swore, and pushed the useless comforter into his pocket.

He had gone up to her room with no great hopes; if anything, he had been depressed, having just given her the printable chapters of his less than successful life story. But his mumbled, would-be jokey fears that his lack of female companionship for the last few years might have blunted his technique – his declared celibacy was stretching a point, but his recent encounters had required no technique – and that his abused body might not have the attraction it had once had, had been allayed by her frankness about the whole thing, and had vanished altogether at the first electric touch of her skin on his.

He turned into the football ground, almost groping his way towards the railings, looking for the gap.

He had never met anyone like Melissa, far less gone to bed with her. He wouldn't have, not in the old days, because she wasn't beautiful; her features were too sharp, her face too long, her hair too short, her breasts too small, her body too angular. But the combination of intelligence and unashamed sensuality had knocked him sideways, and he was a happy man.

Life, he thought, could hold no more surprises, not after Melissa. Until his foot hit something soft and yielding, and he looked down.

Life had one more surprise up her sleeve.

Four

He had phoned Judy eventually, just to make sure she had got home all right, and to say he was sorry. Lloyd always said he was sorry. He always *was* sorry. She had been monosyllabic, which had annoyed him all over again; he had given vent to his feelings, and she had hung up on him. He wanted to ring her again, ask her forgiveness, get her to say more than yes and no. But it was after midnight, and she was probably in bed. She hated having her sleep interrupted. But then she probably wasn't asleep – not when they were still at loggerheads.

A little voice told him that that was whistling in the dark; she almost certainly *was* asleep. Then she had no right to be, not while he was here worrying about everything. Serve her right if he woke her up.

The phone rang, and he smiled broadly. She did feel like he did, he thought, as he picked it up. 'Hello,' he said, his voice contrite.

'Sir? Finch here, sir. We've got an as yet unidentified body in the car park of the Byford Road sports and leisure centre. We've got her bag, but there's no ID. It looks like she's been strangled. The pathologist is on his way, and the police surgeon's already here. The inspector said I should call you,' he added, just to cover himself.

Lloyd's eyes closed briefly. 'Description of the victim?' he said.

'Female – fair hair, about five feet six, apparently aged between twenty and thirty. She was found by someone taking a short cut home.'

'Did he trample all over any evidence that might have been there?' asked Lloyd testily.

'Probably, sir. He practically fell over her. You'll see when you get here – it's pitch dark. Someone's taken a preliminary statement, but I haven't been able to question him yet.'

Lloyd sighed loudly. 'Thank you, Tom. I'll be there in about—'

'There's something else, sir. Mrs Whitworth – the solicitor's wife? Didn't come home from work. He rang the station a while back to check on accidents.'

Lloyd's instantly suspicious mind logged that, as had Finch's. 'Have you got a description of her?' he asked.

'No. He wasn't actually reporting her missing, apparently. It was a more or less informal call to Jack Woodford. We're getting her description, but there's no sign of her car at the ground.'

'Right. I'll be with you in . . . well, what's the weather like?'

'Bloody awful, sir.'

There was a silence after that, which Lloyd broke with the suggestion that neither of them had wanted to make. Rapists sometimes went over the edge.

'Has he gone one step further this time?'

'Can't be sure, sir. Her clothes are disarranged, but it doesn't look like a sex attack. Not at first glance, anyway.'

Lloyd thanked Finch, and put down the phone. He wasn't certain, as he reached for his jacket, whether Finch's final statement was good news or bad news. A rapist turned murderer was always bad news. But two violent criminals in one not very large town was worse.

He drove out of the village, stopping at the roundabout to check for sudden traffic coming out of the void, then drove on, picking up speed as the visibility lengthened and it was possible to remember what driving without a blindfold was like, only to slow down again as another bank of fog rolled in.

At the top of the hill was the grim paraphernalia of sudden violent death. Police cars, ambulance, people milling around, the area being cordoned off. The blue lights blinked blearily through the mist, and Lloyd pulled into the side of the road, a little way away from the crush of vehicles. With just a little reluctance, he got out of the car, and looked at the fog swirling round the orange glow of the street-light, the last one before the football ground, and the unlit bypass.

It was popularly supposed to be on nights like these that Jack the Ripper had stalked Whitechapel, he thought, with the gas-lamps guttering as the hansom cab clip-clopped its way into the mask of smoke and mist, leaving his latest victim on the cobbled street. Shivering, he walked purposefully towards the car park, and the police surgeon loomed out of the darkness as he approached.

'Lloyd – I've certified death, taken temperatures – all the usual stuff. Left notes with your sergeant. Bright lad, that.'

Lloyd nodded.

'Do you want me to hang around for the pathologist?'

'No, Doctor, thank you. It could take him hours to get here in this.'

'Right, I'll be off then.'

Lloyd moved towards the cordoned-off area where the duty inspector was organising the uniforms for a search, and where the victim presumably lay. He carefully followed the path indicated.

'Evening,' said the inspector. 'I've got my lads doing a search of the immediate area in case he's broken in to a building or anything, but I expect he's long gone.'

Lloyd nodded. Close to, he could see her by the fuzzy beam of the inspector's torch-light, half-sitting, half-lying, her head slumped against the thick concrete upright of the fencing, a man's tie tightly wound round her neck.

Finch was taking a call on the car radio; Lloyd looked down once again at the girl, then over at the football ground, and the black shapes of the floodlights in the mist. 'Find someone who can switch these things on!' he shouted angrily. 'I'm not waiting all bloody night for lights to arrive!'

The inspector went off to comply with the request; Finch hastily finished his call, and came over to where Lloyd stood. 'Sorry, sir,' he said. 'I didn't know you were here.' He looked a little anxious, but Lloyd wasn't angry with him. 'I should have thought about getting the lights on,' he said.

After a few minutes, the inspector returned. 'Mr Parker has said he'll get the groundsman out,' he said.

'Good.' Lloyd sighed. 'Thanks.' He turned to Finch as the other man walked away. 'Right,' he said. 'Tell me what you know.'

Finch took a breath. 'I know that we're doing Parker for breach of the peace,' he said. 'And now we're asking him to help us out.'

Lloyd sighed. 'The papers will love that,' he muttered. He glanced at Finch. 'Was that why you didn't ask for the lights to be put on?' he asked.

'No sir,' said Finch honestly. 'I just didn't think.'

Lloyd smiled. 'Neither did I,' he said. 'Parker won't fight shy of the publicity.'

'The fight was over some girl,' Finch reminded Lloyd. 'Their statements just accuse one another of starting it – no one said who the girl was – not to us, at any rate.' He glanced over to where the makeshift shelter was being constructed. 'Do you think that might be her?' he asked.

Lloyd thought about that. 'Could be,' he said, after a moment. 'I want to see Mr Parker if he comes down here. The moment he arrives – and don't let him anywhere near the scene.'

'Sir,' said Finch. He hesitated slightly, then went on. 'It's probably nothing,' he said. 'But when I looked at the body, I could smell sawdust.'

Lloyd shrugged. 'There's a lot of building work going on,' he said.

'Yes, sir – but I can't smell it anywhere else. And I couldn't see any sawdust on the ground.'

Lloyd nodded. 'We'll see what the lab has to say,' he said. 'In the meantime – what else?'

'She was found by a man who gave his name as Gil McDonald,' Finch said.

Lloyd was transported back fifteen, twenty years at the mention of one of his all-time heroes. Gave his name as Gil McDonald. Lloyd looked at the young man – how old was he? Twenty-eight? He would have been about eight years old in the days when Gil McDonald would suddenly come tearing into the box from nowhere at all and volley a ball right past the keeper. He'd assumed that *The Chronicle* article was syndicated, but if it was the same Gil McDonald, then he must have come to live among men right here in Stansfield. Lloyd had always been a terrible disappointment to his Rugby Union obsessed father, with his love of the round-ball game. The real game, he would tell Jack Woodford, when he pointed out that Lloyd wasn't exactly a regular at Stansfield Town matches. The First Division game.

Gil McDonald. Mad Mac. Finch would have been about eighteen when he started his long descent. Couldn't have been a football fan.

'Sir?' Finch was aware that he seemed to have lost his audience. 'Mr McDonald says that he was intending to take a short cut across the ground. Apparently, you can squeeze through a gap in the fencing just there,' he added, pointing, 'and he was looking for it when his foot actually struck the body.'

'Is he wearing a tie?'

'No, sir.'

'Where is he now?'

'In one of the cars, sir.'

'You haven't asked him where he'd been or what he was doing here?'

'No, sir. I was too busy trying to make sure no one else stood on the body.'

Lloyd smiled a little at the hint of defiance in the young man's voice. 'Quite,' he murmured. 'Quite. Carry on with whatever you were doing.'

Finch went off, and Lloyd was pleased to note that he did not immediately go and talk to McDonald. He liked his men to have minds of their own. He sighed again.

His women certainly did, he thought sourly, then immediately felt guilty. She hadn't *done* anything, he told himself again. Neither had his ex-wife, with whom he had also had a difference of opinion, or – come to that – his daughter, over whose actions the difference of opinion had occurred. But all that had to take a back seat; he had his job to do, and at least Judy would understand that, which Barbara never had.

And he didn't like the way this one was shaping up. No identification yet; no immediate lead on why she was dead. A rapist on the loose, and a reputedly millionaire businessman getting himself involved in a fight over a woman. This woman? Jack Woodford said that she had gone off before the police got to them. He'd need confirmation of who the woman was, but she was probably nothing to do with anything.

DI Barstow was setting up the murder room at the station, plucked from sleep like most of the people already hard at work on the case. But they really had nothing to go on, so far. All they knew right now was that there had been two hundred people here tonight, and that meant two hundred potential witnesses, with the consequent huge amounts of legwork and paperwork. Her shoulder bag had been found, complete with purse, which still had money in it, so robbery was unlikely to be the motive. It had no credit cards, no driving licence, nothing to say who its deceased owner was. It had a receipt, dated that day, for clothes she had bought at the superstore, which might be some sort of lead, and a key, which seemed to be to a street door. But they didn't know who she was, and until they knew that . . . He sighed for the third time.

The groundsman arrived, but Parker had not accompanied him. Lloyd watched as the powerful lights began their sequence. When they were all lit, he turned towards the fence. The fog was lifting; the light was good. He sent two DCs to interview Parker about the evening's altercation, and resigned himself to waiting for answers.

He heard Freddie's car long before it nosed its way into the line of cars by the entrance, its powerful engine humming through the stillness as it came along the bypass, growing to a roar as the car made its way towards the ground. Even at the low speed enforced on it by the weather, it sounded angry. It growled to a halt, and Freddie's tall thin frame emerged with some difficulty. In the summer, he would drive it minus its top, and would step out over the closed door.

'No assistant tonight?' Lloyd asked.

Freddie smiled. 'No. She and her police sergeant are off on honeymoon.'

Oh yes. Judy had told him that Bob Sandwell had finally married Kathy. He'd forgotten.

'Well,' said Freddie, still smiling, despite what he was about to do. 'Lead the way.' Freddie enjoyed his work, and would set about it with an enthusiasm that was almost, but not quite, infectious.

They picked their way through the scene of crime officers to the body, and Freddie crouched down to begin his examination. He didn't touch the girl's body until he had noted everything about it and its environment which might be of use to the investigation, writing quickly and neatly. He sketched out the area, the position of the body, the spot where her bag had been found.

He looked at the tie, turning the end carefully to reveal the label. 'If you were hoping it was the tie of a very exclusive club, forget it,' he said, with a grin, looking up at Lloyd. 'This is one of thousands.'

'You needn't look so pleased about it,' said Lloyd. He was all right once the investigation was under way, and the victim was just a name about whom they had to find out as much as they could. But until she had a name, the investigation would be being conducted in a void; Freddie could tell him how she had died, and give him an estimate of when. He and forensic could, with luck, give him pointers on the physical and mental characteristics of the murderer. Her clothes, her injuries, everything would tell part of the story. Perhaps even Finch's sawdust. But every minute they lost before they could circulate her description, before they could start interviewing possible witnesses, the murderer was a minute better off.

He went across to the car in which Finch was speaking to Gil McDonald, and got into the front passenger seat. It *was* the Gil McDonald. He felt the almost schoolboyish pleasure that he always did on meeting a famous face, and always wished he didn't.

'This is Detective Chief Inspector Lloyd,' said Finch. 'Mr McDonald, sir.'

'I wanted my boy to be a footballer,' Lloyd said.

McDonald raised his eyebrows. 'And what does he do?' he asked.

'He's a plumber. Well – he will be, when he's finished his apprenticeship.'

'Good,' said McDonald. He took a slightly battered cigarette from his jacket pocket. 'You don't have a light, do you?' he asked. 'No one smokes any more,' he added, with a hard look at Finch.

Lloyd had a book of matches somewhere, because he'd picked them up in a restaurant yesterday. He always did that, though he didn't smoke either. Judy did. He found them, and handed them to McDonald, who looked pale and upset.

McDonald struck the match which flared with the alarming

suddenness of paper matches, and inhaled deeply, coughing immediately. 'I'd given up,' he spluttered. 'Until tonight.'

When the spasm had subsided, Lloyd indicated that Finch should carry on.

'Can I ask where you had been, Mr McDonald?'

McDonald released smoke without choking this time. 'Nowhere,' he said. 'Walking round in circles.'

Finch looked puzzled.

'I was here earlier to cover the opening. I left after about half an hour, but I got lost in the fog,' said McDonald.

'And . . . when did you leave here?'

'Around eight,' he said.

Finch's fair eyebrows shot up. 'You were lost in the fog for almost four hours?' he asked.

McDonald, cool as you like, nodded. Lloyd didn't speak. He wanted to see how Finch handled the interview, and he wanted to come to terms with the idea that a hero of his might just have strangled someone. He had been wild, in his youth. Mad Mac wasn't just a newspaper epithet because it was alliterative. He had gone at everything hell for leather; if he had felt like killing a woman, he would have been quite likely to do it and damn the consequences.

'You were lost for four hours in a town like Stansfield?' asked Finch.

Judy wouldn't have done that. Finch had asked the last question; Judy would have let it lie there until it got some sort of response other than the nod.

'I might not have *been* in Stansfield all the time, for all I know,' said McDonald. 'I got good and lost.'

'You found your way here, though,' Finch said. 'When you came to the opening.'

'Yes. But I tried to go home a different way.'

'Why?'

McDonald looked uncomfortable for a moment. 'I just wanted to walk for a bit,' he said. 'But I got lost. Eventually, I realised I was in the village. I knew how to get home from there.'

'Where's home?'

'Digs,' he said. His voice was cool, but his hands were agitated, seeking something to do. He fiddled with the wedding ring he wore. He smoked quickly, in short puffs. 'In Buchan Road.'

Buchan Road was on an estate which, like the football ground itself, bordered on the bypass, about three miles further down by road. Crossing the pitch and the public playing fields would indeed be a shortcut.

'Where did you telephone from, Mr McDonald?' Finch asked, as McDonald jettisoned the lit cigarette through the open car window, and drew another cigarette from the packet.

'What? Oh – to the police, you mean? Here.' He jerked his head back at the telephone box by the entrance.

'And . . . where did you get the cigarettes from?'

Good, good. Most of the cellophane was still on the packet, including a ribbon overprinted with the words MACHINE PACK. You didn't get a full twenty from a machine; the pack was obviously new, and he had said he'd given up. Lloyd hadn't noticed; he felt more confident about the young sergeant now. And the question had fazed McDonald; he was making a business of lighting his second cigarette to give himself time.

'The pub,' he said, when he removed the cigarette from his mouth, trying to make it look as though speech would have been impossible before doing so.

'Which pub?'

'The one in the village. What's it called – Sneakers?'

Finch nodded. 'Did you have a drink in the pub?'

'No.'

'Would anyone remember seeing you, do you think?'

McDonald drew deeply on the new cigarette. 'No,' he said. 'I just went in, got cigarettes and came out – there was no one else around. The machine's in the foyer. Do you think I killed her, or something?'

'We have to ask questions,' Finch said. 'It's our job, Mr McDonald.'

McDonald subsided. 'Sorry,' he said.

'How long had you given up smoking?' Finch asked.

'Three years,' said McDonald, looking a little surprised at the question.

'What made you buy cigarettes tonight?'

'Look – I'd been lost in the fog for hours, I had been stood up by the lady I was supposed to be taking to this damn opening, and I was feeling sorry for myself. So I bought cigarettes. It's not a crime yet.'

'No, sir,' said Finch. 'But I'll be honest with you. I find it very hard to believe that you were wandering round for four hours. Why didn't you ask someone where you were?'

'I just didn't. And I want a straight answer. Do you think I did that?' He pointed towards where Freddie worked.

'I don't know,' said Finch.

'Why would I phone the police?'

Finch shrugged. 'People have been known to,' he said.

53

'Who is she, anyway?'

'We don't know that either.'

'You don't know much.'

'No, we don't. That's why it helps if people tell us the truth. For all I know she could be your date.'

'What?'

'Who were you supposed to take to this do tonight?'

'A woman called Donna Fairweather – she works as a typist at *The Barton Chronicle*. She lives on the Mitchell estate – I was trying to find her house when I got lost.'

Going to cover the opening of the new sports and leisure centre, and he hadn't worn a tie? Lloyd thought about that as Finch jotted down the name. 'Thank you,' said the sergeant.

McDonald watched Finch write. 'I tripped over a body, and I went to that phone and rang you. I waited for you, and I've been here for hours, and now I find I'm suspect number bloody one!'

'You've been very helpful, sir,' said Finch. 'Thank you for your time. You just stay here – I'll get someone to drive you home.'

McDonald gave a short laugh. 'Someone to make sure I go home and stay there?' he said.

'Yes, sir,' said Finch, with disarming honesty.

The two men walked away from the car, and Lloyd looked at Finch. 'Well?' he said.

'I'm damn sure he wasn't walking around for four hours,' said Finch. 'But – if you want a personal impression – I don't think he had anything to do with it. I think he was up to something, but it wasn't that. And people don't automatically wear ties when they go out these days.'

Lloyd smiled at the accurate interpretation of his fleeting thought. 'Just something he regards as none of our business,' he mused. 'Yes. I'm inclined to agree. But once we know who the victim is, we'll be in a much better position to question Mr McDonald, and that's just what we'll do.'

The floodlights blazed through the night as the police searched for evidence. The body was taken away, and Freddie roared off; SOCOS took away all manner of things for forensic examination. Odd pieces of building materials lying around from the site, the Coke tins and empty cigarette packets that might just give them a lead; what looked like and probably was a load of rubbish.

The DCs arrived back, and Parker's story had been filled out a little from the one he had told at the police station. The girl he had spoken to was one Sharon Smith, who had worked for him once. She had been heavily engaged in chatting up Barnes when he had seen her at the ground, and the younger man had swung a punch when she left him to talk to Parker.

Sharon Smith answered the description of the dead girl; she lived with her mother, and Parker had supplied her address. Lloyd braced himself for the worst part of all.

Two hours later Mrs Smith had identified the body, and Lloyd was a little wiser about Sharon Smith and a great deal wearier. He drove back via the scene of crime, where they were trying to get prints from moisture-beaded metal railings, examining the tarmac surface of the car park, and the rather more productive grass verges out on the pavement, taking tyre impressions and footmarks before they were obliterated by rain or whatever else the weather might have in store. At five o'clock, he went home to get some sleep and to reflect on the little he had learned.

Sharon hadn't gone out much. She didn't have a boyfriend that her mother knew of. She had always been very quiet; never had all that much to do with men. She had taken a flat of her own at one point, when she had worked for Parker Development, but she had come back to live with her mother when her father had died, and her mother couldn't cope. She had taken the job with Mr Evans then, as it was too far to travel to Parker's. It was Mr Parker who had got her it, really. He'd always been very kind to Sharon. That might have been why she was at the football ground; she certainly wasn't interested in football. Her mother hadn't recognised the key; she thought that perhaps it had something to do with work.

Sharon had loved her family, and had been loved, that much was obvious. But she had kept her feelings and her private business to herself, and her mother and sister had respected that. Which was fine when she was alive, but not much use to him now. They had given him names of people who might be able to tell him more; he had passed them on, and made a mental note to speak to Parker as soon as possible.

He switched on the radio before getting his head down for a couple of hours. The fog would disperse soon after daylight, said the weathermen, but it would be dense and widespread again that evening. This pattern, they said, looked set to continue through the weekend. Lloyd had a feeling in his bones that the forecast might turn out to be more prophetic than the Met Office knew.

He got into bed, looking at the clock, and decided it wasn't too early to ring Judy. She might have been trying to ring him back, and getting no reply. She would surely have been worrying; he thought he really ought to ring.

* * *

In a spacious, old-fashioned flat which had once been part of someone's town house in the centre of Malworth, above the shop into which the ground floor had been turned, Judy turned over in the double bed in which she had spent six warm, comfortable hours, and snuggled down into the duvet, sleeping the sleep of the just, or possibly of the just very selfish, depending on your point of view.

The insistent purring of the telephone penetrated her dreams; she opened her eyes, groped for the light switch, then focussed on the clock, pulling a face. Work. Who else would phone this early on a Saturday morning? It wasn't fair. It was supposed to be her day off.

'DI Hill,' she said.

'Just wanted to say good morning.'

She stared at the phone, then at the clock again. 'Do you know what *time* it is?' she demanded.

'Yes,' he said. 'And for your information, I haven't been to bed at all yet.'

More fool him. Judy hung up on him again, pulled the duvet over her head, and was sound asleep again without so much as a pang of guilt.

At seven, the phone woke her again, and the feeling that she might just have been a little insensitive broke through the anaesthetic of sleep. She picked up the phone. 'Hi,' she said. 'I'm sorry. Honestly.'

There was the tiniest of silences before anyone spoke. When he did, Judy blushed painfully in a way that would have gladdened Lloyd's disenchanted heart.

'DI Hill? Merrill. Sorry to bring you in on your day off, but we've got another alleged rape, and I rather think your bedside manner is called for in this particular case. I'll give you the details when you come in.'

Oh, God. Her new DCI, the God-fearing, home-loving Arthur Merrill. Why, she wondered sleepily, as she got herself ready to face the day, were rapes always prefixed with alleged? Burglaries weren't. Car thefts weren't. Muggings weren't.

Only rapes.

Melissa lay on the hotel bed alone. Mac hadn't wanted to leave; he hadn't understood.

You have to come down from a high . . . wasn't that what Sharon had said? And she had come down from the high that Mac had given her. Talking to a stranger was easier, she had told Mac, a little unoriginally. Perhaps making love to a stranger was even better. Sheer physical pleasure uninhibited by years of day-to-day intimacy; fantasy could take over, and carry the two of you into another sphere. She had taken reckless, shameless enjoyment in Mac, and he in her; it had given them both a kind of release from reality.

But reality had come back, she had sent him away, and had lain naked on the bed, not moving, tears streaming down her face. Eventually, the tears had stopped, and she had slept, waking to the sense of achievement which she had felt with Mac gradually reasserting itself. Daylight was breaking through the mist that still hung low over the town, and she rose with the sun as it burned away the remnants of the fog, taking with it the claustrophobia which had haunted the night before, leaving everything clear and fresh.

She ran a bath, and took her time in its warm, soapy depths. The interlude with Mac hadn't been part of her plan, but it had been good for her, despite the sudden depression. Simon might not want her – Sharon's words again, and undeniably true, again – but Mac certainly had.

Now, she had to decide what to do next. One day at a time, she had told herself. By the time she was dressed, she knew that she was going home. Simon had to be faced.

Lionel drove up Byford Road towards the football ground, and saw the floodlights on in the daylight; his heart sank a little. He had to get it back, but he had rather hoped that he could get it without any fuss. When he saw the police car, his inclination was to drive past without stopping, but he had been signalling the turn, and the policeman was walking towards him.

He wound down the window.

'Sorry, sir – no admittance, I'm afraid,' said the constable.

Lionel swallowed. 'I . . . I wondered if someone could let me in – I left something here last night.'

'Could I have your name, sir?'

He hadn't expected it all to happen this quickly. He felt sick.

Colin's eyes opened with a start at the banging on the door knocker. For a second, he forgot where he was, or why he was there. Then he looked down at his muddy jeans, and remembered, closing his eyes again.

The knock grew louder, more determined. His parents? Oh God, had they come back early? He hadn't had time to clean up. There would be questions; he'd have to think of something.

The knock grew louder still. 'Police!' a voice shouted. 'Open up!'

Colin got up slowly, aching with the effort of moving. The anger

57

had gone; the exhilaration that his foolhardy burn-up in the fog had given him was gone. The nausea, the numbing tiredness had gone. But now he ached. Every inch of him ached.

'Colin Drummond? Police!' Another knock. 'Open the door!'

And he was afraid. He opened the door, and saw two policemen, but it wasn't the same ones as before.

He breathed a sigh of almost giddy relief.

Simon heard the car, and ran to the door, arriving beside Melissa as she got out.

'Where the hell have you been?' he shouted. 'I've been worried sick!'

She reached back in for her bag and swung it out, locking the car. 'I tried to ring,' she said. 'You weren't here.' She walked past him into the house.

'You could have tried again!' he said, running after her. 'I've been up all night worrying!'

She put down her bag. 'Have you?' she asked, her voice cool.

'Yes,' he said, and sat down heavily. 'Where *were* you?'

'I stayed at an hotel,' she said. 'And I did try again, but you still weren't here.'

'I was at work. And I got called to the police station. I didn't get home until eleven. Jake Parker got into a fight at the football match.'

She frowned a little. 'Is that why the police car?' she asked.

'What?' he said.

'There was a police car outside the football ground as I passed,' she said.

'I . . . no. It was just a fight,' said Simon. 'Jake and some man called Barnes started pushing and shoving one another.' He wanted a drink. You couldn't have a drink at nine o'clock in the morning. He got up and went over to the kitchen area. 'Coffee?' he asked, striving to make his voice normal.

'Yes, please. I was going to ring you again, but I fell asleep,' she said. 'I came home as soon as I woke up, rather than ring.'

Simon filled the kettle noisily, and switched it on. 'I'd better ring the police,' he said.

'Whatever for?'

'I – I told them you hadn't come home,' he said. How could she make him feel as if that wasn't a perfectly natural thing to do? 'They came and asked for a description of you.'

'Oh, Simon, for God's sake!'

'What did you expect me to do? I was *worried* – I thought you'd had an accident! They were supposed to be watching out for your car – fine job they did of that, if you've just passed . . . ' He stopped shouting, and went to the phone, while Melissa sighed her impatience with him.

'Stansfield Police.'

'Oh – is Sergeant Woodford there, please?'

'No, I'm sorry – he went off duty at six. Can I take a message for him? He'll be back on at ten o'clock tonight.'

Of course, he'd gone off duty. Simon couldn't think straight. But the last thing he wanted was the police involving themselves with his life, and . . . He licked his lips. 'I . . . he may not have . . . it's just that I told him last night that my wife hadn't come home, and now she has.'

But it wasn't as simple as that. He had to give his name, Melissa's name, their address, the registration number of Melissa's car, and then wait for someone else to come on the line.

'Mr Whitworth? Detective Chief Inspector Lloyd. Could I have a word with your wife, please?'

He held the phone out to Melissa. 'It's a chief inspector,' he said. 'He wants to speak to you.'

'Oh, really!' She took the phone. 'Melissa Whitworth speaking,' she said.

There followed a series of terse replies from her to lengthy questions from the chief inspector.

'So I understand.'

'I tried. He wasn't at home.'

Simon made the coffee.

'No. I work.'

'*Barton Chronicle*.'

'Very well. If you must.'

She slammed down the phone. 'The damn police are sending someone to talk to me at work!' she said angrily.

'Why?' asked Simon, mystified.

'How the hell should I know? You're the one who rang them!'

Simon looked at his watch. 'Oh, look – I've got to go,' he said. They still worked Saturday mornings in Stansfield solicitors' offices.

'Yes,' said Melissa. 'It wouldn't do to keep Sharon waiting, would it?'

Simon frowned. But he didn't pursue her odd response; he had to get to the office, and whatever else Melissa was doing, she was spoiling for a row.

'I'd better ring and tell her I'm on my way in,' he said, picking up the phone as Melissa went upstairs.

But there was no reply.

Jake ushered the chief inspector into the patterned depths of the sitting room, where the curtains still held off the daylight. He put on the light rather than open them.

'Terrible thing,' he said. 'I'd hoped – last night . . . well, I'd hoped you were wrong.'

Lloyd nodded briefly. 'How well did you know Sharon Smith?' he asked.

Jake shrugged a little. 'She worked for me,' he said. 'Sit down,' he urged. 'Would you like coffee or anything? I've just made some.'

The chief inspector declined the offer, and Jake sat down, his mouth dry. Why did this feel like a dawn raid?

'How did this fight over.Sharon happen?' Lloyd asked.

'This character she was with objected to her talking to me,' said Jake. 'He hit me, I hit him – your guys saw it, and came charging over. Other people were getting involved. Someone grabbed me – and you know the rest.'

'In his statement, Barnes seems to think you started it. He says he wasn't with Sharon – she simply asked him for the time.'

Jake didn't think that his smile would do much good this time. It was hardly appropriate. 'Yeah, well,' he said. 'Perhaps I jumped to conclusions.'

'You did start it?'

'Maybe.' Jake looked up. 'Does it matter?' he asked, getting up. He was having some coffee, whether or not his uninvited guest wanted one.

'She's dead, Mr Parker. Of course it matters! I have to know as much about her as possible. Why did you start it?'

Jake went determinedly into the kitchen, and poured himself black coffee. His eye throbbed, his head wasn't together yet. He had to be careful. Lloyd followed him in, and just stood there, while Jake swallowed the strong dark liquid. He wiped his mouth with the back of his hand.

'I take it your relationship with her was more than just a working one?' Lloyd said.

Jake drank more coffee. 'Sure,' he said. 'Why not? We were both free agents. Look – I didn't like the way she was behaving, all right?'

'What did she do when the fight started?'

'She took off.'

'Did she leave alone?'

Jake drank some more coffee. He had been too busy head-butting a policeman to notice; it hadn't occurred to him until now that she might not have. 'After I pushed him away, he came back and dragged me away from her,' he said. 'She walked off. That's all I know.'

'Did you see anyone go with her, or after her?'

'That's *all* I know!' repeated Jake.

Lloyd looked at him for a long time. 'If you're thinking about private justice, you can forget it, Mr Parker,' he said.

Jake finished his coffee, and poured more. 'I've no idea who killed her,' he said, with as much patience as he could muster. 'I've told you everything I know.'

Lloyd didn't believe him. But Jake was getting used to that by now.

Engaged again. Mac put down the phone, and walked briskly back up the street to his digs. He had used the phone box rather than ring in what would almost certainly be his landlady's hearing – but he mustn't start behaving like a criminal, he thought, as he let himself into the house, and took the stairs as quietly as he could.

'Mr McDonald!'

My God, they should use landladies instead of radar. He turned. 'Yes,' he said.

'I'm having to go over to my sister's,' she said. 'She's been taken bad again. There's a hotpot in the fridge that you can heat up for your evening meal – I've left instructions on how to use the microwave.'

'Thank you.'

'I should be back about ten, I think. She's usually perfectly all right – she just panics.'

He smiled briefly. The conversation seemed to be terminated; he turned back and went up to his room.

He'd be as well going to see Melissa at the paper. They didn't want his piece on the opening for tonight's edition, but he could write it up and use it as an excuse. He rang Sheila at the garage, and said that he wouldn't be in until the afternoon.

He had lied to the police. He wouldn't have reported it at all if he'd thought for a moment that they would suspect him of murdering the girl. If you found a body, you reported it; that had been all that he had thought. The questions, the intense interest in what he had been doing – that hadn't occurred to him. Now, on reflection, he knew that it was bound to have made them suspicious of him. But they couldn't prove that he hadn't been walking round Stansfield all evening; they certainly couldn't find anything to tie him in with the dead girl, aside from the fact that he had found her, and somebody had to find the dead bodies that other people from time to time left lying around.

It was usually fishermen, he reflected, as he shrugged on his jacket. Or people taking their dog for a walk. Or kids playing in old air raid shelters. Did they all get the third degree about what they'd been doing? Probably, he told himself comfortingly. But Mac had a nasty suspicion that he would get to know the officers of Stansfield constabulary much better than he had any desire to before this business got itself sorted out.

And he had to tell Melissa that he had kept her name out of it. The paper obviously didn't know yet that he had found the body, or he would have heard from them, but she would, of course, find out. So he'd get some Brownie points for not giving her hobby away, at least. But of course – he didn't have to write up his piece. His having found the body was a good excuse for going to the paper, he told himself, as he set off towards the bus stop. He would go in to report his news, and just happen to talk to Melissa while he was there. Even with the uneasy feeling that lying to the police had given him, he viewed seeing Melissa again with pleasurable anticipation, and he felt almost jauntily certain that a little shuttle-bus would appear as soon as he arrived at the stop, so good a turn did his luck seem to be taking.

And a shuttle-bus indeed did; he took the fifteen minutes or so of the journey to sort out his thoughts. He was, despite joking to himself about updating the sports desk on the available skirt, beginning to doubt that Melissa's behaviour of the night before had been in character, and he was glad that he hadn't told the police about her. If he had, it might all have got out, and he wouldn't have wanted to do that to her. He had never felt chivalrous about any woman before, and he walked in the sunshine towards *The Chronicle* offices with a spring in his step.

Until he saw the police car already there.

Five

'And you thought she was me?' Melissa looked with astonishment at the young sergeant who had arrived on the dot of nine o'clock.

'For a while. The first thing you do is check to see who's been reported missing.'

'But my husband said that he gave you a description of me,' Melissa pointed out.

Sergeant Finch nodded. 'That was after we had found her,' he said. 'We naturally assumed that it wasn't you then, but we did have to make certain.'

Melissa stared at him. 'You thought that he'd done away with me, and got someone to say she was me on the phone?' she asked.

'Stranger things have happened.'

The newsroom had been buzzing with the murder when she had got there; the police, however, had been very cagey, and had so far only released her description and the fact that they were treating it as foul play. Melissa could see the reporters just waiting to pounce on Sergeant Finch when he had finished with her.

They were in the editor's office which Finch seemed to think afforded her some privacy. The glass walls simply had the opposite effect, with everyone looking towards the room, trying to guess what her involvement was.

'Can I ask where you were?'

'No, I don't think you can,' said Melissa. 'I chose not to go home last night – that's surely my business?'

Finch smiled. 'Probably,' he said. 'But my boss might not see it like that.'

'Your boss has no more right to know what I was doing last night than I have to know what he was doing,' she said.

'That kind of depends on circumstances, doesn't it, Mrs Whitworth? I mean – if he had spent last night accepting bribes from criminals, you'd think it was your business then, wouldn't you?'

'And did he?' asked Melissa, only too aware that it was difficult for journalists to make stands on rights of privacy.

Finch shrugged. 'You can ask him yourself,' he said. 'I think you'll be getting a visit from Chief Inspector Lloyd before too long.'

'Good. I look forward to putting him straight about the rights of the individual in this country. Well, if that's all, I really do have to—'

'Just one other thing,' he said. 'Gil McDonald.'

The name meant nothing to Melissa. She frowned. 'Who?' she asked coldly.

'I was told I might find him here.'

Melissa shook her head. 'I've never heard of him.'

'He does a column for you, I believe.'

'Not for me,' she said. 'I'm the features editor – I know our columnists.'

'No – sports.'

'Mac!' she said, startled to realise that she didn't even know his real name. My God, did they have video cameras in hotel bedrooms these days? 'Yes, yes – that's right. I only know him as Mac. Sorry.'

'That's all right. I wondered if you could tell me anything about him, but obviously not. Who would be able to?'

'Barry Houghton,' she said, pointing through the glass, and then saw everyone swoop on him as Mac himself walked into the room. She frowned. 'That's Mac,' she said, pointing to the figure in the middle of the small crowd in the middle of the floor.

Finch sat up a little and craned his neck to see over the filing cabinets. 'Oh, of course,' he said. 'Something of a scoop, isn't it, to have one of your very own columnists find the body?'

Melissa went very cold.

'Perhaps you'd ask Mr Houghton to come in and have a word with me?'

Jake had tried to contact Lionel Evans, without success. Whitworth had told him that he was in Birmingham all day; Jake remembered now that he had said something about that last night. He rubbed his eyes, making himself wince as he disturbed the bruised skin. It only took an hour to get to Birmingham – Evans would presumably be back some time. He would try again this afternoon. He'd keep trying. He would camp out on the bloody man's doorstep if he had to.

He hadn't expected an early morning visit from the police; he had told them all they needed to know about Sharon last night, and had hoped that that might have been that. But Chief Inspector Lloyd had wanted to know more, and had asked questions that Jake

64

hadn't expected; he had thrown him. He wasn't used to being on the defensive.

He'd handled it pretty well though. He *was* used to thinking on his feet. But he had the uncomfortable feeling that so was the chief inspector, and that could prove just a little tricky.

Colin had been brought to Stansfield police station to help with their inquiries. He had been asked about his injuries, and they had suggested that a doctor see him. He hadn't objected.

The police that had come for him had said that they wanted him to answer questions in connection with the murder of a Sharon Smith. He had told them he'd never even heard of her, but they didn't say anything else. At the station, his appearance had given rise to a lot of comment and some excitement. He had said that he didn't want a solicitor, and that he didn't want anyone informed. He had said that he didn't want his own doctor present at the medical examination.

The questions had started then, and he had lied in answer to almost every one. Hot sweats of sheer panic would come over him every time anyone came into the room, but nothing had happened, except the questions. They had brought him something to eat.

Now, he looked up as a new face came in. A man with short, receding hair and a dark complexion. He waited for him to say something, but instead he toured the walls, reading notices, looking out of the window, doing anything but look at him. It irritated Colin.

The man switched on a tape recorder, and told it that the interview with Colin Drummond was in the presence of Detective Chief Inspector Lloyd and DC Harris, then resumed his contemplation of the scene outside the window.

'No views here,' he said, in a Welsh accent. 'Not like Malworth. It's a pretty town. I've a friend who lives there.'

Colin didn't speak, and the man still didn't look at him.

'You were in a bit of a hurry to get home last night, weren't you?' he asked, still absorbed in the lack of view from the window.

'Yes, sir,' said Colin.

He turned then, eyebrows high on his forehead. 'Do you know,' he said, 'I can't remember the last person who called me sir who wasn't obliged to.' He indicated Detective Constable Harris. 'He calls me sir,' he said. 'Well, to my face.'

Colin smiled, not wishing to offend, as did Harris, presumably for the same reason.

'You told my officers that the clothes you were wearing this morning are the ones you were wearing last night,' he said.

Colin nodded.

'Can you say yes or no, Colin?' asked Harris.

'Yes.' Black shirt, jeans, leather jacket, boots. That was what he always wore. They had taken them away, and given him sort of white overalls.

Lloyd nodded. 'Were you at the football ground?'

'No.' Another lie.

'The thing is, Colin, we took tyre impressions from the muddy grass at the entrance to the club. Motorcycle tyres. They match your motorcycle tyres, Colin. Right down to a small flaw in the tread of the front tyre.'

Colin licked his lips.

'So. Were you at the football ground?'

'Yes, sir.'

'Why?'

Colin frowned a little. 'To see the match,' he said.

'There was a fight there.'

'Yes.'

Lloyd nodded, standing behind the chair, his hands holding the back. 'Were you involved in it?' he asked.

'No.'

'Where did you get the bruises, Colin?' Lloyd asked.

Why did he keep saying his name like that? It was getting on his nerves. Too many people had seen the incident at the match for him to pretend he had come by the bruises that way; Colin told the same story that he had told since he had been brought to the station. 'I came off the bike,' he said.

'When?'

Colin shrugged. 'I don't know.'

Lloyd's fingers tapped the back of the chair, and he gave a short sigh. 'The thing is,' he said, 'the doctor who examined you says you couldn't have got those injuries by coming off your bike. He thinks you were kicked and punched. Were you?'

Colin shook his head, his heart beating painfully. Lloyd must be able to hear it.

Lloyd sat down and contemplated him for a long time. Colin looked at him, at the detective constable, and the tape recorder. He didn't speak.

'Did someone kick and punch you last night, Colin?'

He shook his head vigorously. 'I came off my bike,' he mumbled.

'Where?' asked Harris.

'I don't know.'

'The doctor says you get that sort of bruising from fists and feet,' said Lloyd. 'Whose fists and feet, Colin?'

66

He got up then, and walked round, so that he was standing behind him. Colin could feel the hair rising on the back of his neck.

'But there's no real damage,' Lloyd continued. He bent down, and spoke into Colin's ear. 'Sharon Smith was small, slight – she wouldn't be able to do much damage to a big lad like you – especially not if she was losing her strength.'

He threw a plastic bag on to the table with a sudden movement that made Colin jump.

'Is that your tie?' he asked.

Colin shook his head. He never wore ties if he didn't have to. Who wore a tie with jeans, anyway? He wanted to say all that, but he couldn't. He'd told so many lies that even the truth was beginning to stick in his throat.

'How old are you, Colin?'

He wished he would stop calling him Colin like that. He wished they would just let him go. He could have a bath, get rid of some of the aches. He could be home before his parents, if they would just let him go now. 'Eighteen,' he said.

'Were you at the match alone?'

'Yes.'

'Do you have a girlfriend, Colin?'

'No.'

Lloyd sat down. 'Well,' he said. 'They don't usually want to go to football anyway, do they?'

Colin shrugged.

'Where were you on August the fifteenth at about ten thirty at night?' Lloyd suddenly asked.

Colin shook his head. 'I don't know,' he said.

'September the seventh, at about eleven fifteen at night? September the twelfth, at eight o'clock in the evening?'

'I don't know,' Colin said again.

'You have a think,' said Lloyd. 'And tell me where you were on these dates when I come back.' He stood up. 'Interview suspended, ten fifteen a.m.,' he said, and went to the door.

'Are you suggesting that my wife had something to do with what happened to Sharon?' Simon didn't want to think about that.

'No, of course not, sir,' said Sergeant Finch. 'It's just odd. "A little puzzle" my boss calls things like this.'

'Does he?' said Simon.

'Yes,' said Finch. 'Like the key.'

He had shown Simon a key; asked if it was something to do with the office. He hadn't recognised it. He had told him that Lionel might be able to help.

Finch looked round the little reception area where Sharon had worked. 'How well did you know Miss Smith?' he asked.

'Well, I'd worked with her for six months,' Simon said. 'It's a shock. I can't really take it in.' He wished to God that Sergeant Finch would just go away and let him cope with everything that had happened in his own way.

'Only six months? I thought she'd worked here for almost a year,' said Finch.

'*I'm* the one who's only been here six months,' he said. 'Well – not really that. I joined the practice in the second week of May.'

'Oh, I see.' Finch smiled. 'I'm new to Stansfield too.'

'Mr Evans will be able to tell you more than I can,' said Simon, in a desperate attempt to get rid of the man. 'But he's away in Birmingham today.'

'Had you had some sort of row with your wife, sir? That made her stay out all night?'

'No!' Simon could feel his face grow pink. 'I really don't understand why you imagine the two things are connected,' he said, and it sounded false even as he spoke the words.

Finch picked up Sharon's appointments diary and started looking through it. 'We don't imagine they're connected,' he said, almost absent-mindedly, as he checked through yesterday's appointments. 'They *are* connected. You are the connection.'

Simon sat down before his legs gave way.

It was almost an hour before Mac escaped. In the open-plan office, Melissa sat at a screen, apparently absorbed in what she was writing.

'I've just been talking about you,' Barry Houghton said to him, as he passed.

Mac had seen the sergeant talking to Barry in the editor's office. In daylight, Sergeant Finch looked even younger than he had last night. Wasn't that a sign of growing old? He didn't feel old. He felt almost like the old days. Everyone wanted to talk to him, and he had a girl again.

'He wanted to know how long you'd been here, what sort of guy you were, that sort of thing.'

Mac smiled. 'And you told him that I listed my hobby as motiveless homicide in *Who's Who*,' he said.

'I told him you were clean, quiet, sober and industrious. You handed in your copy on time, and you'd been here two months,' said Barry. 'Must have been a bit of a facer, that,' he said more seriously. 'Finding her.'

Mac nodded. He made small talk with a number of people, in

much the same vein, and took in the desk at which Melissa was working.

'You found her?' she said, still keying something in to her VDU, not looking at him.

'Yes.'

'After you left me?' Her voice was quiet; he could only just catch the words.

'Yes. I didn't tell the police where I'd been.'

She looked up sharply then. 'Why not?' she asked.

He felt a little disappointed with her reaction to his gentlemanly behaviour. 'I've been asking myself that ever since,' he said. 'But I just told them I'd got lost in the fog.'

A fleeting smile crossed her lips. 'You were being gallant?'

He shrugged. 'I suppose I was,' he said.

'You might wish you hadn't,' she said.

Mac smiled. 'Yes,' he said. 'Well.'

Someone made an entrance. It was hard to pinpoint *how*, but whereas other people had been coming in and going out all the time, he somehow made an entrance, and everyone turned to look.

'Well, well – we meet again,' he said to Mac.

'Chief Inspector . . . ' Mac tapped his head. 'I'm sorry, it's gone.'

'Lloyd,' he reminded him, with what seemed like a touch of irritation.

'Oh, yes.' Mac thought he'd better use his good excuse. 'I had to come in and give them my story,' he said. 'I'm a newspaper man now.'

'Quite,' said Lloyd, turning to Melissa. 'Mrs Melissa Whitworth?'

To Mac's surprise, Melissa agreed that she was Mrs Melissa Whitworth. She was married. Of course she was married. But she didn't wear a ring; it simply hadn't occurred to Mac that there would be a husband.

'Perhaps we could talk in there.' Lloyd indicated the editor's office, which the sergeant had some time ago vacated.

'I'd really rather not,' Melissa said. 'It creates much less attention if you speak to me here, though why you should find my activities so fascinating, I really—'

'Mrs Whitworth,' he said, his voice low and angry. 'This is a very serious matter, and you may be able to help. I spent a long time last night with the mother of a murder victim. She had to identify her own daughter after she had been strangled. I doubt very much if I would find your activities remotely interesting at any other time, but I do today. And I'd advise you not to try being flippant.'

Melissa's eyes widened, as had Mac's. He couldn't take any

69

of it in to start with. Lloyd seemed to be . . . my God, he seemed to be accusing her of having had something to do with this girl.

'Look,' Mac said. 'I think maybe I—'

Lloyd looked at him; they were the same height, and Lloyd's angry blue stare met his. 'Mr McDonald,' he said. 'I don't wish to be rude, but—'

'No, you don't under—' Mac saw the look in Melissa's eye, and he broke off. She didn't want him to say that she had been with him, that much was obvious.

He watched as Melissa led the way into the editor's office. She was an inch taller than the chief inspector, even wearing flat shoes. That made her an inch taller than him. He sat on the edge of the desk, and watched as the chief inspector made himself comfortable behind the desk, and saw Melissa sit stiffly in front of him. He couldn't see her face.

He wasn't leaving until he could speak to her. He took some coffee from the trolley as it passed, and waited.

'She was taken to hospital,' said Inspector Menlove.

Judy's eyebrows arched. 'Don't you mean allegedly taken to hospital?' she asked.

He sighed. 'Don't jump down my throat,' he said. 'I'm not Merrill.'

Judy smiled. 'Sorry.'

'Anyway,' said Menlove. 'In this case, he's right. The victim insists that there was no rape.'

Judy sat down, and refused the cigarette Menlove was offering her. 'What's the story?' she asked.

'Seems she shares a flat, and when she got home last night, her flatmate says she was in a state, and said "some bastard jumped me" before going straight upstairs. When she didn't come back, her friend went up and found her in the bathroom, out cold, and obviously injured. She called an ambulance, and then called us. With me so far?'

The complication was about to be presented, presumably, thought Judy.

'She came round in the ambulance, but the doctor wouldn't let anyone talk to her last night. He said she had obviously been attacked in the same way as the other three rape victims. We had someone by her bedside, but when she woke up this morning she said that no one had attacked her.'

Judy's eyebrows rose.

'Quite. Detective Chief Inspector Merrill thinks she's either too

70

frightened to report it, or she knows who it was and is trying to protect him, despite what he's done.'

Judy smiled. 'And he's nominated me to find out,' she said.

'Well, his other theory is that she perhaps doesn't want to talk to a man about it. She got upset this morning, and the hospital said no one could even try to see her until lunch-time today.'

'How did she get home last night?'

'Drove herself from wherever she had been. Her flatmate heard the car arriving, and saw her. She thought she looked as though she'd been drinking, which surprised her, so she went to the door. Otherwise she might not have been told what she was told. As it is, she had had her bath before she passed out – she washed away any evidence.' He took a deep drag of his cigarette and stubbed it out. 'She's lucky she didn't pass out in the bath,' he said. 'Or while she was driving home. She had inhaled an unusual amount of carbon monoxide, apparently.'

'Did she try to kill herself?' Judy asked.

Menlove shook his head. 'They don't think so,' he said. 'We all inhale some just walking down a busy road. She had just inhaled more than usual.' He shrugged. 'The attack might have taken place in a vehicle workshop or something,' he said. 'Where engines were running. She won't talk about it.'

'How badly hurt is she?'

'It's just like the others,' he said. 'He uses brute force and plenty of it, but the physical damage will heal. The doctor's not so sure about the mental damage – particularly if she's trying to tell herself it never happened, or it was her own fault or whatever.'

Judy looked at her watch. Eleven thirty – she might as well go to the hospital now. She was not looking forward to it.

'How much longer am I going to be kept waiting?' Lionel demanded of the desk constable.

'Oh . . . Mr Evans, isn't it? I'm sorry sir, we're very busy – Bill – Bill!'

The man whose attention the constable was trying to attract stopped at the door to the CID room, and turned back with a resigned sigh.

'Mr Evans is wondering when someone's going to see him. He's been here for well over *two hours*.' The last two words were in a desperate sort of whisper, as though Lionel couldn't hear him, and didn't already know that anyway.

'Oh – Mr Evans. Yes. Come in. I'm sorry to have kept you waiting for so long.'

Lionel went into the long room, and Bill led him to a paper-strewn desk. 'Forgive the mess,' he said. 'I'm Detective Constable Harris. Now . . .' He scrabbled about in the papers on his desk. 'You were at the football club last night, I understand.'

'Yes,' said Lionel.

'Attending a function?'

'An opening party – a bit odd, since the place isn't really open yet, but I think it was more in the nature of a capital-raising event. I left early. Look – I left my wallet there, that's all. The policeman at the club said that I should come here.'

'Yes, sir. But there was an unfortunate incident at the club last night, and we were wondering if you could help us at all. Where exactly were you?'

'In the executive box.' Lionel felt uneasy. Clearly, this wasn't about a wallet.

'Did you see or hear anything at all odd?'

'Like what?'

'There was a fight. Did you notice it starting?'

Lionel shook his head. 'Do you have my wallet?' he asked.

'Yes, sir. It had slipped down behind a radiator. The constable found it after you reported it to him.'

'Well, if I could just—'

'When did you leave the club?'

'I was with Mr Parker. He saw someone he wanted to talk to, and went down to the ground. I took the opportunity to escape.'

'Was anyone with you?'

'Yes. Mr Parker – we left the box together.'

'I see. You didn't notice what Mr Parker did after he left you?'

Lionel was feeling more and more bewildered. He shook his head. 'No – I just said goodbye, and went to my car.' Fear produced a sort of veneer of boldness. 'If this is about something other than my wallet, please say so,' he said. 'As far as I am concerned, all that happened was that this morning I realised that I had left my wallet in the directors' box. I was *supposed* to be going straight to Birmingham, and so I—'

'Birmingham?' said Harris, as though he had said he had been going to the moon.

'Yes! Birmingham! Is that so odd?'

Harris was distractedly looking through bits of paper on his desk. 'Are you the Evans of Evans and Whitworth?' he asked, his voice rising with disbelief.

'You mean you don't know?' said Lionel, heavily sarcastic.

'Well, I'll be buggered,' said Harris, then gathered himself. 'Sorry,' he said, and stood up. 'Mr Evans, I think we had better go into an interview room.'

Whatever Lionel had said, he shouldn't have said it.

'Why did you go to see this Whitworth woman?' asked Detective Superintendent Andrews, the new head of Stansfield CID.

Lloyd had been a little irked when Andrews had arrived at Stansfield; he had liked being acting head, and he didn't like having to account for every little notion that occurred to him. But the new Chief Constable was fonder of chiefs than of Indians, and both he and Judy had acquired overseers.

'Just one of those little oddities, sir,' he said. 'The victim worked for Mr Whitworth, and Mrs Whitworth was missing all night. I thought it best to check it out.'

'And?'

Lloyd gave a little shrug. 'And I have no reason to suspect Mrs Whitworth of anything other than perhaps a little extra-marital dalliance,' he said. 'Gil McDonald – the man who found the body – and she are both employed by *Barton Chronicle*.'

Andrews picked up his pipe and studied it, rather as though he had never seen it before. 'Perhaps she was the lady with whom he had the date,' he said. 'The one who is supposed to have stood him up.'

Lloyd smiled. 'I think perhaps she was,' he said.

'What about Drummond? Are we getting anywhere with him?'

'Not yet,' said Lloyd. 'But he answers the description of the rapist. Six feet tall, dressed in black from head to foot.'

'Except that he uses a knife to scare his victims, and Sharon Smith was strangled,' said Andrews. 'And we don't know yet if the victim *was* sexually assaulted, do we? I understood that it was unlikely.'

'Yes, sir. But her clothes had been pulled about, and Drummond is very scared of something. We've placed him at the scene, he's lied to us, and he won't account for the bruises.'

'I've got his parents downstairs swearing that Colin has always been a positive saint, and couldn't possibly be mixed up in something like this.' He looked up at Lloyd. 'They want to know why they weren't informed.'

Lloyd indicated the chair, and Andrews nodded.

'Drummond didn't want anyone informed. He's eighteen years old. His parents don't really come into it.'

Andrews ran his hands over his face. 'Well, they have come into it,' he said. 'And they won't go away. We don't really have anything on him, do we?'

'Not yet,' said Lloyd. 'But I'd like to hang on to him until we've got something from forensic and the p–m. I think he could be our rapist – and this one went wrong.'

'Sure. But I don't think you can keep him here while you find them.'

'He was stopped when riding his motorbike in a suicidally reckless fashion, and can't deny that. He's told a cock and bull story to account for the bruising, and wouldn't account for it at all when the traffic lads stopped him last night. I've asked Malworth for a full report of the stop on the dual carriageway and I'm trying to find someone who saw him set out for the match. With a view to discovering whether or not he was wearing a tie.'

Andrews smiled, and picked up his pipe. 'It's all very circumstantial,' he said.

Lloyd shrugged a little. 'Two hundred people were at that match – we ought to get something there. We've had a rough time of death given as three to six hours before she was found, so it could have been going on as the crowd were leaving the ground. Someone might have heard or seen something.'

Andrews raised his eyebrows. 'Are you suggesting that we were busy arresting two men for a minor breach of the peace while this girl was being strangled?' he asked.

Lloyd sighed. 'It's possible, sir. And going on what we know so far, it's even probable. That part of the car park's like a priest-hole with the new building. It juts out into the car park, and leaves a little recess. No one would see anything. And the match was in the process of being abandoned – there were loudspeaker announcements, a fight going on – there would be a lot of noise, a lot of confusion. Our men had their hands full – but someone at the match might just have seen or heard what was going on elsewhere.'

'That's not going to look good, if it is what happened.'

'No,' said Lloyd. 'But perhaps we've got him already.'

The phone rang, cutting off the warning that Andrews was clearly about to give him about jumping to conclusions; Andrews nodded to indicate that Lloyd could leave.

Lloyd stood, and flexed his back as it complained. He must be getting old, he thought, and fairly rattled downstairs to prove that he wasn't.

Six

Finch was never going to leave; it was nearly lunch-time, almost time to close up the office, and he'd arrived before ten. Simon knew that he was already under suspicion, thanks to Melissa's strange behaviour, before they got on to any possible motive.

Why had he phoned the police? It had been a ridiculous thing to do. If he hadn't . . .

'You reported your wife missing—'

'I simply said that she hadn't come home,' Simon corrected, years of magistrates' court training not going amiss. All right, he'd brought all this down on his head, but he was damned if he would let them put words in his mouth.

'You reported that your wife had not come home, and then we find your secretary dead. It's an odd coincidence, isn't it?'

'It's a coincidence, Sergeant. I fail to see that there is anything odd about it at all. It was a filthy night, and my wife decided to stay overnight at an hotel rather than drive home through thick fog. She was unable to get hold of me because I was at your own police station all evening! I was worried precisely *because* of the weather.'

Finch looked reflective. 'You came to the station at about nine fifteen,' he said. 'And left at ten forty-five or thereabouts. Is that right?'

'Yes,' said Simon, trying not to think about any of it. What was Sharon doing at the football ground with Parker *or* this other person? Why was she there at all?

'And before you were called to the station?' Finch asked, breaking into his private misery. 'Where were you then?'

Simon stiffened. 'I was here,' he said. 'Working late.'

'Alone?'

'Not all the time. Sharon was here until about six.'

Finch didn't try to disguise his irritation. 'She didn't leave here until six?' he said. 'Couldn't you have mentioned that earlier, Mr Whitworth? We are trying to piece together her movements yesterday evening, and we thought that she left when the office closed at five.'

'Yes. Sorry.'

'Did she mention her plans for the evening?'

Simon looked up. He didn't want to think about any of this. It was hard enough getting through today as it was. But he would have to think about it. And he didn't want to answer questions until he had. 'No,' he said.

'Did she ever mention boyfriends to you, by any chance?'

Simon shook his head.

'Any men friends that you know of?'

Simon closed his eyes. 'She . . . she was very quiet,' he said. 'Reserved. She didn't . . . she didn't talk much about—'

'So what do you make of Mr Parker's story? Two men fighting over her in public?'

Simon stood up. 'I hope you're not asking me to tell you what passed between me and my client, Sergeant.'

Finch smiled. 'No, sir,' he said.

Finch went, at last, and Simon sat for a long time staring out of the window at the shops across the road, and wondering how in the world he was going to get out of this in one piece.

Sharon hadn't.

Colin had been left on his own again, but now the chief inspector was back. This time his manner was brisk, no-nonsense.

'Someone answering your description was seen at the football ground, walking towards the car park at the same time as Sharon Smith.'

Colin shrugged again. He'd been waiting for this. They had abandoned the match at just about the same time; the people nearest the exits had been leaving. He knew that someone might have seen him. 'I never killed her,' he said.

'Don't you like girls, Colin?'

Colin stiffened. 'I don't know what you mean,' he said.

'Most young men of your age have girlfriends.'

Colin shrugged.

'You're a good-looking lad. Are you shy? I know what women can be like, Colin, believe me. They can make a man feel this small.' The chief inspector indicated with finger and thumb just how small.

Colin's head shot up. They didn't make him feel small. 'They don't frighten *me*!' he shouted. He could feel the chief inspector relax, as soon as he had said the words, and he knew he should have kept his mouth shut. He looked down at the table, and waited for another question.

'Have you thought about where you were on those other dates?'

'I can't remember.'

'I'm sure you can, if you try.'

Colin didn't answer.

Lloyd stood up. 'Let's see,' he said. 'August fifteenth – that was a Thursday. What do you normally do on a Thursday evening, Colin?'

'Watch television,' he muttered.

'Oh? What do you watch?'

Colin shrugged.

'And September seventh – that was a Saturday. Do you go out on Saturday nights?'

'Sometimes.'

'Where do you go?'

'Just out on the bike.'

'And September the tenth – that was a Tuesday.'

Colin looked up at him. 'What's special about those dates?' he asked.

'Women were raped on those dates, Colin. By someone tall, wearing dark clothes – and now a young woman has been murdered, and you turn up.'

Colin went cold.

'Did Sharon Smith speak to you?' asked Lloyd suddenly.

Colin shook his head.

'Where did she go?'

Colin swallowed. 'She . . . she just walked away after the fight started. They said the match was abandoned – I went to my bike. I just left at the same time, that's all.'

'How did you get so battered and bruised?'

He looked down again, and repeated what he had said over and over again. 'I fell off my bike.'

Lloyd stood up. 'We know that's not true,' he said, then reached over to the tape recorder. 'I think you tried to rape her too, but she fought back. So you strangled her. Interview suspended twelve-thirty p.m.,' he said. 'Think about it, Colin.'

Judy looked at the girl who lay on the bed, at the angry red graze down one side of her face, and the even angrier eyes.

'Miss Chalmers? I'm Judy Hill from Malworth CID,' she said.

'I didn't send for the police.'

Judy sat down. 'No,' she agreed. 'But you told your flatmate that someone had jumped you.'

'Did I?' The girl looked away.

'She phoned us and said that you had been attacked.'

The girl swallowed hard. 'She had no right,' she said.

'She has every right to report a crime, and I have every right to investigate it.'

The young woman's eyes looked back at her. 'What crime?' she said.

Judy took a breath. 'Look,' she said. 'You and I are the only people in this room. And we both *know* that you were the victim of a rape.'

'Do we?'

Judy tried to gauge what the girl's reasons were for denying that the rape had happened. There seemed to her layman's eyes to be no psychological block; one look at Bobbie Chalmers was enough to see the impotent anger that she felt. She wasn't denying the experience to herself, only to the police.

'Do you know him?' Judy asked, her voice quiet. 'Were you with him?'

Bobbie's eyes blazed at the suggestion. 'Of course I wasn't with him! He grabbed me from behind! He forced me face down on to the—' She broke off, her bruised face reddening, the fire leaving her eyes.

There was little point in apologising, but Judy did anyway. 'Did he say anything?' she asked.

The girl's lips were pressed together with sheer fury at what Judy had just done; Judy was glad to see the anger, but it meant for the moment that she wouldn't get an answer.

'Was he carrying a weapon?' she tried.

Still, no answer. So Judy just waited. She could hear the sounds of the hospital beyond the side-ward. Someone laughing in a corridor; a television somewhere, with what sounded like a cartoon playing; the lunch trolley going its rounds.

'He had a knife,' the girl said quietly, her eyes blank now, blank with the misery of the memory.

Judy wrote that down. She had no witness to the conversation, and she couldn't use her notes if the girl wouldn't make a formal statement, but everything helped.

'Did you see the knife, Miss Chalmers?' she asked, her voice as quiet and calm as she could make it.

She nodded.

'Can you—?' Judy broke off. 'It's Bobbie, isn't it?' she asked. 'Your first name? Do you mind if I call you Bobbie?'

She shook her head, fighting tears. Judy left her to it for a moment or two, while she looked through her notebook.

'Can you describe the knife?' she asked, once Bobbie had got control again.

'Flick-knife.'

'Did you see his hands?'

'Gloves. Black gloves.'

Judy thought before asking her next question. The other girls had been a different proposition; they had been hysterically pouring out details before anyone could sort them out. Their reticence would start when it finally came to court, but Bobbie's had begun already.

'Could you describe the attack?' she asked gently. Their man had a definite method of operation. 'I have to know if this was the same man who attacked these other girls,' she explained.

Bobbie's lip trembled as at first she shook her head, and screwed her eyes tight shut. Then tears forced their way through the lashes, and she began to speak about what had happened to her, her voice low.

'Did you see his face?' Judy asked, when the girl fell silent. She was trying to sound as much like a machine as she could; everyone was different, everyone dealt with the horror in a different way. Bobbie Chalmers didn't want a comforting mother figure. She didn't want to talk about it at all. She was answering the questions put to her, and the more impersonal they could sound, the easier she would find it to answer them.

She was shaking her head. 'He . . . he wore . . . one of those—' She ran a hand down the length of her face. 'You know. One of those—'

Judy couldn't prompt her.

'Mask things. With holes.'

Judy wrote down *ski mask*. 'Did you see anything else he was wearing?'

The tears were being wiped away, and the girl was fighting back again. 'Dark clothes,' she said. 'I didn't see him – he was waiting . . . ' Her voice tailed off, and she gathered herself together once more.

'Did he say anything?' Judy asked, her voice not betraying the importance of the question.

Bobbie Chalmers nodded, and told Judy what she had been waiting to hear, what all the others had told her. He had said the same thing to each of them.

'Look, Bobbie,' Judy began. 'I know you'll have heard scare-stories about the court proceedings—'

'Are you saying it isn't like that?' Bobbie suddenly demanded, the anger turned once again on Judy.

Judy shook her head. 'No,' she said. 'The defence counsel is trying to get his client off, and he'll use anything they think will work with the jury. But judges don't let them get away with too much – and you have a barrister too, you know – one who's on your—'

'Do you know what I do for a living?'

Now she came to mention it, Judy didn't. She shook her head.

'I'm a hostess,' she said. 'In a night club in Barton. I don't sleep with the customers, but there are some that think I should. And it would be made out in court that I do – wouldn't it?'

'Not necessarily,' Judy began.

'No? You want to see the costume I wear? I'm asking for it, aren't I?'

Oh. Judy didn't have to see it. The question said it all, and she couldn't pretend it was the best background in the world. But this was different. 'Bobbie,' she said firmly. 'You were jumped. From behind. By a total stranger. You were the victim of a particularly brutal rape. Your lifestyle's got damn all to do with it!'

'I'm not going to make a statement,' she repeated.

'Was that where you were last night? At the club? Was it one of the customers?' She remembered the carbon monoxide. 'Was he in the car park?' she asked.

Her eyes widened slightly, but she shook her head.

'Where then?' Judy waited; she had to know where the attack had taken place. They had to track him down from the locations he chose, amongst other things. So far, there were only two constants; what he did, and what he said. The attacks had taken place on different nights of the week, sometimes weeks apart, sometimes only days apart. The more that they could pin down as a pattern, the more likely they were to get him. Eventually, Bobbie would have to say something, like before. Judy wouldn't speak again until she did.

'The Jetty,' she said miserably, after long moments of silence. 'I was getting into my car.'

The Jetty was the local name for the widest of the many alleys which ran through the blocks of shops in Malworth, and which was used as an unofficial car park in the evening. It was a new location; she wasn't sure whether that was a help or a hindrance to the investigation.

'About how far along the Jetty were you parked?'

'*I* don't bloody know!'

No. It just might have made SOCOS job easier if she had known.

'What time did it happen?'

'About ten past nine.'

No hesitation about the time; that was a little unusual.

'Bobbie – *do* you know who it was?'

80

'No,' she said tiredly.

'Then why not help me?'

She took a deep, deep breath and held it for a long time before releasing it slowly. 'I'm going away,' she said. 'Abroad. I'm not coming back here. I'm not going to any court.' She looked at Judy. 'I'm not going to stand up in public and tell some bloody judge what that bastard did to me! So nothing happened. No one raped me. This is how I get my kicks. All right?'

Judy shook her head. 'I can't pretend it hasn't happened, Bobbie,' she said. 'You're his fourth victim. We have to catch him.'

Lloyd was certain that they already had. If Bobbie could be persuaded to attend an ID parade, they would have enough to hold him until they could get physical evidence, which they had in abundance from the other three victims.

One thing had occurred to her about the time; she had to find out. 'OK,' she said gently. 'Just one more question, and I'll go. It's important, or I wouldn't ask it. Have you any idea how long the attack lasted?'

Bobbie looked defeated when she answered. 'Twenty minutes,' she said. 'I thought it was hours and hours, but it was just . . . '

Judy frowned. 'How can you be so sure?' she asked.

'My car,' she said. 'You have to let it run with the choke out for a while or it just dies on you. So . . . ' She bit her lip, then resolutely carried on. 'I started the car, and the radio came on – the news was just finishing – they said it was five past nine.' She took a deep breath. 'I got out and put something in the boot. I'd just closed it – he . . . he pushed me down behind the car.'

And the exhaust was pumping out fumes all the time, thought Judy, closing her eyes for a moment.

'When he went away, I felt sick and . . . ' She blinked away tears. 'I got back into the car, and they were saying it was twenty-seven minutes past nine. I couldn't believe it . . . I couldn't – I thought . . . ' She closed her eyes. 'I thought it must be nearly morning,' she said.

Judy took a card from her bag and handed it to the girl. 'Rape counselling,' she said. 'It's a rape-victim support group.'

Bobbie let it drop on to the cover. 'The hospital already gave me one,' she said.

Judy stood up. 'Ring them, please, Bobbie,' she said. 'You don't have to worry about telling them what happened. It's happened to them too. And it'll help to tell someone. No one's going to take down any details and reel them off in court – you'll be talking to someone who really understands.'

Bobbie looked up at her, and shook her head.

81

Judy shrugged, and went to the door.

'And if I get any more police here I'll tell them you're lying,' she said. 'Have you got that? You can make me go to court, but you can't make me tell them anything!'

Outside the room, Judy found someone whom she took to be Bobbie's flatmate, hovering anxiously. 'Marilyn Taylor?' she asked.

'Yes. Are you the police?'

'Judy Hill. Malworth CID.'

Marilyn looked at her apprehensively. 'Was she mad at me?' she asked.

Judy smiled, and shook her head. 'I don't think so,' she said. 'Does Bobbie have any family round here, do you know?'

'I don't think so. She's got a boyfriend – she's going away with him soon.'

Judy sighed. 'She told me. She's not hoping to keep this from him, is she?'

Marilyn shrugged. 'I said I'd ring him,' she said. 'She wouldn't let me.'

'And I don't suppose I'm allowed to know his name?'

'No. She wants to handle it her way.'

Judy gave in gracefully. In truth, she didn't need Bobbie's evidence; it was exactly the same as the others, and her indignant rage wouldn't go down too well with some judges, who seemed to think that it couldn't have been that bad if the victim was still together enough to be angry.

She just hoped Bobbie *could* handle it.

Melissa had found as many things to do as she could, and still Mac waited. Eventually, she came back to her desk, and sat down.

Mac looked at his watch. 'It's after one,' he said. 'Why don't you let me buy you a long lunch?'

She looked up at him. 'I'm not hungry.'

'Neither am I.'

She frowned, a little puzzled for a moment, then closed her eyes briefly. 'Don't be silly,' she said sharply.

'What's silly about it?' he asked, his voice urgent. 'My landlady's away for the day. We could go to my digs.' He looked to see if anyone was overhearing them, but the office was practically empty as people went about the business of news-gathering, with some real news to gather, so she had no protection.

'Mac,' she said. 'I'm married, I've never done anything like that in my life before . . . I'd had too much to drink on an empty stomach. Can't we just forget it?'

Mac shook his head, smiling. 'I'll never forget it,' he said.

The truth was that neither would she, but this was just too much to take. 'Look – that policeman is practically accusing me of murder, and you want to—'

'Why is he?' asked Mac.

She gave a long, shuddering sigh. 'She worked for my husband,' she said resignedly. 'And my husband reported me missing last night. So they want to know where I was. In case Simon and I are part of some plot to kill the girl, presumably – I don't know.'

'What did you tell them?'

'I said I was at the hotel alone. I didn't have much option, did I?'

'Did he believe you?'

She shrugged. 'He seemed to accept it.'

'So forget it. They'll get whoever really did it, and we can all relax.'

'Last night was a one-off situation,' Melissa said in a fierce whisper. 'It's not going to happen again, all right?'

The editor came back in. 'Am I actually allowed to use my own office now?' he asked. 'Oh – Melissa. Dig up what you can on the victim, will you? Schools, work, that sort of thing. Her address is on the board – her name's Sharon Smith.'

The name seemed to echo round the empty newsroom as Mac's eyes flicked towards her. She stared at the VDU; the editor went into his office, and closed the door.

'I think we should have lunch now, don't you?' Mac said quietly.

Jake came out of the suite of offices that he rented from Malworth Borough Council, but allowed business acquaintances to believe he owned, and pulled a packet of cigarettes from his pocket, lighting one on the steps.

The whole morning wasted because Evans had gone to Birmingham. Jake hadn't bargained on Evans simply disappearing; if he didn't come back, Jake would be running a considerable risk, and he had no intention of running any more risks than he had to.

He started up the car, and pointed it homewards. Evans had to come back sooner or later, and he couldn't say what he wanted to say to him with the security man eavesdropping. He accelerated away, the cigarette clamped between his lips, mentally rehearsing what exactly he was going to say when he did locate Evans.

But waiting for him on the mat as he unlocked the front door was a note from his driver-cum-minder Dennis to say that he had been unable to get a reply from Bobbie's flat that morning, and had seen no sign of life.

Jake stared at the note, all thoughts of what he was going to say to Evans driven out by this new crisis. He dialled Bobbie's number; the phone rang out for long minutes before he hung up, his face tense and worried.

What the hell had gone wrong now?

Melissa finished what she was doing on the VDU. She hadn't looked at Mac, hadn't spoken. Then she picked up her bag. 'I'll be at the bus stop,' she said quietly. 'Don't leave with me.' And she walked out of the room.

Mac read the notice board for a few moments, then left, calling cheerio to Donna, who had at least presumably confirmed to the police that he had been going to take her to the opening, and that she wasn't dead.

He walked towards the bus stop, where Melissa's red car sat, and got in beside her. 'You didn't give the police that tape,' he said. 'Did you?'

'I told her that what she told me would be confidential,' Melissa said, pulling away from the stop. 'Which way?'

'Turn right at the end,' said Mac. 'And don't bullshit me.'

'I'm not. Just because she's dead doesn't mean that her private—'

'You had that tape in your bag yesterday. You couldn't have been back to the office since interviewing her, or it would be in your tape rack, which it isn't. Which means you interviewed her yesterday. The day she died. Left.'

She pulled out on to the bypass, where wisps of the ever-present mist still floated amongst the haystacks.

'Did you tell Mr Lloyd that?' Mac asked.

'No.' She overtook a tractor, and pulled savagely back into the left-hand lane. 'Why don't you join forces with him?' she asked. 'Since you're such a good detective?'

'Is it still in your bag?' he asked, twisting round to the back seat.

The car squealed to a halt as he felt around in the bag, and she pulled his hand away. 'Leave that alone!' she said, her eyes blazing.

'Come on, Melissa, let's hear it,' he said, pushing her hand off his arm, and rummaging in the bag again, bringing out the tape. 'Let's hear what Sharon Smith had to say for herself the day she died.'

She snatched it from him. 'What business is it of yours?' she shouted.

The tractor sounded its horn as it pulled out round them.

'I found her! And the police think I'm just as likely to have done it than you or your husband or anyone else. I don't believe in coincidence either. So I want to know what she said that's so bloody secret!'

She looked at him for some moments, then silently handed him the tape.

He took it out, taking a moment to work out how it went into the car stereo. 'It's left at the roundabout, first left again then third on the right,' he said, as he pushed it in.

Melissa switched on the hazard warning lights and the car stayed where it was, she staring straight ahead while he listened to every word that the predictably shallow Sharon had had to say. Then he got to the bit that mattered.

'. . . *where do you go for privacy?*'

'*The office, usually.*'

So that was it. He looked at Melissa; her face held the pink blush of anger that it had when he had first seen the tape.

'*Well . . . I think that's all I need. Thank you for giving me your time.*'

'*Is that it?*'

'*Yes.*'

The tape went dead, and Melissa slowly turned towards him, the flush gone. 'So you see,' she said. 'What happened with you and me was . . . ' She searched for the right words. 'A simple act of revenge. Nothing more.'

Mac released the tape, and put it in his jacket pocket. 'It'll be safer with me,' he said.

Melissa said nothing.

'It's left at the roundabout, first left again then third on the right,' Mac said again.

Melissa's eyes burned with resentment as they slowly left his. She put the car in gear and pulled away.

'DI Hill, Malworth, for you,' said Detective Inspector Barstow.

Lloyd took the phone. 'Yes, Judy,' he said.

'Two things. I understand we're faxing the report on the Drummond stop to you now, and I can tell you that Drummond isn't the rapist after all.'

Lloyd closed his eyes. 'Are you sure?' he asked, but he knew there was no point. Judy didn't make statements like that without hard evidence to back them up, and already he was rethinking his strategy concerning Drummond.

'The rapist was going about his business at the far end of Malworth at about five past nine last night. The assault went on for over twenty minutes,' she went on, her voice brisk. 'The speed trap clocked Drummond at nine thirty-two, almost ten miles away, coming from the opposite direction.'

That was hard evidence, Lloyd conceded. 'So we've got four rapes now?'

'Yes, but she says she'll deny that anyone raped her if I pursue it, and she means it. There would be no useful purpose served in forcing her to give evidence.'

Lloyd frowned. 'Why won't she co-operate?' he asked.

'She thinks she'd get raped all over again in court,' said Judy succinctly. 'And she's leaving the country soon. She just wants to get away.'

'Are you sure she was raped by the same man? Sounds more like she knows who raped her, and isn't saying.'

'It was the same man,' Judy repeated, her voice firm and uncompromising. 'The papers know about the mask and the knife, but we've never released what he says or his MO. Whoever attacked Bobbie Chalmers had that off to a tee.'

So Sharon's murder hadn't been a rape gone wrong. There had, he supposed, been very little evidence to support his rather shaky theory that Drummond was the rapist. But Drummond was still his man for Sharon's murder. Perhaps Drummond was yet another of Sharon's boyfriends that she didn't have. He had seen two men brawling over her in public; perhaps that hadn't met with his unqualified approval.

'How is she?' he asked belatedly, of the rape victim.

'As well as can be expected,' said Judy crisply.

Lloyd said goodbye, and hung up. Judy always held him a little to blame just for being a man after she had dealt with this sort of thing. Still – perhaps dealing with a series of rapes would put her off the idea of applying for promotion to the planned rape squad, about which there had been more rumblings, of course, since this lot had started.

If it didn't put her off, the experience would mean that she'd walk into the job, if the squad ever did get set up. Lloyd sighed.

'A Mr Evans in the interview room, sir – Harris says you'll want to see him.'

Lloyd doubted that.

Mr Evans sat at a table with Detective Constable Harris; Lloyd glanced at the constable.

'Mr Evans of Evans and Whitworth, sir,' said Harris, and turned to Evans. 'He was at the football match too.'

Evans looked pale. 'I . . . I can't believe that Sharon's dead,' he said.

Lloyd sat down. 'I'm sorry, Mr Evans,' he said. 'I know it must be a shock to you, but the more we can find out about Sharon, the better. She came to work for you ten months ago, is that right?'

'Yes. She was very good – worth much more than I was paying her. She was a secretary, receptionist, office manager – she had made herself virtually indispensable.' He looked away. 'I shall miss her very much,' he said simply.

'Did she talk about her private life at all? Boyfriends, that sort of thing?'

Again, Evans shook his head. 'I don't think she had a boyfriend,' he said. 'She never mentioned one.' He looked back at Lloyd. 'She was a very nice girl,' he said.

Lloyd smiled. 'Nice girls have boyfriends,' he said.

Evans coloured a little. 'Oh – of course they do. I just meant . . . she wasn't the sort to . . . to . . . '

'Get herself strangled?' offered Harris.

Evans coloured more deeply. 'She was a very nice girl,' he said again, defiantly.

Lloyd thought about that. It was the impression he had got from the family, and the friend who had come to look after Mrs Smith. It was the impression Finch had got from Whitworth. But it wasn't the impression he was getting from her behaviour. Damn it, she had had boyfriends all right, and Drummond was probably one of them. That was why all the lies, all the discrepancies.

'One more thing,' he said. 'We found a key in Miss Smith's handbag – her mother doesn't recognise it. Did you perhaps give her a key to some cupboard, or . . . ?'

Evans was shaking his head.

Lloyd stood up. 'Thank you, Mr Evans,' he said. 'Detective Constable Harris will show you out.'

He went into the murder room, where there was a buzz of activity that he hoped meant that they were actually getting somewhere. People talking on the phone to would-be witnesses, some of whom would have useless information, some of whom would be attention-seekers, and one, every now and then, with real information, like the one who had seen Drummond follow Sharon into the car park.

On the wall was a plan of the Byford Road Sports and Leisure Complex, with the little recess in which Sharon's body had been found marked with a cross. On the blackboard were lists of names: people who had been interviewed, people who still had to be interviewed, people who could conceivably be suspects, people crossed off.

Sharon's description was there, and what they knew of her

movements. Cross-references might lead them off in another direction, but for now he only had Colin Drummond. The system had worked well to produce him as quickly as it had; the computer had logged the stop on the dual carriageway into Malworth of one Colin Drummond, driving in a reckless manner from the direction of the old village, which was also the direction of the football ground.

Lloyd remembered the bike roaring through the village now; remembered wondering vaguely and unoriginally, in the midst of his miserable evening with Judy, where the fire was. When Drummond was brought in with a cut lip and a black eye, having noticeable difficulty in moving, and answering the descriptions they had been given of the rapist, they had all thought that they could pack both the rape and the murder incident rooms up again.

'The tie,' he said to Detective Inspector Barstow, when the inspector got off the phone.

Barstow unlocked a cupboard, and produced the tie, which was enclosed in clear plastic.

'Are the parents still here?'

'They're not leaving without Colin,' said Barstow, mimicking what Lloyd assumed was Mrs Drummond's voice.

'We'll see,' said Lloyd.

Perhaps the Drummonds might be a little more forthcoming about Sharon. Perhaps quiet, unassuming Sharon who had no discernible boyfriends wasn't quite what her nearest and dearest thought she was. Or said she was, at any rate. It had always seemed quite remarkable to Lloyd how many of the young women who died violently had been quiet girls with no boyfriends. But that was a male chauvinist thought, he supposed.

Mr and Mrs Drummond were in reception, looking drawn and anxious.

'How long are you going to keep Colin here?' Mrs Drummond demanded as soon as Lloyd had got them into an interview room, by dint of turfing out the occupants.

'Well, that depends on Colin,' said Lloyd. 'You see, I have to know what went on.'

'We had to find out from a neighbour that Colin was here!' she said, her voice shrill with anxiety. 'She said Colin could hardly stand up straight when he got home last night! What's been going on?'

'That's what we're trying to find out,' said Lloyd, 'as I've just said. Has Colin ever mentioned a Sharon Smith to either of you?'

'Is that *her*?' asked Drummond.

Lloyd raised his eyebrows in a query.

'Is that this girl that's got herself strangled?'

Lloyd nodded. 'Yes, Mr Drummond,' he said.

'No, he hasn't.'

Lloyd ran his hands over his face. 'Maybe you should take some time to think,' he said.

'I don't need time. And if you can't do better than this, you'd better release him. Now.'

Lloyd produced the tie. 'Do you recognise this?' he asked.

Mrs Drummond looked at it, shaking her head. 'No,' she said.

'Could it be one of Colin's?'

Drummond laughed. 'Colin's only got one,' he said.

'No, he hasn't!' said Mrs Drummond, stung. 'But he doesn't wear them, except for work,' she said. 'We only came back from holiday this morning to . . . to all this.' She blinked away the tears.

'Does Colin have a girlfriend?'

'That's his business!' said Drummond.

'Ssh, Desmond,' said Mrs Drummond, soothingly, as one might to a grizzling baby. 'No,' she said. 'Not yet. He's only a boy.'

Lloyd thanked them, and went back to the murder room, where Barstow was tearing off a fax from the lab.

'Right,' said Lloyd to the assembled company. 'Drummond isn't the rapist, so I was wrong about that. But I'm going to have one last attempt to make him tell us how he came by his bruises. Meanwhile – see if we can't dig up a girlfriend that Sharon Smith might have spoken to about her love life.'

'Please God, there's some DNA evidence on her body,' said Barstow, handing Lloyd the report. 'Her clothes aren't going to be much help. They were new. But Finch was right about the sawdust,' he added. He looked at Lloyd, a look that Lloyd was not unused to getting. 'I think we're taking a bit of a flyer with Drummond,' he said. 'Sounds like she was inside one of the buildings at one point – it could have been one of the workmen.'

Lloyd smiled. 'DNA evidence would be nice,' he said. 'But we managed without it before, and I expect we can manage without it now.'

He looked at the report. New leisure suit, velour. New shoes, trainers. Traces of mud, of blood (her own), of builders' sand. Traces of sawdust. The mud and sand were present where her body was found; the blood was from a small graze on her arm. The sawdust was unaccounted for as yet. Scene of crime officers would be examining the interiors of all buildings.

Good for Finch, he thought. Who needed forensic scientists when they had Finch's nose?

He looked at the list of site workers, most of whom had been interviewed, none of whom had admitted still being there at that time in the evening, and he hoped they weren't going to have to interview them all again.

Drummond was in the interview room by the time he got there, looking scared stiff, as he had all along. His eyes rose to Lloyd's as he came in. Lloyd sat down, and clasped his hands behind his head, tipping his chair back on two legs, just a tiptoe between him and disaster. It always disconcerted people, he'd found. It was worth the risk. He didn't speak at all.

After long moments, Drummond looked up from the formica which he had been studying. 'I never killed her,' he said.

'Were you at the match with her?'

'No. I didn't know her.'

'Have you got a girlfriend, Colin?'

Colin looked a little puzzled. 'No. I've already told you.'

'I think you did have a girlfriend,' said Lloyd, swinging gently backwards and forwards, his eye on the ceiling. 'I think Sharon was your girlfriend. I think you saw her at the match, saw two men fighting over her. I think you followed her to the car park, and dragged her round the corner, where no one could see. You wanted to know what was going on with her and Parker. She was struggling and kicking – she was probably saying things – you couldn't take it. So you strangled her.'

There was silence after he'd finished speaking; Lloyd didn't look down from the ceiling. He rocked slowly back and forth. 'Is that why you strangled her? Because she'd been playing around with Parker again?'

Colin shook his head slowly. 'It's them you should be talking to,' he said. 'They're the ones who were fighting over her. I didn't know her.'

'Nice try, Colin. But unfortunately they were in police custody from then on. And you're the one who left with her.'

'I just . . . I just went after her,' said Colin. 'I never killed her! I just – I saw her in the car. I never killed her.'

At last, at last. Lloyd didn't dare move, and just hoped the chair legs were stronger than they looked. 'What car?' he asked.

'I never killed her! She was in the car, and she started taking her clothes off! I never killed her!' Colin was growing ever more agitated, then stopped speaking suddenly, his face white.

Lloyd's eyes came slowly down from the ceiling, and the crack in the brand-new plaster, to rest on Colin Drummond.

Drummond visibly got himself under control, his eyes growing less afraid and more wary as he thought the whole thing through. And in that instant, Lloyd had lost him, he knew; Drummond was beginning to realise how little they really had on him.

'Slow down,' Lloyd said, trying to rescue the situation by switching strategy. 'And begin at the beginning.' His voice was friendly, his manner that of someone who understood. But when Drummond started to speak, Lloyd wondered just who was kidding whom.

'I thought she might talk to me. But she just walked away. I went and got the bike. I followed her. A car picked her up.'

Lloyd shook his head. 'She never left the football ground, Colin,' he said.

'She did! She did. They went *back* to the football ground! It was dark by then. Empty. They parked right over at the far side – it was obvious what—' He swallowed. 'I waited for a while,' he said. 'Then I just got on the bike and went away. I must have forgotten the lights.'

Lloyd let the chair down slowly. He still waited for Drummond to carry on with his story. For that's what it was, and soon, he'd trip himself up on his own fiction, even if he had stopped himself spilling it all out this time.

'I got stopped on my way into Malworth by the police. That's it. That's all.'

'Not quite all, Colin.'

Drummond swallowed. He wouldn't look at Lloyd.

'When did you fall off your bike?'

The question lay there between them. Drummond had swung wildly between lies and truth about everything, but now Lloyd had the faxed report of the officers who had stopped Drummond on the dual carriageway; the end was in sight. A nice, speedy arrest, a confession, a charge, a prosecution. Then it was up to other people to decide what to do with him. Not his problem, thank God.

'There was no car, Colin,' he said, his voice gentle, almost sympathetic. 'No one picked Sharon up, because Sharon never left the ground. You dragged her back, behind the wall. You did know her, didn't you, Colin? And when Parker and Barnes began fighting over her, you realised that she wasn't quite what she made herself out to be – and you lost your temper, isn't that it?'

Drummond was pale, the bruises on his face standing out.

'And you didn't fall off your bike. You got those bruises because Sharon kicked and punched, not by falling off a bike. You had them when the police stopped you. We *know* that, Colin – there's no point in denying it.'

'She left the ground. She got into a car,' Colin repeated mutinously.

Lloyd looked back at the ceiling.

'There was a car,' said Drummond. 'There *was*. I swear it.

91

Someone picked her up, they took her back there. They did. That's who killed her, it must be.'

'Colin . . . ' Lloyd began wearily. 'If you didn't know her, why were you so interested in what she was doing in—?'

'But I didn't fall off my bike,' Drummond said suddenly, interrupting Lloyd's question.

'What did happen?' asked Lloyd.

'I got beaten up.'

Lloyd sighed. My God, he didn't give up. 'By whom?' he asked.

'By the traffic cops,' said Drummond.

Now he'd heard everything.

Lionel arrived home, and reached the front door as the phone started ringing. Panic made him unable to find his front-door key; when he did, he dropped the bunch. By the time he had retrieved them and found them again, Frances had answered the phone.

'Oh – hold on,' she was saying, as he practically fell into the house. 'He's just come in.' She looked at him. 'Someone called Jake Parker,' she said, handing Lionel the receiver. 'He's been trying to get you all day.'

Lionel closed his eyes briefly, and took the phone, waiting pointedly until she had gone back into the sitting room and closed the door before he put it to his ear. 'Hello,' he said, cautiously.

Parker's voice was low and menacing, and it took Lionel a moment or two to take in what he was saying.

'You stupid bastard, Evans,' he said slowly. 'What the hell did you have to kill her for?'

Seven

'You wanted me, sir?'

Merrill waved a hand to indicate that Judy should sit down. 'How did you get on?' he asked.

'Officially, nothing happened to her,' said Judy.

'So I understand. And unofficially?'

'She was his fourth victim. But she's a dyed-blonde night-club hostess who titillates men for a living, and she's emigrating or something soon, so she just isn't about to go into the witness box to be pulled to pieces. I'm not so sure we should try to make her – she could be something of a liability.'

Merrill rubbed his eyes. 'Anything new for us to go on?'

'Only the location – the Jetty, this time. Exactly the same MO, same description. I've given the incident room what I got, but it won't help much.'

They had to find him; it was as simple as that. Once they had a suspect, there would be no problem of identification. They had the physical evidence, the DNA fingerprint just waiting for a match. All they needed was the suspect, and there were a great many officers doing nothing but looking for him.

'We're going to have to go through the previous offenders again,' said Merrill. He looked at her for a moment before speaking again. 'What do you think of psychological profiling?' he asked.

Judy shrugged a little. 'Paying someone to tell you that he's a loner with a chip on his shoulder seems a bit odd,' she said. 'But we've done a spot of amateur profiling. The lack of a pattern seems to indicate someone who doesn't have to be anywhere in particular in the evenings, so he probably isn't accountable to a wife. The times and the places suggest that he is definitely local, rather than someone who visits the area on business. The attacks all took place in the evening – he's probably a nine to five man rather than unemployed or a shift-worker.' She shrugged. 'Professionals might be able to gather a lot more from what we've got than we can,' she said. 'To be fair to them.'

Merrill grunted. 'Let's do a thorough job on the previous

93

offenders first,' he said. 'According to the computer, there are three most likely. I want to interview them again.' He moved some papers about his desk. 'Now,' he said. 'Re Sharon Smith. This boy Drummond lives in Malworth . . . there's his address. Can you get someone to make discreet enquiries about whether or not he left for this football match wearing a tie?'

Judy frowned. Why discreet? They'd been questioning him all day – there was nothing very discreet about that.

'We don't want it to look like harassment,' explained Merrill, in answer to her frown. 'He has come back with something of a counter-charge against two Malworth officers, and the complaint has to be investigated, which does, as you will, I'm sure, understand, make the whole thing a little delicate.'

Merrill was all right, but more than a little pedantic. Besides, Judy still felt a little awkward about her greeting to him on the phone that morning. She wished he would get to the point and let her go away again.

'He's made a complaint against the officers who stopped him for the traffic offence, and that will of course have to—'

Judy interrupted him. 'What sort of a complaint?' she asked. She was a witness, though another police officer wasn't much use in these circumstances.

Merrill rubbed his eyes, and flexed his back, and did other things to indicate that he had had a trying morning, and that the afternoon was turning out no better, with people asking him questions that they should know better than to ask, and that he wasn't supposed to answer. Judy imagined he'd at least had some lunch, instead of a painful interview with a rape victim. And he must know her well enough by now to know that she wasn't asking out of mere curiosity.

'He says they worked him over,' he said bluntly, once he had decided to answer her.

'What?' said Judy. 'But I saw them. After they stopped him – some considerable time after, I think.'

Merrill stared at her. 'You *saw* them?'

'Yes. I was on my way home.'

'Did you stop?'

Judy felt a little guilty. 'No,' she said. 'I was tired, and—'

'And you'd had a fight with your boyfriend?' suggested Merrill, with a slight twinkle.

Judy blushed again. 'Yes,' she said. At least he didn't know who her boyfriend was, she thought. She had to be thankful for small mercies.

'So you didn't get a good look at Drummond,' said Merrill.

'But I did,' she said. 'I wasn't going at any speed in the first place because of the fog. And I can assure you sir, that there was nothing at all wrong with Drummond when I saw him. Of course, he might be saying that it happened after that – but if he isn't, then—'

Merrill looked hard at her. 'Are you one hundred per cent certain about that?' he asked, interrupting her. 'He had no facial injuries – he was having no difficulty walking?'

'I'm quite sure. I actually looked at him carefully, because I'd heard the siren some time before, and I did think there might have been an accident. But he was fine – pacing up and down while they examined the bike. I know the complaint investigator will think it's just police officers sticking together, but it's the truth, I promise—'

'No,' said Merrill, interrupting her. 'He won't think that.' He sighed heavily. 'The officers concerned said in a written statement that Drummond was in that state when they stopped him,' he said quietly, 'and when asked how he had come by his injuries would give no explanation. That's why Stansfield were so certain Drummond was their man,' he said.

Oh, no. Judy looked away from him.

'It wasn't a trap, Judy, believe me,' he said. 'I had no idea that you had seen them.'

She didn't speak.

'Out of my hands now,' said Merrill. 'I'll send a report to the DCC. You'll almost certainly be called as a witness in the disciplinary proceedings, I'm afraid. And any criminal proceedings which may result.'

Judy nodded. Giving evidence against fellow police officers. Life, at the moment, was a bitch and a half.

Merrill leant forward. 'See if the grapevine knows why these two had it in for Drummond,' he said, almost to the blotter, almost as though he wasn't speaking at all.

Judy wished Sandwell was there. He would have known already. She wished she had never got up. She wished she hadn't had the row with Lloyd, because then she wouldn't have been going along that road as early as she had been, and she wouldn't have known what state Drummond was in when they stopped him.

And she wished, with all her heart, that she didn't feel like that. They had no excuse for doing what they had done. A policeman losing his temper with a suspect was wrong, but understandable; two of them setting about a defenceless young man was quite another.

And yet she didn't know for certain that she would have mentioned her trip home at all, had she known the whole story.

If anything, it had been even better. Again, Mac had felt a moment's awkwardness when the bedroom door actually closed behind them, but Melissa's total lack of coyness didn't allow for awkward moments; she made him feel like superman, like Mad Mac again, diving for the low header and slotting it into goal. Running towards the fans, arms above his head, listening to the roar.

Mac threw his arm out of the bed, feeling for his jacket, and took out the cigarettes and Lloyd's book of matches. The tape was still in his pocket; she hadn't asked for it back.

'Everything was fine. Really. We've been married for nine years, and we were happy. He fancied a move – he got the partnership here, and we found a cottage – oh, it's right on the main road, but it's beautiful. I couldn't have been happier. I really couldn't. For maybe a month,' she added bitterly.

'What happened then?'

Mac lit a cigarette, and wondered if he'd have to give up sex again in order to give up smoking. Why did you buy them? the sergeant had asked. Because he had been fed on a diet of movies in his formative years, and that was the only way the director could indicate what had taken place off-screen. Nowadays, it was the smoking that shocked people. He had needed a cigarette last night to complete the act, as he had always done. He hadn't wanted to smoke after his recent loveless encounters; this was different. He smiled, reminded of an old joke. *Do you smoke after intercourse? I don't know, doctor, I've never looked.*

'I have to get back to work,' she said. 'It's quarter past three.'

'To find out all about Sharon?'

She was already dressing, as eager to put space between them as she had been before; she didn't answer.

Mac reached over for his empty coffee cup, and dropped the cigarette into it. The smoke rose and spiralled in the air. 'Maybe you'll find out who killed her,' he said. 'What will you do then? Or does that depend on whether or not it was Simon?'

She looked a little surprised. 'What?'

'She said he hated her sometimes. You think he killed her, don't you?'

Melissa smiled a little, and shook her head, but she didn't actually deny it.

Mac got up after she had left, and looked out at the quiet street. He knew Sharon Smith. Oh, he'd never met that particular one, but they were all the same, her type. Some of them were his neighbours, with their semi-detached houses and semi-detached husbands. Coiffured hair, feminine, made up to the nines. And it was all for show. Sex was just power to them; in the days when he was watching couples have their post-coital cigarette, girls like Sharon would withhold their favours until you put a ring on their finger. These days, it was a little more subtle. The ring came afterwards. But it came. The problem in Sharon's case was that Simon Whitworth already had a wife. All that stuff about preferring married men was rubbish; you could hear the lies. She preferred men with a bit of substance, a bit of money in the bank, maybe. And they tended to be married.

Simon's choice had been simple; Melissa or Sharon. Sharon had been a bit on the side for Simon – a change, an adoring little distraction who told him how clever he was, and who had pulled a fast one on him. So he'd made sure that Sharon couldn't foul things up for him. Mac didn't blame him in the least; Melissa was worth a hundred Sharons. A hundred Sandras. A hundred of any other woman he had ever met.

'You can't hang on to him now.'

Lloyd felt, and looked mutinous. For no good reason, he had to admit. He knew he couldn't hang on to him.

'Lloyd – your case, such as it was, and *you're* the one who thought it had to be strengthened, has just been blown away.'

'Just because he seems to have told the truth about one thing, it doesn't necessarily—'

'Release him, Lloyd. His parents are still here, and I want them all to go before they think of anything else to accuse us of.'

Lloyd loathed two fellow officers whom he had never met. There was no reason to suppose that Sharon's attacker would bear the marks of a struggle, but their behaviour had made certain that any such marks on Drummond had been well and truly disguised. In his opinion, that was no reason to cross Drummond off that list of names in the murder room.

'Drummond knew her,' he said stubbornly. 'Or at the very least, he knows a lot more than he's saying.'

'You have no proof that Drummond ever set eyes on Sharon Smith before last night,' Andrews said. 'And you only thought that he might have been involved with her once you knew that he wasn't the rapist.'

Lloyd hardly needed to be told all this.

Andrews sat back. 'Your case against him was influenced by your belief that he was the rapist, and he isn't. In my opinion, that belief has slowed down both of these investigations. I suggest you leave the rapes to the rape inquiry, and conduct this *murder* inquiry in a more ordered and rather less inspired fashion.'

He was on the carpet. It wasn't the first time, and he didn't suppose it would be the last.

'I still have to talk to Drummond, sir,' he said. 'I've been given no description of this car he's supposed to have seen, never mind who was driving—'

'Because you were convinced he was lying! You didn't ask, did you?'

'No, sir.' Lloyd still thought he was lying. That was why he wanted to hang on to him.

'By all means continue to investigate his involvement – I'm not warning you off, for God's sake! But it isn't cut and dried, and it never was. We'll have to hope that at least one of your two hundred witnesses saw something. Isn't it time you were doing something about getting them in here?'

Lloyd was dismissed, and went back to the office, where he immediately phoned the path lab to beg Freddie to give him anything he could as soon as he could. Freddie told him that the post-mortem would be being done that afternoon, which was something.

Tom Finch sat at the other side of the desk, shaking his head.

Lloyd smiled as he replaced the receiver. 'It is, as they say, a rum do,' he said.

'Rum? Whitworth's wife was staying at an hotel a mile away from the sports ground. Whitworth's partner was at a function in the sports ground. And Whitworth's secretary gets herself murdered in the car park *of* the sports ground. Gil McDonald – who just happens to work with Mrs Whitworth – was at the bloody place *twice*, and just happens to find the body on his second visit.' He drew a breath.

Lloyd still smiled.

'Evans and Whitworth represent the owner of the ground at which all this was happening – he's involved in a fight at the same time, and it's Whitworth who turns up to bail him out! It's ludicrous!'

'What about Colin Drummond?' asked Lloyd.

'Well he's not in the frame any more, is he? Not now that we know what really happened to him. He's our best witness now.'

'We don't know what really happened to him,' said Lloyd quickly. 'Not officially.'

'No, sir. But we do. So let's not beat about the bush.'

Lloyd was beginning to like Finch more every day, but he disagreed profoundly with his snap decision. 'I accept that we have to take rather more notice of his story now,' he said. 'But I still believe the whole business with the car is a figment of his imagination, and that he knows more about Sharon than he has so far told us. I agree that he's our best witness – but perhaps for different reasons.'

Finch nodded. 'Yes, sir,' he said. 'Sorry.'

'But since we're not beating about the bush, I'd like to know why two of our esteemed colleagues found it expedient to beat him up.'

Finch looked up. 'Well, the word is that he's a cocky little bastard,' he said.

'If we all took to beating everyone who answered that description, we'd never do anything else.'

He had got a glimpse of the cockiness when they released him. The fear of being beaten up again had gone, and the arrogance which suited him rather better than his humble act had returned. 'See you in court,' had been his parting shot.

Lloyd got up, and looked out at the view of the car park. Malworth did have much better scenery, he thought. Judy was lucky to work there. He felt badly about the row. And he felt badly about how he had spoken to Mrs Whitworth. The woman had got on his very exposed nerves, that was all. But then, all women were doing that at the moment, come to that.

He turned back to Finch, acutely grateful that he was male.

'So you want background on the two who beat him up?' Finch asked. 'Unofficially?'

Finch had grown about ten years older since last night, Lloyd thought. They all had, he supposed. But the rigours of a murder investigation suited Finch. It had just given Lloyd a bad back. 'Of course I do,' he said. 'I'm not crossing Drummond off just because two barbarians chose to attack him and have made it impossible to say whether or not he had been in any sort of struggle before they got their hands on him.' He looked at his watch. Half-past three. 'Have you eaten?' he asked.

'No. I've been running round like a blue-arsed fly all day.'

'So have I. Let's continue this discussion over whatever the canteen has to offer.'

Tom didn't look too enthusiastic about a working lunch, or whatever it was called mid-afternoon, but he walked with Lloyd to the old building, and the canteen, where he had hamburgers piled with tomato sauce and mustard.

'I don't like Drummond's story,' Lloyd said. 'It's too pat. A car picked her up and conveniently took her back to the football ground. I ask you.'

Finch said something that Lloyd had to translate into English from hamburger.

'All the others?' he said, with a smile. 'What about them?'

Finch swallowed. 'They were all there, sir. Or thereabouts.'

Lloyd looked disparagingly at his ham salad, and wished he'd had hamburgers too. But he was trying to keep the weight off that had developed a habit of creeping on. It was bad enough being bald, and feeling his back twinge every time he stood up. He didn't have to be fat as well.

'Evans, Mrs Whitworth, McDonald. And Whitworth was . . . I don't know. Edgy, when I spoke to him.'

'His wife had been missing all night and his secretary had been murdered,' said Lloyd. 'I don't suppose you'd have been too sanguine in his shoes.'

'But—'

'What's the alternative, Tom? A conspiracy? Parker starts a fight to keep the police busy while Mrs Whitworth dispatches Sharon? Mad Mac McDonald is deputed to find the body, and Whitworth comes and bails Parker out? Drummond was an innocent bystander?'

Tom didn't look in the least chastened as he finished off his first hamburger and started on his second. 'Why was Melissa Whitworth staying in an hotel when she was only a couple of miles from home?' he asked.

Lloyd smiled again. 'I could hazard a guess,' he said. 'But I won't. She says that she didn't fancy becoming a statistic on the bypass, even if it was only two miles. She'd already had one close shave with the traffic, and she didn't want another.'

Finch looked sceptical, as well he might.

'I did some checking up,' said Lloyd. 'She booked in at the hotel at about half-past nine, and about an hour after that was joined by someone answering McDonald's description. They had a couple of drinks – the barman didn't notice them leave the lounge, but he came out to serve two salesmen just after eleven, and they were gone.'

'You think that Mad Mac was getting his leg over,' said Finch, indistinctly.

'Precisely. I wouldn't have phrased it as inelegantly, but that is indeed what I think. What I don't think is that she was giving him directions to where she'd left the body.' He swallowed some tasteless salad. 'He happened to know Mrs Whitworth, and he happened to find the body. And that's probably the only coincidence we've got.' He deliberately didn't say why he was of this opinion; he wanted to see what the young man did about that.

Finch did nothing but eat his hamburger, so Lloyd ate his salad, then told him anyway.

'Parker used to employ Sharon,' he said. 'And he became

100

involved with her – he's told us that. For whatever reason, Sharon went back to her mother's, and Parker got her the job at his solicitors. It was his opening do – naturally, his solicitors were invited. And naturally, *The Chronicle* sent McDonald to cover it. Mrs Whitworth and McDonald have made a date, and they end up at the hotel – arriving separately to allay suspicion.'

Finch frowned, his mouth too full to allow him to voice his obvious objections, so Lloyd steamed ahead.

'Meanwhile Sharon arrives at the ground – possibly she was actually with Barnes, or possibly she just chats him up.'

'We can't shake his story that she just asked him for the time,' said Finch. 'I left his statement on your desk.'

Lloyd put on his glasses and picked up the papers he had brought with him. He found the statement, in which Barnes maintained that Sharon had asked him the time, and before he could answer, Parker was pushing him away, and seemed to be about to set about Sharon. The gallant Mr Barnes had pulled Parker off, and the fight had begun.

Lloyd looked over his glasses at Finch, and grunted. 'Well,' he said, 'whatever she did, she needled Parker, as a result of which he finds himself in a police cell. Who else would he ring but Whitworth? He's his solicitor.'

'Why did he *want* a solicitor?' asked Finch, having swallowed the last of his hamburger.

Lloyd sipped his cold tea. 'Parker is a back-street thug who has made money,' he said. 'He likes having the power to snap his fingers and have Whitworth come running. That's all.'

Finch wiped his hands on the paper napkin. 'I'd be prepared to swear that Mrs Whitworth had no idea who McDonald was when I spoke to her this morning,' he said.

Lloyd stood up. 'I want to know exactly what Sharon Smith did between leaving the office and getting herself murdered. All we've got to go on is that she was at the football match, for some reason. There were two hundred other people there, so someone must have seen her. Her movements shouldn't be that hard to trace.' He finished his tea. 'If she wasn't the victim of a random killing, then someone wanted her dead. We have to find out why before we can find out who.' He walked towards the door and turned back. 'And I want to know what that key opens,' he added.

Back in the office, he formulated an appeal to the football loving public to come forward with any information they had, however insignificant it seemed. Finch had gone tearing off to confirm with Parker Lionel Evans's account of his actions during the evening, giving himself indigestion at the very least, and probably storing up ulcer trouble while he was at it.

Lloyd took things at a rather easier pace. He wanted badly to see the results of the forensic examination of the buildings, and while he could not be said to want it, he needed the result of the post-mortem, which Freddie was doing even now. He had toyed with the idea of sending Finch, but the lad had been working himself ragged, and he thought that it would perhaps be less than fair. He would go himself.

The super was out of the office; Lloyd left the draft appeal on his desk, and went off to join Freddie at Barton Hospital morgue, a procedure which never did his temper much good at the best of times.

Still, he thought, brightening a little even as his steps took him towards the room, with its dreadful smell of antiseptic and other, nameless horrors, at least Freddie was also male. Even Kathy was on her honeymoon, as he was reminded when he saw Freddie prepare to dictate his findings to a cassette.

'Lloyd,' he said, not looking up before beginning his work.

Lloyd spent a lot of time not looking at anything; he could hear what was being dictated, but Freddie's notes were largely incomprehensible to the layman, so he waited for the abridged version.

'That's that,' said Freddie cheerfully, switching the machine off with his elbow and a great deal of difficulty. 'She died from asphyxiation. Several contusions and abrasions, none very serious. Time of death is between three and six hours from when she was found, give or take an hour or so.'

Lloyd pulled a face. 'Thanks,' he said.

Freddie shrugged. 'There's a Nobel prize waiting for the man who can find a way of ascertaining the precise time of death,' he said. 'Temperature isn't much of a guide in asphyxiation deaths, so the whole thing becomes even more of a lottery.'

'OK,' said Lloyd.

'She was fit and healthy. She hadn't eaten for some hours before death, and she hadn't been drinking. She was less sexually experienced than you would expect for a woman of her age. These days, anyway,' Freddie added.

Lloyd smiled. 'Once upon a time,' he said, 'single meant virgin – eh, Freddie?'

Freddie's eyes widened. 'Did it sound disapproving? I didn't mean it to. I really meant the opposite.'

Lloyd was grimly pleased that the evidence was going some considerable way towards disproving Drummond's story of her having it off with someone who picked her up in a car.

'But she had had recent intercourse,' said Freddie, with what seemed to Lloyd like malicious timing.

Lloyd sighed. 'How recent?'

Freddie smiled. 'I don't know, Lloyd, I wasn't there. Recent enough for it still to be detectable. Half an hour before, say. I've taken samples for DNA.'

Time for another rethink on Drummond. Andrews' unspoken warning about jumping to conclusions was, Lloyd grudgingly conceded, entirely justified, and his rap over the knuckles for dismissing the young man's story was probably less than he deserved.

'An observation,' said Freddie, breaking into Lloyd's morose thoughts.

'Go on,' said Lloyd, tiredly. Just a few more years until he could retire and let someone else take on the human race in its less lovable moments.

'These days, more and more people are using condoms if they go in for casual sex. One wasn't used in this instance, as you'll have gathered.'

'So – taken in conjunction with her below-average sexual experience, you think she in all probability actually had a steady relationship with whoever she was with?'

Freddie beamed at him. 'I don't think anything. I have made an observation. I will go so far as to say that she possibly knew the person quite well. But you think what you like.'

Thanks, thought Lloyd sourly. The only person with whom he knew Sharon had had a relationship was the only one who couldn't possibly have been in that car with her.

'I think I want the result of Drummond's blood test,' he muttered.

'It's gone off to the lab, Lloyd. I can do no more than that,' said Freddie. 'It'll be at least two weeks before we get the result.'

A line from an old song was running in Lloyd's head, despite his efforts to ignore it. *You can't make love on a cycle, Michael, like you can in an automobile.* So perhaps the car story was true. Another scenario began to present itself. He wasn't alone in jumping to conclusions – Parker had admitted that he might have done. Sharon had gone to meet someone; whoever it was had failed to turn up, and she had checked the time, to make certain that she wasn't early. Parker, seeing her speaking to Barnes, thought that he was the new boyfriend, and caused the trouble from which Sharon walked away. The person she had expected to meet at the match had arrived late, to find that the match had been abandoned. He had driven away from the ground, and had caught Sharon up. She had got into the car with him.

Why go back to the football ground? Well, he had known it would be deserted, and perhaps they didn't have much choice about where they met. A married man? In any event, despite Parker's apparent belief, Sharon had been far from promiscuous, according to Freddie. That had to make it relatively easy to find out who was in the car with her, surely? The thought brightened him a little.

But then there was Drummond. Watching all this. And reacting very strangely indeed. Lloyd couldn't shake Drummond off, couldn't cast him in the role of innocent bystander. If Finch found any connection at all between Drummond and Sharon, Drummond would be back in custody, complaint or no complaint.

'Do you think she put up a fight when she was attacked?' he asked.

'Hard to say. She was strangled from behind – not much opportunity to fight back. She certainly struggled – some minor grazing and bruises, as I told you, so she might have left her mark on him.' He smiled. 'But then again, she might not have.'

'Was she definitely killed where she was found?' Lloyd asked.

'Nothing to suggest otherwise, apart from the sawdust – which she could have picked up when she was alive, of course. She could have been killed in situ.'

He smiled again and Lloyd waited patiently for the punch line.

'But then again, she needn't have been,' said Freddie.

Pathologists were such a comfort.

Melissa left Parker's offices in Malworth, got into her car, and checked over the notes she had got on her investigation into Sharon Smith's background. She had gone to Sharon's old school straight from Mac's so that the editor didn't find out just how long her lunch-hour had been.

The notes weren't up to much. Sharon had left school at sixteen, having taken five CSEs and passed them, but she wasn't what you would call academic. She had played games, but not to any particularly high standard. The woman was clearly having trouble remembering who she was, which was reasonable, given the seven-year gap since Sharon had left, but it was evident that Sharon had not made her mark on school life.

She had forced herself to ring Simon and get the details of her background. The police had been to see Simon too, of course. No, he had said, they hadn't been too bad. He had tried to telephone her, but she had been at lunch.

Melissa thought again about her lunch-hour, and the high came back, just like before, despite the fact that her hand had been forced. It had been blackmail, but it had been therapeutic blackmail, if such a thing was possible.

The Parker Development offices were closed on a Saturday, and the security guard had never heard of Sharon. Mr Parker had been in earlier, but he had left.

Melissa drove through a misty Malworth, checking her watch. She mustn't be late for the vet; she had to pick up Robeson. She was waiting to come out of a side street when she saw Detective Inspector Hill; she had seen a lot of her when she did the column on the aftermath of rape, in the wake of the recent attacks. She had been very helpful.

Melissa frowned as she watched the inspector take a note from under her windscreen, read it, then screw it up and throw it into one of the bins that adorned every other lamp-post in Malworth in its attempt to regain the Best Kept Town trophy. Then she tried to get into her car, but the key didn't seem to work.

There was a hooting from behind, and Melissa, much to the annoyance of everyone around, cautiously changed lanes and turned right instead of left. She pulled up beside the inspector. 'Can I help?' she asked.

Detective Inspector Hill turned quickly, startled by her voice. 'Oh,' she said. 'It's you. I . . . I can't unlock the door.'

'Have you tried the passenger door? The lock's probably collapsed or something.'

She had seen Detective Inspector Hill very angry – angry enough to say things about the judicial system which Melissa had felt it prudent not to publish; she had seen her relaxed. She had seen her control a quite sizeable press conference. She had never seen her flustered.

'I . . . yes. No – it's silly. Someone's superglued the locks.' Her face was pink, her eyes bright. She tried to laugh it off without much success.

Melissa opened her passenger door. 'I'll give you a lift,' she said.

She looked as though she was going to refuse, but she got in. 'Thank you,' she said. 'It's kind of you.'

'Can I give it to the news desk as a filler?' asked Melissa. 'Vandals strike at copcar?'

'If you like.'

Melissa smiled. 'Just a joke,' she said. 'I won't tell them if you don't want me to. I'm not paid to give them news.' She pulled back out into the traffic, occasioning more hoots. 'Where to?' she asked.

'Oh – I live on the High Street. It's not far.'

Melissa wondered about the note under the windscreen. If she was a newshound, she would drop off the inspector and come back and fish for it in that bin. But she wasn't a newshound, and she had a cat to fetch from the vet's. Besides, police officers were probably always having this sort of thing done to them by those whose lives they had made less comfortable.

She glanced at Detective Inspector Hill, who sat stiffly beside her, her cheeks still burning, her eyes fixed firmly on the road ahead.

She didn't suppose it always produced that reaction, though, she thought, and sneaked another look at her watch. Between five and six, the vet had said, and she didn't have any spare time. Perhaps she could telephone Simon, get him to go to the vet. Or even come back after she'd taken Robeson home.

As the thought crossed her mind, she heard the hum and beat of the street-sweeper as it made its noisy way along the wide pavement, saw the driver get down and empty one of the bins into its trailer. He would obviously beat her to it, whatever she did.

Oh, well. She wasn't a newshound anyway. She pulled up as instructed, outside a shop, and Detective Inspector Hill got out.

Few women could make her feel that she didn't do enough with herself, as Lionel had observed when making a clumsy pass at her during her own housewarming party. She was very confident of her womanhood; girls like Sharon Smith didn't make her question herself at all, unless they had just told her they were sleeping with her husband.

But Detective Inspector Hill could manage it, even when she was uncharacteristically agitated, without saying a word. She wore as little make-up as Melissa, and her hair was short and natural too. But she looked elegant and *right*; she was somehow dressed for early autumn, not in summer jeans and T-shirt and an old cardigan in case it got cold. Her skirt and jacket were autumn coloured; the crisp shirt was a perfect contrast, the shoes, even the bloody tights were right. She could have understood if Simon had wanted someone like her. Someone with a touch of class, someone who made more of herself without making herself a dressmaker's dummy.

And now she was covered in cat hairs, which she was absently attempting to brush from her skirt. Melissa felt awful.

'Sorry about that,' she said. 'I had to take the cat to the vet yesterday afternoon – I'm just on my way to pick him up.'

'That's all right,' she said. 'And thanks. I'm sorry I wasn't very good company.' She looked a little ashamed. 'I believe Sharon Smith worked for your husband,' she said. 'It must have been a shock for him.'

'I expect it was,' said Melissa, speaking before thinking. The bitterness was evident. But for once, the usually sharp Detective Inspector Hill hadn't seemed to notice.

The fog was closing in again as Colin straightened up from his task, and looked out of the garage door. He stretched; the aching in his bones was wearing off now that he could relax.

He had checked the bike minutely, just in case it had been 'accidentally' scratched or otherwise abused when it was in police care, but it seemed to be all right. He was getting away from his parents, who had spent every minute since they had got home demanding to know what was going to happen.

How did he know? He had made an official complaint; that wouldn't make him any more popular with the constabulary, but he had had no choice. After he had told him, the chief inspector had just looked at him; Colin had seen the disbelief, and the anger. Then he had terminated the interview, and left him with a uniformed sergeant and Constable Harris.

His mind had been prepared for all sorts of reprisals, but they had given him a complaints form to complete, and then he had been dumped back in the cell. It had seemed to have changed nothing, but something must have happened, because a little later he was being taken away by his parents, and the fear had at last left him. He was going to enjoy watching these two getting their comeuppance.

And Lloyd. Patronising him, calling him Colin all the time like that, so convinced that he was her boyfriend, for some reason. Why he thought that was a mystery to Colin. And he still didn't believe him about the car.

'Colin?'

Colin moved the powerful beam of the portable light in the direction of the voice, dazzling Chief Inspector Lloyd, who shaded his eyes.

'Mr Drummond to you,' said Colin.

'I'd like to ask you some questions about the car you saw,' he sa.d, walking in further.

Colin still held the beam pointing at him. 'You believe me now, do you?' he said.

'I have my job to do,' he said, lowering his hand as his eyes grew more accustomed to the bright light. 'You weren't telling the truth, and I knew you weren't.' He was blinking, but he didn't put his hand back up.

'I thought I might end up in hospital if I did,' said Colin.

'I can't discuss that with you. But I need to know about that car – if you really saw one.'

Colin was on his own private territory. In the garage, with its faint, ever-present smell of oil and petrol, the stone floor on which the soles of his boots made a scraping sound when he walked, its shelves full of boxes of spark plugs and spares. In summer, the air was perfumed by the damp grass that clung to the mower; that had faded into the heavy autumn smell of newly oiled machinery, put away for the winter. Lloyd had no right. No *right*.

The beam cut past Lloyd, out into the fog. Colin put down the lamp, and the garage was lit again, distorted shadows on the walls, on the floor, on Lloyd's face.

'I just saw its rear lights,' he said.

'Did you get a glimpse of the colour – an impression of the size? Did you see any of the number?'

Colin shook his head, and the huge shadow on the wall moved with it.

'You said you followed her – why did you do that?'

Colin picked up a rag and crouched down beside the bike, polishing the paintwork. Before, he had been too scared to think straight. But he wasn't scared any more, not now that he was back where he belonged. He shrugged, the cloth moving slowly over the mudguard until it gleamed. 'I just wanted to see she was all right,' he said.

He looked up at Lloyd, and reached up for the lamp, bringing it down to his level. It made Lloyd look like a devil now, his features lit from underneath. He moved to address the petrol tank, polishing it with the same lazy stroking motion.

'Why didn't you just talk to her? Why follow her?'

Colin's hand stopped. 'I didn't know if she'd want me to talk to her,' he said. 'After what had happened. I wasn't sure what to do. Then the car picked her up.'

'Where?'

Colin smiled. Lloyd should have asked these questions a long time ago. He must have been chewed out. Sent round here to get told what he would have been told if he hadn't been so convinced that Sharon had been his girlfriend.

'Byford Road.'

'Whereabouts in Byford Road?'

'About halfway down towards the village.'

'When?'

He thought about that. 'About half eight, just after.' He snapped off the light, and for a moment, the darkness seemed impenetrable. Then light from the fog-obscured early evening skies filtered in, and he could see Lloyd. 'I'm finished in here,' he said, walking out past him.

Lloyd came out, and Colin pulled down the door.

'Why did you follow the car?' he asked.

'I thought she might be getting a lift home,' said Colin. 'I thought I could talk to her when she got out. But the car went back up to the football ground and parked.'

'And she began to remove her clothing?'

Colin was turning away from him as he spoke; he checked the movement, and turned back with a smile. 'Not then,' he said. He walked towards the side door of the house, where the kitchen light gleamed in the misty twilight, through the glass of the door. The truth, lies. Colin smiled. Lloyd would never know which was which. Only he knew. 'After they'd been there about ten minutes,' he said. 'So I left. Wasn't much point in staying, was there?'

'But you didn't just leave, did you? You drove off without lights, at eighty miles an hour, in thick fog.' Lloyd walked up to him. 'And you want me to believe that what she was doing in the car didn't bother you?'

'I didn't drive away from there like that. I just drove round for a while. Then I fancied going fast.'

Lloyd looked annoyed with himself. That pleased Colin.

'So when did you actually leave the football ground?'

'About nine,' said Colin. 'I reckon.'

'And she was still in this car when you left?'

Colin opened the kitchen door. 'Sod off,' he said. 'I've had enough of answering questions.'

Jake Parker's eyes widened. 'You're the last person I expected,' he said.

He had thought that it might be the police again, but he had not thought that he would find Lionel Evans offering himself up. He might have preferred Evans' office, or better still, his car. But he was here now, and Jake wasn't about to waste any time.

'I had to come,' said Lionel.

'Did you?' said Jake shortly, and walked into the living-room, where he lit a cigarette, doubtless ruining the Laura Ashley soft furnishings.

Lionel closed the door quietly and followed him in. 'Jake – you accused me of killing Sharon!'

Jake turned to face him. 'So I did,' he said.

'You can't believe that!' Lionel was pale; his eyes were wide with fear.

'What do you expect me to believe? I tell you that she came to see me – next thing she's dead!'

Lionel was shaking his head. 'No. No, you're wrong, Jake. You're wrong. I didn't even see Sharon last night!'

'What?' Jake removed his cigarette from his mouth. 'You were on the balcony *with* me, Lionel! If you're going to lie, watch who you're lying to.'

'But . . . but I—' Lionel sank down on to the sofa, then looked up. 'The police have got someone,' he said. 'It's in tonight's—'

'What are you trying to tell me, Lionel? Someone else conveniently took it into his head to kill her? They pick up anyone remotely suspicious after a murder – that's why they've got him. He had no motive – you did.'

Lionel looked bewildered. 'Why shouldn't I think it was you?' he said. 'You had as much to lose as I did.'

Jake took a puff of the cigarette, and some pleasure in releasing smoke in the direction of the swathes over the curtains. 'When we saw her,' he said slowly, 'I went to talk to her. She was talking to this guy as though nothing at all had happened, and I lost my rag – I grabbed her and pushed him away. I'd have knocked the little bitch's head off if he hadn't pulled me off her.'

Lionel blinked at him. 'If . . . if you were that angry with her,' he said, 'why aren't the police questioning you?'

'Because I got arrested for disturbing the peace,' said Jake. 'I was in a bloody cell all evening. But where were you?'

What colour Lionel had had left drained away. 'Home,' he said. 'I went home.'

'You panicked, and killed her, that's what you did. And do you know what that means? That means I get some chief inspector here before breakfast wanting to know what my little difference of opinion with her was all about!'

'What did you tell him?' Lionel asked, alarmed.

Jake closed his eyes. 'I made out I was jealous,' he said. 'I saw her chatting up a bloke, and I told the chief inspector that I was jealous. All right?'

'But she wasn't,' said Lionel, still trying hard to hold on to the threads. 'Was she?'

'I don't know,' said Jake, with another sigh. 'I didn't ask.'

Lionel looked worried. 'It would hardly have been like her,' he said.

Jake snorted. 'Who says it wasn't like her? She wasn't the goody two-shoes she made out, Lionel. Whitworth could tell you that.'

'*Simon?*' Lionel squeaked. Jake didn't think his voice could move up any more registers.

'Simon,' he confirmed. 'Didn't you know?'

Lionel shook his head slowly, wonderingly. 'How do *you* know?' he asked accusingly.

'She told me.' He sat down. 'They've been turning your office into a regular little love-nest, Lionel.'

It had been his own fault, Jake supposed, for sending her there in the first place, in what had been one of his few acts of selfless generosity. Evans had needed someone to look after the office, and she had wanted to work somewhere closer to home.

'Are you *sure*?' asked Lionel.

'Oh, yes.' Jake got to his feet again, as anger once again swept over him. 'I did her a favour, ungrateful little cow, and that was how she repaid me.' He leant down towards Lionel. 'But killing her was a very bad idea,' he said, shaking his head.

'I didn't! You can't think I did!'

No. Jake didn't think that at all. But he very much wanted Lionel to think that he did. The law were sniffing round, and he had a proposition to put to Lionel. But he had to get him good and scared first.

'Who, then?' he asked. 'Your fairy godmother?'

'Let him go?' said Simon.

Melissa nodded, and stroked Robeson, who was sleeping off the anaesthetic.

'But why?'

She sat down at the table, and picked up her knife and fork. 'They don't confide in newspapers,' she said, with a shrug.

Simon felt irrationally as though Melissa was somehow responsible, because the evening paper for which she worked had told him that a man was being held, and now she was telling him that he wasn't. 'Was it the wrong man?' he asked.

'I don't know!' She began to cut up her chicken. 'They wouldn't say yes or no when they were asked if he had been eliminated from their inquiries,' she said, her tone conciliatory. 'Which probably means that he hasn't been – they're usually quick to point out if someone really isn't a suspect any more.'

Simon looked at his plate. 'Do they know why she went to the match?' he asked.

Melissa swallowed. 'They haven't said.'

Simon pushed his plate away. 'I didn't tell them everything,' he said.

Melissa's face coloured a little. 'What do you mean?' she asked sharply.

'I said she hadn't told me her plans,' said Simon. 'But she did, sort of. She said she was meeting someone.'

Melissa put down her knife and fork. 'What did she tell you?' she asked.

'Just that.'

'It won't be much use to the police, then,' she said.

Simon should have told the police about Sharon's appointment, but everything was so confusing; he had needed time to think. Then, when he saw the headline in the paper, he had thought that his information wouldn't have helped. Now Melissa was telling him that nothing was settled, and he had to make a decision.

'It might have been him she was meeting,' he said, with a nod at the paper, and very little conviction. 'This man that they've had to release.'

'So what?'

'I think I'd better tell them,' he said.

Melissa pushed her plate away too. 'I don't see the fact that she was meeting someone has got anything to do with it,' she said.

Simon shook his head. She wasn't usually illogical. 'Don't you?' he said. 'I think the police will.'

'Oh, do what you like!' she said, and ran upstairs.

Simon looked after her, puzzled by her reaction. He had thought he might get an argument, given the police's unwarranted interest in her movements, and her current dislike of them; he had thought she might think that he had already told the police something which had led them on a wild goose chase, and that he should leave well alone.

He hadn't expected her to be angry.

Lionel felt mesmerised; he watched as Jake moved, lithe as an athlete, across the room, watched as he opened a drawer, and almost passed out when he pointed a pistol at him.

'I've been warned not to take the law into my own hands,' he said conversationally.

He was walking towards Lionel with the gun trained on his head. Lionel couldn't speak, couldn't think; his vital functions seemed to freeze into immobility, for which he could only really be grateful. The gun was placed at his temple, and he still didn't, couldn't, move.

'So we can do it legal,' he said. 'I can ring the police, tell them what Sharon told me.'

Lionel spun round, almost knocking the gun from Jake's hand, but not quite. He doubted if he would have been quick enough to do anything even if he had. 'You *can't* do that,' he said.

'I can. You've landed me right in it, Lionel. Because now that she's dead, they're going to be poking and prying into her affairs.

Finding out what she did, who she saw, who she knew – what she knew.' He pulled the clip from the gun.

It was empty. Lionel breathed again. He ought to run for it now, while he had a chance, but . . . he had to know what Jake was going to do.

'I can give them an edited version of what Sharon told me,' he said. 'Leave my name out of it, and it doesn't look good for you, does it?'

Lionel stared at him. 'Do you seriously think that *I'd* leave your name out of it?' he demanded.

Jake smiled, shaking his head, and reached into his pocket. 'No,' he said. 'But you'll go to prison, Lionel. If they believe you, and can prove anything, I'll go to prison too – but I didn't kill her. You did.'

'I didn't!' Lionel was beginning to wonder if he could prove that Parker had had anything to do with the fraud at all. He was beginning to suspect that he had been set up as a fall-guy from the very start. He was beginning to realise what a fool he had been.

Jake was still smiling as he took the bullets out and inserted them in the clip. One by one, they clicked into place. 'Or there's suicide,' he said, pushing the full clip home, and holding the gun at Lionel's temple again.

Lionel didn't believe he was going to shoot him. That sort of thing didn't happen. 'Why would I come here to commit suicide?' he asked.

'You came to plead with me to give you time to get the money back where it belongs,' said Jake. 'I'll tell them that I knew nothing about it until Sharon told me yesterday. I'll deny telling you anything. I'll tell them that there was only one way you could know that I had found out, and that was if you had talked to Sharon.'

The pistol nudged Lionel's temple, and he almost passed out.

'I was very close to Sharon,' Jake continued, smiling. 'I told the Chief Inspector. We had a good thing going, me and Sharon. You had murdered my beloved, Lionel, and I told you there was no way I was giving you time to pay the money back. I was going to the police. You pulled out a gun and shot yourself on my rented shagpile.'

It sounded almost plausible. With a loaded gun at his temple, there was no doubt that Lionel was in a less than enviable position. But neither alternative had much in it for Parker. Lionel waited for his third choice, and was not disappointed.

'Or,' said Jake.

'Done,' said Lionel. 'Whatever it is. Just take that gun away, for God's sake.'

Jake's smile vanished. 'Thanks to you,' he said, 'I'm going to have to leave much sooner than I meant to, with a lot less money.' He shook his head. 'I could have worked something out with Sharon,' he said. 'A deal – something. She just wanted to protect Whitworth – she wasn't bothered about the investors.'

Lionel was still having trouble coming to terms with this altered image of Sharon. He could believe she had been involved with Parker, just. He was a bachelor, so there was no reason why she shouldn't have had a relationship with him. But Simon? Sharon and a married man? But then he thought of all the times they had stayed at the office together, working late. Someone other than him would have tumbled weeks ago. Melissa had – that was why she had rung him, asking about Simon's overtime. Served her right. She should make more of herself. She could be quite a good-looking woman if she tried.

'I'd have worked something out,' Jake said again. 'You didn't have to kill her.'

Lionel shook his head. 'I didn't,' he said.

Jake took the gun away, and held it loosely as he looked at him. 'I'm prepared to make it obvious that I was involved in the fraud,' he said. 'Once I'm safely out of the country.'

Lionel stared at him.

'There's a catch,' said Jake. 'In return, I want it all, and I want it on Monday. Today would have been much better, but you did a bunk.'

'I didn't – I . . .'

'Then I leave, and you do what you can to get yourself clear.'

That was more like it. A solution that left Parker somewhere the law couldn't touch him, and Lionel with nothing to show for six months' hard work, holding a time-bomb. 'But if we withdraw all that cash at once—' he began.

'It'll look very suspicious,' said Jake. 'Tough. You can still do what we planned,' said Parker. 'More or less.'

'Who's going to believe me, if you've already gone? The whole point was that the cash would have disappeared bit by bit, and you would still be here – you would be backing me up.'

Jake shrugged. 'That's your problem. Though,' he added thoughtfully, 'if you really *didn't* kill her . . .'

At last. He believed him. Lionel hadn't relished the idea of Parker believing him to be the author of his misfortune. If the police got on to him before he could do his disappearing act, that gun wouldn't be for ornament.

' . . . and I don't really think you did – you don't have the guts –

then there is the question of who did kill her, and you know what they say, don't you?'

'What do they say?' Lionel asked wearily.

'Murder is almost always done by your nearest and dearest,' said Jake. 'Maybe Sharon and Simon had a barney, and he ended up doing her in.'

Somehow, that seemed rather likelier than their having a liaison in the first place, Lionel thought.

'Someone killed her. If it *was* Whitworth, that would strengthen your hand, wouldn't it? She knew too much, so he killed her.'

The phone rang, and Jake fairly leapt across the room to pick it up. 'Hello. Oh – Marilyn. Thank God – where the hell is Bobbie?'

Lionel watched as Jake Parker listened, his eyes at first disbelieving, then wide with shock.

'No,' he said. 'No – you did right. I'll be there. I'm coming now.'

He put down the phone and stared blankly at Lionel. 'I – I've got to go,' he said. 'Something's . . . I've got to go.'

It seemed inappropriate in the extremely odd circumstances to inquire politely if anything was wrong, but Lionel would not have believed that anyone holding a loaded pistol could ever have looked so completely vulnerable.

Eight

Lloyd got home, his virtually sleepless night beginning to catch up with him. Just driving was tiring in this weather, peering through the mist. He wanted to get in, have a night-cap, and fall asleep to an old film on video.

He listened to the sole message on his answering machine, and left the flat again, driving straight to Judy's through the ever-thickening fog.

She opened the door a little guiltily. 'You look tired,' she said.

He smiled. 'I'll survive,' he said. She looked worried, as he had known she would. She was smiling, trying to pretend that nothing was wrong, but she was hopeless at that, and the three-word message she had left him had merely confirmed what he had feared.

'Have you eaten?' he demanded, as he removed his coat and hung it up on the hooks which had suddenly made an appearance in her small hallway.

She shook her head. 'I'm not hungry,' she said.

'Did you have lunch?'

'No.'

'Right.' He went into the kitchen, snapping on the light. 'I'll do you an omelette. Have you any cheese?'

'I couldn't eat it, honestly, Lloyd.'

He raised his eyebrows. 'Nonsense,' he said, opening the fridge, and finding cheese, rather to his surprise. 'Anyone can eat an omelette. I'll share it with you.' No need to inquire about eggs; there was always a plentiful supply. Judy was a bacon and eggs for breakfast woman, which was just as well, because she didn't seem to eat anything else unless he fed her.

She grated cheese while he broke eggs into a bowl, salting and peppering them. Black pepper was always available now; his next task was to get her to buy a pepper-grinder instead of using the ready ground stuff.

He had news for her which he was diffident about imparting, and she clearly had problems which she didn't want to admit. The

116

result was a very rare slightly awkward silence, which Judy broke just as he was about to take the plunge.

'Did you go to see Drummond again?' she asked.

A reprieve. He put two plates into the oven to warm up; he wasn't sure he wanted a reprieve. In his book it was always better to get bad things over with. 'I did,' he said, finding a fork, and gently beating the eggs. 'He is one very weird young man. And Finch is right. He *is* a cocky little bastard, when he isn't frightened of being beaten up.'

He saw Judy's back stiffen, and her grating hand stop for just a moment before continuing to attack the cheese. He couldn't believe that he had said it. Freudian. It had to be. He wanted to get it over with, so he had introduced the topic without even thinking.

'Someone superglued my car locks,' she said. 'And left me a note to explain why.'

So that was it. Lloyd sighed. 'Forget it, Judy,' he said. 'It's a piece of juvenile behaviour that you should just ignore.'

The cheese was on a hiding to nothing. Lloyd put the frying pan on the gas, and introduced an enormous knob of butter to it. He cleared his throat a little.

He hadn't felt as bad as this since he was six, and he'd had to confess to his dad that he'd eaten all the strawberries out of the patch in the garden. He could still feel the soft earth, warm beneath his bare, scuffed knees, as he had had just one, and then another, and just one more, until they had all been gone.

'Merrill will be ringing you tomorrow morning,' he began, 'but I might as well tell you now.'

She turned to him, her face apprehensive. 'Ringing me about what?'

The butter began to sizzle, and Lloyd moved the pan, sliding the melting gold across its surface. He didn't use a non-stick pan himself – he had inherited a cast-iron beauty that was coming up to its telegram from the Queen. But he supposed if they said they were non-stick, then they were. Modern cooking utensils were probably the only new-fangled things with which Lloyd did not hold.

Her question wasn't repeated, but it was hanging about, waiting to be answered. He was often very grateful that he wasn't a miscreant trying to pull the wool over Judy's clear eyes. And he had brought the subject up, so he had no option but to answer.

'Andrews thought we could do with beefing up the murder-room team,' he said, turning the gas up full, and standing by with his bowl of eggs. 'Barstow's the incident office manager, so I can't have him on the streets. Besides, if he gets this job he's

117

after, he'll be whipped off to patrol a desk at headquarters any minute.' The eggs hit the almost-burning butter, and they didn't stick.

'Finch is a good lad,' he continued. 'He's bright, and keen . . . but he doesn't have the experience, or the rank.' He reached across her for the plate of vanquished cheese. 'Andrews thought we could do with another DI, and your name was suggested.' He lifted the edges of the omelette, adjudged the moment right, and popped in the cheese. 'Merrill has agreed to second you for the duration.'

There. He'd got it out, and had made the omelette, all in one go. Now Judy was looking at him, her dark eyes resting on his for a long time before she spoke.

'Who suggested it?'

'What?' he asked, playing for time, as he flipped the omelette over, and took the plates from the oven, neatly producing two halves of omelette, and putting them down at the table.

'My name was suggested,' she said patiently, opening the drawer. 'Who suggested it?' she asked, holding out his knife and fork to him.

Lloyd wanted to look away from the steady brown gaze, but he didn't. 'I did,' he said, taking his cutlery. 'One thing about our beloved chief constable throwing everyone up and seeing where they land is that the gossip hasn't got to the current top brass at Stansfield. I thought I could get away with it, so I just—' He shrugged a little and sat down.

'Why?' she demanded, joining him.

'Why what?' he asked.

'Why did you suggest my name?'

He could tell her that he missed the totally unimaginative logic which she possessed, and which provided checks and balances for his own inspirational (as Andrews had rather nicely called it) guess-work, keeping him off the carpet on more than one occasion. He could tell her that Finch wasn't, for the moment, at any rate, a suitable sounding board for his theories; he would either act on them, which would be disastrous, or think that Lloyd was off his head. He could tell her that neither living with her nor working with her was getting him down, and he had seized the chance of having her around. It would all have been true, but it was for none of those reasons, and Judy knew it.

'Because I knew your life would be made hell at work,' he said, and began to eat.

She looked away then.

Well, Lloyd thought stoutly, he could weather it. He'd done it now, so she would just have to put up with it. Maybe he was a chauvinistic pig who thought that all he had to do was ride up on his charger and rescue the damsel in distress whether she wanted to be rescued or not. Maybe he did have a nerve thinking that he could interfere in her business, in her professional relationships with her colleagues. But he wasn't going to stand by and watch her . . .

He shouldn't have been eating the strawberries at all, never mind all of them. But he had seen them just lying there, red and plump, and he had crawled under the netting, just to taste one. It had been delicious. Sweet and juicy and slightly warm; he could taste it now. They had all been delicious.

'Thank you,' she said, turning back, and smiled.

He stared at her. 'I'm not in trouble?' he asked.

He hadn't been last time either; his dad had laughed. 'Never mind,' he had said. 'Were they good?'

'You had no right to interfere,' she said. 'But I wasn't looking forward to next week.' She paused. 'And you didn't lie to me,' she added.

Was that why his dad had forgiven him too?

Lloyd smiled back at her, but already she was fixing him with a stern eye. 'Was it honestly Andrews' opinion that you needed another DI?' she asked.

'Cross my heart. Ask him.' After a little subtle prompting, perhaps. But the actual suggestion had issued from Andrews' lips, and he had *thought* it was his opinion, at least.

'Then you'd better fill me in on Sharon Smith,' she said.

'We're supposed to be off-duty,' he reminded her.

'We can be off-duty when we've eaten,' she said.

As they ate, he told her what they knew; no more. No half-baked theorising, not yet. Not so soon after being proved wrong about Drummond. By Judy, of course. It would be good to have her back in harness with him.

'The lab have confirmed that there *were* traces of sawdust on her clothes, and SOCOS will be at the site tomorrow to see where it might have come from,' he finished.

She nodded, and got up from the table, switching the kettle on. 'Tea or instant coffee?' she asked.

And a coffee-grinder. He'd civilise her if it was the last thing he did. 'Tea,' he said. It would be tea bags, of course, but that wasn't as bad as instant coffee.

'So there you are,' he said. 'Two little puzzles. The sawdust – and this key that no one knows anything about. Any observations?' he asked, when she had made the tea.

'Just one,' she said. 'A leisure suit and trainers are very sensible things to wear at a football match, but I'd like to know if that's what she was wearing at work.'

Lloyd beamed, and stood up, putting his arms round her as she closed the teapot lid. 'That's my girl,' he said, and got smacked on the hand.

'If Drummond's telling the truth,' he said, instantly forgetting his resolution not to theorise, 'I think Sharon had a married man tucked away somewhere. Arranged to meet him at the match, and he didn't turn up. But she spoke to Barnes, and Parker got the wrong idea.'

Judy nodded, and reached past him to pluck two mugs from the tree on the worktop.

'Then the boyfriend saw her, picked her up, and they went back to the ground, because it was deserted, and they wanted privacy. They didn't know they had a voyeur taking notes.'

'It's possible,' said Judy. 'I suppose. But why did this married man kill her?'

Lloyd shrugged. 'Search me,' he said, with a grin.

They took their tea into the living room, and Lloyd looked round the flat. He hadn't been here very often; the last time, the walls had had the previous tenant's wallpaper still decorating them, the paint work had been a dingy pink, the floor had been partially covered with a large rug of an indeterminate colour, a brownish reddish darkish sort of colour. He had been told that that didn't matter because she wasn't going to be in the flat that long.

Now, the walls were newly painted in white with a peach tinge, the paintwork was sparklingly new and brilliant white, the rug had been replaced by several smaller scatter rugs on floorboards which had been sanded and varnished.

'When did all this happen?' he asked.

She looked round. 'Oh – I just did things here and there,' she said.

Without mentioning it to him, he thought. 'You varnished the floorboards?' he asked, disbelievingly.

'Well, no – I got a man in to do that. He was very good – he only took a couple of days.'

Lloyd drank some tea before he spoke. 'You don't mean to leave here, do you?' he asked.

She sighed. 'Lloyd,' she said. 'Do you think we could discuss this some night when we don't have a whole extra hour to do it in?'

'Do the clocks go back tonight?' His impromptu night-shift had disoriented him.

She nodded.

'But you don't, do you?' he persisted.

'I think I've got a book somewhere about coping with rape,' she said. 'From when I did that course – I think I should take it into Bobbie Chalmers, if she won't have counselling.'

'Fine.' Lloyd put down his mug. 'But I thought we could be off-duty once we'd eaten? I have no desire at all to discuss work.'

'It's better than discussing us,' she said. 'We don't have rows about work.'

Oh, God. He didn't want a row. He was much too tired to have a row, for one thing. He joined her on the sofa. 'Sorry,' he said, putting his arm round her. She smelt of bath-oil; her hair was soft against his face.

He woke up at four in the morning to find himself covered with Judy's spare duvet. She had left a little lamp on for him. He smiled, and got up stiffly from the sofa, feeling his back, switched off the lamp, then tip-toed in the darkness out into the hallway and crept into the bedroom.

He undressed and got into bed beside the sleeping Judy, which was something he always found very reassuring, and just one more thing that he missed now that she didn't live with him.

Mac lay on the bed, headphones on, listening again to Sharon Smith's words.

Melissa had carried that tape around with her after the interview. Had she gone home? Had she told Simon what his girlfriend had done? Had she perhaps even played it to him? It was no honest mistake on Sharon's part, Mac was certain – she knew who she was talking to, all right.

Mac took off the headphones and thought for a moment. He could hear the lies; he'd noticed it before. A kind of rehearsed precision in her answers that you didn't get when people were really baring their souls. But why would she lie?

Could it all have been some sort of fantasy? Some sort of revenge for a slight? Like sending someone a Valentine to get them into trouble, only much, much worse?

He looked at the tape, and he wondered. If there was no truth in it, then Simon might have *felt* like killing her, but he wouldn't have. He might have sacked her, but he wouldn't have killed her.

He ran the tape back, and listened again, his face growing sombre. Sharon Smith was telling lies; he was sure of it.

But Melissa had believed her.

Judy blinked as the morning sun came through the thin curtains, waking her as it had all week, and found Lloyd beside her. Good, she thought sleepily.

She hadn't thought twice about what to do when she had left Melissa Whitworth's car and run up to the sanctuary of her flat; she hadn't thought at all. Instinct rather than conscious decision had prompted her to reach for the phone and dial Lloyd's number. His latest gadget had answered, saying that he couldn't come to the phone, but he'd be home sooner or later. She had waited impatiently for the tone, and said 'Please come over,' before she had given herself up to the tears.

At first, when she had seen the note under her windscreen she had thought that they had come and painted more double yellow lines when she hadn't been looking. Then, when she had unfolded and read it, she had been unable to see how its unpleasant contents could refer to her. The anonymous writer, she had thought, must have got the wrong car. But then she had realised, with a stab of guilt, what it was all about.

Her confidential chat with Merrill had got round with the usual staggering speed of station rumour, and this was her first taste of retribution. She hoped she hadn't made too much of a fool of herself with Melissa Fletcher. At least she hadn't burst into tears then, which was all she had felt like doing.

What made it all so much worse was that she couldn't imagine a single one of the dozens of male colleagues with whom she had worked over the years being reduced to tears by a malicious trick and a few unlovely adjectives. But it wasn't so much the manner in which the message had been delivered that was upsetting her, she knew that. It was what it had said, and she hadn't told Lloyd that, because it was that that had made her feel guilty.

Six forty-five. She frowned. This was too early, she thought. On the other days, it had been time to get up when the sun had invaded her sleep. Gradually, her brain stirred itself. The hour. It was really *seven* forty-five. She should be up, she thought, pushing back the covers, then another few brain-cells kicked in. No. It was Sunday, of course. She relaxed back on to the pillow, then sat up again. Lloyd had said that Merrill would be ringing; she had better get ready to go in to work and sort things out, if she was joining the murder team. And there would be no day off today. She pushed back the covers again, and got as far as swinging her legs out of bed. No, no. It *was* really six forty-five.

'Mm? What? What's wrong?' Lloyd opened one reluctant eye.

She smiled. 'Nothing,' she said, lying back down, pulling the cover back.

He opened both eyes. 'What time is it?' he asked.

'The extra hour,' she said, snuggling up to him.

'If you want that sort of thing first thing in the morning, you'll have to go elsewhere for it,' he mumbled.

She did, rather. But Lloyd was not a morning person in that respect or in any other. He had conquered his desire to stay in bed until noon by waking up as late as possible, getting shaved and showered and dressed as quickly as possible, swallowing coffee, and getting to the car. Then, and only then, did his system adjust to the new day, which it did with startling, and usually irritating rapidity.

She liked mornings, though until her inherited ultra-thin curtains she had usually slept until the alarm woke her. But she liked watching the dawn touch the sky, and hearing the birds call, and listening to the sounds of the world waking up. She enjoyed the semi-reality of early morning, the slow adjustment.

'You *don't* want to leave here, do you?' Lloyd said.

She sat up. 'If you're awake enough to start a row, you're awake enough to—'

'I don't want a row. I want an answer. Please, Judy.'

She thought about her answer before she gave it. He didn't hurry her; he wouldn't like it, and he knew it. He would probably rather she didn't answer. But she did. 'I've never lived on my own before,' she said. 'I'm thirty-eight years old, and I've never lived on my own.'

A flick of his eyebrows indicated that that wasn't so unusual. She knew it wasn't. People lived at home, then married and set up home with someone else. But it hadn't been quite like that with her. She had met Lloyd, complete with wife and children, and her story might have been more like Sharon Smith's, if she hadn't been afraid to have an affair. Lloyd's theory of the married man seemed likely to her; hence no discernible boyfriend. But there she went again, thinking about work because it was easier than thinking about them.

'I lived with my parents,' she said, at last. 'Then I met Michael, and I wished all the time that I was with him. Then I met you, and that was hopeless, so I married Michael, and wished all the time that I was with you.' She paused. 'I know what I'm like, Lloyd,' she said. 'And I'd rather be on my own, wishing I was with you, than with you and wishing I was on my own.'

His blue eyes looked directly into hers, daring her to deviate one centimetre from the truth. 'And when you *were* with me?' he asked. '*Did* you wish you were on your own?'

She shook her head. 'But I'd never been on my own then,' she said. 'Not properly. Not somewhere that was mine, and no one else's.' She took his hand. 'And we weren't together long enough for the bloom to wear off,' she said.

He gripped her hand tightly. 'Who says it has to wear off?' he demanded.

'Oh, Lloyd. It always wears off. It has to.'

He sat up. 'You married Michael because you wanted to pretend that I didn't exist,' he said. 'Of *course* the bloom wore off!'

Judy stood her ground. 'And you and Barbara?' she asked.

He looked down.

'I'm sorry, Lloyd. But it's true. You married Barbara because you really wanted to – not as a substitute for what you couldn't have. It was fine to start with – right?'

'Yes,' he said, looking up again. 'But there were children, and money worries, and my peculiar working hours – this wouldn't be the same!'

The sun inched up the sky; a patch of light shone through the thinnest patch of material in a hazy splash on the duvet. Judy looked at it as she spoke. 'It would be,' she said. 'There would be different causes, but it would be the same effect.'

'No!' He pulled her round to face him. 'You and I have meant this much to one another for seventeen years, Judy – don't try to pretend that we haven't.'

'I'm not,' she said, alarmed that he might think that, even for a moment. 'I . . . I just think that that's because we haven't lived together. I don't want to spoil what we've got.'

He flopped down on to the pillow. 'For God's sake,' he said.

She looked down at him. 'Lloyd,' she said, 'I love you. I know I don't say it very often. Do you need to be told?'

He shook his head, with a little smile.

'You mustn't ever doubt that. It's not like I felt about Michael – that was to do with him being the first. This is real. And nothing's going to change it.'

He looked exasperated. 'But you've just said that living with me would change it.'

'I wouldn't stop loving you. But you—'

'That's crazy!' He shouted to stop her finishing the sentence, and sat up again. 'It's nonsense.'

'No.' She shook her head. 'You're a romantic. You think it'll be roses all the way, and it won't.'

He gasped. 'Why would I think that? It isn't roses all the way now!'

'But you think that my marrying you would end all the rows and the hassle – and it wouldn't! They'd just be different rows – and the only difference would be that I couldn't just get up and walk out on them!'

He stared at her. 'You're wrong,' he said.

124

She wasn't making a very good job of explaining. She had avoided this conversation for weeks because she knew she would never make him understand. 'I like things the way they are,' she said.

'I don't.'

She smiled at him. 'But you're the unselfish one,' she said.

He held her close to him. 'All this is a smoke-screen,' he said. 'You always do it. Give yourself good reasons for what is simply a fear of committing yourself to anything that might alter whatever nice cosy rut you've—'

She kissed him. 'You're awake now,' she said.

Sunday. Colin got up, and risked shaving now that his lip had gone down a little. It hurt, but he looked rather better than he had.

His mother hadn't stopped; Colin would swear she had been going on all night, full of righteous indignation about what they had done to her Colin. His father, on the other hand, was deeply suspicious of the whole business; he inclined to the chief inspector's belief that Colin had been involved with Sharon Smith in the first place.

Colin was glad that they had been away on the actual night; they may have been given a report by their ever-vigilant next door neighbour, but at least they had missed him staggering home, using the bike like some sort of Zimmer frame as he had pushed his battered body along.

If his mother had seen that, she would have been camped out on the chief constable's doorstep. She hadn't asked him or herself why the police officers had done it, but his father had, obliquely. Colin had shrugged. He wouldn't be able to shrug when it came to a court hearing, but he would think of something.

He wished, almost with a smile, that he was black. Racists, he could say. All police are racist. And they would have swallowed that. As it was, he was white, middle-class, late teens, in gainful employment in one of his father's shops, and hardly what a court of law would see as a natural target for corrupt coppers.

And he almost wished that his father would do more than simply look sceptical and grunt the odd question to which he did not expect an answer, and even that only out of his mother's earshot. He should stand up for himself, not let himself be brow-beaten by her into agreeing with her every word. Colin didn't. But then again, if his father suddenly found some backbone at this stage it would be very awkward all round, so it was possibly just as well.

He went out, opening the garage door, smiling at the bike which gleamed in the sun that had already broken through the mist. He still felt stiff, but he thought he could ride her now.

He pushed the bike out on to the street, and started her up.

He'd told the chief inspector what he had seen. Twice. And he still didn't believe him. He didn't like having his word doubted. And Chief Inspector Lloyd had seen him scared; Colin didn't like that, either. And he'd thought he could scare him again, turning up without warning. Coming round to the house like that, coming into the garage. How dare he come into the garage? It was private. It was Colin's space, where he could get away and work on the bike and think. His father used it to put the car away and take it out again, but for nothing else. How dare Lloyd invade his privacy like that?

He drove, mindful of speed limits and lights, into the centre of town, and had turned into a deserted High Street when he saw Lloyd and some woman coming out of one of the alleys which ran along the side of the shops. He slowed to a stop before they saw him, his foot on the kerb, revving the bike gently, as he watched them get into a car.

His curiosity overcame his desire to get out on to the open road and drive to where he could open the bike up and put her through her paces; instead, he followed them at a discreet distance, using what sparse traffic there was to keep out of sight, to find out where they were off to so early on a Sunday morning.

Malworth police station, as it turned out. She didn't look as though she was going to help with their inquiries. Then he saw her wave to a couple of policemen who were going on duty. She obviously worked there, and he was dropping her off.

He liked the idea of spying on Lloyd going about his private business, just as he had probed into his. *Have you got a girlfriend, Colin*? What business is it of yours, Chief Inspector Lloyd? He continued to follow Lloyd's car as he headed towards the river. At the lights, he took the Stansfield turn, and Colin went the opposite way, out into the countryside, to the disused airfield where he could let the bike go.

It was dangerous; the concreted wartime runways were crazed and broken, and high, strong weeds pushed up through the cracks, making the surface uneven, with sometimes as much as six inches between paving slabs. The old huts had been all but destroyed by wind and weather and vandals, and sheets of rusted corrugated iron lay unseen just beneath the grass. The bike would buck and rear like an untamed horse, threatening to throw him. But it wasn't enough, not now.

He sat on the bike, looking round at the desolation. This morning wisps of mist still hung almost motionless in the air, giving the derelict buildings a ghostly air. It was easy to imagine it busy and full of suppressed excitement, as the pilots waited for the next mission. He'd have liked to have been a wartime pilot. The airfield would have been blacked out when they got the call to scramble; he imagined himself climbing into the cockpit, in charge of a machine that would take him soaring into the air to join a skyful of others on a night raid. No lights; just menacing dark shapes moving against the stars, droning steadily through the night to rain their deadly cargo on the enemy.

He worked in one of his father's clothes shops.

Sometimes he would pretend, on the bike. He had never got caught before. Once, they had chased him, but he had lost them, weaving through Malworth's lanes and alleys where the car couldn't follow, back to the garage and safety. Engaged by enemy fire, but mission successful. This time he had been shot down in enemy territory, but that had happened to the best of them. And he had escaped, like the best of them. He was ready for another sortie.

His father had two shops; one in Malworth, and one in Barton. He hated his job; he hated the customers, hated his father for the calm way in which he had accepted his son's being turned down by the air force. You can always work in the shop until you know what you want to do, he had said.

He had longed to be out there in the heat and dust of the Gulf, flying low-level precision-bombing raids, banking away from the explosion which would light up the night sky behind him as he flew back to base over white moonlit sands to a desert runway and a hero's welcome.

You wouldn't have been out there, his father had said. These men have trained for years. They're not eighteen-year-old kids. He hated his father.

And the police. He felt again the helplessness when the policemen stood over him as he lay on the pavement. Not doing enough to hospitalise him, and have people asking questions. Just enough to hurt. Then the dread when two more of them arrived at the house. The day-long fear at the police station, and Lloyd, tricking answers out of him, asking personal questions, coming into his garage without asking, without waiting for an invitation that he would never have got.

And it had been early, he realised. Very early, when Lloyd and that woman had come out of that alley, talking and laughing together. Perhaps she was his wife. Colin smiled to himself, and started the bike again. But then, perhaps she wasn't. *Have* you *got a girlfriend, Chief Inspector Lloyd?* He got on to the road, and drove back into Malworth.

Perhaps it would be worth finding out a little more about her.

* * *

Jake had never felt helpless in his life; he had always been the boy the other kids were afraid of at school. He had always had an answer – he had even had an answer to Sharon's little bombshell. There was always a way out – helplessness was for people like Lionel Evans, born losers; it wasn't for him. But he felt helpless now.

Marilyn had rung him against Bobbie's express wishes, and had told him as much as she knew. Bobbie wouldn't see him last night, and he had eventually taken the nurse's advice, and gone home to get some sleep, though he would hardly classify the guilt-ridden night of tossing and turning as sleep.

She had finally agreed to see him that morning. To start with she had been almost businesslike, apologising for not being available when Dennis called, explaining that she had been unable to fulfil her commitments, as though she had been caught up in a traffic jam. She was trying desperately, heart-breakingly, to build a wall of indifference to what had happened, her eyes bright with anger and pain.

But the wall thankfully crumbled; she started telling him, speaking in a low monotone, and he listened, his helplessness growing. He didn't know how long it would be before she could travel; he didn't, he realised, even know if she still wanted to go. He could never make it up to her; he could never take the memories away. He had made promises he could no longer keep, but he could still give her a better life than she had had, if she would let him.

He said he was sorry, over and over again. He tried to take her hand, but she pulled it away. Bobbie, who didn't quite accord with the image he had been creating for himself in Stansfield, was the only woman for whom he had ever given a damn, and it was his fault that this terrible thing had happened to her.

She wouldn't let him touch her, and he didn't have the words to tell her how he felt about her.

'Do . . . do you still want to come away with me?' he asked eventually.

She nodded; he was relieved, but it wouldn't help in the short term. He had to sort that out for himself. Everything had changed yet again, and the plan would just have to change with it. He knew how to sway with the punches, but this was below the belt.

There was a brisk knock, and a woman of about his own age came in. The kind that would have suited his image, the kind that would find him vulgar, and would bore him stiff.

'Who are you?' he asked suspiciously.

She glanced at the bed, and smiled briefly. 'My name's Judy,' she said. 'I'm a friend of Bobbie's.'

He looked at Bobbie for confirmation; she nodded slightly.

'I'll go, then,' he said, feeling awkward. He supposed a woman friend was a better idea, in the circumstances. He stood up, and bent down to kiss Bobbie's cheek, but she stiffened as he got close to her. He picked up the keys that she had left for him on the cabinet by her bed, and tried to smile, but he wanted to cry.

He walked from the room, and tried to remember that he was Jake Parker, and Jake Parker was *never* helpless.

Simon Whitworth was shown into an interview room, where two men already sat. One of them he recognised as Sergeant Finch.

'Mr Whitworth – thank you for coming in,' said the other man. 'I'm Detective Chief Inspector Lloyd – I believe you've met Sergeant Finch. I met your wife briefly, yesterday.'

Oh. Melissa hadn't said. She had seen Sergeant Finch, like he had. She hadn't mentioned any other visits from the police.

'It may be nothing,' he said. 'But Sharon told me that she was meeting someone on Friday evening.'

'Why didn't you tell me that?' Finch demanded to know.

Whitworth tried to excuse himself, but they were lame excuses, and the chief inspector indicated as much. He hadn't thought it was important, he had forgotten, he had meant to mention it, but somehow . . .

He gave up, worried about the impression he was giving. He was more worried by the time Lloyd had finished with him; if he had any more information that could help the police and was keeping it to himself, it would give him sleepless nights from now on. It would; but for the moment, it was information that he still had no intention of imparting.

'Did Sharon ever mention someone called Colin Drummond to you?' Lloyd asked.

'No,' said Simon. That must be the one they'd been holding.

'And she gave no indication of who she intended meeting? Or where?'

'No. She just said she had to meet someone.'

Finch looked slightly bored. 'So that's it, is it? She was meeting someone? And she left at six?'

'Yes,' said Simon.

'What was she wearing to the office, Mr Whitworth?' asked Lloyd, suddenly.

Simon knew precisely. But he didn't suppose that bosses usually knew. He'd never noticed what his secretary in his previous job had been wearing.

'I couldn't be sure,' he lied.

'Dress, skirt, trousers – think, please, Mr Whitworth.'

He swallowed. 'Skirt,' he said. 'And a blue blouse. Yes. A skirt with a sort of blue check, and a blue blouse.'

Finch got up and left the room. Simon looked at Lloyd, convinced that he knew, that he was only making matters worse by trying to keep it quiet. He just hadn't had time; he hadn't had time to sort out his feelings. He didn't think he could cope with Melissa's hurt on top of everything else.

Finch returned with a sort of jogging suit in a clear plastic bag. 'Have you ever seen Sharon wearing this?' he asked.

Simon shook his head.

'And she was wearing the skirt and blouse when she left the office at six?'

He nodded. His face was growing pink; he could feel it.

'Do you remember what shoes she wore?'

Blue leather court shoes that matched the blouse, with a tiny little fabric bow of darker blue. 'Sorry,' he said, miserably. 'Why are you . . . was she wearing this when you found her?' he asked.

'Yes,' said Finch. 'She must have changed her clothes at some point, and she didn't go home – would you know where she might have gone?'

No. Simon was beginning to think that he didn't know her at all. 'Wherever her appointment was, I suppose,' he said.

'Yes,' said Lloyd. 'Thank you for coming in, Mr Whitworth.'

Was that it? Simon looked at Lloyd, but he seemed to have lost interest in him. He was looking thoughtfully at the plastic bag.

'I'll . . . er . . . go, then.' He left the room, and the police station, and found himself almost running in his desire to put as much space as possible between it and him.

Melissa put down the phone, her heart heavy. She had no option but to do what Mac had asked. Simon had gone off somewhere without saying where he was going, probably just to get out of the house, where the atmosphere was becoming unbearable, so thankfully she had been alone when Mac had rung.

He was at the garage, he said. He wanted to see her. She saw him waiting on the forecourt, looking out for her as she drove through the business park, and she viewed him with an odd mixture of pleasure and anger. She could have driven past, but she didn't care for the possible consequences, so she pulled in.

'I can't stay long,' she warned him. 'I have to get Sunday lunch.' How she could tell such a lie without blushing, she didn't know. Simon had had his last Sunday lunch when he married her.

'I'll bet,' he said.

She smiled. 'Why am I here?' she asked, walking with him into the showroom.

'Because hardly anyone comes in on a Sunday, and I wanted to see you again,' he said. 'I run to coffee and biscuits.'

She sat down, resigned to being at Mac's beck and call as long as he had the tape. And it was a lot easier than being with Simon, when all was said and done.

'Why don't you have a game of golf?'

Lionel raised his eyes to heaven. 'I don't *want* a game of golf!' he said.

'You should do something,' said Frances. 'Take your mind off it.'

Oh, sure. Hitting a golf ball would take his mind off it.

'Why don't you tell me?' she asked.

'Tell you what?' He felt the alarm seizing his throat, making his voice sound odd.

'Whatever it is that's bothering you.'

'Sharon Smith has been killed!'

Frances sat down with her cup of tea. She never ate the huge, late Sunday breakfast that she always cooked for him. He had eaten; worry increased rather than decreased his appetite.

'But that's not it,' she said. 'You've been like it ever since you came back from that do at the football club.'

Lionel stared at her. He couldn't remember this many words passing between them since they had stood at the altar. But it didn't surprise him that she could tell the difference between normal long silences and worried long silences. Frances always knew.

'I trust you're not going to say that sort of thing if the police come here,' he said.

She frowned. 'Why should the police come here?' she asked.

'You've heard that announcement!' Frances always had Radio Barton on from the moment she got up until the moment that she switched on the television for the early evening news; they had heard the police appeal for witnesses about six times already.

'But you didn't see Sharon there, did you?' she asked.

Lionel closed his eyes. 'No,' he said.

'Well, then. You can't tell them anything.'

Frances never asked questions. She would snoop and pry, and she found things out, but she never asked questions. Why now? Why in God's name now?

'They know I was there,' he said. 'I was on the guest list.' Even Frances couldn't find out that he hadn't been on the guest list, surely. But he had to account for the fact that the police would

131

be coming here; they had said so, when they had given him his wallet. Someone would call, they said. He hadn't told her about his wallet, because he never told her anything much. After his visit to the police station, he hadn't wanted to tell her.

He had to worry about the police, and Parker. He didn't need to start worrying about Frances as well.

Nine

Colin had watched as Judy Hill had come out of the hospital and got back into a Panda car. She sat in the front with the driver, and after waiting for a break, they moved out into the growing day-tripper traffic. Colin let a few cars go by, then pushed away from the pavement, weaving in and out, keeping an eye on the police car.

Even on a Sunday, the road from Barton was busy. But the sight of a police car made everyone drive at the forty miles an hour laid down, despite the dual carriageway; it wasn't easy to keep well out of their way, but he did.

They didn't go back to Malworth police station, as he had expected; the car had signalled left halfway along the Malworth Road, and taken the turn into Stansfield village. In order not to be spotted, Colin had to carry on, and take the next left, risking a few moments of speeding to arrive by a different route at the village, stopping just before the first exit they could take, if they hadn't got there before him. He waited by a storage depot, where he wouldn't be noticed, and smiled with triumph as he saw the car, signalling the turn into Byford Road.

He moved when it did, and had a satisfactory number of vehicles ahead of him as he watched the unlit blue lamp on the car make its way up to the roundabout, and go straight across.

They must be going to the football ground, he thought. He was following a car up there just like before. The thought excited him; he wished he had the cloak of fog and the anonymity of an unlit bike in darkness. But it was broad daylight, with the sun climbing in the sky, heating up the ground so that the drop in temperature would bring the mist again by evening. He hung back, watching until the car's indicator proved him right; when it went out of sight, he revved the bike and sped through the traffic until he too reached the ground.

He pulled in, and stopped the engine. Bumping the bike over the pavement, he pushed it to where the high hedges would give him cover, and watched.

She got out of the car, and it drove off again. After about five minutes, Lloyd's car drove in. Colin ducked down then, and pretended to be working on the bike as he watched through the gaps in the privet.

He smiled. He had just had an idea.

Judy looked out of the picture window that ran the length of the room, at the mist which still hung, wispy now, over the pitch, weaving through the tall floodlight columns and the golden autumn trees that ringed the ground. Following the pattern of the previous day, the sun had broken through; it would be a beautiful day again. She had handed her case-load over to Detective Chief Inspector Merrill with relief; the atmosphere at Malworth was not one that she would have relished working in. Lloyd had told her to go straight to the football ground when she was free, and now his car was down below her.

She watched him speak to the groundsman; he was doing his Welsh boyo act, she thought, able to tell from the body movements. The groundsman had regarded her with deep suspicion, even after she had shown him her ID; he was talking to Lloyd as if he had known him all his life.

She heard feet on the stairs, and the door opened with a suddenness that had once upon a time made her start, but to which she had grown accustomed.

'Detective Inspector Hill,' he said, smiling broadly. 'How nice to have you with us.'

Judy smiled.

'I wanted you to see the scene for yourself,' he added. 'Maps and plans are all very well, but it's better if you can visualise the actual place.'

Out on the gallery, he again described the events of two nights before, indicating the two points at which there had been incidents, reminding her that though the ground had been floodlit, the fog had been so bad that the match had been abandoned, and that once the lights had been put out, the place was in near-total darkness.

'But,' he said, 'the sawdust is *inside*. In the big building.'

Judy looked across at the half-completed centre. It was comprised of several linked blocks, some of which were finished, some of which still had builders working.

'And the buildings had been secured for the night before Sharon ever left the office,' Lloyd said. 'In her skirt and blouse,' he added, with a little bow of acknowledgment. 'So perhaps we've solved the little puzzle of the key. And we're checking with the shop to see if that receipt is for the clothes she was wearing. The superstore's only ten minutes' walk from Evans and Whitworth, so I expect it is.'

'Good,' said Judy, though she had rather been assuming that to be the case all along. It didn't seem to help much.

'Parker's meeting us here,' he said. 'If that key is to one of these buildings, we have to know how she got hold of it.'

'But Drummond says they stayed in the car,' she said.

Lloyd snorted. 'Personally, I don't believe a word that Drummond says, but I've been told not to jump to conclusions.'

'It's your theory,' Judy pointed out indignantly. 'Not mine.'

'It's my scenario based on Drummond's account of what happened. But if you ask me, it's an account which isn't borne out by common sense.' He looked at her. 'You don't take your clothes off if you're having a bit of nooky in a car. You just . . . well – remove any actual obstacles to progress, don't you?'

'I wouldn't know,' she said, with mock primness. But the statement was true enough, as Lloyd well knew.

He grinned. 'Take my word for it,' he said.

'But she must have changed her clothes,' said Judy, thoughtfully. 'Couldn't that have been what Drummond saw her doing?'

Lloyd was shaking his head. 'She was wearing the leisure suit at the match,' he said.

'So she was.' Judy subsided a little, and realised that she had better write up everything Lloyd had told her last night, or she would forget things. 'Perhaps she was changing back into her other clothes,' she said hopefully, though she couldn't imagine why she would bother. 'And whoever she was with killed her before she could.' She smiled at herself. 'I'm getting as bad as you,' she said. 'And quite frankly, Sharon doesn't strike me as the type to have men flying into uncontrollable rages at all, never mind twice in one evening.'

Lloyd laughed. 'But perhaps Sharon isn't quite what she seemed,' he said.

It was what she had thought this morning. But then she had thought that Sharon seemed to have been a little like her herself; still hardly the type to inspire jealous rage. She leant on the rail, and watched as a sleek car made its way up, the groundsman waving to its driver. Her eyes widened as she saw him get out. 'What's he doing here?' she asked.

Lloyd looked down. 'That's who we're meeting,' he said. 'Jake Parker.'

Judy nodded down at him as Parker walked towards the building. 'He was with Bobbie Chalmers in the hospital,' she said. 'He's the one she's going away with.'

Lloyd frowned, looking from Parker to the half-finished building, then round the rest of the ground. 'Going away, is he?' he said, and went back into the room, to wait for him. 'You wait out there,' he instructed, pulling the curtain across far enough to mask her presence. Judy sighed. Lloyd was fond of theatricals.

Parker came in; Judy heard him pass the time of day with Lloyd in confident modified Cockney tones that entirely suited the camel coat and identity bracelet image he projected without actually wearing either of these items.

'I'd like you to meet my colleague,' Lloyd said. 'Detective Inspector Hill.'

Judy felt as though she were coming on to a stage as she stepped through the sliding window.

Parker looked at her, then made a contemptuous noise. 'I thought you said you were a friend of hers,' he said.

'I hope I am,' said Judy steadily.

His eyes lost their hostility, and their certainty. He looked like Bobbie had; impotently angry, not quite, but almost, defeated. 'Yeah,' he said. 'Sorry.'

'We'll find him,' she assured him. But it was never easy. Crime – real crime, was difficult enough. But there were informants and neighbourhood-watch hawks; there were honest citizens prepared to help. Serial rape was different. No network of petty criminals to give them information, wittingly or otherwise. No members of the public, because it happened in lonely, deserted places. And often, very often, someone protecting the criminal. Still, they would get him. For the moment, it was no longer her immediate problem.

'Miss Chalmers won't make an official complaint, I understand,' Lloyd said.

'Do you blame her?' asked Parker.

Lloyd gave a little shrug. 'I'm wondering why,' he said.

'She knows why.' Parker jerked his head at Judy.

'Mr Parker,' said Lloyd quietly. 'I don't believe that you have told me the truth.'

Parker looked from one to the other, then walked out on to the balcony, his back to both of them, his shirt-sleeved arms spread along the rail, his back tense.

Lloyd moved to the open window. 'Sharon was in one of the buildings under construction,' he said. 'Either before, during, or after her murder.'

Parker's shoulders hunched, and his hands gripped the rail. Then he turned to face them. 'She came to see me,' he said.

'When?'

'I don't know. I was getting things ready for the party. About half six, seven. Something like that.'

'Why?'

'Just to say hello.'

Lloyd's eyebrows went up slowly. 'She came all the way here from her office just to say hello?'

Jake shook his head. 'She was meeting someone here,' he said.

Judy looked at Lloyd.

'She had been shopping,' Jake said. 'She asked if there was somewhere she could change. I gave her the key to the centre.' He nodded over to it as he said the word. 'Changing rooms,' he said, with a shrug. 'That block's complete.'

Judy thought that Lloyd might explode. When he spoke, his voice was as low and as Welsh and as dangerous as he knew how to make it. 'I want to know why you didn't tell me this before, Mr Parker,' he said.

Parker wasn't moved by Lloyd's evident anger. 'I didn't want to discuss it,' he said.

'You preferred to waste police time?'

'I wasn't trying to waste your time,' he answered evenly. 'But what we discussed was private.'

'Private? After she had been murdered?' Lloyd's blue eyes blazed, but his voice was controlled.

'I thought you'd got him.'

Lloyd went out on to the balcony and stood directly in front of the much taller man. 'I saw you first thing yesterday morning, Mr Parker,' he said. 'I don't believe you knew then that we had anyone in for questioning. I had only just been told myself. And I want to know why Sharon was here, and why you didn't tell me that she was here.'

'It's still private.'

'Do you have the key to these changing rooms?'

'No. I'd forgotten about it, to be honest with you. I didn't see her again until the carry-on on the terraces.'

Lloyd produced the key from his pocket. 'Is this it?' he asked.

Parker nodded. 'The groundsman will show you which building,' he said.

Lloyd left Judy with him, indicating as he went out that she should continue the questioning in the same vein.

'Were you and Sharon still seeing one another, Mr Parker?' she asked, joining him on the balcony.

'No.'

She looked down at the terracing. 'But you got involved in a fight because you didn't like the way she was behaving?' she asked.

137

He sighed. 'She was trying to provoke me, and she succeeded,' he said.

Judy frowned. 'But if it was all over . . . '

He turned away, back to his contemplation of the pitch. 'I always was too possessive,' he said. 'That's why we split up.'

'Where does Bobbie fit in?' she asked.

'Leave Bobbie out of this, all right?'

'All right,' she said, amiably. 'But if Sharon could still provoke you, there must still have been something there.'

He turned. 'We were still friends,' he said. 'I got her that job.'

'We have been told that Sharon was picked up by someone in a car after she left the ground on Friday evening, and brought back here,' Judy said.

'Is that right?' He was endeavouring to look as though this didn't interest him, but his voice betrayed him.

'Well – it's so far unconfirmed,' Judy went on, deciding to take the matter further, to see if she could produce a definite reaction. 'But we do know that she had sexual relations with someone shortly before she died,' she said. 'So it seems likely.'

He was thrown by that, she could see. She had got her reaction, and she pushed the point home before he had time to recover himself. 'Was she meeting a man here?' she asked.

He turned away again to hide his confusion. 'Christ,' he muttered to himself. 'I don't know,' he replied. 'She didn't say.'

'But she changed out of her working clothes?'

He turned back, and nodded. 'Maybe she wanted to impress him,' he said. 'You could be right.'

Lloyd came back with a carrier bag containing the clothes that Whitworth had described Sharon wearing when she left the office.

'Why did Sharon leave these in the changing room?' he asked, dumping the bag on the table, coming out on to the balcony.

'I've no idea,' he said. 'She must have meant to pick them up after the match.'

'You didn't notice that she left without them?'

'No,' he said. 'I was otherwise engaged when she left, if you remember.'

'Did she tell you who she was meeting?'

His head was shaking almost all the time. 'No,' he said again. 'I've just told her that.'

He had come in oozing East End charm and hair gel; now, he was on the defensive. Judy was certain that he did know who she was likely to have been meeting, but she couldn't shake his denials.

On their way back to the station, Judy told him what had passed between her and Parker, but Lloyd barely seemed to be listening. She glanced across at him as he drove, and saw the film of sawdust on his dark suit.

'Another little puzzle solved?' she said, with a smile, as she brushed his shoulders with her hand. 'The case of the Mysterious Smell of Sawdust?'

'Another little puzzle,' he agreed. 'But there are a lot more than these two, aren't there?'

'I guess she was with her boyfriend in the car,' said Judy. 'Whatever the protocol is about removing clothing. And I think Parker knows who the boyfriend was,' she said. 'I think he knows who picked her up.'

'I think she was with *him*,' said Lloyd. 'Parker himself.'

Judy frowned. 'But she couldn't have been – he was under arrest at the time, remember?'

'No.' Lloyd said. 'Before that. Before the party started.'

Judy frowned. 'Doesn't that make it too long before the time of death?' she asked.

'Only if you believe Drummond, and I don't. I think she never left the ground. I think she was killed just after she walked away from the fight.'

'I've lost you,' she said.

Lloyd waited at the roundabout. 'I don't believe that that car exists,' he said. 'I don't think she was chatting up Barnes, and I don't think Parker thought she was either.' He broke off as he negotiated a particularly tricky layout of mini-roundabouts. 'I think,' he said, as he accelerated up the hill towards the station, 'that Parker is out to deal with this his way, and that we had better find out exactly who picked a fight with whom at that match. Jake Parker wants us to think that he started it, but I'm not so sure about that.'

Lloyd was working on something, and he wasn't sharing it with her. That always tended to make Judy more than a little apprehensive. He had done another about turn in his theorising. 'Are you going to let me in on this new theory?' she asked.

Lloyd signalled left, and pulled into the car park of the police station. He switched off the engine, and released his seat-belt; Judy opened her door, thinking they were going in, but he turned to face her, stopping her getting out of the car. 'Let's talk here,' he said.

She sat back down again, more apprehensive than ever.

'Someone started the trouble at the football match,' he began. 'Parker originally said that Barnes started it, but he changed his mind after he found out that Sharon had been killed. Perhaps someone put Barnes up to that, and killed Sharon before she ever left the ground.'

Judy frowned. That wasn't quite her reading of the situation. 'We don't know for certain who started it,' she reminded Lloyd. 'And why would Parker want us to believe that it wasn't Barnes who started it if it was?'

'Because he wants to deal with it his way,' said Lloyd. 'And the one thing we do know for certain is that whoever started it, it got Parker out of circulation for three hours. During which his ex-girlfriend is murdered, and his current girlfriend is raped.'

Judy's eyes widened. 'Coincidence,' she said.

'How many coincidences are we supposed to accept? I'll buy McDonald and Melissa Whitworth. But one of Parker's girlfriends being raped at the same time as another is murdered?'

Judy stared at him. 'Oh, come on, Lloyd,' she said. 'Of course it was a coincidence. We've got a rapist,' she said. 'His victims are going to be someone's girlfriend, or wife – and the same man raped her as raped the other women. There's no question about that. That would be more of a coincidence than ever.'

Lloyd smiled. 'True,' he said. 'But I think that Parker's up to something with that building project, all the same. The building's months behind schedule. People have started muttering, so the work starts again and he holds an opening in the only finished building there is.'

'The recession,' said Judy.

'And now you tell me that he's planning on leaving the country. It's not beyond the bounds of possibility that he's got someone's back up.'

'I think it's a domestic,' said Judy. 'Pure and simple. Sharon's new boyfriend lost his temper.'

'Oh, before I forget,' said Lloyd. 'I arranged for your car to be taken to a garage.'

Judy sighed. 'Did you, now?' she said.

'Well, you couldn't leave it there for ever with its locks jammed up, could you?'

'No, but I would have rather liked to have—'

'I thought perhaps we could pop over there,' he said, getting out of the car. 'Once we've dropped these clothes off.' He opened the car boot, and pulled out the carrier bag.

He was sometimes really too much, she thought, getting out. 'Where is my car?' she asked him.

'Green's garage,' he said.

'I see,' said Judy, nodding. 'Because Gil McDonald works there?'

'Mm.'

They walked towards the building.

'Why?' asked Judy. 'Because he's a famous footballer, or because he found Sharon's body?'

Lloyd grinned. 'A little bit of both,' he said, opening the door for her.

'Are they open on a Sunday?'

'They are if you want to buy a car,' he said.

'Lloyd! I can manage my own affairs quite well, you know!'

But she didn't really mind. He was right; there was no point in spending more money on the old one, which only went when it felt like it. And the illicit use of police resources in getting it to the garage was something that would never have occurred to her.

She would look at cars.

Things were getting way, way out of hand. Jake Parker drove out of the sports ground on his way to the village where Lionel Evans lived, and looked across at the centre, at the delayed building work which had been put in hand again with the application of as little hard cash as possible, in order to stop the investors getting fidgety too soon. But now it wasn't the investors he had to worry about. It had always been a huge risk, with huge rewards if he pulled it off, and a prison sentence if he didn't.

And he wasn't pulling it off, despite his desperate attempt to salvage something from the mess. He lit a cigarette, and contemplated the scheme that had been going to make him a millionaire. He simply had to cut his losses. Lloyd was already suspicious, and would soon be demanding answers to his questions, not just letting them go. It was turning into a race against time, and time had a nasty habit of winning.

He thought about that. Lionel knew altogether too much, and Jake had failed to scare him as thoroughly as he had hoped to; he was made of slightly sterner stuff than Jake had realised. Getting rid of Lionel seemed the obvious route, but it was a non-starter. Lionel had known that, once he had realised that Jake was not seeking revenge for Sharon's death, but merely a way out of the mess. There was no way the police were going to accept Lionel's sudden demise as being coincidental to everything else.

Jake didn't understand what was happening; he was used to pulling the strings, to making things happen. But things hadn't happened that he had thought would, and had happened that he hadn't, could never have foreseen.

And now Detective Inspector Hill had told him that Sharon had been with someone. He could have foreseen that, but he hadn't. He let the half-smoked cigarette fly out of the quarter-light in a shower of sparks. Sharon had to have been with Whitworth, of course, but

Jake hadn't told Inspector Hill that, because then the police would have taken Whitworth in for questioning.

And Jake had other plans for Simon Whitworth.

Lloyd was still inclined to the opinion that Melissa and Mac were a coincidence, and nothing more, but they were on their way to Green's garage not just to get Judy to buy a newer car, but to let her talk to Mac, whom she hadn't met, to see what she thought of him. He had been proved wrong once too often already; he couldn't just ignore them. And he had great faith in Judy's judgement.

He was still convinced that Drummond's story about the car picking her up was a fiction, and had instituted what inquiries he could on that front. Even a negative response would help. If no one else at all had seen this car, Andrews might be a little more receptive to Lloyd's belief that Drummond was a wrong 'un, and in this business up to his neck. And he had dispatched people to talk to the other lads involved in the disturbance at the match. He very much wanted to know who had really started that fight. They had seemed a little surprised at being asked to make further inquiries into a minor disturbance at a football match; Lloyd had not enlightened them as to the purpose, mainly because he wasn't too sure himself.

While he was in Malworth, Finch would be seeing what he could pick up about the two officers who had beaten Drummond up. Merrill should have known that Judy couldn't find out anything; she had been disconnected from the grapevine the moment she had told him what she had seen. But Finch, with his guileless schoolboy looks and his one-of-the-boys rank was just the man to find out one way or the other.

They drove into Green's Garage, and he parked beside a brown Ford Escort. 'Right,' he said, indicating the showroom. 'Take your pick.'

'I can't afford a new one!' she said.

He grinned. 'The used ones are round the back,' he said, getting out.

Judy emerged after a reluctant moment, and looked across at the sea of vehicles.

'Chief Inspector Lloyd? Can I help you?'

Lloyd turned to see Gil McDonald coming out of the showroom, and smiled. 'Not really,' he said. 'It's Detective Inspector Hill here who would like your help.'

McDonald came up to her. 'Gil McDonald,' he said, holding out his hand. 'Is it about the girl who was murdered?'

Judy shook his hand. 'Well, I am working on that,' she said, 'but it's not strictly why I'm here.' She gestured towards the battered, world-weary Mini parked by the workshop door. 'That's mine,' she said.

'Oh – I did explain on the phone – there's no one here today who can work on it, I'm afraid. Not until tomorrow.'

'No,' she said. 'I'm . . . ' She glared at Lloyd. 'I'm thinking of buying another,' she said.

McDonald smiled, and glanced at the Mini. 'I'm not surprised,' he said.

Judy looked a little offended; what she saw in that heap of junk, Lloyd failed to comprehend. She had never bought a car that actually had all its equipment in working order in her life; her idea of a new car was anything that started on the third try as long as it wasn't raining.

'Will it be worth anything in part exchange?' she asked.

'I'm sure we'll be able to come to some arrangement,' said McDonald. 'Would you like to come and have a look at what we've got? I'm assuming that you are looking for a used model.'

Judy nodded, and went off with McDonald.

Lloyd waited until they were on their way, then wandered into the showroom to play at being a customer for one of the cars with so much electronic wizardry that it would hardly seem like driving at all. One day, he told himself. One day, when he won the pools.

Melissa Whitworth sat at one of the tables, apparently engrossed in a brochure; Lloyd smiled. He didn't suppose that she was any more a customer than he was, and at least one of his theories seemed to be right.

'Mrs Whitworth,' he said. 'I'm glad I've bumped into you.'

'Hello,' she said, a little coldly.

Some sort of backing-down was in order, Lloyd decided, especially since he felt that she had indeed had her privacy invaded for nothing. The fact was that he was about to invade it again; he had to be able to cross that particular little puzzle off if he was to give his undivided attention to sorting out the other puzzles. So he had better get on a better footing with the woman if he could.

'I . . . I hope I didn't seem too impolite when we met yesterday,' he said. 'I can only plead lack of sleep and a natural aversion to mortuaries.'

She smiled a little. 'I think we were both a little on edge,' she said.

He sat down beside her. 'I'd like to put a few more questions to you,' he said.

She sighed, and looked resigned. 'Feel free,' she said.

* * *

143

'Oh, yes,' said Mac. 'Italy. Making time and money, that was Italy.'

Detective Inspector Hill smiled. 'What I want to know is why do you all come back?' she asked. 'What brings you back to rainy old Manchester or wherever?'

Mac gave the question serious consideration. 'Homesickness, of a sort,' he said. 'Sunshine's for fun, if you're British born. It's what you get if you're lucky at the seaside when you're a kid. It's what you get on a package tour to Benidorm. But it's like wearing funny hats and drinking cheap brandy. It's all right for a fortnight in the summer, but you couldn't take it all year round.'

She paused by a two-door hatchback. It was a good little car – a few miles on the clock, but a nice runner. Mac told her so, and she opened the driver's door speculatively.

'I thought the stock answer was pressure,' she said, as she got in. 'Italy's too rough for our gentle flowers.' She smiled.

'Oh, there's enough of that, too. Football's a religion over there. A fundamental religion at that. You get spat at if you don't come up to scratch.' He smiled. 'And – let's face it, in the end I didn't. They didn't want me to stay. That's basically why I came back.'

She laughed. 'Are you being candid in order to indicate how truthful you are?' she said, adjusting the driving seat. 'So I'll believe you about the one careful lady owner?'

'No,' said Mac, honestly. 'I gave up kidding myself years ago.'

'But not the police,' she said, her tone of voice not altered one whit from the pleasant chat of a moment ago.

Mac was startled by the sudden change of subject. 'What?' he said.

'You think you can kid us,' she said, putting the car through the gears, investigating the dashboard.

Mac felt as though he had been had. 'I'm sorry,' he said, 'I really don't know . . . '

'Someone answering your description was seen with Mrs Whitworth at the Marriot Hotel at ten thirty on Friday evening,' she said. 'You told Sergeant Finch that you had been lost in the fog all evening.'

Mac gave a short sigh.

'Well?' she asked, getting out, putting the driving seat back as far as it would go, then pushing the back down and getting into the rear passenger seat. She somehow managed to do that elegantly; Mac was impressed. Under other circumstances, he would have been more than pleased to be doing business with her.

She sat in the back, testing the leg-room, looking up at him, waiting for him to say something.

'Well . . . ' Mac looked down at her. 'Yes,' he said. There wasn't much else he could say.

'Yes?' she repeated, opening windows, testing seat-belts.

'Yes, I was at the hotel with Mrs Whitworth,' said Mac, like a child reciting lines.

She got out again. 'Does it really go well?' she asked.

'It'll go better than that Mini,' said Mac, not sure why she was keeping up the pretence of looking at the car.

'Had you been with Mrs Whitworth all evening?'

'Yes,' he said. He wasn't about to tell them what had really happened. He glanced anxiously over to the showroom, and could see that Melissa had been joined by Lloyd; he closed his eyes. They were being subjected to a neat two-pronged attack, and he hadn't suspected a thing.

'Perhaps I could have a look under the bonnet?' asked Detective Inspector Hill.

Mac reached into the car and released the bonnet catch with a vicious tug. 'Help yourself,' he said.

Turning his back on her, he employed the most useful skill he had picked up in his sojourn abroad. Under his breath, he swore long and hard in Italian.

'Where were you before nine thirty?' Lloyd asked.

Melissa had patiently answered the same questions that both he and Sergeant Finch had asked her before, still maintaining that the last two miles of her trip had seemed too difficult in the fog. He still didn't believe her, but now he wanted to know where she had just driven from.

'Barton,' she said. It was the first thing that came into her head; some of the offices at Barton were still open, to serve the local population. She did interviews all over the county; she could have been anywhere. So Barton would do.

'So you had driven . . . what – twenty miles? And the last two were just too much for you?'

'Yes,' she said. Damn it, surely it was entirely up to her how many miles she was prepared to drive in thick fog? She was beginning to believe it herself; it lent her answers an air of righteous indignation.

'How long did it take you to drive the twenty miles?' he asked.

'Over an hour and a half,' she said.

Lloyd sucked in his breath as he did a calculation. 'At that rate it would have taken you another ten, fifteen minutes to get home,' he said. 'But you chose to stay in an hotel instead.'

'That's right,' she said.

Lloyd got up and walked around, looking at cars, brochures, bending over to read the small print under the price tags.

Melissa looked in vain for rescue; Mac was obviously giving Judy Hill a part by part tour of the internal combustion engine.

'I'm not inquiring into your private life for the hell of it,' he said, turning towards her and leaning on a huge four-wheel-drive off-road vehicle painted a quite startling metallic maroon.

'Then why are you?'

He pushed himself away. 'You know why, Mrs Whitworth,' he said, looking out of the window at Mac and the inspector, then back at her.

Melissa swung round and looked out at the view behind her; at yet another business park, for such everyone had had to learn to call these strange collections of offices and factories and showrooms and workshops, with pools and fountains instead of useful shops. The sun was bright, reflecting off the water in the pool, and making little rainbows in the spray from the fountain.

'Because Mac found the body,' she said.

'Is that who you were with at the hotel? Mr McDonald?'

She hoped Mac had given up his attempt at being gallant, because he was doubtless being asked the same questions. Had Lloyd really 'bumped into' her as he had said? He must have, unless they were following her. But maybe they were. 'Yes,' she said.

The chief inspector didn't comment; Melissa continued to look out of the window as her private life was being ripped open for him to have a peek inside.

'Were you with Mr McDonald earlier in the evening?'

'No.' The truth; as much of it as she was prepared for them to know.

'Had you arranged to meet him at the hotel?' he asked, then, sounding puzzled.

'No. I'd met him once before in my life, and I didn't even remember that,' she said. Let him think what he liked about her morals.

'And was Mr McDonald at the hotel with you from half-past ten onwards?'

'Yes.' She turned then, defiantly facing him. 'I went to bed with him, chief inspector,' she said. 'He left at midnight, and he found Sharon Smith's body. The whole thing was a coincidence, nothing more.'

He nodded. 'I'm inclined to agree,' he said. 'And thank you for being so co-operative.'

He left the showroom; that was obviously the signal for Detective Inspector Hill to stop pretending to buy a car. It was with surprise

146

that she saw her come back to the showroom with Mac, and make arrangements for a test-drive, and for someone to come and give the car the once-over for her.

At last, their car drove off, and she and Mac were alone again. He swivelled round in his chair to look at her. 'Do you think they knew you were here?' he asked.

She shrugged. 'I don't care,' she said. 'What did you tell her?'

Mac looked a little apprehensive. 'That we had arranged to meet,' he said.

Melissa closed her eyes. 'Then we won't have seen the last of them,' she said, and got up. 'I told him the truth.'

'Oh. Sorry – I just wanted to . . . '

'To protect my reputation?'

'Yes,' said Mac. 'I suppose so.'

'Please *stop* trying to protect my reputation,' she said, and went out, getting into her car and slamming the door.

Protecting her reputation, she thought, reversing out of the space, and crashing the gears as she tried to move off. That somehow didn't sit well with the blackmail.

Lionel felt a little envious of Parker. He seemed all wrong, somehow, sitting in Lionel's own living-room, on Lionel's own sofa, dark and dramatic, a designer crook. He had seemed to bring his own colour with him; the drab monochrome of the Evans homestead was suddenly technicolour. Lionel had never altered a room by his presence.

He wondered if that was what had made him go in with Parker in the first place; if it wasn't so much the promise of all that money, which he didn't need, and didn't particularly want come to that, but the excitement, the danger of it all.

He hadn't really believed that Parker was going to kill him, but he had never known anyone who possessed a hand-gun, never mind being prepared to point it loaded at someone's head. It wasn't nice, but it was exciting. Because Parker could have pulled the trigger, if it had been in his interest to do so; Lionel knew that. It ought to alarm him. It ought to make him run to the police and tell them everything, to keep himself safe. But he didn't want to be safe.

'Something else has happened,' said Parker, taking out his cigarettes. 'Will your missus mind me smoking?' he asked, as he lit up.

'No,' said Lionel. Of course she would.

'I can't leave,' said Parker. 'And I've had Lloyd sniffing round again this morning.'

That alarmed Lionel. More than his life being threatened had alarmed him, because his life wasn't really in danger.

147

'He and his lady sidekick have started wondering why Sharon should have been a target.'

'I swear, Jake – I had nothing to do with it!'

Jake nodded. 'I believe you,' he said. 'But the water's got murkier, and I have to change my plans again.'

Oh, dear God. Lionel glanced anxiously out of the window. Frances was at church; she would be back soon to cook lunch. What now?

'So I don't want you to do anything with the money,' said Parker.

Lionel let out the breath he'd been holding. 'Just leave it where it is?' he said, hardly able to believe that some unexpected development had actually got him off a hook rather than hung him on one. 'That's a much better idea, Jake,' he said. 'If we took it all out at once—'

'Just leave it where it is, Lionel. We're going to lie low, you and I. We have no option.'

Thank God for that. 'What's happened to change your mind?' he asked.

'The less you know, Lionel, the better.'

It wasn't entirely reassuring.

Simon and Melissa hadn't exchanged a word since their discussion about Drummond's release; he felt like death, and she didn't look much better. She had been out when he had got back from the police station, and he was upstairs packing a case when he heard the car. He hurriedly pushed it under the bed. He had to leave, obviously, but he didn't have to hurt Melissa any sooner than was necessary.

He came down to find Melissa sitting on the arm of her chair sooner than disturb Robeson. 'Have you had the police again?' she asked.

'No,' he said, alarmed. 'No. Why – should I have done?'

'No,' she said. 'I just wondered.'

He sat down opposite her. There was no point in pretending that nothing was wrong between them. It had been getting worse and worse for weeks, and now it was impossible.

'Melissa,' he said. 'Why did you stay at the hotel on Friday night?'

'You know why,' she said, stroking the cat.

Simon looked down at his feet. How had she found out?

'As far as the police are concerned,' she said, 'you simply worked with Sharon. And we're keeping it that way, aren't we, Simon?'

148

'She . . . she wanted me to tell you,' he said, his voice no more than a whisper.

'Did she?' she asked coldly.

'I didn't have the guts,' he said.

'Well, you'd better find some from somewhere,' said Melissa crisply. 'Because the police aren't going to let this go.'

Ten

Lloyd and Judy positively winced as they walked in to a barrage of messages from those manning the murder room.

'Malworth want Detective Inspector Hill to ring Inspector Menlove.'

'We've found something in those clothes you brought in, Lloyd – I think you'll be interested.'

'We've got anonymous confirmation of a car having picked Sharon up – a male voice – reckons he heard the appeal on the radio. Still no make or number, but he thinks it might have been red or brown.'

Judy, dialling Malworth, glanced at Lloyd when she heard that.

'Anonymous confirmation is no confirmation at all,' he said. 'It could have been Drummond himself.' But it was an automatic last-ditch defence of his stance over Drummond.

She spoke to Menlove, and hung up, looking a little puzzled.

'What?' said Lloyd.

'Some children blackberrying along the Stansfield Road found a flick-knife in the bushes,' she said. 'And now a search has turned up the ski-mask.' She frowned. 'He's never got rid of them before,' she said. 'Or at least, we haven't found them if he has.'

'Any prints on the knife?' Lloyd asked.

'Lots. Of the children who found it. They were playing with it, would you believe? But the mask might give us something to go on.'

Lloyd sighed. 'Perhaps,' he said, and turned his attention to Barstow. 'What have you got?' he asked.

'We found a cutting from a newspaper in the pocket of the skirt. We've sent it for prints – here's a photocopy.' Barstow picked up a sheet of paper, and handed it to Lloyd. 'One of your theories looks good,' he said, with a smile.

Lloyd took the paper, and read.

150

> ## Are you the Other Woman?
>
> This newspaper is doing a
> series of articles on marriage
> and morals, and would like to
> hear from women whose men
> belong to someone else. Your
> contribution would be held in
> the strictest confidence, and
> nothing will appear in print
> which could in any way
> identify you or your partner.

There was a Stansfield phone number at the bottom. It wasn't the general number for *The Chronicle*, which had recently moved to brand-new offices in Stansfield from Barton, swopping hot-metal type for electronics, but it was close to it, and he suspected that it was a direct line. It seemed unlikely that it would belong to anyone other than *The Chronicle*'s feature editor, who had assured him less than an hour ago that she had never met the girl.

Judy rang the number, ready to launch into her Other Woman act. After listening for a moment, she hung up. 'Melissa Fletcher isn't there to speak to me right now, but if I'd like to leave my name . . . et cetera, et cetera,' she said. She looked at Lloyd.

'She told me she'd never met her,' said Lloyd.

'Perhaps Sharon never rang her.'

Perhaps. But Melissa Fletcher, or Whitworth, or whatever the damn woman's name was, had gone missing on Friday night, and her boyfriend had found Sharon's body. What Lloyd had confidently dismissed as coincidence was looking decidedly odd again. The versions of events given by Melissa Whitworth and Gil McDonald were at considerable variance not only with one another, but also with Simon Whitworth's.

But if Melissa Whitworth and Gil McDonald were somehow involved in Sharon's death, wouldn't their accounts of events have given one another an alibi, rather than the opposite? And, quite apart from anything else, their joint reason for murdering Sharon Smith utterly eluded him.

And there was Drummond. There was always Drummond, whom Lloyd kept trying to cast in role of witness rather than suspect, but without success. He looked at the copy of the newspaper cutting, and shook his head. Too many little puzzles.

He doodled on the blotter in front of him. There was one way that they could get it over with quickly. One way that would frighten the life, and the truth, out of McDonald and Melissa Whitworth. He glanced at Judy, who was talking to Finch, who had just come in. Above their heads was the board where a picture of Sharon Smith smiled at him. They would be releasing it to the press tomorrow; it would be on *The Chronicle*'s front page by late afternoon, and the trickle of response to the radio appeal might gather some momentum; he didn't want still to be messing around with the Whitworths and Mad Mac if they had nothing to do with it.

'My office,' he called over to them, and strode out of the murder room. Judy would argue with his proposed strategy; he would just have to pull rank.

They came into his office, and sat down. Lloyd raised his eyebrows at Finch. 'Did you get anything from Malworth?' he asked.

'Not yet,' he said. 'But I'm having a drink with some of the lads tonight – I might be able to pick up the rumours.' He sighed. 'And I'm sorry, sir,' he said. 'But so far I can't find any connection at all between Drummond and Sharon Smith. They really don't seem to have known one another at all.'

'No,' said Lloyd, resignedly. 'I didn't think they would have.'

Finch seemed disconcerted; Judy smiled.

'Don't worry, Tom,' she said. 'You'll get used to it.'

Lloyd frowned a little. Used to what? 'Lunch-time,' he said, standing up. 'Team talk. Canteen.'

He watched Finch and Judy exchange glances, and raised his eyebrows. 'I want us all to know exactly where we're going on this,' he said, ushering them out of the room. 'And what we're doing this afternoon.'

'Oh, but sir, I was rather hoping to take the kids to—'

The kids? He had *children*? He was barely more than a child himself. 'Whatever you were hoping to do this afternoon, Finch, you're working,' said Lloyd.

The young man accepted the order with an air of resigned martyrdom, and another covert, but not covert enough, look at Judy, who smiled.

Lloyd felt like a school-teacher taking slightly unruly children on an educational trip as he walked along behind them to the canteen. He wanted to get the Whitworth connection settled one way or the other, and he wanted it settled now; they could listen while they ate, and they would do what he told them to do, whether they liked it or not.

He'd teach them to make veiled allusions about some aspect of his personality which seemed to amuse them.

Mrs Smith, thin and colourless, admitted Lionel, who had belatedly realised that with all his other troubles, he hadn't yet been to pay his respects. Wanda Smith sat on a sofa, a younger version of her mother, her eyes pink-tinged with grief.

A photograph of Sharon was on the bookcase, which had no books in it. Just photographs and ornaments. Sharon had been good at her job, and she had made an effort; always smart and well-groomed, the family tendency to a lack of colour made up for with skilful make-up. Lionel always admired that in a woman.

But then, the other two Smiths probably didn't look like this all the time, he reminded himself.

'If there's anything I – or the firm, of course – can do, Mrs Smith,' he said.

She shook her head. 'There's nothing anyone can do,' she said.

No. Lionel had never had to talk to anyone who had been bereaved by murder before. By road-accidents, by illness, by suicide, even, and God knew that was hard enough. But murder? He hadn't come to terms with it himself, and he had only known the girl for just over a year. What Mrs Smith must be going through was unimaginable.

'Obviously, if you have any legal . . . well, you know. Just ring myself or Simon . . . Simon Whitworth. And—' He wasn't sure how to say this in order not to give offence, but Sharon had moved back with her mother to help out financially after her father died; he had to say it. 'And – well, don't . . . don't worry about money, Mrs Smith.'

'I'm all right, thank you, Mr Evans.'

There was a photograph on the television of a man in his fifties. Lionel sighed. The Smiths had had more than enough to cope with; they probably didn't need his presence making matters worse. He had said what he had come to say.

He got up. 'I'm dreadfully sorry,' he said.

Mrs Smith accepted that with a slight inclination of her head. Her eyes were dull with misery. 'She said she'd be home by seven,' she said. 'I had her tea ready.' There was a hint of what he had heard before from the suddenly bereaved; a feeling of having been let down. Sharon hadn't said that she was going to die.

'If . . . if you need any help with anything at all, please don't hesitate,' he said. He meant it, but it didn't matter how he said it, it still sounded like the automatic reaction to death; meaningless and pointless. 'I'll see myself out,' he said.

He was on his way home when what Mrs Smith had said struck

him. Sharon was at the football match; why would she have said that she would be home by seven?

It probably meant nothing, he thought. She'd changed her mind, that was all. But he couldn't see Sharon doing that without warning her mother not to get her tea ready. Still . . . he wouldn't have thought that she would have been in any way personally involved with someone like Jake Parker, never mind having an affair with Simon Whitworth, so it just went to show that you didn't really know people at all.

But falling for someone was a bit different from deciding to go to a football match, he argued with himself. Anyone might behave uncharacteristically where the emotions were concerned. But going to a football match – especially one involving Stansfield Town – was hardly a great emotional upheaval. Unless Simon had changed his mind, and gone after all. Perhaps they'd had a row; perhaps she had followed him up there . . .

He should go to the police. Tell them what he thought. Tell them, at least, what Mrs Smith had said. But could he really do that to Simon? Why not? he argued with himself. What did he know about Simon Whitworth? Next to nothing. He had answered the advertisement, so he'd got the job. For all Lionel knew, he might be perfectly capable of losing his temper to a murderous extent.

And Lionel had known Sharon well enough to be certain that if she really had been having an affair with Simon, then as far as she was concerned, it would have been serious. Simon had presumably just been bored with his unglamorous wife; Sharon could have become an embarrassment to him.

He slowed down as he reached the road that would take him home, or up the hill to the police station. He took the turning for home. Odd, he thought. He had taken Whitworth on purely and simply to implicate him in a fraud, without a qualm. But he didn't feel that he could go running to the police with this.

Parker had pointed out that if Whitworth was suspected of having murdered Sharon, that would rather strengthen Lionel's hand; perhaps that was why the guilt. He couldn't be sure of his motives in going to the police. Implicating him in a fraud – shifting suspicion – was one thing; accusing him of murder was quite another.

He would have to give it serious thought.

They hadn't spoken; Melissa sat with Robeson on her knee, staring at the sports programme on the television, not watching it.

Simon asked if she wanted coffee, and his voice came out hoarse from misuse. She said she did; that was something.

As soon as he moved towards the kitchen door, Robeson was off Melissa's knee like a shot; he hurtled towards the closed door, trusting in Simon to open it before he hit it, which Simon did, with precision timing that would have done justice to the Red Arrows. 'All right, all right,' he said, getting out his plate and the cat-food. Merely watching the can being opened sent Robeson into ecstasies; he rolled on the floor, then righted himself, and wound in and out of Simon's legs, purring loudly enough for Melissa to hear him.

'I think food has always been his real passion,' she called through, in an attempt at lightening the prevailing mood. 'I don't think he'll care what we've done to him, as long as we feed him.'

Simon laughed, to try to help out, but silence reigned again, and it was only Robeson's purr and the clink of his identity disc on the dish that was heard until the doorbell rang.

Simon went into the living room as Melissa answered the door, and she came back with a woman whom she introduced as Judy Hill. At first he thought she was a friend from work, and was relieved; then Melissa said that she was a detective inspector, and he had to work hard at not allowing the dismay to show. This was quickly followed by the intelligence that she was investigating the rapes, and he breathed again, his stomach feeling as though he was on a roller-coaster.

'Not at the moment,' said Detective Inspector Hill, correcting Melissa. 'I'm here about Sharon Smith.'

The roller-coaster dived again, and Simon sat down on the arm of the sofa. His heart could sink no further.

'You ran an advertisement,' the inspector went on, addressing Melissa. *'Are you the other woman?'*

It could sink further, and did. An advertisement?

'Yes,' Melissa said, eventually, after what had been a very long time to think about her answer. 'I'm doing a series of articles on marriage,' she added. 'It was to get copy.'

Simon almost laughed. He had seriously thought that Melissa had put a personal ad in the paper, trying to find out what had gone wrong between them.

'And Sharon Smith replied?'

All manner of terrible possibilities went through Simon's head during the long, long silence that followed.

'Did Sharon Smith reply?' repeated the inspector, and Simon realised that Melissa hadn't answered her question.

'Yes.'

The inspector nodded. 'Did you interview her?'

Melissa's eyes flicked for an instant to his; they held a warning, an indication that he was not to contribute to this conversation. 'Yes,' she said.

'Were you aware of her identity when you interviewed her?'

'Yes, of course. I imagine that she wasn't aware of mine, however.'

She had to have been, thought Simon. She knew Melissa's name, knew what she did for a living.

'I'd like to know what passed between you during the interview,' said the inspector. 'Presumably she was having an affair with a married man.'

'Naturally, since that was the point of the article.'

'Did she mention a name?'

'No.' Melissa's eyes slid towards Simon. 'He might be one of many,' she said. 'Sharon preferred married men, apparently. She said single men were too possessive.'

Simon couldn't believe he was hearing this.

'And you were aware that she was the victim of the murder about which Sergeant Finch and Detective Chief Inspector Lloyd interviewed you yesterday morning?'

'Yes.'

'When you denied ever having met her?'

'Yes.'

Simon realised that his mouth was open. Why? Why would Melissa pretend she hadn't met her if she had? Knowing she was dead? Knowing what the police would think if the truth was discovered?

The inspector looked distinctly uncomfortable. 'Melissa Whitworth, I am arresting you on suspicion of the murder of Sharon Smith on Friday the twenty-fifth of October. You are not obliged to say anything, but anything . . . '

Simon watched, as though it was a scene from a play. In a moment, the stage would go dark, the lights would come up, and they would take their bows.

But all that happened was that Melissa got her bag, and her coat, and was taken out to a car. The inspector said something to him; he didn't know what. He couldn't move from the spot.

Mac was sitting on the end of the bed; the sergeant had the easy chair. Finch had been called to the phone, and Mac's landlady had come tripping upstairs to tell him; Mac was lucky if she bothered shouting up to him.

They both had tea, provided by his landlady, with whom Finch had flirted outrageously, until she looked about seventeen instead of almost seventy. Mac knew that the tea was for Finch's benefit;

he, who could never have been bothered with the hard work of flirting, got nothing that wasn't in the agreement.

Finch had wanted to know where he had gone when he left the football match. Mac had told him that he had realised that Donna Fairweather lived on the Mitchell Estate; he had originally been trying to find her house, hoping that he might get invited in, but instead he had become hopelessly lost in the fog.

Finch came back in. 'I am arresting you on suspicion of murder, Mr McDonald,' he said. 'You are not obliged to say anything, but anything you do say may be given in evidence.'

Mac stared at him.

'Now, Mr McDonald,' he said, and they were going downstairs, out of the door, walking out to the waiting car.

The afternoon had a dream-like quality, as though it was being filmed with a soft-focus lens. The young sergeant, who had changed from being a boy who could wrap old ladies round his little finger to a man who dealt with human disaster, sat beside him in the back of a car driven by a uniformed constable.

Neighbours were peering from windows, ducking back if anyone looked in their direction. His landlady was watching, looking on with a mixture of horror and pleasure. He was being driven through Stansfield to the police station, past rows of neat semis and terraced houses, along the road that separated the red and gold of the old wood from the tall pines of the new. Through the rash of mini-roundabouts, past older, larger, more opulent houses. Another mini-roundabout, and up the hill to the police station, square, solid and sixties.

The dream became more pronounced as they went into the station, Finch on one side, the constable on the other, and Mac was taken into a room where Inspector Hill stood at a table with Melissa. A uniformed sergeant sat at the table, and Melissa was emptying out the contents of her huge bag, a procedure which had evidently already taken a great deal of time, and had just finished.

'Empty your pockets, please, Mr McDonald,' said the desk sergeant. 'These items will be returned to you.'

Mac slowly emptied his pockets, one of which still contained the tape. He placed it on the desk, Melissa's handwritten 'Sharon Smith' all too visible.

Melissa could have stayed for ever in the groves of Academe, eventually getting a department of her own, losing more and more of her budget every year like her own head of department had. She could have lived in the sort of part-time ivory tower still afforded to caps and gowns during term-time. She could have written learned biographies instead of fashion hints, something she had very little right to do. She had thought long and hard before making the offered move into journalism, at first serious, then – as she discovered that she liked it much more – human interest.

And if she had, would she ever have met the woman who sat opposite her now, waiting like patience on a monument for an answer to her question?

Mac. He must have told them after all. But why? She had gone to the house with him. She had even enjoyed every minute of it, which was more than most blackmailers could hope for. But he was here too, so he must have told them.

'Is this your notebook?' she said again.

'You took it away from me,' she said. 'You know it's my notebook.'

'And the entry dated twenty-fifth October contains notes relating to your interview with Sharon Smith?'

'Yes.' Melissa looked away. Why, Mac, *why*?

'Why did you tell my colleagues that you had never met Sharon Smith?' she asked.

Melissa gave a sigh. 'Sharon met me as a feature writer for *The Barton Chronicle*,' she said. 'I had never met her in my capacity as Simon's wife, which is the one in which I was being interviewed by Mr Lloyd. I didn't think it was relevant.'

The inspector was giving her a very dubious look, which was fair enough, in the circumstances.

The inspector handed her the book. 'Could you read your notes, please?' she asked.

Melissa read back her shorthand. A note of what she was wearing, the odd remark about her mannerisms, her expression when she answered the questions, which were indicated by numbers. Then, normally, she would play the tape, and match the two. Not this time.

The inspector listened. 'They don't seem very extensive,' she said.

'They're not meant to be. We promised interviewees complete anonymity. These are just notes on how she struck me. I tape the actual interview, as I imagine you know.'

The inspector glanced at her own notebook. 'Is that the tape which was in Mr McDonald's possession?' she asked, marking something off.

Damn him. Damn him to hell. Was that what he was going to tell her when he told her to come to the garage? That he was going to go to the police with it? They hadn't had a chance to speak before Lloyd and Judy Hill had turned up. Or was that when he'd told Detective Inspector Hill about the tape? When they had been having their tête-à-tête over the car? He'd made her look a liar, then told them about the tape. Why?

'Is that the tape which was in Mr McDonald's possession?' she asked again. There wasn't the usual slight raising of the voice when repeating a question, the hint of impatience that most people employed. Just exactly the same question, in exactly the same tone of voice, as before.

'I expect so,' said Melissa.

'Can you tell me what is on that tape?' she asked.

Melissa felt her cheeks go pink. 'I've no doubt that you have played it,' she said.

'Yes, we have,' said Detective Inspector Hill. 'But I'd still like you to tell me.'

Melissa looked at her. She didn't know Judy Hill at all, not really. A purely professional acquaintance, but none the less she was someone whose ability Melissa admired. 'Why am I here?' she asked. 'I don't believe you think I killed her, whatever she and my husband were doing.'

Was there just a hint of surprise in the brown eyes? Surely not. Just more game-playing, and Melissa was tired of it.

'Don't pretend you haven't worked it out,' she said. 'I'm sure her reference to "the office" left you in as little doubt as it did me. Sharon made it very clear that she was having an affair with her boss, and her boss just happens to be Simon, as you very well know.'

She remembered Judy's parting shot when she had given her a lift home, about Sharon working for Simon. Had she known then?

'When did the interview take place?'

Melissa wanted one of the men back. Either of them would do. Sergeant Finch, so suspicious of her that he might as well have brought handcuffs with him. Chief Inspector Lloyd, angry and looking for someone to blame. Anyone but Detective Inspector Hill, whose brown eyes looked so implacable now.

But of course. She hadn't put a time on her notes, or the tape. Or a venue. 'I'm not certain now,' she said. 'Some time after lunch, I think.'

'No,' said the inspector, shaking her head.

Melissa looked at her. She *couldn't* know, however certain she sounded. Only she and Sharon Smith knew for a fact when that interview took place. Sharon was dead, and she hadn't told anyone. 'Yes,' she said. 'It must have been – I was in Barton in the afternoon.' She had to remember the lies. She had driven home from Barton, therefore she had to have got there in the first place.

'You interviewed her some time after six o'clock in the evening,' said the inspector.

Melissa flushed.

'You describe her clothes in your notes,' said the inspector. 'They're the clothes she was wearing on Friday evening.'

My God, that would be no clue in her case, thought Melissa. But Sharon Smith wouldn't wear the same outfit all day and all evening any more than Detective Inspector Hill would. Judy Hill probably thought that no female person was capable of such a wanton act of dowdiness. But it hardly constituted proof.

'The clothes were brand new. Bought that evening,' said Detective Inspector Hill. 'We have the receipt, timed at 6.13 p.m., and the salesgirl remembers the purchase.'

'Then I expect it was the evening,' Melissa said. She was in trouble. Real, real trouble, and she didn't know how to get out of it. She was used to being one jump ahead of other people in the quick-thinking stakes, but she was overmatched.

'You know it was the evening,' Detective Inspector Hill said steadily. 'And it was the night you spent at the hotel.'

'I don't see what—' Mac found the body. Damn, damn, *damn* him. If she hadn't met him . . .

'Where did you meet Sharon?'

She doubtless knew the answer to that too. She seemed to specialise in asking questions to which she already knew the answers. Melissa gave up, and told the truth.

'At the football ground,' she said. 'Where she was later found. By Mac. With whom I had just been—'

'What time was your interview?' asked the inspector, interrupting Melissa's angry reply.

Again. Just a question. Not a repeat of one which she had just answered with a pack of lies.

'Just after seven,' she said wearily. 'We spoke in my car. She left just before the match kicked off at seven thirty.'

'Did you see where she went?'

'Into the ground.'

She wrote that down. 'Sharon left you at seven thirty, to go into the match. You booked into the hotel at nine thirty or thereabouts.' She looked up. 'You told Detective Chief Inspector Lloyd that you spent that time driving back from Barton,' she said.

Melissa looked down.

'Where were you between seven thirty and nine thirty, Mrs

160

Whitworth?' There was something infuriatingly calm about Detective Inspector Hill. She didn't get annoyed with the lies, or impatient for the truth. She just asked polite questions, to which she mostly knew the answers.

Did she already know where Melissa was, too? Or was this where the fishing really began? 'At home,' she said, to test the water.

She wrote that down, as she had every other blessed word. If Melissa took notes like that, her interviews would never finish. She wondered if this one ever would.

'Not according to your husband. He rang the station to say that you hadn't come home.'

'I went home after I interviewed Sharon,' said Melissa, 'and I came back out and went to the hotel. Simon must have just missed me.'

She wrote that down too.

'I didn't want to be there when Simon did come in,' she said. 'When I got to the hotel, I met Mac. I know he told you that we'd arranged to meet, but that's just because he thinks it sounds better than the truth.'

'Why didn't you tell us the truth in the first place?' she asked. 'Or even the second place?'

Melissa could see the end in sight. 'Because I didn't think that my private life had anything to do with you,' she said. 'Because I didn't want to have to answer these questions. Because it's none of your business!'

Detective Inspector Hill didn't reply. 'Sharon gave you no clue as to who the single man was? The one who was too possessive?'

Melissa frowned. 'No. I got the impression that she was just generalising. Didn't you?'

Judy Hill closed her notebook, and switched off the tape that had been recording this interview. All over the place, it seemed, there was magnetic tape recording Melissa's private life.

'You're free to go, Mrs Whitworth,' she said. 'No charges are being brought at the moment.'

She looked a little tired as she spoke. Melissa stood up. 'I'm sorry I messed you around,' she said. 'But . . . ' She sighed. 'I do have my own life to consider,' she said.

She was given back her bag with its belongings intact; it was the first time in years that she had even known what exactly was in it. She walked out of the police station, into a late afternoon where the horizon was once again obscured by mist, and into Mac.

'Are you all right?' he asked.

She gasped. 'Oh, that's good. That's really good, Mac.'

161

He frowned. 'I mean – are you out on bail, or what? I didn't know what was happening—'

'No, I am not out on bail. I haven't been charged with anything.'

'Neither have I. Let's go somewhere,' he said.

She stared at him. 'What?'

'The hotel – somewhere. Anywhere.'

She shook her head in disbelief. 'It's finished, Mac,' she said. 'You can't blackmail someone once you've played your ace!'

He gaped at her. 'Blackmail?' he said.

'What would you prefer me to call it?'

'*Blackmail?* Is that what you thought? Is that why you came to the house? Is that—'

But she was walking away towards the taxi rank, getting in and slamming the door as Mac came running up, thrusting his hand through the slightly open window, dropping something into the cab.

The driver twisted round as she pushed the window up, very nearly trapping Mac's fingers. She wished she had.

'Just drive,' she said. 'Drive!'

'Play it!' Mac was shouting, his voice muffled. 'Play it!'

She felt around on the floor until her hand closed over the cassette, and she put it back in her bag, where she should never have put it in the first place.

She didn't look back.

Jake had gone to the hospital again in the afternoon, to be told that Bobbie had discharged herself. She hadn't asked him to come and get her; she hadn't even told him. My God, he thought, as he drove into Malworth, Lloyd had been going on about private justice – if he knew where to start, he would dispense private justice all right. But he didn't. He didn't know how to cope with this at all.

Marilyn answered the door, and told him that Bobbie was in bed.

'Is she asleep?'

'No,' said Marilyn. 'At least, she wasn't when I looked in.'

Jake stood awkwardly in the hallway. 'I just want to talk to her,' he said. 'I won't stay if she doesn't want me to.'

Marilyn looked a little dubious. 'Let me tell her you're here first,' she said.

He nodded, and went into the living-room, where he paced up and down until Marilyn came back.

'She does want to see you,' she said, looking relieved.

Jake went along the narrow hall, and tapped on her door before going in. The colour was back in her cheeks; the puffiness on her face had gone down. He went in a little further; not too close.

'Are you feeling any better?' he asked.

She shrugged. 'They let me come home,' she said.

He advanced a step further; she didn't seem to mind, so he took another step, bringing him to the end of the bed. 'Can I sit down?' he asked.

A nod.

He sat down gingerly. 'Do . . . do you have to stay in bed?' he asked.

'No. I just felt a bit tired.'

Jake felt slightly cheered. And relieved. 'Do you think you're well enough to travel?'

'Where?'

'France,' he said. 'You've still got the ticket, haven't you? It's still valid.'

'That was before—' She pressed her lips together, and blinked hard, but the tears came all the same.

Jake wasn't good with tears. 'I know,' he said quickly. 'I know. But you said you still wanted to go.'

'Not yet.'

Oh, God. Jake ran a hand down his face. As far as he was concerned, persuasion consisted of a backhander, financial or physical, whichever he deemed appropriate. And until now, the women in his life had needed no persuasion, or he simply didn't bother with them. It had been as simple as that. Bobbie had always done what he'd asked, and kept any questions to herself. But everything had changed since Sharon, and he didn't know how to go about persuasion of the gentler variety.

'I'll be there before you know it,' he said. 'I told you. Just a couple of things that I'll have to clear up here, that's all. I don't know how long they'll take.'

She looked at him, her eyes widening. 'Alone?' she said. 'You want me to go alone?'

'That's what you were going to do before,' he said.

She didn't speak, just sat, propped up on one elbow, her eyes cast down at the duvet.

'But I'll be there as soon as I can. Then we can really go. Jetting off to the sun, Bobbie. You and me, and—' He broke off. You, me, and a pile of money. That was what he'd always said before. But the money wasn't coming. 'Well – you and me, anyway,' he said. 'But you have to go first thing tomorrow,' he said.

'No.'

163

He licked his lips, and tried again. 'Dennis will pick you up at six o'clock, take you down to Dover—'

'No.'

She had to go. He couldn't expose her to more danger than he already had. She had to go. 'You're going,' he said. 'No arguments.'

'What sort of trouble are you in, Jake?' she asked.

Deep trouble. Jake smiled. 'No trouble.'

She shook her head. 'I'm not going,' she said.

'You won't be alone. I'll tell Dennis to go with you – he'll stay with you. He'll make sure nothing—'

'I'm not going.'

Jake rubbed his eyes. 'Look – Dennis is going to be here at six o'clock tomorrow morning—'

'I'm not going.'

He knew when he was beaten. 'All right,' he said. 'All right. But promise me you'll stay here. In the flat. Promise me.'

'What's going to happen if I don't?'

He looked at her. 'Just promise me,' he said.

For a moment, he thought he had lost even her trust, as she just looked back at him, a question in her eyes if not on her lips.

She nodded slowly. 'I promise,' she said.

He got up, relieved and suddenly desperately tired, as if the adrenalin on which he had been surviving had suddenly been withdrawn. He reached out to pat her hand.

She pulled it away, with a shudder.

It was almost dark by four o'clock now that the clocks had gone back. It got dark earlier and, at the moment, it got foggy earlier. That was good. On a Sunday, Malworth High Street was deserted; the wide thoroughfare that on weekdays and Saturdays was lined with parked cars and thronging with shoppers and office workers was quiet and empty. The shops were closed and, in some cases, shuttered.

But Colin wasn't interested in the shops. He was looking at the window of the flat above the greengrocer's, waiting for a light to go on. The street lamps had come on; dusk was growing into night. As he watched, a light appeared in the window of one of the other flats; in the alley, the lamp over the door to the flats was switched on. But her flat remained in darkness. She wasn't home yet. But she would be coming home.

Colin pushed the bike across the road, watching the reflections of the street lights play over the polish. It was black. Black, and shiny and fast. He pushed it into the alley, right along to the other end, where the lane at the back led to the riverside area that they had redeveloped now. When he was a child, he used to come down here and play in the derelict warehouse, climbing crumbling walls until adults chased him off.

He left the bike in the deep shadow of the block of craft shops and luxury flats; no one would see it there as darkness fell. Across the road, across the park, down to the river side, where the muddy bank could be relied upon to provide him with the implement he needed. He gouged a large stone from the soft earth, and washed it in the river before carrying it back with him.

Walking back to the alley, he paused at the lane end, but there was still no one about. At the other side lay High Street, dead and deserted, wisps of misty vapour twisting round the white light of the street-lamps. The alley was dark now, save for the splash of light above the door. He checked the name-plates. No one called Lloyd. Two couples, and a married woman. That had to be her, and she wasn't his wife. She was someone else's. But she seemed to live alone, so the chances were that she would come home alone. He stood back a pace, and pitched the stone swiftly and accurately at the light.

The tinkling of glass, and darkness. He moved quickly out into the street, but no one came to the door. After a few moments, he strolled back into the alley and waited in the shadow.

Everything was ready for her.

Lloyd had finally let Tom go at about half-past four; half an hour later, Judy escaped from the station. She let herself into Lloyd's car, and waited for him, having a sneaky and much-needed cigarette with the windows down. Smoke drifted out, already creating a little patch of smog beside the car as it hung in the mist.

Eventually, the door opened, and he got in beside her.

'Well?' she said.

'Well what?' He started the car, and began to manoeuvre his way out of what seemed to Judy like an impossible position in the car park.

'Well, I don't suppose Andrews congratulated you on your super wheeze,' she said.

'At least it worked,' said Lloyd, looking over his shoulder. He turned the wheel very fast to his right, and straightened the car just before it made contact with the Superintendent's.

'What about the tape? Don't you think that that's just a touch suspicious? And Melissa Whitworth didn't know what had happened to it, I'm sure.'

Lloyd signalled right. 'For the moment, we can't prove that it's anyone's business but theirs,' he said. 'And I don't think we ever will. Mad Mac and Mrs W have lied in their teeth so that no one found out about their tuppenny-ha'penny romance.'

Melissa wasn't that sure. The post-mortem suggested that it had to have been Simon Whitworth who picked Sharon up and went back to the ground with her. But she let that go for the moment.

'So – are you still a chief inspector?' she asked.

'Just about. Andrews was going on about their being quite likely to sue for wrongful arrest, her husband being a solicitor and all that – but I doubt if her husband's opinion will be sought.'

'But you didn't for one minute think that either of them had killed her, never mind both of them,' said Judy. 'You still don't.'

'No. I just thought they would be frightened enough to tell the truth, and they were.'

Of course they were. Threatening to boil them in oil would probably have frightened them too. Their tuppenny-ha'penny romance, she thought, a little sadly. Lloyd had a good line in putting people down. But what about Sharon's tuppenny-ha'penny romance? Didn't he even think that that was worth pursuing? It *had* to be. She had been with someone, and her relative inexperience in these matters hardly suggested that it would be anyone other than Whitworth.

Her boss. They really should have thought of that in the first place. She looked at Lloyd from under her lashes, so that he wouldn't see her looking at him, and watched as he leant forward over the wheel, waiting for a lorry which laboured up the hill. She had fallen for the boss. It was the one thing that irked her about it, really; it was so clichéd. Cars. Other people's flats. Hotel bedrooms. That's what married men meant. And Sharon preferred that? It had to have been a fairly recent preference, if the post-mortem findings were anything to go by. But McDonald had listened to the tape too, and he had confirmed that that was what Sharon had said – and that she had said Simon Whitworth sometimes hated her. But he had also said that he thought she had been lying.

Judy thought she must have been lying too, at least about preferring to have an affair. No one could prefer it. In fact, the sheer logistics of having an affair with a married man had been one of the reasons that Judy hadn't done so seventeen years ago when she first met Lloyd. Amongst other things, none of which were concerned with morality, the idea of furtive couplings had not appealed. And it hadn't appealed to Sharon all that much, presumably.

'Surely it has to have been Whitworth?' she said. 'This man in the car? Or are you still convinced that Drummond's lying about that?'

166

Lloyd smiled. 'No,' he said. 'Not now. But if he's telling the truth, then it wasn't Whitworth.'

'Who else?'

'I don't know. But at the time Drummond was doing his Peeping Tom act, Whitworth was being telephoned at home by none other than Jack Woodford.'

Oh. Judy hadn't known that.

'It must have been one of her other non-existent boyfriends,' said Lloyd, pulling out.

'She wasn't sleeping around with married men,' Judy said firmly.

'Whatever she told Melissa Whitworth. Not according to Freddie's findings.'

'No,' said Lloyd. 'But I think that might have been a slight exaggeration on Mrs Whitworth's part. McDonald said that she had been asked why *a married man*, and she said that she preferred that to a possessive single man. A brief romance with Parker, and then Whitworth. Just two,' he said. 'Which makes sense with Freddie's findings.'

Just two. The sum total of Judy's relationships. And Sharon had gone to see Jake Parker; had Lloyd been right in the first place? Had *they* made love when Sharon visited him? Judy tried to put herself in Sharon's place, something she was finding increasingly easy to do. If the circumstances were conducive, could she imagine being persuaded to make love to Michael again? If he were hurt, or in trouble, or miserable . . . if she felt he needed her? With painful honesty, she knew that it wouldn't be out of the question. Was that what Sharon had done?

'Perhaps she was with Jake,' she said.

'Not if Drummond really did see a car,' said Lloyd. 'And I am reluctantly coming to the conclusion that he did.'

But that meant a third man, thought Judy. Someone who had never had much to do with men suddenly juggling three of them? For Freddie to have remarked on her inexperience, she really had to have had very few sexual encounters, and yet it couldn't have been Whitworth in the car. Her eyes widened a little.

'Sharon didn't actually come right out with it to Melissa Whitworth,' she said.

'What?' Lloyd waited at the junction, signalling right.

'She seems to have given her enough information to put two and two together – but she didn't actually say that it was Simon Whitworth she was talking about. Supposing it wasn't?'

Lloyd grew interested.

'She made it clear she was having an affair with the boss – but which one? Couldn't it have been Evans?'

Lloyd nodded slowly. 'But it wasn't Evans who claimed not to know what she had been wearing at work and then described her clothes with total accuracy,' he said. 'And it wasn't Evans who gave Colin Drummond a beating.'

Judy frowned. The two incidents seemed to her to lack a connection. 'Whitworth didn't beat him up either,' she said.

'No,' said Lloyd thoughtfully. 'Two policemen did.'

'Anyway – I thought you just said you believed Drummond?' she asked.

'I know,' Lloyd sighed. 'But every time I say it, my instinct shakes its head.'

She smiled.

'I don't believe that Sharon died as the result of a lover's quarrel,' he said. 'I *don't* believe Drummond, and I'm damn sure that Parker knows more than he's saying.' He flicked the indicator down, and began signalling the left turn. 'So let's call on Jake Parker,' he said.

So much for getting home early.

Eleven

'Look – I want to know if I'm getting paid for this!' demanded the taxi driver, jerking his thumb towards the meter.

Melissa sighed, and felt in her bag for her purse, opened it, and thrust a twenty-pound note into his hand. 'All right?' she said. 'Now, just . . . drive round. I don't *care* where you go.'

He looked at the note, and at her, and shrugged. 'God, I get them,' he muttered, as he turned back to the wheel, and carried out his instructions. 'They're never going to believe this one.'

'Does this thing close?' Melissa asked, tapping the glass partition.

He closed it.

Melissa sat back, and took a deep, calming breath. Once, there would have been cigarettes and matches in that bag, but she had given up. She looked for a moment at the back view of the disgruntled cabby, but decided against it. She could survive without nicotine.

What was in her bag was her tape-recorder, and the tape. Play it, he had shouted. Melissa pulled out the recorder, and opened the cassette housing. It took three goes before she got the right tape; it took some time to establish the fact, having to wait, as she did, until the taxi went under some sort of illumination.

Sharon Smith.

Her hand trembled slightly as she put it in; she waited for more light, found the play button, and pressed it.

' . . . *his first cap for England. Rob Bailey spoke to him at his home . . .* '

She ran it on.

' . . . *to bring on young tennis players, because until we do we can't bleat about there being no British singles players in the tournament after the second round . . .* '

She switched it off.

Dear God, things just went from bad to worse. She put the tape-recorder away, and tapped on the window again.

'Buchan Road,' she said.

Jake put down the decanter without pouring his drink, and thought
for a moment before walking slowly towards the door. It was
Sunday; he was unlikely to have any business callers, and he didn't
have any other kind, except police. It was survival of the fittest in
this game, as Lionel Evans would shortly find out. He opened the
door to Chief Inspector Lloyd and the inspector whom Bobbie said
had been all right.

Lloyd smiled. 'Good evening, Mr Parker,' he said. 'I think
perhaps we need the answers to some questions.'

Jake had known that Lloyd wouldn't let him continue to declare
that his conversation with Sharon was confidential, but he was
a little taken aback by the approach. He had grown used, in
his younger days, to being bundled into cars and taken in for
questioning; of recent years, with his growing affluence, he had
even met the odd bit of forelock-tugging. He had known eminently
corruptible police officers, and rigidly unbending police officers. He
didn't know at which end of the range to put the pleasant, smiling,
but ever so slightly sinister Mr Lloyd.

'Come in,' he said. 'I've been expecting you.'

They went into the living room; Jake switched on the light, and
waved a hand at the floral three-piece suite. Inspector Hill took
the armchair. Lloyd didn't sit.

Jake took out his cigarettes and offered one to Lloyd, and the
inspector, who both shook their heads. 'You don't mind if I do?'
he said.

'Not at all,' said Lloyd. 'It's your house, Mr Parker.'

Jake lit the cigarette before he spoke again. 'I've not been entirely
straight with you, Mr Lloyd,' he said.

'No,' said Lloyd, gently touring the room, not looking at Jake.
'I didn't think you had.' He stood looking at the owner's choice
of prints. 'Are you going to be straight with me now?' he asked,
taking out spectacles and looking more closely at one picture.

Not exactly, thought Jake. But then you don't imagine for
one moment that I would tell you all my business, I'm sure,
Mr Lloyd.

'Sharon Smith didn't just come to say hello,' he said.

'No,' said Lloyd, looking back at him, removing his glasses as
he did so.

Jake reached across for the ashtray, and rolled the tip of his
cigarette round to remove the ash. 'No – but it wasn't what you
thought, either,' he said to the inspector, then turned back to Lloyd.
'I misled you a bit about that,' he said.

'About what?'

'Sharon and me. There was nothing between us. Sharon worked for me, that's all.' He smiled. 'She was very quiet, very shy – not really my type at all. And I don't suppose it's too likely that I was hers.'

'Why did you mislead me?' asked Lloyd, sitting down at last.

'You wanted to know why I wanted to talk to Sharon, so I gave you a reason.' Jake was glad that he too could sit; he wouldn't before, so as not to be at a disadvantage.

'Why not the real reason?'

'Because she came to tell me something,' Jake said. 'And as far as I was concerned, it was my problem – not yours, not anyone else's. Just mine.' He got to his feet again. 'I'm forgetting my manners,' he said to the inspector. 'Can I get you something to drink – I was just going to have one.'

'No thank you,' she said. 'Not on duty, and all that. But you go ahead.'

'Ah. Coffee, then.'

'That would be very nice,' she said, smiling. 'Thank you.'

'Mr Lloyd?'

'Yes – black, please. No sugar.'

Jake stubbed out his cigarette, and went through to the kitchen, busying himself with the coffee, with finding out how the inspector took hers, with producing biscuits, while he worked out how best to tell his story. He would have preferred to have gone to the police himself, with it all rehearsed, but he had underestimated Mr Lloyd again. If anyone had ever told him that he would be producing coffee and biscuits for the Bill, he would have laughed. But they were being polite and civilised, and he would be too.

He put everything on a tray, and brought it into the living room, where Lloyd had irritatingly resumed his inspection of the artwork. Jake set the tray down on the coffee table. 'It seems Sharon was using the computer at work, and happened to get into an accounts programme that she didn't recognise,' he said.

Lloyd turned to look at him as he spoke. The inspector picked up her coffee. Neither of them said anything.

Jake carried on. 'You'll appreciate that a lot of money is held from time to time on behalf of Parker Development by Evans and Whitworth until it can be released.'

Lloyd nodded.

Jake picked up Lloyd's coffee cup and placed it on the silly table with the spindly legs beside the armchair. Lloyd smiled, and gave up his art appreciation to sit down.

'Well,' said Jake, sitting. 'Sharon was puzzled. Money had been leaving those accounts and going to holding companies that she knew nothing about. She worked for me, remember – she knew most of my business. She could see no reason why such large sums of money should be being moved about – and she thought it all seemed a bit fishy.'

Lloyd had begun to look sceptical, but that was all right. He could be as sceptical as he liked; Jake was certain that nothing could be proved against him. Lionel had done it all.

Jake picked up his own coffee. They sat around like WI ladies at afternoon tea, and yet he felt as though this was a sword fight in which only he was participating. 'She thought I might be trying a tax dodge, but she doubted it. So she came to me, and asked.' He tried to keep the edge of desperation out of his voice, but he wasn't convinced he was succeeding.

At last, Lloyd spoke, but not until he had picked up his cup and saucer, sipped his coffee, set it down again, and looked at Jake a bit like he had been looking at the prints, with a measure of distaste.

'Why would she doubt that you were dodging taxes, Mr Parker?' he asked.

Jake smiled, unruffled by the implication, just glad that he was no longer making a speech. 'She knew how I operated,' he said. 'It didn't smell right.'

'Not your usual style of tax evasion?'

'Avoidance,' said Jake.

He carried on, in the absence of another question. 'She said she was meeting someone – I don't know who. She asked if she could change – well, I've told you all that. Anyway – I sent a last minute invitation to Lionel to come to the do – he never passes up the chance of free hospitality,' he added. 'I thought it had to have been Whitworth – he's only been there a few months, and Lionel's as straight as a die, or so I thought. I wanted to talk to him about it. He came, and I told him what Sharon had told me.'

Lloyd picked up his coffee, and drank half the cup, black, sugarless, and still piping hot, as Jake had discovered. He hardly seemed to be listening, but the inspector was jotting down notes while he spoke; Jake smiled at her when she looked up.

'When did you see Sharon?' she asked.

'We were out on the balcony, and I saw her down on the terraces. I thought we should both talk to her, try to get to the bottom of it. We went down to the terraces – I thought Lionel was with me, but when I turned to speak to him, he had gone.'

'But you still spoke to Sharon?'

Jake nodded. 'I was going to tell her that I'd spoken to Lionel, but before I got the chance, this bloke launches himself at me. I fought back, and then I was grabbed from behind – and you know the rest.'

Lloyd looked at him speculatively. 'I don't think we do,' he said.

Jake smiled. 'I don't know what you mean, Mr Lloyd,' he said. 'In the early hours of Saturday morning you were told that Sharon Smith had been murdered,' said Lloyd. 'And you lied to me. You had started the fight, you said – you were jealous. Why did you do that, Mr Parker?'

'You know why,' Jake said. 'I thought maybe someone had put him up to it – I wanted to find out who.'

'Private justice,' said Lloyd quietly.

'Not for Sharon,' said Jake. 'I won't try to kid you, Mr Lloyd – Sharon meant nothing to me. But she was dead, and the only person who knew that she had been to see me was Evans.' He lit another cigarette. 'I don't like being cheated,' he said.

It was quite a convincing story, he thought, given that he hadn't really had time to prepare. He was admitting that he had lied to the police, and that he had intended dealing with Evans himself. The fact that his motive for going after Evans wasn't quite as stated would be unlikely to occur to anyone, but even if it did, they couldn't prove it. Giving up his dream of the good life had been the difficult bit; this bit was easy compared to that.

'You think Evans killed her?' asked Lloyd.

'He denied it,' said Jake. 'He reckoned she must have told Whitworth what she was going to do, and he got rid of her.' He was pleased with that – he hadn't rushed it. He had waited for the opening.

Lloyd raised his eyebrows. 'And you believed him?'

Jake drew on the cigarette. 'I don't know,' he said. 'It could be true – or they could all three have been in on it.'

Lloyd nodded, and finished his coffee, saying nothing at all. It was the inspector who spoke next.

'Why are you volunteering this information now?' she asked. 'Why have you abandoned private justice?'

Jake had hoped that the information would be of sufficient interest for that question not to be asked, but this one was sharp. Not too sharp, he hoped. He drank some coffee, and took a long pull on his cigarette, and told the unvarnished truth. 'I've got other problems,' he said. 'I want to get Bobbie away from here. Get her to the sunshine somewhere.'

Lloyd was walking about again; it unnerved Jake when he did that. He didn't speak, and he still didn't seem very interested.

'But you were already planning to leave,' the inspector said.
'Bobbie told me herself.'

Ah. She always seemed to be one jump ahead of him – Jake
wasn't used to that. 'Yes,' he said.

'When did you make the arrangements to leave?' asked Lloyd.

Christ. Well – it wasn't a crime to arrange to leave the country.
He could prove nothing. And he could find out what he wanted
to know soon enough, by going round the travel agents.

'Last month,' he said. 'I know what you're thinking, Mr Lloyd –
and I don't blame you. Whatever Evans or Whitworth or all three
of them were up to, I'd much rather have been a part of it. But I
wasn't. I just knew that it wasn't working out – I wanted to sell up.
Evans must have got worried, because the money began to shift in
much larger amounts after I'd told him that I was jacking it in –
that's when Sharon noticed. Or got greedy. Or scared.'

Lloyd frowned. 'Mr Evans could simply move this money at
will?'

'Sure. Either of them could – in fact, Whitworth was the one
actually dealing with my business. He could release it as and
when – it was supposed to make for smoother negotiations,
and make sure it was earning money for the investors while
it was tied up. But it wasn't smoothing things – now I know
why.'

'Mr Parker, you realise that you will have to make a statement
concerning all that you've just told me?'

Jake nodded briefly.

'And that the fraud squad will be called in, and will be looking
for any discrepancies which could indicate your involvement?'

Jake crushed out his cigarette. 'Sure.' He didn't feel as confident
as he sounded; Lloyd knew it, and the watchful inspector knew
it. But he'd been careful. And Evans was an amateur. He'd be
all right.

'You wouldn't still be thinking of leaving the country while all
that was going on, would you?' asked Lloyd.

'No,' he said. No, he wouldn't. If he could persuade Bobbie
to, he'd feel a whole lot better, but one thing was for certain. Guilty men ran. He was the victim of this fraud, and
he was staying to see it through. He could almost believe it;
and before he knew where he was, Evans would almost believe
it too.

They left, at last, and he poured himself the drink he had been
going to have before they arrived.

Let them sort that lot out, he thought.

* * *

'I was right about the building development, anyway,' Lloyd said smugly, as they got back into the car, and the headlights reflected back against the fog.

'Mm.' It didn't do to praise Lloyd.

'Evans now,' he said, and set off slowly.

'I can't see why Evans would have killed Sharon,' she said. 'He knew she'd already told Parker everything she knew.'

'You don't believe for a moment that Parker wasn't involved, do you?' said Lloyd. 'Evans could well have panicked, and killed Sharon, thinking that if he got rid of Sharon, he and Parker could carry on. But Parker knew that Sharon's death meant that the police would be investigating his affairs. And he knew, when he'd stopped being angry and thought about it, that something untoward happening to Lionel would be viewed with suspicion. So he's getting out from under, and leaving Evans to carry the can.'

It all made sense. Whatever Sharon had really told Parker, and whatever Parker had really told Evans, Evans was in trouble up to his neck if the accounts were examined.

And Lloyd had been right about the fight, come to that, she thought. 'Do you think Lionel put Barnes up to it?' she asked. 'To get Parker out of the way?'

Lloyd shook his head, and took the car out on to the fog-bound road to the village where Lionel lived. 'No,' he said. 'If it was him, he didn't have time to organise something like that.' He grinned. 'So perhaps Drummond did see a car,' he said. 'I'm not always right.'

'Oh, surely you are,' said Judy.

Lloyd chose to ignore the sarcasm. 'It fits Drummond's story,' he said. 'Sharon left the ground at the same time as Evans did,' he said. 'He could have seen her, pulled up, asked if they could talk, and taken her back up there on the pretext of including Parker in the discussions. Perhaps that was even what he meant to do.'

And if that was what had happened, then it *was* presumably Evans that Sharon was having an affair with, because whoever it was made love to her when they got there. The ground had been dark and deserted. Perhaps Evans had thought that his relationship with Sharon would save his skin. She didn't know that Parker had told Evans; when she realised that she was being manipulated, she had apparently sealed her fate.

Lloyd slowed to a crawl as he watched for the turn-off to the bypassed village. 'Where the hell is this place?' he muttered, as though someone had deliberately tidied it away when he had left it on his desk.

Judy wound down the window, admitting trails of mist, as

she tried to recognise a landmark that would stop them getting hopelessly lost.

'And Drummond was an innocent bystander,' said Lloyd, but the statement still lacked conviction.

Judy sighed. It seemed likely enough to her. The voyeuristic Drummond had not left when the action started in the car; he had watched enviously, then consoled himself with his reckless ride on the bike. When he was stopped, he had presumably been a cocky little bastard, as Finch would have it. The police officers' response to that had been swift and painful, and their lies had dragged Drummond into the murder inquiry.

'You still don't believe him?' she asked, as a sign loomed out of the mist, and Lloyd indicated the turn.

'I'll reserve judgement until I hear what Evans has to say,' said Lloyd.

She was sitting in the armchair, saying she was sorry for having misjudged him.

Mac didn't feel in the least offended; my God, she had only known him two days. All that mattered was that she had listened to the tape, and she was here, in his room. His landlady had admitted her with deep suspicion, and had only allowed her to come up because it was still early evening, and she knew that people didn't get up to anything like that until after ten o'clock at night.

Not that they had got up to anything; Melissa had sat very properly in the visitor's chair, and he had perched on the end of the bed, almost as though nothing had ever happened. It wouldn't be sensible, anyway. One twang of a bedspring, and he would be out on his ear.

'I'll get a flat,' he said. 'Not in Stansfield – the waiting list's years long. Malworth maybe – they've got privately let flats there.'

'Yes,' she said. 'Good idea.'

'I'll be installed in one before you know it.' He carefully didn't say 'we'; he didn't know what sort of relationship Melissa had in mind, and he didn't honestly care whether she wanted to stay with Simon or not, just so long as some of her time was his.

She smiled a little uncertainly. It was funny, Mac thought, that this should make her shy, in view of what had gone before. He wanted to chase away her awkwardness as she had done his, but not here.

'Can we go somewhere?' he said.

'What?' She seemed startled.

'The hotel, maybe. I could just about afford to stay the night there so that it didn't look too much as though we—'

'No, Mac,' she said, as though he had already asked three times and wouldn't take no for an answer.

He frowned. 'Well – all right. It's just that . . . ' He pointed down through the floor. 'She won't miss a trick – and I was warned when I came here. Any hanky-panky and I was out. I can't really afford to get chucked out.'

It was Melissa's turn to frown. 'Mac,' she said firmly. 'I told you in the first place. I'm married. What happened is not going to happen again.'

He felt as though she had punched him. 'But – you . . . I thought – why did you come here?'

She sighed. 'To say I was sorry for believing that you had blackmailed me,' she said.

No. No – he couldn't have been that wrong. She hadn't been like someone acting under duress. 'But it was wonderful,' he said. 'You know it was.'

'It wouldn't be like that again,' said Melissa. 'I thought I had no choice – that removed the guilt, somehow. I didn't have to have a conscience about it. I was doing it for Simon, because he was there, Mac. I saw him. And you had the tape – I thought . . . ' She sighed. 'And now they know anyway,' she said.

He hadn't been doing it for bloody Simon. If he had thought that it would have got rid of Simon, he'd have given the police that tape without a moment's hesitation. He got up and looked out of the window, his back to her.

'You didn't think I was blackmailing you at the hotel,' he muttered.

'No. I'd had nothing to eat and too much to drink. I'd been hurt – really badly hurt. Mac, I love Simon! I don't *want* to have an affair. I just want to keep him out of prison.'

So that's all it had been. The result of too much booze on an empty stomach. He had been right in the first place. It might just as well have been one of the reps. 'Then get out,' he said.

She did.

Lionel had been watching television when Chief Inspector Lloyd had arrived with yet another police officer. A woman this time – very nice, too. It hadn't surprised him to see Lloyd at the door; they had said that someone would call. But they had asked if there was somewhere private, and that had surprised him a little, and alerted him. If they thought that Frances shouldn't hear, perhaps he and Parker weren't lying low enough. But they couldn't know about that, he thought, as he took them into the sewing room that he sometimes used as a makeshift study.

177

They said it was about Sharon; Lionel tried not to sigh aloud with relief. But he hadn't gone to them with what Mrs Smith had said about Sharon being expected home, and he ought to have told them. Anything, they had said. Anything that might help. If he told them now it would look a little . . .

'What did you do after you left Mr Parker at the football ground on Friday night?' Lloyd asked.

'I went home,' said Lionel. 'I think I told the police officer who spoke to me next day.'

'No – I want to know exactly, Mr Evans. You left the executive box with Parker – he went to talk to Sharon, and you left the ground. What did you do then?'

'I went to my car – I went home.'

Lloyd perched on the edge of the sewing-machine table. 'But you had just had a very nasty shock, hadn't you?' he asked.

Oh, God. Lionel licked his lips. 'What?' he said evasively.

'Mr Parker had just informed you that Sharon Smith had found irregularities in the accounts held on behalf of Parker Development,' Lloyd said steadily.

Lionel knew that his mouth was opening and shutting. 'He said something about . . . yes,' he said, hoping that the perspiration that he could feel trickling down the back of his neck was not as evident to his inquisitors as it was to him. 'So Sharon said, at any rate.'

Inspector Hill looked interested. 'Do you think it's likely to have been a mischievous allegation?' she asked.

He had been over this. He had known that this had to happen some day – that was part of the plan, after all. All that was happening was the questions were coming sooner than he had expected. But he had prepared the answers. With great difficulty, Lionel took himself in hand.

'Well, I find it hard to believe that . . . ' He stopped, as though unwilling to put into words the thought that had crossed his mind. That was better than blaming Whitworth straight out. Defend him. Defend his integrity. Nice chap. Clever wife. Doesn't make enough of herself though, so not really so surprising that he took to the fetching, if dull, Sharon.

Detective Chief Inspector Lloyd was apparently engrossed in the intricacies of Frances's sewing machine, but he joined in the conversation none the less. 'Find what hard to believe, Mr Evans?'

Lionel took his eyes away from the inspector, and focussed on Lloyd. 'That there could be anything wrong with the accounts,' he said. 'I took on Mr Whitworth for his expertise in these complex development projects. I'm fine when it comes to doing land searches for semis, but . . . '

Somehow, without Parker's voice saying it, it didn't sound so clever. It didn't sound so likely. And it didn't sound good. For the first time, the very first time, Lionel was alone with only his conscience. No devil perched on his left shoulder, telling him what he could do with his share of the loot; no street-smart Parker to make it all sound like an exciting game with high stakes. Just a dreadful feeling that it wasn't going to work, and an even worse feeling which, if it did work, he would have to live with for ever.

'Is that what Sharon thought? That it was Whitworth who was cooking the books?'

Lionel frowned. 'I . . . I don't know,' he said.

'So you had had a nasty shock, as I said,' said Lloyd. 'But you just went to your car, and drove away?' he asked.

'Well – no. I couldn't believe it – I didn't want to believe it. I sat there for a few minutes. I heard the announcement that the match was being abandoned, and people began to come out. That's when I left.'

'And when did you see Sharon?' Lloyd looked up from the sewing machine, his face the picture of innocence as he asked his deadly question.

'I didn't,' said Lionel, now thoroughly alarmed. 'I didn't see her at all.'

'You must have done,' said Lloyd. 'You were on the balcony with Parker. And Sharon left moments before the match was abandoned – moments before you did.'

Lionel shook his head. 'I must have missed her,' he said.

Lloyd pushed himself away from the table, and handed over to his colleague with a slight raising of his eyebrows.

'You must have wanted to speak to her, Mr Evans,' she said. 'You must have wanted her to explain what she had found.'

Lionel nodded, shrugged. He had known what Sharon had found, and he hadn't been thinking all that clearly at the time.

'So when you saw her, you drove up to her, and asked her to go back with you to Parker, and you would all discuss things rationally – work out some sort of solution.'

It might have been a good idea, if it had occurred to him. Or if he'd seen Sharon. But it hadn't, and he hadn't.

'Isn't that what happened?' Lloyd asked. 'You saw her walking back down Byford Road, and you picked her up, and took her back. But the place was deserted, and you thought perhaps you could persuade her not to blow any whistles. But it didn't work, so you panicked, and killed her.'

It was so ridiculous, it didn't even alarm him that the chief

179

inspector was accusing him of murder. 'I didn't see her,' he said. 'I didn't pick her up.'

The door opened and Frances came in with a tray on which she had put a pot of tea and a plate of biscuits. Everyone fell silent until she had left, closing the door behind her.

'Someone did,' Lloyd said. 'Someone picked her up, and took her back to the ground. She was in the car with whoever it was until at least nine o'clock. Someone made love to her, and we think that that same someone killed her, Mr Evans.'

Lionel's mouth was permanently open. 'You think I . . . you think Sharon and I were—' He almost laughed with relief. 'Here,' he said, pointing to the tray. 'Help yourselves. Sharon and me?' He felt light-headed, breathless. 'It wasn't me she was having an affair with,' he said. 'It was Whitworth. I didn't see her – whoever picked her up must already have done it. Try Whitworth. Sharon's mother was expecting her home at seven o'clock – she had got her supper ready. What made her go to the football match instead of going home? Whitworth, I'll be bound. If anyone picked her up and . . . and . . . well, if anyone did, it had to have been Whitworth, if what Parker told me about them is true.'

'We know where Mr Whitworth was when Sharon was in that car,' said Lloyd. 'We want to know where you were, Mr Evans.'

The moment's euphoria at their mistaken assumption left him as suddenly as it had come. It didn't get him off any hooks. And he might as well be accused of Sharon's murder. It was his fault it had happened. If he hadn't gone along with Parker's plans, if he hadn't wanted whatever it was that Parker seemed to be offering him, then Sharon would still be alive, because she would never have been at the football ground in the first place.

'I was here,' he said.

'Can someone confirm that?'

He smiled, calmer now than he had been for the last two days. 'My wife. But I don't suppose that's good enough for you.' Certainly not if they knew her, it wouldn't be. She would say he was there at any time he cared to name. He wondered where his marriage had all gone wrong. He hadn't been sleeping with his secretary, not like Whitworth. Frances didn't have to ring people up to check on where he was when he said he was working late. Then he remembered.

'Melissa Whitworth,' he said. 'She can confirm it. She rang me here not long after nine o'clock.'

Lloyd's eyes widened.

'You know how long it took you to get here, Chief Inspector,' he said. 'I can hardly have been strangling Sharon at nine o'clock and back here by ten past.'

Lloyd picked up his tea and drank it thoughtfully. 'So you are saying that Mr Whitworth was having an affair with Sharon Smith, that Mr Whitworth has to have been responsible for any discrepancies in your accounts, and that Mr Whitworth in all probability murdered Sharon when she discovered this, and unwisely told him what she'd found?'

He ought to agree. He ought regretfully to agree that was indeed what he thought. Parker had said that if Whitworth really had killed her it would strengthen his hand. But he didn't want his hand strengthening. It had offended him; he wanted to cut it off.

Lionel closed his eyes. It was an odd way in which to see things clearly for the first time, but that was how it was. It had to have been Parker himself who had told them what Sharon had discovered. This had always been going to happen. Parker had had to initiate the investigation himself because of what had happened to Sharon, but that was the only difference. Whenever and however it had come about, Lionel would have been on his own.

Parker had always been going to sit back and watch Lionel jump through hoops. Of course Lionel couldn't incriminate Simon. He had neither the guile nor the sheer wickedness, and Parker had known that. He had simply employed Lionel to do all his dirty work, and then he would have skipped with the money.

It gave Lionel some satisfaction to know that since Parker had had to make the allegations himself, rather than waiting until the money had been laundered into safe and secret accounts, the proceeds would all be impounded, and Parker wouldn't get a penny either. And Lionel could at least make an attempt to have him put where he belonged.

'Parker says she was having an affair with Simon,' he said, his voice expressionless. 'It is perfectly possible, but I have no personal knowledge of the situation. Whitworth was not involved in the fraud. I have no idea who killed Sharon, and I want to make a statement,' he said. 'Parker was just as involved in this fraud as I was.'

'Not my pigeon,' said Lloyd, putting down his cup. 'This needs people who can read balance sheets and spot errors. Fraud squad stuff. I've no doubt you'll be hearing from my colleagues very soon. I am only concerned with it in as much as it precipitated the murder of Sharon Smith. If it did.'

Lionel stared at him. 'You don't still think that I did it, surely?' he asked.

'I don't know, Mr Evans. That rather depends on who else has been lying to me.'

They left, and Lionel closed the front door on the foggy night, squaring his shoulders, and preparing himself to tell Frances what was about to happen to them.

Lloyd eased out of the Evans's driveway, and settled in for the long, tiring journey back to Stansfield. 'The Whitworths?' he said.

'It's getting very late,' said Judy. 'And we really only have the word of two very doubtful witnesses as to what Whitworth was doing – you've already arrested his wife today.'

Lloyd smiled. 'The Whitworths,' he said. 'We have to find out if Mrs Whitworth confirms Evans' alibi, don't we?'

Judy sighed. 'They might be in bed by the time we get there,' she said.

Lloyd grinned. 'It'll make a change for them to be in bed with one another if they are,' he said.

'And if she does confirm his alibi?' asked Judy.

Lloyd blinked, as though that would clear his vision, but the damp clouds of fog remained. 'Then first thing tomorrow, we get Drummond back in,' he said grimly. 'And ask him why we have been chasing all over the countryside in search of his phantom bloody car!'

There was no car, he was sure of it. Drummond had been lying from the start. And if that was the case, then Lionel's alibi was no good to him, because Sharon Smith had been murdered before she ever left the ground.

Judy yawned. 'When we've seen the Whitworths, we call it a day – yes?'

'Yes,' said Lloyd.

They drove for a few minutes in silence, as Lloyd tried to push the theory that was evolving to the back of his head. If Whitworth wasn't involved in the fraud – and there seemed little doubt that he had been selected as the fall guy – then Judy had been right all along, and it was a domestic. Why had Sharon said she would be home at seven? Her appointment with Melissa Whitworth was at seven. And had she seen Whitworth at the match? If so, he might have seen her. And what had he seen? Sharon in deep consultation with his wife. And did she tell him what she had just done?

Perhaps they could wrap it all up tonight, and he could forget the little voice that nagged him about Drummond, and the police who had it in for him, and the coincidental rape of Parker's girlfriend.

'I spy,' said Judy, boredly, 'with my little eye, something beginning with F.'

Lloyd smiled.

'Talk to me,' she said. 'I hate it when you're strong and silent.'

'I'm trying to see where I'm going! What about?'

'Anything.'

'The occult? Gardening. The eruption of Vesuvius in 79 AD. South Africa – is apartheid truly dead? Flemish art. Charles Edward Stuart – how valid was his claim to the throne? Astronomy. Simone de Beauvoir—'

'She'll do,' said Judy.

He had told her everything he knew, and made up a great deal that he did not, about Simone de Beauvoir before the orange lights of Stansfield were close enough to penetrate the fog, and they were on the bypass on which the Whitworths inexplicably chose to live. Both the Whitworths' cars were parked on the grass verge; garages were a thing of the future when the cottage had been built, and its preservation order prohibited building. Lloyd drove on to the lay-by, and pulled in behind another car.

He frowned. 'No one else lives within miles of here,' he said.

'Probably broken down,' said Judy. 'It's a bit beaten up – maybe it had an accident.'

Probably. He couldn't let his wild theory take him over, he thought. But he made a mental note of the number, all the same.

'Come in,' said Whitworth, looking strained and anxious, as did his wife, who hovered anxiously at the living-room door.

The room was untidy; there was evidence on one of the cushions on the armchair of a cat's presence, but the cat itself wasn't to be seen. The television was on, with the sound too low to be of any use; that always irritated Lloyd. In fact, he thought that the Whitworths were the most irritating couple he had ever met. And even the cat had had enough of them, or Lloyd might have had someone sensible to talk to.

'Did you speak to Mr Evans at all on Friday evening, Mrs Whitworth?' Judy asked.

Lloyd had become convinced, during his impromptu and wildly unreliable lecture on the French lady of letters, that this whole thing was a waste of time. Time that he was once again spending with people whose selfish lives really didn't interest him.

There had been no car; Drummond had wasted even more of his time.

'Yes,' said Mrs Whitworth. 'I telephoned him to see if he knew where Simon was.'

'Can you remember what time that was?'

'Nine, or so. I can't remember to the minute.'

Judy took him a little by surprise then. 'Where did you ring from?' she asked.

'Here,' she said, guilelessly.

Judy consulted her incredible notebook. Whatever it was, she hadn't forgotten it – it was doubtless what *she* had been thinking about all through the lecture, but her dependence on note-taking had given her a prop, too, like his glasses had given him. They all did it, unconsciously acting, using power-play and body language to gain the upper hand.

'But in your last statement you said that you had left Sharon Smith going into the match just before the kick-off, and gone home,' said Judy.

'Yes,' said Mrs Whitworth, still quite unaware of the snare that Judy was holding open for her to walk into. Lloyd was unsure of the nature of the snare, but he recognised one when he saw it, unlike Mrs W.

'And that you must have just missed your husband,' said Judy.

'Yes – look, I'm not too sure what all this is about,' she said.

Neither was Lloyd.

Judy looked up from her notes, her expression politely puzzled. 'It's about when exactly you left this house, Mrs Whitworth,' she said. 'You see, you said that you left here and went to the hotel.'

Melissa Whitworth looked at Lloyd then; Lloyd couldn't help her. All he could do was look as though he knew what Judy was getting at.

'Yes,' she said. 'I left at about ten – quarter past nine, I suppose. Right after I'd phoned Lionel.'

'And got to the hotel at nine thirty?'

'You know I did.'

'But Sergeant Woodford rang your husband at this number at eight forty-five, Mrs Whitworth. And later, your husband said that you hadn't come home at all, so I must assume that you weren't here then.'

'No, I . . . '

'Where were you between seven thirty and eight forty-five?' Judy asked.

'I don't know! I must have . . . ' She tailed off. 'I don't know,' she said.

The silence that followed was tangible; Simon Whitworth sat on the arm of the sofa, his eyes on his wife. Judy waited, pen poised, for a reasonable answer to her question. Lloyd was wondering how he had missed that discrepancy in her statement, and knew that it was because of his obsession with Drummond.

'All right,' Mrs Whitworth said, almost huffily. 'I did come home when I said I did, after I'd left Sharon Smith. I was very upset – and I thought at least Simon would be here, because for once I knew he wasn't "working late", which is his unoriginal euphemism for screwing his secretary.' She shot a look at her husband.

Whitworth had the grace to blush, and look down at the arm of the sofa, on which he seemed to have found something that required his earnest attention.

'But he wasn't here,' she said, her eyes still resting on her uncomfortable husband. 'I waited for ages, but he didn't come home. I tried the office, and there was no reply. So I decided to go there. If she had gone back to the office, I might even catch them in the act of working late.'

Whitworth was a painful brick-red.

'I drove down towards the village. Then . . . I saw her. Walking down to the office, presumably. So I drove alongside her, and wound down the window.'

Lloyd stared at her.

'I offered her a lift – she didn't want to take it, obviously, but I just crawled along beside her. She had to get in. I was embarrassing her.'

'Where did you go?' Judy asked.

'She asked me to take her back up to the football ground,' said Melissa.

'Did you ask why?'

'No, but she volunteered the information that there had been a bit of a fight, and she had left. She wanted to go back because she had to speak to someone.'

She glanced at Lloyd, who was busily trying to reorganise his thoughts on Drummond, who had been telling the truth, blast him.

'When we got there, the place was in darkness,' she said. 'And I told her what I thought of her.'

Whitworth looked up at his wife, who turned and addressed him directly.

'I knew as soon as she'd gone that it hadn't even been an honest mistake! She did it quite deliberately! How you could possibly have wanted to have anything to do with that unprincipled little bitch—' She blinked away tears. 'She pretended not to know what I was talking about, and that just made me angrier. Then she said that my husband obviously didn't want me, and he did want her, though she used rather more basic language than that. I told her to get out.'

Whitworth was staring at her now, his mouth open. 'That isn't true!' he shouted. 'She wasn't like that – she wasn't!'

'What happened then?' said Judy, ignoring Whitworth's protestations.

'I drove away. I came back here. I didn't understand where Simon

185

had gone, so I rang Lionel. Then I didn't want to be here when Simon did condescend to come home, so I picked up a change of underwear and my toilet bag, and I went straight to the hotel.'

'Is there some reason why you didn't tell us this in the first place?' asked Lloyd.

'I wasn't terribly keen to tell anyone! I got drunk – I made a fool of myself, all right?' She turned to her husband. 'And don't flatter yourself that it was because of you!' she shouted. 'I'd nearly run over some idiot on a motorbike – I was shaken up, and I drank too much. And what happened at the hotel,' she said, bringing Lloyd back into her line of fire, 'was completely unplanned – and I might add, entirely unprecedented, whatever you may think of me!'

'What – what did happen at the hotel?' asked Whitworth, angry and bewildered, but no one enlightened him.

'An idiot on a motorbike?' Lloyd said wearily, as if he didn't know. There could hardly have been two idiots on motorbikes abroad on Friday night.

'Some cretin who didn't even have his lights on,' she said.

Lloyd closed his eyes briefly. Drummond. Here was Drummond. Again. Perhaps Tom was right in his jaundiced summing-up of the problem. Perhaps it was one giant conspiracy.

Judy's clear, quiet voice broke into the lull that had followed Mrs Whitworth's outburst. 'In your previous statement, you said that you must have just missed your husband,' she said. 'What did you mean?'

Melissa Whitworth frowned. 'What do you think I meant?' she asked, her temper rising again. 'I had been home, and gone out again. Then I came back, by which time Simon had been home and gone out again. I missed him. That's not too difficult to grasp, is it?'

'*Just* missed him,' Judy corrected, not at all ruffled by Mrs Whitworth's anger. 'How did you know you had "just" missed him, Mrs Whitworth?'

Melissa Whitworth's cheeks grew pink.

'How did you know that you had just missed him?' Judy asked again, infuriatingly.

'I saw his car turn into Byford Road as I left the football ground,' she mumbled, and turned to him again. 'You told me you got called away from the office! But I had *seen* you.'

Simon Whitworth leapt to his feet. 'I was on my way to the police station!' he shouted.

'I know that now!' she yelled back. 'But I didn't know it this afternoon, when I was being questioned, did I? I thought—'

Whitworth advanced on her. 'You thought what? That I'd killed her? Is that what you thought? Why? Why in God's name would I have killed her? I loved her! Don't you understand? I loved her!'

'Loved her! Would you like to know what she thought of that – what she thought of you?'

'I don't want to hear any more lies,' Whitworth said, railing against what was all too obviously the truth. 'I don't believe a word of it.' He sat down again, a muscle working in his temple as he contained the anger.

He may have to, Lloyd thought. The atmosphere simmered and bubbled as he asked Simon his next question. 'I take it you admit having an affair with her, Mr Whitworth?' It seemed a little unnecessary, but it was as well to have everything spelled out.

'Yes.'

So, he could forget about delicacy. 'Did you see Sharon earlier, when the match was on?'

'No! I wasn't there.'

'Sharon Smith had sex with someone less than half an hour before she died,' Lloyd said. 'Was that you, Mr Whitworth?'

Whitworth looked up, his eyes wide. 'I don't believe you,' he said.

He would have to believe someone some time. 'Was that you?' Lloyd repeated.

'I don't believe you! You're lying – you're all lying! Why are you telling all these lies about her?'

'Are you saying it was someone else?'

'There wasn't anyone else!' Whitworth shouted.

'Are you saying that it was you? Were you at the football match, Mr Whitworth?'

'No I was not!'

Lloyd sighed. 'Then she was with someone else,' he said.

'No! I don't believe you – I don't believe a word of this!'

Evidently not, thought Lloyd. But she had been with someone whether Whitworth liked it or not. And it was becoming very important that they find out who. Drummond loomed large in Lloyd's thoughts again. The whole thing could have happened after Melissa Whitworth had left Sharon stranded.

'We will be requiring you to take a blood test, Mr Whitworth,' he said.

Whitworth sat silently fuming at his wife, his anger a coiled spring waiting to be released as soon as they had gone.

Judy looked a question at Mrs Whitworth, who gave a little nod of reassurance.

'You think we have rows?' said Lloyd, as they saw themselves out, and walked to where the car was parked.

The other car was still there; Lloyd strolled over to it, looked in, and round it. There was no need to be suspicious of it, really, he scolded himself. Even if his theory was right, it only meant that the Whitworths were what he had assumed them to be in the first place. A monumental waste of time.

He got into the car, and wearily put it in gear. God, he hated the fog. His eyes were aching with the effort of simply trying to see, as he turned into the now famous Byford Road, and headed down the hill. He thought about asking Judy just to come to the flat, which was much closer, but she hadn't got anything with her to wear tomorrow, and that would mean driving her home in the middle of the night, which he could do without. Malworth it was.

'So where does that leave us?' asked Judy.

Sharon had once again proved to be rather less quiet and unassuming than her nearest and dearest had believed her to be. Someone other than Whitworth had been with her, and Drummond was still the favourite, in Lloyd's book. Acting alone, or, he thought darkly, in concert with whoever wanted Jake Parker to come to heel. Or possibly . . . he didn't speak again until he pulled up outside the shops in Malworth High Street.

'Money,' he said. 'There are enormous sums of money involved in all of this.'

'You don't think it was a crime of passion, I take it?'

Lloyd shook his head. 'Why did Barnes start that fight? Why did Drummond follow Sharon? Why did Parker change his story?'

Judy released her seat belt. 'Do you still think someone deliberately got Parker out of the way?'

'Yes,' said Lloyd. 'And I still can't believe that Drummond isn't involved – and I still can't believe that the rape was a coincidence.'

'There's no other explanation, Lloyd.'

Lloyd turned away from her, and looked out of the window at the fog curling round the old-fashioned street-lamps. 'Isn't there?' he asked.

'You can't honestly believe that a serial rapist is somehow mixed up in property fraud,' she said.

Lloyd shook his head. 'I just don't think Bobbie Chalmers was one of his victims,' he said quietly.

'She has to have been. I've told you. No one knows what he does, or what he says, but the victims and him.'

'I am the Stealth Bomber?' said Lloyd.

That was what the rapist said to his victims, over and over again. They had been careful not to release that to the press, or the papers would have called him by it, which was just what the rapist wanted.

'No,' he said. 'No one knows, but his victims. And me,' he added.

188

'And you. And Finch. And anyone else who's entitled to open the files.' He turned back to look at her reaction.

Judy blinked at him. 'A police officer?' she said. 'Are you seriously saying—'

'Drummond,' he said, interrupting her, 'was beaten up by police officers.' He looked at her. 'Wasn't he?'

'Yes,' said Judy. 'But that doesn't mean . . . ' She shook her head.

'And couldn't that have been a gentle reminder by two of the boys in blue to keep his mouth shut about his involvement?' said Lloyd. 'Or is that a coincidence too?'

She nodded her head obstinately. 'Yes,' she said. 'Yes, it is a coincidence too. I *know* these men! I hold no brief for what they've done, but it was one of those things! They aren't part of some web of corruption, Lloyd.'

Lloyd wished that he could be as certain. 'This time – and only this time – the rapist throws away his mask and knife?' he said. 'Coincidence?'

Judy didn't speak.

'And the fight at the ground? Another coincidence? You said it yourself! Sharon just wasn't the sort of girl to whip men up into jealous rages – she was killed for a *reason*, Judy.'

Judy thought about that. 'I'm not certain what sort of girl she was,' she said. 'It depends who you listen to. But suppose I accept that Sharon was killed for a reason. Why in God's name would they do that to Bobbie?'

Lloyd looked serious. 'It wouldn't be the first time that rape has been used as a weapon of terror,' he said quietly. 'I think someone was giving Parker a very severe warning as to his future conduct. Whoever did it made it look like one of the series of rapes, that's all.'

'And you think that corrupt police coached him?'

'I don't know, Judy,' he said. 'I hope I'm wrong. But look what happened to you with your car.'

She took a deep breath. 'You said that that was a juvenile reaction that I should ignore,' she said.

'It probably was and is. But . . . ' He shrugged.

'Have you told anyone else your theory?' she demanded.

'No.'

'Good,' she said hotly.

He smiled. 'You're supposed to be picking holes in it,' he said. 'Not taking offence.'

'I will,' she promised him. 'But I think I'd better sleep on it first.' She smiled. 'Are you staying?' she asked.

189

'Better not,' he said.

She was disappointed, and showed it before she had time to disguise it. He wasn't often allowed a glimpse of her feelings; he rather liked it when he was.

'Sorry,' he said. 'But I am in charge of a murder inquiry, and you are a member of the team. I can hardly leave this number as where I can be reached in the middle of the night, can I?'

She stared at him. 'You are unbelievable,' she said. 'I'm only a member of the team because you pulled strings!'

He thought he had better look sheepish. 'All the same,' he said. 'We'd better not rock any boats at this stage.' He was aware that rocking boats was something that was done when he felt like it. Still, she was a bit on the irritating side too, so she could put up with that minor fault.

She smiled again. 'Say goodnight properly, then,' she said.

Simon slammed the front door, and got into the car, firing the engine and driving off into the fog before he had time to think about what he was doing.

It was lies. It was all lies. She had started lying this afternoon, with all that rubbish about Sharon preferring married men, and then . . . His face burned as he remembered the dreadful things she had said once the police had gone.

He couldn't see where he was going. He forced himself to calm down, to slow down, and with the lessening of speed came the voice of reason, which he didn't want to hear. Why would Melissa lie? What would be the point? Besides, he knew Melissa. He knew that she wasn't lying. And what had he really known about Sharon? What she had told him, what she had chosen to show him.

But he had loved her. And even if their unsatisfactory situation had brought out a side of her that he didn't recognise and didn't like, it would never alter that.

Colin had had a very long wait, but he had never once thought of giving up. Not until daylight would he have left his post; the longer the wait, the sweeter the moment. He had stood at the mouth of the alley, in the shadow, watching the road. By day it was busy, but at night it was lonely. And tonight his friend the fog was back, licking round the edge of the alley. It was perfect.

And then when he had seen Lloyd's car pull up he had thought that he'd have to try another night. Perhaps he lived there after all. Or perhaps he was spending the night there, at least. He had stood there for a few minutes, trying to come to terms with the disappointment.

But they hadn't got out of the car, and Colin had reasoned that in that case, Lloyd might not be staying after all. It looked like he had been right, because in the muted glow from the street-lamps, he watched them say a long goodnight.

His heart began to beat quickly as he walked silently into the darkness of the alley, and took the ski-mask from his pocket, pulling it on. Then he took out the knife. Knives scared them. Scared them witless.

He heard the car door open, heard the murmur of voices, and flattened himself against the wall, holding his breath. The alley was wide; wide enough for vans to park and turn at the far end, so that they could unload at the rear of the shops. She would pass him without noticing a thing until it was too late, because he was invisible.

The car door closed, and he listened as her high heels clicked along the pavement.

She couldn't see him, but he could see her, as she paused for a moment at the mouth of the alley, backlit by the street lights. She came out of the mist, and into the blackness; she was quite alone.

And he was the Stealth Bomber.

Twelve

Lloyd might have gone, had it not been for his bladder; he shouldn't have had the tea on top of the coffee. It was his urgent need for her facilities that had changed his mind, though he wouldn't tell Judy that. He caught her up as her footsteps started down the alley.

'Hey, Jude,' he called to her retreating backview, almost ghost-like in the misty darkness.

She turned.

'You've persuaded me.' He quickened his step again to catch up with her almost ghostly presence. 'Aren't there any lights in this place?' he asked.

'There's one over the door,' she said, trying to sort out her keys. 'It's not much use at the best of times, but it must have gone.'

'Tell your landlord to change the bulb,' he said. 'This is danger-ous.' He crunched some glass underfoot, and then tripped over the step he had forgotten was there as the door opened into the equally dark entrance. 'See?' he said.

'Yes, sir.'

She closed the door and kissed him in the dark; he was glad he'd changed his mind, but he wished she would hurry up.

'I'm letting you in on one condition,' she said, as she put on the light, and started upstairs.

'What's that?'

'That you leave the job here.' She smiled, and carried on up, until she stopped, and turned. 'It could have been Whitworth,' she said.

She was going to stand here and discuss it. It served him right for being hypocritical. 'He was at the police station by nine fifteen,' he said.

'He could just have done it. He sees her, finds out that she's told Melissa all about it, kills her in a rage, then carries on with what he was going to do – people have done that before.'

They had. But perhaps with a touch more time at their dis-posal. And Lloyd didn't believe that Whitworth had killed her. Whitworth's illusions were being shattered even as Lloyd had watched; he hadn't found out all about Sharon on Friday night.

192

'And perhaps he *was* at the football match,' she said. 'Perhaps that's why she hung on to the key to the changing room.'

Lloyd shook his head. 'If you ask me, the Whitworths' sexual liaisons have nothing to do with this. I want the result of Drummond's blood-test.' He tried to usher her upstairs.

Judy frowned. 'You think he was with her?' she asked.

'Yes. After Melissa had left her stranded. He knew Sharon all right – that's why he followed her. He's her possessive boyfriend.'

Judy wasn't instantly giving him The Look. He put his predicament out of his mind, and carried on with his scenario.

'He was with her in the changing-rooms. And he may not have killed her, but he saw who did. That's what made him take off like that. That's why he got beaten up – to make sure he kept the knowledge to himself. And Jake Parker knows who killed her too, only he wants to deal with the matter himself. That's why *he* sent us on a wild-goose chase,' he added. 'Or hadn't you noticed?'

Judy shook her head obstinately. 'I don't believe the police are involved in this,' she said.

Fine. Lloyd put his arm round her, and headed for the flat and its plumbing. 'Well,' he said. 'Let's do what you said, and sleep on it. We'll see what it looks like in the morning.'

Jake got back into the car, starting the engine, and pushing in the cigar lighter as he shook a cigarette from the pack.

His heart had all but stopped when the headlights that had loomed out of the fog, and which he had expected to sweep past him as all the others had done, had suddenly been glaring into the car. He had thrown himself across the front seat, and waited until he heard the murmur of voices that meant that the Whitworths' visitors had been admitted.

Then he had recognised the car that had sat in his own driveway a couple of hours ago. Lloyd. God Almighty, did the man never knock off for the day? He had left the car then, and stood in the shadow of the trees that lined the road, until at last Lloyd and Inspector Hill had emerged.

Lloyd had had a good look at the car; he had doubtless taken the number. It was Dennis's car – Jake's Mercedes was too flamboyant to park anywhere unobtrusively, and Dennis's car had a surprising turn of speed for what looked like an old banger.

If Lloyd made inquiries, he'd find Dennis's name on the logbook. And that would mean nothing to him at all.

The lighter popped out, and Jake applied the glow to his cigarette, inhaling deeply before easing off the handbrake and driving off into the fog.

Colin had never had to abort a mission before. He had been an inch from discovery; a millisecond from launching himself at her, when Lloyd had appeared, and he had had to stand still, unbreathing, not daring even to think, until they had shut the door.

He had hardly been able to get to the bike, his legs quivering, his heart pounding at the near-miss. Swooping down on the target only to have to bank away from a barrage of anti-aircraft fire, and return to base.

He sat on the bike, breathing hard. Then he removed the mask, stuffing it back in his pocket, wrapped round the knife. He pulled on his helmet, then pushed the bike on to Riverside, and started her up. He cruised at first, hoping to find another one; fog lay along the river, obscuring the view of the far side where they sometimes took shortcuts on their own through the wood. It was a perfect night for it, and he wanted one badly.

But that might, he supposed, be pushing his luck. So he swung the bike round, and took the road to the airfield, to do the runs in the dark.

His speed and the fog made him almost miss the turn-off for the airfield, causing him to skid on the damp road. He righted the bike, steadying his speed, then slowed, and stopped at the single track road which led on to the old RAF station. He took off the helmet and carried it, half-riding, half-walking the bike on to the old runway, where he laid the helmet down, switched off the headlight, and roared away from a standing start into pitch darkness, the wind on his face, in his hair, wind that he was creating as he hurtled forwards through the still air.

The bike's front wheel flew up as it struck a join in the paving; he rode it on the back wheel, bumping down, wheeling round, revving the engine as he made the return pass, going further each time before he leant into the turn, so that he was moving faster. Faster, faster, smelling hot rubber, jumping with the bike as it met the hidden obstacles, landing, accelerating away again, his jacket billowing out. Wheeling round, head down, the engine screaming in protest, into the pall of exhaust fumes hanging in the motionless air. But it seemed to fuel the anger, and increase his frustration; he stopped before he damaged the bike.

He was on his way home when he saw one of them, all on her own, walking home through Malworth's empty streets. He drove a long way past, bumped the bike into an alley and stopped. He removed his crash helmet, smoothed down his hair, pulled on the mask, and waited.

She didn't make a sound once she saw the knife, and he told her who he was.

Simon watched the stars appear in the pre-dawn sky through the office window as he sat in the darkness at his desk, as he had all night. He had slept fitfully in his swivel chair, waking up at every creak of the old building, every night sound. The fog had gone, moved on by the same wind that was sending clouds to hide the stars almost as soon as they had appeared.

Six months, since he had first regarded this desk as his. Six months since they had come to Stansfield, in response to Lionel's advertisement for a partner. Simon had spent his working life in big partnerships in big cities, where his presence or absence from his desk had been of no concern whatever to his clients. They had simply seen another partner.

The first big city had been where he had met Melissa; he had been dragged to a party at the university, and had taken her to be a student, only to find that she was a lecturer. The youngest lecturer since God knows when. She had of course had a sparkling academic record, unlike him. He had asked her out, once a couple of drinks had made him brave enough to take the rejection, but to his surprise she had agreed, even sounded enthusiastic about it.

They had seen quite a lot of one another; he never lost the faint feeling of surprise. The first time they spent the night together, he had expected to be the last; she was clearly better versed in such things than he. The first time she went home to visit her parents, he expected never to see her again. But back she came, turning up at his flat as though she really wanted to be with him. She had been writing the odd article then, doing the odd book review. His circle of acquaintances had included university professors and literary editors, with whom he had always felt a little awkward, because they had expected him to be as bright and expressive as Melissa.

She had been offered a job on a literary magazine, then, and had switched careers effortlessly, while he had still worked doggedly to improve his lot in his. They had married not long after that, he just a little surprised that she turned up. Then, he had found himself at literary lunches and book launches, chatting to editors and publishers and authors that he had to pretend to know, sometimes even to have read. Then a glossy women's magazine had come head-hunting her. It had meant a move to London; she had asked him how he felt about that, but working in a big practice in a big city was the same job, wherever the city; they had moved to London.

Her brief had altered; then it had been best-selling authors and marketing junkets, trips to Wimbledon and Grand Prix races. He had rather liked that; he had been able to escape from the suffocating hospitality tent and watch the sport. Then she had moved into more general journalism, and he had found himself accompanying her to parties where everyone was a household name.

And still he had been a minor partner in a major partnership. The only difference that Simon had been able to detect had been that the legal work was almost exclusively on inner city development, and even more boring than before.

When he had seen Lionel's advertisement, he had had to read it twice to make certain. Here was someone who wanted *him* – his expertise, his field, his line of country. Until that time, he hadn't really thought of himself as having one. And Melissa hadn't thought twice; she had given up her job at the magazine, and offered her services to the local paper in Stansfield, who were bowled over to have her, as they should be.

He had finally achieved something. He was Whitworth of Evans and Whitworth, not Whitworth in the Conveyancing Department. He had something concrete to offer Lionel, and he hadn't even had to put money into the business. Melissa enjoyed working for *The Chronicle* more than she had the other magazines, because she was the features editor, and could instigate projects, and because she met real people, not packaged celebrities.

He had met a real person too. He had met Sharon, who had at first been a little shy of him, then opened out a little as she realised that she had to show him the ropes. He felt tears prick his eyes. Why would they all lie? Melissa, the police . . . but they couldn't all be lying.

She had seemed so . . . so innocent. So honest. She had never read a piece of literary criticism in her life; she hadn't been so much as on nodding terms with anyone remotely distinguished or famous. She had thought that he was clever and knowledgeable, and he had had the sheer luxury of not having to run just to keep up with her.

He supposed she had massaged his ego, but he couldn't believe that she had employed deliberate guile in so doing. He had fallen in love with her, and she with him. She hadn't liked the deception; she had begged him to tell Melissa and get it over with. Perhaps she had despaired of his ever doing that; perhaps that was why she had done what he had to believe she had done.

Though that hardly explained the things she was supposed to have said, and what the chief inspector had said about her having been with some man half an hour before she died. He wouldn't lie about a thing like that.

He had been taken in. But why?

Mac lay fully clothed on the bed as the sun, obscured by cloud, rose invisibly in the sky, casting a grey light into his room. He hadn't slept; he had smoked all his cigarettes. He had heard the rain come just after it got light; it was drizzling miserably against his unshaded window.

It had meant nothing to her, nothing at all. And he had lied for her right from the start. He had lied, first for her reputation, and then for her freedom. He had wiped that tape, he had been arrested, he had been interviewed by the police every day since it had happened. He believed that she had killed Sharon Smith, and it made no difference at all to how he felt about her.

He had been born again somewhere in the few brief hours he had spent with Melissa; he had seen hope steal over the dark horizon; he had thought, just for a moment, that he could hear someone cheering him on, that he had emerged from the desperate obscurity and become Mad Mac McDonald again. But that could never be. He had a past, but he had no future; Mac had already been down that road, and he was damned if he was going down it again.

He grabbed his jacket, rattled downstairs, and slammed the door before his landlady had time to get out of bed to see what he was up to.

Lionel pulled up outside the office. It was very early; he didn't know how soon the fraud squad went about the business of freezing accounts and descending on suspicious solicitors.

Frances had been . . . well, she had been strong. And she had been supportive. She hadn't just behaved as though he was telling her that he'd bumped the car, which he had been afraid of. She hadn't packed her bags to get out before the disgrace, which he'd have understood. She hadn't asked him how he could have done such a thing to her. She had listened, and she had said that Lionel must know who the best man was to defend him. He ought to put that in motion, she said, as soon as possible.

She had told him to go to the office early. She had advised against any more creative accounting in an attempt to absolve himself from blame; she thought he should simply tell them the truth. That he had been tempted, and had done what Parker had suggested. But she did think that he might want to take anything private, anything he didn't really want policemen or anyone else picking up.

So that was why he was here. He was about to be charged with attempted fraud and embezzlement and goodness knows what all; Parker would probably get off scot free. Lionel would go to prison, almost certainly. And would be struck off without any doubt. His career, his life, was in ruins.

And yet he felt more at peace with himself than he had for the last twenty years. He frowned as he inserted his key in the door; it was already unlocked. Well, if they had done some sort of dawn raid in his absence, he would at least be able to challenge all their evidence.

But there was no sign of policemen. Burglars? Surely not. Lionel walked quietly through the office, checking each room; he literally jumped off the ground when Simon's door opened.

He looked like death. Unshaven, crumpled, bags under his eyes.

'What are you doing here?' Lionel asked.

Simon looked at his watch. 'What are you?' he asked, and went back into his office, dragging himself back to the desk.

This hardly seemed the moment to tell him, but he might not get another chance.

Judy and Lloyd slept late; the rain had stopped the sun performing its wake-up service, and they had forgotten to set the alarm. Lloyd was always impossible when he was behind schedule in the morning; his routine for waking up was disturbed, and as a consequence it was as well to ignore him as much as possible.

Judy grabbed at the skirt that she had uncharacteristically left over the back of the chair on Saturday, when she had changed her clothes and had a bath and tried to pretend that she hadn't been the victim of a pathetic act of revenge. She pulled her clothes on, and glanced at herself in the mirror as she raced past, coming out into the hallway to hear the hum of her battery shaver now that she had vacated the bathroom, which Lloyd had considered was not a moment too soon.

That would be wrong too, she thought. He didn't have time for a wet shave, and that ridiculous shaver wouldn't take the fuzz off a peach. She was proved right when he emerged from the bathroom, declaring that he looked like Desperate bloody Dan, and that they were going to the Whitworths again.

Judy stopped in the act of putting on a shoe while hopping about on one foot. 'If we're not going straight to work, why are we killing ourselves to get out?' she asked.

'I rang Tom while you were in the bathroom,' he said, ignoring her question. 'It gave me something to do while I was waiting. And

I've brought him up to date on what we were told last night – he'll pass it on to Barstow for the team-talk.'

Judy put on her shoe. 'And why are we going to the Whitworths?'

'Because either they are involved in this or they're not, and I have to know one way or the other,' he said, draping his tie round his collar, and looking round for the mirror that had been in the hall until she had put the pegs up. 'Bedroom,' she said.

He stood in front of the wardrobe, and called out to her as she hastily applied make-up. Clearly, calling on the Whitworths was to make their exit from the flat no more leisurely.

'On the one hand,' he said, 'I've got Freddie telling me this girl was inexperienced with men. On the other, I've got Melissa Whitworth telling me she was a vamp. On the whole, I think that Freddie is less biased.'

'So?' said Judy, cautiously.

'So at best Mrs Whitworth's distress is exaggerating her impression of Sharon – and at worst—' he came out of the bedroom— 'she's lying. I have to know if that's for her husband's benefit or ours.'

'Or Sharon was lying,' said Judy. 'To Mrs Whitworth.'

'Why?'

Judy dabbed lipstick on to a hankie. 'To make damn sure she broke up the marriage,' she said.

Lloyd looked interested, and then remembered that he was in a bad mood. 'And,' he went on, 'in view of her inexperience, it's reasonable to suppose that the man that Sharon was with was Whitworth.'

Judy shook her head in wonderment. 'I said that last night,' she said. 'You said it was Drummond!'

'And that if it was Whitworth,' Lloyd continued, as though she hadn't spoken, 'then he is lying about not being at the football match. And there seems little reason for him to do that, unless he saw something that he wants to keep from us. Like his wife, who was supposed to be at home at the time. Perhaps she didn't just happen to see Sharon and pick her up again. Perhaps she was watching, and waiting.'

'So you've changed your mind about police corruption and Drummond seeing the murder?' she asked mischievously.

Lloyd scowled. 'No, since you ask. But I mustn't have tunnel vision. Besides, we know these two were both involved with Sharon on Friday night, and we don't have an ounce of proof that Drummond was. Yet.'

Judy sighed, and they went out to face Monday morning and the Whitworths. A drizzle that was barely visible, blown by a persistent wind, was soaking into everything; the warmth that had lifted the other days after the pre-dawn fog was no more. Clouds were streaking, grey and dismal, across the sky.

A lot of little puzzles, Lloyd had said, thought Judy, as they drove out of Malworth. She took her notebook from her bag, and looked through the notes, pausing at each query. Some had been resolved.

Wearing leisure suit to work? That had a cross beside it, and a description of what she had been wearing to work. And it was reasonable, Judy supposed, to change out of working clothes and into something more suitable for watching a football match. Why should that entail actually buying clothes specially? That had seemed odd, but perhaps they had the answer now.

Newspaper cutting. It had been in the pocket of Sharon's skirt; that should have suggested to them that the appointment with Melissa Fletcher/Whitworth had been made during the course of the day, and from what Evans had said, it seemed that it must have been; she had told her mother that she would be home at seven, and that would explain the change of plan. But someone who was solicitous enough of her mother's feelings to move back in when her father died had not rung to stop a meal being made for her? Still – she would have been under some emotional stress, given what she was going to do. And perhaps she had wanted to wear something new, something special, to boost her confidence.

Along the dual carriageway, through the village, past Lloyd's flat, over the roundabout, and up Byford Road, where Melissa had picked up Sharon Smith. And she had wanted to be taken back to the ground, but not, it would seem, in order to collect the clothes she had left there, though she still had the key.

Key. Parker had lent her the key, and she had kept it, intending to go back and pick up her other clothes. And perhaps the altercation between Barnes and Parker had alarmed her enough to forget them. But when she went back with Melissa Whitworth? Surely she would have remembered by then? And yet, she hadn't mentioned them, or given that as her reason for wanting to go back. That was also a little odd.

Past the old post office, its grassed surrounds no longer on the Council mowing list, and obviously not on the new owner's either. The tall, yellowing grass shifted wetly in the dismal wind. The road at the rear that once had led to Mitchell Engineering now led nowhere, and cars were parked along it, belonging to those who worked in the little offices and shops of the village. This was where Melissa Whitworth had had her close shave.

Almost ran over an unlit motorbike. That had to be Drummond.

He had said that he had left the football ground at nine, and had been driving around. In which case, what had made him decide on his death or glory ride? Perhaps Lloyd was right; perhaps he had seen the murder. Or perhaps he had been murdering Sharon Smith himself. But there was nothing, either on his clothes or Sharon's, to suggest that he had been anywhere near her; no witness, no shred of evidence. Finch couldn't find that there had ever been any kind of connection between them. Logic said that he didn't know her, and her history suggested that she did not have quickies in the changing rooms with men she had never met. So he had not been with Sharon after Melissa Whitworth had left her. But what *had* he been doing?

Further on, and the football ground was on their left, already back to normal. No blue and white ribbon, no cars and vans. Much the way it had been when Sharon went back up there with Melissa Whitworth.

Football ground. Parker and Evans were involved in a fraud over the development at the football ground. Melissa Whitworth had met Sharon at the football ground. There had been a fight at the football ground. Whitworth even took Parker back there when he had been released.

Why did Barnes start the fight? Lloyd's question. *Did* Barnes start the fight? Judy wouldn't take Parker's word for anything.

Why did Parker change his story? Lloyd's question again. To keep the police out of what he regarded as his business, Parker said.

Why did Drummond follow Sharon? Because he knew her, according to Lloyd. Because perhaps he was the over-possessive single man, about whom she may not have been generalising. But that didn't accord with the evidence.

And all of them there, at the football ground. There were an awful lot of coincidences, she thought gloomily. She could see why Lloyd thought that Bobbie Chalmers was just one too many, and turned to her notes on the rape.

Lloyd was wrong. She wouldn't allow herself to believe that someone had leaked confidential information for such a purpose. And yet, he had got rid of the mask and knife this time; why? Why was this time different? But Lloyd couldn't be right. He couldn't. Merrill might be right – Bobbie might know who the rapist was.

'Are you not speaking to me?' Lloyd asked.

She smiled. 'Sorry. Just reviewing the situation.'

'The situation is that we are having to go and waste more of our time with these . . . ' He made a dismissive noise when, for once in his life, he failed to come up with a word.

'You're letting them render you speechless,' she said, with a smile. 'You really do disapprove of them, don't you?'

'Don't you?' he asked, signalling right at the top of the hill, on the home stretch to the Whitworths' house.

'No, I don't think so,' said Judy. 'Melissa Whitworth's all right. I don't know him.'

Lloyd took his eyes off the road, the better to show Judy his astonishment. 'We are about to question her for the fourth time about her movements on Friday night,' he said. 'For all you know she strangled that girl!'

'With a man's tie?'

'Probably her husband's tie,' muttered Lloyd sourly. He didn't like it when his theories were dented, even when he didn't go along with them himself. 'She went home to get it specially.'

'According to your last bit of deduction, she didn't go home at all. And I don't believe she killed her,' said Judy. 'Any more than you do.'

Lloyd sighed loudly as the house, perched on its own on the edge of acres of fields, came into view in the distance. 'How can you say she's all right?' he asked. 'All you know about her is that she jumps into bed with total strangers.'

Judy laughed. 'She jumped into bed with someone that she had met briefly. When she had had too many drinks and too much to put up with from her husband – marriage is like that sometimes.'

'I see,' said Lloyd. 'You're back on that, are you?' On the exposed bypass, he flicked the wipers to full speed as rain misted his windscreen. 'If you married me, I could look forward to your hanging about hotels getting drunk and looking for rough trade, is that it?'

Judy smiled as they heard the siren; she turned to see the area car, lights flashing, indicating that it was going to overtake. It squealed to a halt outside the Whitworths' house, and its two occupants met the man who was running down the path towards them.

Lloyd pulled in behind the police car, and Judy leapt out to see that it was Gil McDonald, of all people, who had run to meet it.

'She's dead!' he was shouting. 'She's dead! Just . . . just the same way. She's . . . '

And he sank to the grass verge on his knees, his head in his hands.

202

Thirteen

A police car. Lionel had thought that they might at least turn up in an unmarked car. The village would be buzzing by mid-morning at this rate. He frowned. Two uniformed constables? He had rather been expecting a tough, gimlet-eyed chief inspector, with two sharp young detective sergeants in tow. Surely two constables weren't about to examine his accounting records?

No. They'd be there with the warrant or whatever. And Simon thought he had problems, just because he'd had a spat with Melissa and lost his job. There were times when he would have given almost anything for Frances to start yelling at him. And what wouldn't he give never to have seen the inside of a solicitor's office in the first place? But it had been expected. That was what his family had always done.

Evans and Son and Grandson – that was what his grandfather had called the firm when Lionel joined it. Fortunately – in some respects, because he had really been rather fond of his grandfather – the old man had died not long afterwards, and Lionel's father had contracted the name to Evans and Evans. Which was what it had continued to be called even after his father's death. Until Simon came along. Lionel had realised that having his name on the brass plate meant more to Simon than his percentage; it had been the lure that had hooked him.

Lionel had tried to make Simon go home and have a shave and some breakfast, but he was just sitting at his desk, staring into space. He could hardly have been expected to be any too pleased at Lionel's news, of course. It was hard to know how to tell someone that there had never really been a job for him anyway, and now that the Evans part of Evans and Whitworth was about to be publicly disgraced, the Whitworth part should think about moving on.

That had seemed to upset him more than anything. Much more than the bust-up with his wife – more even, than Sharon's death, in a way. He'd hidden his feelings about that in the vain hope that his wife wouldn't find out. But he couldn't hide his feelings about losing his job.

There had been no knock on his office door. If they were looking through the stuff in the secretary's office without so much as telling him that they were on the premises . . .

He walked across the room, and stepped out into the corridor. The policemen were taking Simon out. They stopped, one either side of Simon, almost having to hold him up.

'Melissa's dead,' Simon said, his voice expressionless.

Lionel's eyes grew wide. 'Dead?' he repeated.

'I think,' said Simon very slowly, 'that they think I killed her.'

'No one said that, sir. We just have to ask you a few questions, that's all.'

'Oh, my God – what happened? When did it happen?'

Simon looked at the policemen, who looked at Lionel.

'Do you want me to come, Simon?' Lionel asked, forgetting for the moment his own appointment with the constabulary.

Simon shook his head. 'I didn't kill her,' he said.

'No, of course not. I just thought—'

But Simon shook his head again, and was escorted to the waiting car.

'What were you doing there?' Finch asked.

Mac couldn't think straight. She was dead. She was *dead*. He looked at Sergeant Finch. 'I . . . I just went to see her,' he said.

Finch looked disbelieving. 'Odd time to visit someone, wasn't it?'

'She came to see me yesterday,' he said, still unwilling to believe what he had seen with his own eyes. It was some sort of cruel joke. It was a mistake, it wasn't true. She wasn't dead. She wasn't.

'What happened when she came to see you?'

'Nothing,' said Mac, shaking his head, bewildered. She had sat in the armchair, he had sat on the bed. Nothing had happened.

'Why were you at Mrs Whitworth's house at eight thirty in the morning?'

Mac looked up at him. 'Do you have a cigarette?' he asked.

'I don't smoke. Answer the question.'

He needed a cigarette. They'd brought him tea, but he needed a cigarette.

'I wanted to see her.'

Finch sat down with a sigh. 'What about?' he asked.

Mac shook his head. He couldn't talk about it. He couldn't think about it. The last thing he'd said to her was get out. Get out. And now she was dead, and he couldn't answer questions about him and Melissa. It was private, it was his hurt – he didn't want to share it.

204

'Why did you go to see her?'

'It's got nothing to do with you!' Mac shouted.

'You have found two bodies in four days, McDonald! I think that's got something to do with me. Why were you there?'

Oh God, he needed a cigarette. 'She – she told me she didn't want to see me any more,' he said.

'When? When did she tell you that?'

Mac looked at him with eyes that wouldn't focus. He had to think about every word before he understood it. 'Please, can you get me a cigarette?' he asked.

Finch shook his head. 'When did she tell you she didn't want to see you any more?' he asked.

'Yesterday,' said Mac, now that he had sorted out the question.

'Why didn't she want to see you any more?'

'She – she thought I'd been blackmailing her,' said Mac.

'She didn't want to see you because she thought you were blackmailing her?'

Mac shook his head. 'No – no, she didn't want to see me because I *wasn't*,' he said.

'Make sense, McDonald!' he shouted.

Mac licked his lips. He needed a cigarette. 'She saw her husband,' he said, trying to explain. 'That's why she didn't give you the tape. She thought I was . . . ' He ran out of steam. Finch would never understand anyway.

'And this morning?' Finch ran his hands over his face. 'What time did you get there?'

Where? Mac needed a cigarette.

'What time?' Finch picked up his paper cup, screwing it up, throwing it into the bin as he spoke.

Mac frowned, and drank some more tea, but it was cold, and he wanted a cigarette. 'I don't know,' he said. 'I walked. I don't know.'

'Were you angry?'

No. He hadn't ever been angry with her.

'What did you do when you got there?'

Where? Mac had lost the thread.

'Answer the question, McDonald.' Finch stood up, and opened the door in answer to a knock. He held a brief conversation with someone, but Mac couldn't hear what they were saying.

'What happened when you got to the house?' asked the other man, who until now had stayed silent.

'I've told you.'

Finch left the room, and Harris recorded the fact.

'I went in.'

'Did you see anyone else?'

Mac shook his head. 'Her car was outside, but it was the only one there. Her husband must have gone to work. I wasn't going to go in if he was there – I didn't want to get her into . . . The door was open, though. I knocked, but no one answered. So I went in. And she was . . . she was lying there. Just like on Friday. Just the same. Exactly the same. I thought I hadn't been awake all night after all. I'd fallen asleep. I was dreaming. I . . . ' He took a deep breath to steady himself. 'And I phoned the police,' he said. 'Again.'

'You're sure that's how it happened? Maybe she was there when you arrived. Maybe she opened the door to you. Maybe you asked her to reconsider, and she wouldn't. Isn't that what happened, Mac? Did you have a row? Did she tell you to get out?'

No. No. He'd told her to get out. He closed his eyes.

'Did Sharon upset you too?' he asked.

Sharon. Sharon Smith. A name on a tape. That was all; he didn't even know what she looked like. Just a name on a tape. Had she caused all this?

'Did she say she didn't want to see you any more either? Is that what it is? Women don't appreciate you, do they, Mac?'

Mac shook his head slowly. The rain that had fallen steadily all morning, soaking him on his long walk to Melissa, brushed dismally against the window, blown on the wind.

'Tell me again about this morning.'

Mac stared at him. 'I've just told you,' he said. 'I've told you over and over again. He must have killed her.'

'Who?'

Mac made little patterns on the formica with his finger as he spoke. 'Whitworth,' he said.

Harris looked sceptical. 'Why would he do that?' he asked.

'Because of Sharon Smith,' Mac said. 'Because of me. I don't know.'

'We have to ask you to stay here, Mr McDonald,' said Harris. 'While we make further inquiries.

Mac nodded. 'Can someone get me cigarettes?' he asked.

Harris sighed. 'I'll see what I can do,' he said.

Simon sat in the interview room, unshaven, unmoving, unblinking, as Chief Inspector Lloyd and Sergeant Finch waited for some sort of explanation that he couldn't give.

The two people who meant most to him in his life were gone. People survived that; they lost families in accidents, in natural disasters. In unnatural disasters, like bombs on planes. But someone

206

had singled out Sharon and Melissa, and he didn't know who, or why. Or how to survive it.

They thought he had done it. Perhaps he had. Perhaps while his mind told him he had been driving along a street or sleeping in a chair at his desk, he had in reality been strangling the two women he cared for.

This was the interview room where he had seen Parker on Friday night. He had been in dozens in his time; in the early days, he had inclined towards criminal law. He had enjoyed it; there was a pleasing camaraderie in the weekly magistrates' court sessions. A kind of shorthand evolved between solicitors and justices, and even between the justices and regular petty offenders.

But there had been more money in conveyancing. You would never get fat on legal aid.

'Did you murder your wife, Mr Whitworth?' Finch asked.

Whitworth shook his head slowly.

'You were very angry with her, weren't you?'

The shake turned into a nod. 'Yes,' he said.

'Why?'

He lifted his eyes painfully to Lloyd's. 'She said such dreadful things about Sharon,' he said.

Lloyd nodded.

'And they weren't true. I know they weren't.'

Lloyd sat down. 'Why would she lie?' he asked.

Whitworth dropped his eyes again. 'I think . . . ' He stopped, and shook his head again. 'I thought,' he amended, 'that she must have – you know. Killed her.' It hurt him physically to say the word.

'What made you think that?' Finch asked.

Lloyd stood up, and feigned interest in the cabinet of the cassette recorder. Simon looked over at him. He knew police tricks at interviews. Asking sudden questions, non sequiturs, in an attempt to catch people off guard. That was why he had wandered off; he wanted to listen, then throw in a question to catch Simon out.

'I didn't believe that Sharon had said those things,' he said. 'That she preferred married men – that I needed the excitement. That I hated her.' He was shaking his head again, as he spoke. 'She said that, you know. After you'd gone. That Sharon said I felt so guilty that I hated her. I thought Melissa was making it all up.'

Lloyd seemed to be paying no attention, but he was, of course. Simon knew that, and almost gave him the answers to Finch's questions, so much in charge was he of an interview in which he appeared to be taking no part.

'But you believe it now, Mr Whitworth?' asked Finch.

Lloyd was watching him closely as he answered. 'I believe she said it,' Simon conceded. 'But it wasn't true. I was the first man she had ever been with. I know I was. And we'd only made love a few times. She . . . she didn't like using the office. She was always afraid Lionel would come back for something.' He smiled sadly. 'We'd stay late, but sometimes – most times – we would just talk. Get to know one another.'

'But you had sex with her on Friday, didn't you?' Finch said.

'Yes,' Simon said, miserably. That made it sound so sordid, and it wasn't. It wasn't.

'Whose idea was it to use the changing rooms at the sports ground? Hers?'

Simon frowned. 'We didn't,' he said.

'Sharon got the key from Parker, saying she wanted to change her clothes – did you meet her there?'

'No,' he said. 'We were in the office.'

'But she left the office at six,' said Lloyd. 'We know she did. She went to the superstore and bought the clothes she was wearing.' He walked over to Simon, coming close, making him shrink back a little in his chair. 'Did you meet her at the ground?' he demanded. 'Did she engineer it all? Get both you and your wife up there, hoping to bring something to a head?'

'No.' Simon groaned.

'It all looks as though it was arranged, Mr Whitworth.'

Simon covered his face with his hands. 'I loved her,' he said. 'And I didn't want to hurt Melissa – I didn't want to hurt either of them!'

He heard Lloyd sit down again. 'But you did hurt them,' he said, his voice gentle. 'Didn't you?'

'They're dead,' Simon said distractedly, his face still buried in his hands. 'They're dead. They're both dead. I don't understand.' He bent over the table, in physical pain.

'But you didn't mean to hurt them,' said Lloyd. 'We understand that.'

The pain went; Simon knew that tone of voice. Lloyd thought what he'd said was some sort of confession. He sat up. 'I didn't kill them,' he said.

'What did you mean when you said you didn't want to hurt them?'

'I just meant . . . I thought I could . . . ' He shook his head. 'You know,' he said. He had thought he could have his cake and eat it. Have both of them, hurt neither of them. 'But I did hurt them,' he said. 'If Sharon really did say those things to Melissa – she must have been desperate. She must have wanted to break us up any way she could. Because I didn't have the guts to tell Melissa I was leaving.'

208

'You thought your wife had killed her?'

He nodded.

'Is that why you killed your wife?'

Whitworth sighed. 'I didn't,' he said. 'I didn't. I don't understand. Someone . . . '

'What happened last night after we left?' asked Lloyd.

'She . . . she kept saying things about Sharon. I just walked out. I slept in the office.'

Lloyd got up. 'All right, Mr Whitworth,' he said. 'We'll leave you to think very hard about what happened last night. Then we'll talk to you again.'

No. No, he couldn't bear to talk about it any more. 'I'm not answering any more questions,' he said, surprised at the firmness of his own voice now that he had come to even as negative a decision as that. 'I've told you what happened. I'm not obliged to say anything.'

'Neither you are,' said Lloyd abruptly. 'Interview terminated.'

He was taken to a cell. He sank down on to the bench, and doubled up with the pain again.

'Do you need a doctor?' the constable asked.

'No,' said Simon.

He supposed he needed a solicitor. But he couldn't bear the thought of anyone he knew seeing him in this condition. If only he knew why they had died. Why Sharon had said those things to Melissa. He couldn't have been that wrong about her. She couldn't have been that good an actress. And even if she had been – why would she have bothered?

The money? This money that Jake Parker and Lionel were misappropriating? Dodgy share certificates, bogus land deeds – his head had still been spinning with Lionel's confession when the police had come to tell him about Melissa.

Sharon surely hadn't been mixed up in that.

Dennis Parry. Lloyd looked at the name of the registered owner of the car he had seen outside the Whitworths', and sighed. Someone who had broken down, as Judy had said. Nothing to do with this. He glanced out of the window, and saw Judy's car pull in.

He waylaid her before she went diving off anywhere else. 'Judy,' he said, and jerked his head towards his office.

She followed him in, shaking rain from her hair.

'Anything?' he asked.

She shrugged a little. 'Freddie says that it is an exact copy of Sharon's murder,' she said. 'Well – he wasn't as definite as that, but

209

that's what he meant. He'll be doing the post-mortem tomorrow –
he can't fit it in today.'

'I've seen Whitworth,' he said. 'He denies everything, of course.
I've left him to stew for a while.'

Judy sat down. 'We couldn't have known,' she said.

'You saw him! He couldn't wait for us to leave so that he could
get his hands on her!' Lloyd shouted. 'You checked that it was all
right for us to leave!'

Judy nodded. 'And she said that it was,' she reminded him.

Lloyd sat down, little comforted by her words. Andrews would
be here any minute, and he wouldn't think that they couldn't have
known what Whitworth would do. 'How long had she been dead?'
he asked.

She looked a little unwilling to impart the information. 'Freddie
saw her half an hour ago, and his estimate is eight to ten hours.'

About five minutes after they left, in other words. And he had
made a joke about rows. He had discounted the Whitworths and
their petty affairs because he was so certain that the fraud must
have been at the bottom of it, so convinced that Drummond had
been lying. Andrews had warned him about that, which was the
only reason he had gone to the Whitworths again that morning.

'Lloyd,' Judy said sternly, reading his thoughts. 'If she didn't
think she was in danger, why should we have done?'

'Because that's our job,' he said.

But he had to snap out of the comforting self-pity, and he had
more news to impart to Judy. She would like this news, though. It
was one of the few things he didn't feel guilty about. He got up
and went over to the door, closing it. 'Speaking about jobs,' he
said. 'I got a wink tipped this morning.'

Judy twisted round to look at him, her eyes instantly suspicious,
just from his tone of voice.

He smiled. 'Barstow's got that job – he's going as soon as we
can find a replacement.'

Her eyes were wary now.

'Apparently,' Lloyd said, 'HQ need Barstow very soon – and want
the post here filled without a gap. In the circumstances, they think
it sensible for you to transfer permanently.'

Eyes widening, as she tried to fathom his reaction. She frowned.
'And you didn't block it?' she asked.

He smiled. 'As if.'

'But if I worked here, we'd have to continue the way we are,' she
said. 'Domestically.'

Lloyd nodded. He knew when he was beaten. They were going
to continue the way they were until Judy decided otherwise. In the

meantime, he'd rather have her working with him than never see her at all. And it really had come from headquarters this time.

'And you don't mind?' she said.

He shrugged. 'Not if you don't. You'll hear officially this afternoon, I understand. It won't affect your chances of promotion – they just think you'd be better off not at Malworth.'

What his informant had actually said was 'After promotion is she? Well, she's good – the Chief likes her. She could go far in personnel, admin work – but she's gone as far as she's going in CID if you ask me – you want a small wager on it?' Lloyd didn't tell Judy that bit. Especially since he hadn't taken the bet.

He put on a cassette of Whitworth's interview, and let Judy hear it. She listened, her face thoughtful, until he switched off the machine.

'What do you think?' he asked.

'He's a mess,' she said.

'Mm,' said Lloyd. 'But is he a mess because his wife and girlfriend have both been murdered for no apparent reason, or is he a mess because he murdered them?'

She shrugged. 'That's what we have to find out,' she said. 'The lab or Freddie might come up with a bit more this time.'

'What does your instinct tell you?'

She smiled. 'It tells me it hasn't got the faintest idea,' she said. 'But while there might have been another motive for Sharon's murder, I can't see that there's one here. This has got to be domestic.'

'Yes,' said Lloyd, heavily, sitting down.

'Perhaps he thought if he killed them both, that would solve his dilemma,' she said.

Nothing would surprise Lloyd. 'Either way, it looks as if he killed his wife after we left last night,' he said. 'I'd better go and confess to Andrews.'

Finch knocked and came in. 'Am I interrupting, sir?' he asked.

'I welcome the interruption,' said Lloyd.

Finch pulled a chair from the wall. 'OK?' he said.

Lloyd nodded. It was the same fine line that he himself walked with his superiors; the minimum of deference. He liked it, but he didn't think it would go down too well with Andrews. He hoped that Finch had some native cunning in these matters.

He sighed aloud. He had had the CID to himself for six months until Andrews had arrived. He had already been told that he mustn't let subordinates become too familiar, that he mustn't encourage the use of first names. No fear of that, sir, he had said with utmost honesty. Even Judy didn't know his first name, so he was damn sure Finch wasn't going to. He'd been chewed out about his fixation with Drummond, and now . . . Now transfer to traffic was staring him in the face. Judy would probably get his job – he should have taken his HQ mole up on his wager.

Finch looked anxiously at him, and Lloyd realised that it was the sigh that had caused him to delay saying whatever it was that he had been going to say. He smiled. 'Fire away, Tom,' he said.

'I've got the strength on what went down on Friday night with Drummond,' he said. 'If you still want it, that is.'

The strength on what went down. Oh, well. Finch was observant, and reasonably literate; he was bright, and he wasn't a yes-man. You couldn't expect an elegant turn of phrase into the bargain. 'Yes,' he said. 'I still want it.'

'Back in August, these two were on traffic duty in the centre of Malworth, which consists mainly of catching people running the red lights in the evening,' he said. 'It has to be the most boring shift in the history of policing.'

Lloyd nodded.

'Then what should they see but a motorbike without lights going through on red at about sixty miles an hour. So they give chase – but you know the Chief's orders about high-speed chases in built-up areas. They don't radio in.'

Lloyd shrugged acceptance of that.

'Then he starts ducking down alleyways and up steps and all sorts of daft tricks, and they lose him.' Finch leant forward a little. 'The first rape took place that night, but they don't make any connection, because it was in Stansfield. But then on Friday night, they're operating a radar trap on the dual carriageway just beyond where the speed limit comes down to forty. And along comes a motorbike, without lights, doing about eighty. They give chase again, and he isn't far enough into Malworth to get the opportunity to do his trick riding, so they catch him.'

'And beat him up because he gave them the slip last time?' said Lloyd.

Tom wrinkled his nose. 'Not exactly,' he said. 'They've stopped him for speeding, and riding without lights. They've warned him that he might be prosecuted for reckless driving, and they should have just let him go. But they want to get a bit of their own back, so they hang on to him, in the hope of finding something. The bike's his, his insurance and licence are in order, he's not drunk – they search him for drugs, and find out that he's dressed in black from top to toe. Jacket, sweater, jeans, boots, gloves.'

Lloyd waited.

'By this time there have been two more rapes, and the girls had all described someone wearing black. But you can't arrest someone for wearing black,' said Tom. 'So they ask him where he's been – and they ask him about the previous time they saw him. He catches on to the fact that they didn't report chasing him that first night, so he knows they're on dodgy ground. He starts saying things on purpose to make them think he's the rapist, but nothing they could hold him on. They go back to the car. Then he calls out something about getting their wives, and what he'll do to them. One of them lost his rag, and the rest you know.'

'They believed Drummond was the rapist, and didn't even mention it to the incident room?' Judy said.

Finch shrugged. 'They were in too deep by the time they'd thumped him,' he said.

Lloyd sighed. 'Thanks, Tom,' he said.

Tom left, and Lloyd looked at Judy. 'What do you think of their story?' he asked.

'Sounds just about stupid enough,' she said. 'And Drummond sounds just about weird enough to fantasise about being the rapist,' she said. 'From what you've said.'

He was indeed. Well weird enough, as Finch would say.

'He dresses like him,' she said. 'He follows girls, he watches people in cars . . . he wanted the traffic men to think he was – he wanted you to think he was. Too bad for him that he's the one person we know it isn't.'

So Drummond got beaten up because they thought he was the rapist, not because he'd been with Sharon, and then seen her murder. He was just a voyeur, as Judy had said. And when nothing at all had happened in the car, he'd made something more exciting up. And that meant that Lloyd was in deep trouble, because it had been a domestic all along; he had left Mrs Whitworth in extreme danger, while he pursued a shaky, unsubstantiated theory of his own.

'You were right,' he said to Judy. 'I was wrong. Simple as that.'

Judy never looked smug when she had been proved right. He did. He knew he did. The phone rang, and he picked it up with a shrug, expecting an angry summons upstairs.

'Lloyd? Ron Merrill.'

'Hello, Ron – what can I do you for?' said Lloyd, sounding as though he hadn't a care in the world.

'We caught the bastard. Well – two fitters coming home from doing a double shift did. Running back to his bike after he'd attacked a girl. And you were right all along.'

Lloyd frowned. What had he been right all along about?

213

'It was Colin Drummond,' said Merrill.

Lloyd stared at the phone.

'No one's had a squeak out of him yet, but I'm about to have a go, and I'll make the little bugger think hard about the mess he's in.'

An apt description of Mr Drummond, thought Lloyd, still tongue-tied. If Merrill had been in the room, he would have kissed him.

'Are you still there?' asked Merrill.

Lloyd smiled. 'Yes,' he said. 'I'm still here.'

'Tell Judy, will you?'

'Oh, yes,' said Lloyd. 'I'll tell Judy.' He hung up.

'Tell Judy what?' she asked.

He told her.

'But it can't be him,' was Judy's instant, illogical, and un-Judy-like response. 'How could he be in two places at once?'

'He wasn't,' said Lloyd. That was the whole point, as he had told Judy last night. Drummond *hadn't* raped Bobbie Chalmers; someone else had, someone who knew exactly what Drummond's MO was. Lloyd, who had hoped all along that he was wrong about that, was now a very relieved man. He sat back, hands behind his head, thinking it through.

Judy got out her notebook, and turned the pages, shaking her head. 'Maybe he has an identical twin,' she said, with a reluctant half-smile.

Lloyd smiled. 'It answers all the puzzles,' he said. 'Sharon spent the first half – as it turns out, the only half – of the match in the changing room with someone. Whitworth, presumably. I think he's denying it because he caught a glimpse of his wife, and he thinks she killed Sharon. If he admits that he saw her there, it'll look like he killed his wife for revenge.'

'That is what it looks like,' said Judy.

'Barnes got Parker out of circulation.' He closed his eyes. 'And Drummond was waiting for Sharon,' he went on. 'He probably followed her there. He certainly followed her when she left.'

'Why didn't he rape *her*?' Judy asked. 'He had plenty of opportunity. What was different about Sharon?'

Lloyd tipped the chair back, as his new improved scenario unfolded. 'Drummond followed her because he was going to *kill* her,' he said slowly. 'Not because he was going to rape her. That was the one thing he had no intention of doing to her.'

Judy frowned. 'Do you still think he knew her?' she asked.

Lloyd shook his head. 'He didn't know her at all,' he said. 'He had been offered a deal.'

214

'By us?' She shook her head as obstinately as ever.

'By them,' said Lloyd, careful to preserve the distinction between the good guys and the bad guys. 'By corrupt police officers. They are not "us" – not to me, they're not.'

Judy looked irritated. 'Nor to me,' she said. 'I just don't think—'

'He followed Sharon, waiting for his chance. But Melissa Whitworth came along and picked Sharon up, and he had to hang fire until she had driven away, leaving Sharon on her own.'

He was thinking aloud now. Thinking aloud, and tipping his chair back on its hind legs. Two dangerous things to do, but if he was any judge, it was worth the strong possibility of his achieving the feat of falling flat on his back and flat on his face at one and the same time.

'He killed her, then rode off on the bike. He *knew* he was going to be stopped by the police; it had all been arranged. He rode the way he did to give them something to stop him for, because the stop on the dual carriageway – at that particular time – was going to ensure that we believed him to be the one person who couldn't be the rapist.'

Judy's permanent frown grew deeper, and she shook her head.

'Meanwhile,' he said, 'someone in Malworth was making sure that Parker understood that he and his were vulnerable, covering his own traces with his impersonation, and at the same time eliminating Drummond from the rape inquiry.'

'Why?' she asked.

'In return for getting rid of Sharon, who had found out what was going on. It could be,' he added, 'that the quiet, shy, retiring Sharon was trying her hand at a spot of blackmail. She must have shown her hand some time ago for all this to be arranged.'

'Who?' said Judy. 'Who was she blackmailing?'

Lloyd didn't answer. 'What Drummond hadn't bargained for was being beaten up,' he said, taking the whole thing through to its logical conclusion. 'These two took the opportunity to mete out a little punishment for his misdeeds, since he wouldn't be having to answer for them anywhere else.' He rocked gently as he spoke. 'And what *they* hadn't bargained for was someone picking up the incident on the computer, connecting it with Sharon's murder, and bringing Drummond in for questioning.'

'Why did they put themselves in such a dodgy position in the first place?' she asked. 'If they had wanted to beat him up, they could have done it any time. Why choose a time when you know you've already reported stopping him? It's much more likely that they just lost their tempers, if you ask me.'

'Whatever,' said Lloyd airily. 'It all got very messy. Drummond told us about the car, and added his artistic touches about her taking her clothes off to make us believe that it was a man who was in the car with her. But he knew that it was a woman – and someone else knew who it had to have been.'

Judy looked unconvinced. 'You can't blame police corruption this time,' she said. 'You and I and her husband knew that it was Melissa Whitworth who picked her up,' she said. 'Last night. No one else knew. So – are you accusing me of being behind all this, or making a confession?'

He smiled.

'No one else knew,' she repeated.

'McDonald knew,' said Lloyd.

Judy sat back a little.

'McDonald,' said Lloyd. 'Who was "lost" for two hours on Friday night, when Bobbie Chalmers was attacked. Who has a very low opinion of women in general, something to prove, and access to any car that happens to be in the garage where he works. Mr Parry's car, for instance.' He sighed. 'And we're hanging on to McDonald until I've checked it out.'

She looked at him seriously. 'Do you really believe that police corruption is at the bottom of all this?' she asked.

Lloyd sighed. 'I don't want to,' he said. 'But someone is. Someone with access to confidential police files.'

'Not necessarily,' said Judy, thoughtfully. 'One of the victims could have told someone what happened to her. Someone who carried out a copy-cat attack.'

Lloyd gave her a look this time. 'At precisely the right moment to give Drummond an alibi?' he asked, getting up. 'Let's go.'

'Where?' she asked.

'Green's garage,' he said. 'To eliminate McDonald, with any luck. I don't want to believe he could do a thing like that.'

'I can't see anyone at all doing it,' she said, standing up, and tutting irritably as she picked at something on her skirt. 'Damn,' she said. 'I remember why I didn't just hang this up in the wardrobe, now.'

Lloyd never ceased to wonder at Judy's tidiness. He never hung things up in wardrobes until he ran out of surfaces to drape them over. But she knew *why* she hadn't.

'I meant to brush it,' she said. 'It's covered in hairs from Mel—' She stopped mid-word. 'Sharon met Melissa on Friday evening,' she said.

He didn't know at what, but his gun dog was pointing; Lloyd congratulated himself on getting Judy on to the inquiry, and convincing Andrews that she was needed on a permanent basis. He needed Judy at work just as much as he needed her in his life. All he had to do was fire off his blunderbuss imagination, and she would spot any shot that hit home.

'Identical . . . ' she said, her voice far away. 'It *was* all a performance.'

Lloyd stared at her. 'You're not seriously suggesting that Drummond does have an—' he began.

'She had shown her hand . . . of course she had. The money started going in bigger amounts.' She looked triumphantly at Lloyd. 'Do you have the forensic report on Sharon's clothes?' she asked.

'Not yet – they won't even have started on them yet, I don't think,' he said.

'No – the ones she was wearing when she was found. I haven't actually seen it.'

'Yes.' He went back to the desk, and dived into the pile of papers, extracting the report with the expertise of the truly orderless.

She practically grabbed it from him, and read through it, her eyes darting from line to line. Then she pushed some stuff over on his desk to make a tiny, tidy oasis, and started checking through her notebook, frowning now and then, then making definite ticks, her brow clearing as she sat back, nodding slowly.

'What?' he said, coming round to her side of the desk, looking over her shoulder at the undecipherable Judyscript, unable to bear the suspense any longer. 'What is it?'

She looked up. 'We were both wrong,' she said. 'And we were both right.'

He had never been in Malworth police station before. He had followed Lloyd and his girlfriend there yesterday, but until last night, he had never been inside. It wasn't like Stansfield. It was an old building, with heavy varnished doors and big door handles. Its cells were like something you'd see in an old film. He'd told them not to tell anyone he was here.

Now he was in an interview room, with a constable, waiting to be asked more questions. He hadn't said a word so far. They couldn't prove it was him, and he'd be walking out of here like he'd walked out of Stansfield. He'd ditched the knife when he heard people coming after him, and it wasn't against the law to wear a ski-mask. Two of Malworth's traffic division had beaten him up, so he would say they'd set him up if they tried to hold on to him. He'd be leaving here very soon.

The door opened and a heavy-set man came in, and sat down.

'I'm Detective Chief Inspector Merrill,' he said. 'You know why you're here, don't you, Mr Drummond?'

That was better. None of that Colin stuff. And Merrill didn't move around all the time. He just sat down like everyone else. Colin shrugged.

'A young girl was raped last night,' said Merrill. 'She was the fourth rape victim in recent weeks. What can you tell me about that, Mr Drummond?'

Colin looked uninterested. He was uninterested. It was the next one that interested him.

Mrs J. Hill. That was what it said on the name plate on the door. It had been exciting, planning it for a particular target, rather than the opportunist raid that he had finally carried out. Watching them until one strayed off alone was all right, but he still liked the idea of a planned strike. He'd be out of here in no time, and this time he would get her when she was really alone.

Or thought she was.

They stood outside Bobbie's flat in Malworth, in a tableau of determination and frustration, the drizzle seeping into everything, covering the cars in a glaze of tiny drops. Lloyd hadn't come up to the flat; Judy had pointed out that whatever else Bobbie Chalmers might be, she was still a very recent victim, and a man's presence might not help the interview.

What interview? Bobbie Chalmers had said nothing from the moment Judy had cautioned her. Nothing at all. Judy had tried everything she knew, but her success on her first visit had been the result of Bobbie's having to talk about what had happened to her to someone. Now, she was out of hospital, and Judy was beginning to realise what strength she must have when she had not just been brutally attacked.

She had shown Bobbie the search warrant, asked to look in the boot of the car, and gone down to tell Lloyd that she had got nowhere. Now he stood beside the car, watching as Bobbie Chalmers sorted out the keys on her ring.

Judy had hoped to keep the two incidents separate, but if it was the only way to get answers, then it was. 'I know who raped you, Bobbie,' she said.

There wasn't even a vestige of a pause as Bobbie selected the key. 'I wasn't raped,' she said.

It was the first time she had spoken, but Judy didn't feel the little surge of adrenalin that she usually did on producing a response, because she knew this one was going to get her no further. Even she didn't need her notebook; that was going to be the extent of Bobbie's statement.

'Open the car boot, please,' she said, with the resigned air of one who knew that there would be nothing in the car boot. But she had got the search warrant, so she might as well search.

Bobbie opened the boot; Judy looked through the oddments, and stood back. 'You can close it now,' she said.

Lloyd had been watching the performance with an air of what could only be described as amusement; Judy glared at him. They needed answers, and they hadn't been given any; needed evidence, and they hadn't found any. It wasn't funny. She closed her unused notebook. 'We may want to ask you more questions,' she said.

Bobbie nodded.

Lloyd walked up to her, and smiled. 'Well, thank you, Miss Chalmers,' he said, with his very best Welsh accent. 'Nice to have met you – oh, incidentally – Mr Parker can vouch for someone called . . . ' He made great play of finding a piece of paper, and his glasses, and what he was looking for. 'Ah, here it is. He can vouch for a man called Dennis Parry, can he?'

Dennis Parry had denied ever having heard of Jake Parker, of course.

Bobbie frowned slightly. 'You'd better ask him,' she said.

'We tried, but we can't contact him. He's not at home, and he's not in the office. Parry said you knew him, but obviously you don't – we'll just have to go ahead and charge him.'

Judy found Lloyd's facility for lying a little disturbing at times.

Bobbie looked flustered for the first time. 'What – what's he supposed to have done?' she asked.

Lloyd put on the expression that suggested he was worried that he might have put his foot in it. 'Look,' he said, transparently changing the subject. 'You shouldn't be standing out here in this weather. You get back inside, and keep warm.'

'He works for Jake,' Bobbie said uncomfortably, throwing the information over her shoulder as she turned back towards the doorway. 'Sort of.'

They got back into the car, with Lloyd being intolerably smug. 'You met your match at last,' he said. 'I knew you had to, one day.'

'Pity you didn't try your technique sooner,' said Judy.

'She isn't going to say a word about Friday night,' he said. 'Not to anyone.'

No. Judy sighed. She could see this whole thing going down as unsolved. And she was damned if that was going to happen.

'Jake Parker next,' said Lloyd. 'I think we'll take Finch with us, though.'

They wouldn't find anything there either, Judy thought gloomily. 'She'll be on the phone to him right now, warning him,' she said. 'I don't suppose your insistence that he was somehow uncontactable will stop her.'

Lloyd shrugged. 'Probably not,' he said. 'But if I know Mr Parker, he will have removed every shred of evidence already, so what difference does it make?'

None.

Jake tore up the last of the evidence that could point to him in any way at all, put it in the log-burning Aga, and watched it go up in flames. He'd hated that pretentious bloody thing when he'd moved in. Having to get logs out of their plastic covering in their wooden log bin like some gentleman farmer when he was in the middle of an industrial town. Having to work out how to boil an egg on it. Now, he loved every inch of its rustic body.

But he was hot. He peeled off his shirt, and went along to the bathroom, whistling softly to himself as he undressed. At least it wasn't a log-burning shower. He had just stepped into it when he heard the phone ring.

Oh, to hell. Let it ring.

He felt better once he had showered. As he turned off the water, he heard the banging at the door, and frowned. He knew who knocked like that, and it wasn't double-glazing salesmen.

'All right, all right!' he shouted. 'Don't knock the door down, boys. I'm coming.'

He plucked his bath-robe from the door, and wrapped it round himself as he walked along the corridor, and opened the door.

'Mr Parker,' said Lloyd.

'Mr Lloyd. And Detective Inspector Hill – perhaps I should get dressed, since there are ladies present.'

'This is Detective Sergeant Finch,' said Lloyd, as all three walked in past him.

'We've met,' said Jake. He wished he had put some clothes on. He felt very vulnerable. He closed the door, and walked into the living-room, where Finch was already opening drawers in a swift and professional search of the bureau. Too late, thought Jake, glancing at the warrant that Inspector Hill was holding up for his inspection.

'I thought it would be a different department who was dealing with this,' Jake said pleasantly. 'You won't find anything, Sergeant Finch,' he added. 'I wasn't involved.' He smiled. 'But I suppose you have to look,' he said.

220

'Your offices are also being searched,' said Lloyd.

Jake nodded. 'I thought they would be,' he said. That was why he had gone in on Saturday morning and destroyed anything and everything that might connect him with the scam. He had covered his traces. He knew how the police worked.

And because he did, he was just a little worried. Lloyd and his lady inspector were on the murder inquiry.

'It would be a month ago, would it?' said Lloyd. 'When Sharon came to you and told you what she had discovered?'

Jake took a cigarette from a box on the drinks table, and lit it with the heavy table-lighter. He sat on the sofa. 'No,' he said. 'It was Friday. Just before the opening do.'

Finch had moved on to the bookcase, pulling out books, holding them by their covers, shaking the pages.

'Then too,' said Lloyd. 'But I rather think her first visit was about a month ago. And she told you that she knew what you and Evans were up to.'

Jake still smiled, and poured himself some whisky. Guess-work. This was guess-work. He had taken care of everything – they could guess till they turned green, they couldn't prove a thing.

The inspector had her notebook out again. My – she had been busy since yesterday afternoon.

'She came to you first, rather than go straight to the police,' said Lloyd. 'Blackmail?' He raised his eyebrows in a query. 'Perhaps,' he went on. 'But from what I've heard of her, I think not. You had been good to her – you had got her the job with Evans when she had to move back to Stansfield. She didn't want to make trouble for you if she could avoid it.'

Jake drew smoke deep into his lungs, and released it in a blue stream. 'Sorry,' he said. 'The first I knew about it was Friday.'

Lloyd sat down, while the industrious Finch began on the hi-fi cabinet, with its LPs and cassettes and videos and compact discs. He'd be there all day. And he would find nothing. Jake reached across to the ashtray, but the ash fell from his cigarette on to the flowered upholstery. Shame. 'If you don't mind, Mr Lloyd, I'm a busy man. I should be at work – so perhaps you'd come to the point.'

'Mrs Melissa Whitworth was murdered last night,' said Lloyd.

'Simon Whitworth's wife?' asked Jake.

'The very same,' said Lloyd.

'Well,' said Jake. 'Still waters and all that. I mean, what the hell made him do a thing like that?'

'We don't think he did. Do you know anyone called Dennis Parry?'

'Parry . . . Parry . . . ?' Jake frowned. 'No,' he said.

'That's odd,' said Inspector Hill. 'Bobbie says he works for you – on a sort of unofficial, untaxed, uninsured basis, I suppose. But he works for you, all the same.'

Jake took another drink. It wasn't a sip. More a gulp. He'd have to watch that. He smiled at her. 'Old habits,' he said. 'Deny everything. Yeah, all right – he works for me. What's he done?'

'His car was outside the Whitworths' house last night,' said Lloyd.

'Yeah? Didn't know he knew them.' Finch should get some sort of medal for sheer persistence, Jake thought, as he watched him. He felt almost sorry for him, as he worked his way through the owner's record collection. 'You should be talking to Dennis, in that case,' he said. 'Not me.'

'We have. His memory seems to be as faulty as yours – he couldn't recall your name either.'

Good old Dennis. 'So what was he doing at Whitworth's place?' asked Jake.

'Oh, he wasn't. He was somewhere else with a dozen witnesses – almost as though he knew he might need them. And he can't think who might have borrowed his car.'

Jake smiled. 'And how can I help?' he asked.

'We'll come to that,' said Lloyd. 'In the meantime, I would like to ask you some questions concerning the murder of Sharon Smith. You are not obliged to say anything, but if you do, anything you do say may be given in evidence.'

Jake smiled. 'Do you think I had something to do with it?' he asked.

'I think you did it, Mr Parker,' said Lloyd.

'I was in one of your own cells when Sharon was murdered – ask him.' He pointed at Finch, who had stood up from his task, and dusted himself off.

'Nothing, sir,' Finch said.

'No. I thought not,' said Lloyd. 'It was worth a try.'

'Shall I . . . ?' Finch nodded in the general direction of the rest of the house.

'No,' said Lloyd. 'I'm sure Mr Parker has destroyed anything and everything which connects him with the fraud.'

Jake was very glad to hear Lloyd's decision, but less than happy with their response to what he had just said. They couldn't go accusing him of murder, and then ignore him when he pointed out that they had been holding him at the time.

'I said I was in your cells,' he repeated.

'No,' said Inspector Hill. 'You weren't.'

Jake turned to face her.

'You were in our cells when Bobbie was raped,' she said. 'But not when Sharon was murdered.'

He began to breath too quickly, too shallowly, and forced himself to slow down, and think. He mustn't let what happened to Bobbie throw him. That's why she had mentioned it, to make him lose his concentration. They were trying to trick him. They had talked to Bobbie; she'd told them about Dennis. But she had no reason to think that she shouldn't tell them about Dennis. She wouldn't have told them anything else, he knew that.

He got up slowly, and poured himself another drink. Slow down. Slow down, Jake. Don't let them panic you. 'Your blokes carted me off in a van when the match was abandoned,' he said. 'Sharon was still alive then. So – she died after I was released, is that it?'

Inspector Hill shook her head. 'She died about a quarter of an hour after she left the office,' she said. 'She died the moment she kept her appointment with you. Because she had threatened your financial future.'

Take it easy, Jake, take it easy. Sit down. They know, but they need proof, and that they haven't got. Not now. He sat down, and took a long, calming draw on the cigarette. 'Even if you were right that I was involved in this fraud – which you're not – why would I kill her? It's because she's dead that you know about the fraud at all.'

'We know about it because you told us, Mr Parker,' said Lloyd. 'And you told us because your girlfriend was raped, and your hand was forced.'

Jake closed his eyes. He'd never forgive himself for letting Bobbie in for that. And they had no right to keep bringing it up like that.

'Sharon left the office, and walked straight up Byford Road to the football ground,' the inspector went on. 'That would take her twenty minutes at the most – the weather was quite clear then. She went to where she had arranged to meet you. The changing rooms. You were waiting for her. You killed her, you removed her outer clothes, and you got her into a brand-new leisure suit as best you could. You left the newspaper cutting in her skirt, and the key to the changing rooms in her bag.'

Jake laughed. 'You'd have a hell of a time taking that to court,' he said. 'Considering she was at the match two hours after that.'

Inspector Hill carried on. 'Meanwhile, Bobbie Chalmers had made another appointment. To meet Mrs Whitworth. At the football ground. And just after six, she went into the superstore and bought an exactly similar leisure suit.'

223

He had got rid of that. Bobbie had locked it in the boot, and he had retrieved it yesterday morning, once he'd picked up her keys. It had gone straight into the Aga. It was gone. There was no evidence.

Remember that, Jake, he told himself, in the face of the inspector's brown gaze. No evidence. No proof.

No case to answer.

Fourteen

They had just come in and told Mac he could go. They had spent hours accusing him of murdering Melissa, and then, calm as you like, someone had come and told him he could go now. Thanked him for his co-operation.

Downstairs, his landlady was hoovering. Next, she would be washing. It was Monday. He had met Melissa on Friday night, if you didn't count the introduction at the paper, and he didn't. She hadn't even remembered meeting him.

He had found her on Friday, and lost her by Monday. But he had lost her anyway. He had never had her. He picked up the packet of cigarettes the constable had finally obtained for him – making him cough up the money for them – and shook it, but he had smoked them all.

He wondered what had happened, that they had let him go. Nothing had changed from his point of view. He was still the man who had found two bodies in four days, and instead of sympathy all he had got was suspicion and questions. And no explanation.

The paper kept ringing up, trying to speak to him, but he had told his landlady he wasn't speaking to anyone, and she was better than a pit bull terrier if you wanted to discourage someone. He wasn't going to talk to them about what had happened. He still couldn't believe it himself. Didn't want to believe it.

He needed cigarettes. He heaved himself off the bed, and pulled on his jacket. He could go to that pub across the road from the police station, he thought. That was where the court reporter hung out, because he picked up bits of information from the police who would go in there when they came off duty. He might find out what had happened. Why it had happened.

He didn't suppose he would ever know why it had happened to him.

Lloyd and Finch kept a close eye on Parker as Judy told him what they had pieced together. Lloyd was watching for his emotional reactions, in the hope of trapping him into an admission. Finch was watching for his physical reactions; Parker was handy with his fists, and Judy was likely to make him very angry.

'Bobbie kept the appointment with Melissa Whitworth, calling herself Sharon Smith,' said Judy. 'She said all the things that you had told her to say. That there had been a possessive boyfriend – that was to make it easier to believe that you had started a fight just because she was speaking to another man. That Whitworth sometimes hated her, so that he would be a candidate. And of course, the revelation itself would give Mrs Whitworth a motive. The more the merrier. Anything to muddy the waters.'

Parker stayed silent.

Lloyd felt less than confident of success. It was obvious that Bobbie had learned her technique from Parker, as he listened without any visible reaction to what Judy was saying. The only emotion he had shown at all was when Judy mentioned the rape, and he had got that under control. If he didn't condemn himself, they were done for.

They needed proof. So far, they hadn't even found anything to connect him to the fraud, never mind the murders. And Bobbie Chalmers would obviously go to her grave without telling anyone. She hadn't even slipped up after she had been raped; this morning she had denied it had ever happened, and would clearly continue to do so.

'Bobbie went into the ground when the interview was finished,' Judy continued. 'You probably gave her some sort of signal from the balcony, to get the timing right. You made sure Lionel Evans was there too, and you told him Sharon was on to you. That gave him a motive too. Then you said she was down on the terraces, but Evans didn't see Sharon – only you. And you didn't invite Evans to come with you to talk to her. You went down, and she asked Barnes if he had the right time. You started a fight in full view of the police, and you hit a policeman to make certain you were arrested.'

Parker finished his drink, and looked unconcerned.

'So as far as we knew, Sharon was alive and well when you were taken away by the police, and dead before you were released. Then you set about making it look to Lionel Evans as though her death was a body blow to your financial operations. But of course, it wasn't her death that meant you had to get out, it was the fact that she had found out. You had already made certain over the previous month that as much money as possible would be available for your departure.'

Parker smiled. 'It's a nice story,' he said. 'Do you have any proof?'

No, thought Lloyd. But you keep talking, Jake. Then we'll get somewhere.

'And last night,' Judy carried on, in her clear, no-nonsense voice, 'you killed Mrs Whitworth. Who was going to be next? Barnes? He's got police protection now, Mr Parker.'

There was a silence after Judy had finished speaking, and Lloyd prayed that Finch had learned not to break it.

'Are you serious?' Parker asked, at last.

'Yes,' said Lloyd.

'You're arresting me for murder on that rigmarole?'

'We have evidence,' said Judy.

Parker shook his head, and got himself another drink. It was early to be drinking; that was good, thought Lloyd. And Judy's bald statement was bothering Parker. She wouldn't elaborate, and if he was any judge . . .

'What sort of evidence?' asked Parker.

'We can prove that Sharon Smith was never in Melissa Whitworth's car,' Judy said.

'How? The woman's dead.'

'Cat hairs,' she said.

Parker turned, the bottle in his hand. 'What?' he said.

Judy gave him a little smile. 'Cat hairs,' she repeated.

Lloyd looked relaxed, but his soul was on the edge of his seat.

'There is no way that anyone could possibly have been sitting in the passenger seat of Melissa Whitworth's car for half an hour without getting covered in cat hairs,' Judy said. 'She took her cat to the vet on Friday afternoon, and the seat was still thick with the things the next day. I checked the forensic report.' She shook her head. 'No cat hairs on the suit that Sharon was wearing. Not even one.'

Parker turned back and poured his drink. 'Is that right?' he said. 'Fancy. But that only proves that it wasn't Sharon Smith who gave the interview to the paper,' he said, and picked up his drink and sat down again. 'Not that Bobbie or anyone else did.'

They knew that. They had rather been counting on the fact that Parker wouldn't think of it in the stress of the moment. But apart from the drinking, Parker was showing very little sign of stress.

'No,' Judy said evenly. 'That's true. But we have an eyewitness in Bobbie's case.'

Last-ditch stuff, thought Lloyd. If the cat hairs hadn't thrown him, this wouldn't.

Parker took a sip of whisky. 'What sort of an eye witness?' he asked. 'Barnes? That would get thrown out at the first hearing. He saw a woman for about ten seconds in the dark, in the fog. So

227

he says he doesn't think it was Sharon Smith – so what? All he'd have to go on would be a photograph.' He smiled. 'And anyway, it was Sharon, as I keep telling you.'

'Not Barnes,' said Judy.

Lloyd was as surprised as Parker.

'We have another witness. He was arrested last night. A witness who followed Bobbie out of the ground, who saw her being picked up by Melissa Whitworth, and being driven back to where she'd come from. Who watched her get out of the car again, and start walking back down Byford Road to her own car, which I imagine was parked on the road behind the old post office. Who watched her change back into her own clothes, waited for her to close the boot and then overpowered her and raped her repeatedly. He'll want that taken into consideration, Mr Parker.'

The blood drained from Parker's face, and he took out another cigarette, reaching over for the lighter as he got himself under control again.

'Not Bobbie,' he said, with difficulty. 'Some other poor kid, maybe. But Bobbie wasn't there. She was in Malworth. Ask her. Ask her about any of this rubbish. She won't confirm it.'

Lloyd knew that was all too true. Judy had tried to rattle him, and had failed.

'No,' she agreed. 'She's saying nothing, Mr Parker. But she can be identified. And it would make a change, wouldn't it? The rapist walking down a line of women, picking out his victim? Bobbie would love that, wouldn't she?'

Parker's mouth fell open, and his eyes grew wide with horror.

'Of course, you could save us some time, and save Bobbie the trauma.'

Parker stared at her.

'Don't think I wouldn't do it, Mr Parker,' she said, her voice like ice.

He leapt to his feet. 'But . . . it – it would *kill* her! She – she can't even bear me to go near her! You can't let that bastard—' Parker was deathly pale.

'She'd do it, too, wouldn't she?' Judy went on. 'In the hope that he didn't recognise her. She'd do it. For you. Are you worth it, I wonder?'

Parker shook his head. 'Bobbie didn't break any laws,' he said. 'Leave her out of this, and I'll make a statement. Everything. The scam – Sharon, everything. But you have to promise to leave Bobbie alone.'

'She impersonated Sharon Smith while you murdered her,' Judy said. 'That makes her a murderer too. We can't leave her alone.'

'No,' said Parker, his voice agonised. 'No. She didn't know why she was doing it. I told her Whitworth had cheated me. I said I was trying to make trouble for him. I swear to God that's all she thought she was doing! She'd never have done it if she'd known – you've got to believe me! She knew I was in trouble about money, that's all – I told her she mustn't say she'd been anywhere near the ground. That's why she said the rape happened in Malworth.'

He appealed to Lloyd, having given up on Judy. 'Leave Bobbie out of it,' he pleaded. 'I'll tell you everything if you promise to leave Bobbie alone.'

Lloyd took a deep breath, and thought about it. He believed Parker, though it might not be too easy to convince other people. But he could try. 'All right,' he said. 'As far is I'm able.'

Parker let out a huge sigh of relief, and sat down again, heavily.

'Sharon wanted me to give the money back. She guessed we were going to make it look like Whitworth's doing, and she didn't want him to know anything about it. Three million pounds, and she wanted me to give it back! I tried to explain, but she wouldn't listen.'

Lloyd frowned. 'Explain what?' he asked.

'That it was *Evans* who would carry the can, not Whitworth! Only an idiot like Evans would ever think Whitworth could really be put in the frame. I conned Evans into believing he could get away with it, and taking Whitworth on was part of the con. That's all.'

'All,' repeated Lloyd. It sounded like quite enough to him.

'Evans was greedy,' Parker said. 'Like all the others. You can always con greedy people – not one of these investors checked that I could really deliver what I was promising, because all they could see was a fast buck. I just had to spend enough to make it look like something was happening, and they were throwing money at me.' He sighed. 'But maybe I got greedy too,' he said. 'I should have got out sooner.'

Lloyd raised his eyebrows at the rare moment of honesty.

'But Sharon wouldn't budge. She didn't want her boyfriend finding out that he was just window-dressing, not if he didn't have to.

'A month, she said. Or she would tell Whitworth, and they'd go to the police. Ungrateful little bitch. I just wanted to . . . ' He closed his eyes. 'I thought of it when I saw that advertisement in the paper,' he said. 'It seemed a fair bet that it would be Whitworth's wife who was writing the article – I rang the number, got her answering machine, and . . .' He shrugged. 'To start with, it was just a way of giving you more suspects,' he said. 'But then I saw its potential.'

'And the whole thing was arranged for Sharon's benefit?' asked Lloyd. 'The opening, the match – everything?'

Jake nodded. 'I arranged it for a Friday, because that way the Saturday paper would only have the bare details. You wouldn't have released her name or photograph. I'd have more time that way.'

Parker's years of street-violence had not been frittered away, Lloyd thought.

'I told Sharon I was prepared to talk about it, and to meet me at the ground before six-thirty. And I spun Bobbie a tale,' he went on. 'She agreed to do it – but I swear to God she didn't know why. She was never going to know – she was supposed to leave next morning,' he said. 'Dennis was taking her to the ferry. She'd have been abroad – she would never have known what had happened.'

Lloyd frowned. 'What about you?' he asked.

'I was going to get my money on the Monday morning, and I'd have been away by the time the paper got Sharon's photograph, and Whitworth's wife blew the whistle.' He looked at Judy again then, his eyes bleak. 'Bobbie didn't know what to do when Whitworth's wife pulled up beside her,' he said. 'She thought going back to the ground was the best thing. But the place was shut down – so she made some rude comments and got herself thrown out of the car.' He gave a long, shuddering sigh. 'She thought she was safe then,' he said. 'But that bastard got her.'

Judy looked away from him as he continued

'And she was in hospital. She couldn't leave. I had to kill Whitworth's wife before she saw Sharon photograph. You knew Bobbie! It would take you thirty seconds to put two and two together. I had to get her out of the way.'

If they stayed here much longer they'd be agreeing with him that murdering two women was an eminently reasonable way out of one's problems, Lloyd thought, and stood up. 'James Edward Parker, I am arresting you for the murder—'

Parker got to his feet slowly, waving away the caution. 'I have to get some clothes on,' he mumbled.

'Finch,' said Lloyd. 'Go with him.'

When they had left the room, Judy looked up from her notebook. 'I'm not very proud of that,' she said.

'It worked,' said Lloyd, with a shrug.

'I'm not sure you understand the seriousness of your situation, Mr Drummond,' said Merrill.

Colin still didn't speak.

'When you were in custody on Saturday, you permitted a doctor to carry out a medical examination, during which you agreed that a blood test could be done,' said Merrill, slowly and carefully.

Colin shrugged again.

'Do you ever read the papers, Mr Drummond?' he asked. 'Or watch the news?'

He read motorbike magazines. Nothing else. Nothing else was worth reading. Above the bike magazines in the newsagents, there were these girlie ones. A waste of money. They were ten a penny on the street – why look at pictures of them in magazines when you could have one any time you liked? He'd sooner look at a 750cc any day. You didn't see them every day. And he watched videos mostly.

'Have you ever heard of genetic fingerprinting?' asked Merrill.

Colin raised his eyebrows a little. Fingerprints. They were trying to catch him out. They were trying to make him say that they couldn't have found his fingerprints, because he wore gloves. Merrill must think he was stupid.

'It's a sort of extra-special blood test,' said Merrill. 'It can distinguish one person from another, just like fingerprints can, but you get the match from blood, or skin, or hair – or semen. You know what that is, do you, Mr Drummond?'

Colin could get annoyed with this. He didn't answer. If Merrill wanted to believe he was stupid, let him. Lloyd knew he wasn't stupid. And Lloyd's girlfriend would know he wasn't stupid, too. Soon.

'I assume you do,' he said. 'And with violent crime – with rape especially – that means it might as well *be* a fingerprint.' He leant forward a little. 'We get the samples from the victims,' he said, 'and we take blood tests from possible suspects, and look for a match. They tested a whole town once before they got who they were looking for. They got him in the end, though. But we were lucky – we didn't have to do that – you fell into our laps, as it were.'

Colin's eyes grew thoughtful. It sounded as though they weren't going to let him go.

'It's a legal means of identification, Mr Drummond. And really, it's better than a fingerprint. You might touch something at the scene of a crime in all innocence. But there's no inadvertent way to leave a genetic fingerprint, and no way that this wasn't out and out rape. If you raped these women, we can prove it,' he said. 'Do you want to make a statement?'

231

Colin nodded. In a way, he didn't mind. He wanted people to know what he'd done. He'd like to tell them he'd done five of them, not just four. But the one he did on Friday was dead; they'd say he'd killed her, and he hadn't.

He'd leave that one out.

Jake dressed slowly, with Finch chivvying him. He opened the shirt drawer, and took out a shirt, gathering up the pistol at the same time, slipping it in his pocket, very grateful to Lloyd for not continuing the search for incriminating evidence of his involvement in the fraud.

He opened the wardrobe, and chose one of his specially imported Chinese silk ties from the rack.

'I see you didn't waste any of those beauties on your victims,' said Finch drily.

Jake looked at himself in the mirror, carefully knotting the tie, and spoke to Finch's reflection. 'Too identifiable,' he said. 'I bought one at a chain-store. I hadn't done that for ten years – you know that? And then before I knew it, I had to buy another for Mrs Whitworth. Thank God for Sunday trading, eh?' He smiled at his own joke, though he didn't feel at all like smiling.

'Ready?' said Finch impatiently.

'Ready,' said Jake, turning and drawing out the gun. 'Keep your hands where I can see them,' he said. 'And turn round.'

'Don't be stupid, Parker,' Finch said, raising his hands, his eyes wide with apprehension before he reluctantly turned his back on him.

'Now – can you feel that?' Jake asked, touching the back of Finch's neck with the gun.

'Yes.'

'The moment you can't feel it, you're dead. Walk very slowly out of the room,' said Jake.

Lloyd was in the hallway; he froze when he saw Finch emerge.

'Tell her to come out here where I can see her,' said Jake. 'Slowly, with her hands up. And yours.'

Lloyd never took his eyes off him as he relayed the message, his voice unnaturally calm.

She appeared in the doorway, closing her eyes for a second, as though the situation might have altered when she opened them again. But it hadn't.

Jake controlled his breathing, and his tendency to shake, before he spoke. 'We're leaving here. If you want to keep him alive, you won't try to stop us. Out,' he said to Finch.

'Parker – where is this going to get you?' Lloyd asked.

'You don't think I went into this without making sure I could disappear? You would have been looking for me once the photograph went to the paper. So I can vanish, and I will. Move,' he said, pushing Finch in the back, making him stumble. 'Stop!' he shouted, as they lost contact. He released the safety catch; Finch was much more careful as they made slow progress past a grim-faced Lloyd and a pale, frightened Inspector Hill. Jake wished it was her he had at the end of the pistol.

He had to get Bobbie, then get far enough away to dump Finch, and get out of this. There was no way he was going to prison for years. No way he was leaving Bobbie to them.

'I have to open the door,' said Finch. 'Look – it's locked. I need to use both hands, and I might lose contact – I don't want you shooting me just because I was trying to open the—'

Jake doubled over in the middle of the explanation as Finch's elbow suddenly thrust into his solar plexus, and he felt the gun slip from his grasp, saw it kicked out of his reach. Someone pulled his hands behind his back and handcuffed him.

'It's over, Jake,' said Finch, scooping up the gun, making it safe, handing it to the inspector.

Jake, coughing and spluttering, was lifted to his feet by the two men. He shouldn't have had the other drink. It had slowed his reactions. Had he jeopardised his deal? He looked at Lloyd, and decided that he trusted him. 'You promised,' he said.

Lloyd nodded. 'I promised.'

It was the fraud squad now, all right. Turning the office upside down, carting off boxes and boxes of files and accounts and computer discs.

Lionel's father and grandfather would be turning in their graves, of course. And he supposed it was a dreadfully ignominious end to almost a hundred years of exemplary legal practice.

But he was very, very glad that it was over.

Simon Whitworth got out of the police car and stared at the mean little house, standing on its own, with no neighbours. They had asked if there was someone they could get to be with him, but he had said no. He wasn't staying. He would go home. Back to his mum and dad, like a child. He needed his mum and dad. But he didn't want them coming here. Not here.

They'd have liked Sharon. Some of the terrible weight that had been pressing him into the ground had been lifted when they had told him what had really happened. Sharon had just been Sharon. She had been exactly what he thought she was. She had never met

Melissa, never said those things. She had loved him. Too much to tell him what she had discovered, because then he would have known why he had been taken on by Evans, and she had known that that would have hurt him. That was why she'd gone to Parker instead of to the police. Because of him. And the weight had come pressing down again, harder than ever.

And Melissa. She had been protecting him, too. Was that all he could inspire? He had left her alone, and Parker had come and snuffed her out too. All because of him. No Melissa. No Sharon. He didn't think he could get his mind round that. His case was already packed, and there was nothing else he wanted from this place. He opened the door.

Robeson yelled indignantly that he hadn't been fed since yesterday, and Simon went into the kitchen, Robeson weaving through his legs. He spooned catfood on to a plate, then went up to get his suitcase. He dragged it out from under the bed, and threw a few more things into it. He couldn't think about what he was going to do. He didn't know if he would ever be able to do anything again. He couldn't think about inquests and funerals and trials. He was going home, that was all he knew.

Downstairs, he could hear the rattle of Robeson's disc on the plate as he cleaned it. Simon went out, leaving the door open, and went to the car, throwing the case in the back. He looked back at the house. He had to do something with the cat. He could take him with him, but he didn't know if he would come. Look what happened to him last time.

'Robeson,' he called. 'Here, puss.' He opened the passenger door; Robeson ran down the path and jumped on to the passenger seat, curling up. Simon patted him. Robeson had, after all, proved that he hadn't killed anyone.

But they had died because of him. And Robeson couldn't make that better.

Judy had taken a statement from Drummond; now that he knew that his fourth victim had not been murdered, he was pleased to give details. He had raped Bobbie Chalmers, then driven off afterwards, as he always did, with the bike unlit. He had heard the police siren, and known that they would catch him, so he had jettisoned the mask and the knife.

He had been quite upset about that; he had been unable to get another flick-knife, and had had to make do last night with a kitchen knife. She, he had informed her, had been within an ace of being his fifth victim, and he made her a promise that she would be his sixth.

She drove back to Stansfield, thinking about the girl who had been raped in her stead, thinking about the total lack of remorse on the young, handsome face as he had told her what he had done, what he had intended doing to her, if Lloyd hadn't changed his mind.

Barstow was packing up the personal stuff in his office, which consisted of a tiny space partitioned off from the CID room; he wasn't going until the end of the week, but Judy had moved in with him already, and elbow-room was severely limited. She sat down at the quarter of a table which she had been allocated, and began the mountain of paperwork that the morning had produced.

'Two results,' said Barstow, encouragingly. 'Good ones, at that.'

Judy tried to smile, but she had never felt less like doing so. Parker's greed had ruined too many lives to feel any uplift about his arrest.

Barstow went out, and Lloyd came in about two minutes later, closing the door.

'Parker is being as good as his word,' he said. 'A full confession. It seems he killed her in the changing rooms, left her there, then simply collected her once Whitworth had driven him back to the ground, and left her where Mad Mac found her.' He shook his head. 'Bobbie Chalmers had slipped the receipt for the clothes under Barnes' seat – Parker picked it up and put it in Sharon's bag. So I don't think I can keep my promise,' he added, with a shrug. 'She was an accessory at the very least.'

'You just promised to do your best,' said Judy, dully. 'You've done that.'

'Are you OK?' he asked.

She nodded.

He contrived somehow to find a space on the overcrowded table to perch. 'No, you're not,' he said.

She looked up at him. 'That note,' she said. 'The one that was left on the car?' She gave a short sigh. 'It said – in effect – that I had lost two good men their jobs. And I have, haven't I? Drummond deserved a lot worse than they gave him.'

Lloyd looked at her for a long time before he said anything. 'They lost their own jobs,' he said quietly, when he did speak. 'The moment they took the law into their own hands. They have no right to wear a police uniform, and you have no right to condone what they did.'

God, he could be a pain sometimes. 'Have you read this?' she asked, pushing the statement over to him.

'No. And I don't care what it says. If you want the right to beat someone you stop in the street, go and live somewhere where people disappear because they have the wrong politics, where society is frightened of its police. Because that's what you're advocating, if you think anyone deserves to be abused by people in authority.'

He was angrier than Judy had ever seen him. He lost his temper, lost his patience with her, all the time. But he had never been this angry with her.

'I was going to be next,' she said in her own defence. 'That girl last night was raped because I wasn't.'

'I *know* you were!' he shouted. 'Merrill told me. And that girl was raped because these two broke the rules. I'm not pretending I don't bend them and stretch them – everyone does sometimes. But you don't do what they do. So don't let me hear you saying that he deserved it – what he deserved was to be safely in custody, where he would have been if they had been doing their jobs – not lying in wait for you, not raping anyone!'

Finch knocked and came in. 'I wondered if anyone would like to go for a drink,' he said.

Lloyd looked at him. 'Now that it's just the three of us,' he said, still angry, 'I have to say that that was a very stupid thing to do.'

'Yes, sir,' said Finch.

'If someone is holding a gun on you, you do what he says,' said Lloyd. 'The safety catch was off – you could have had your head blown off!'

'Sir,' said Finch. 'But it's just that if there is one thing that worries me more than a villain with a gun, it's a cop with a gun. And I wasn't about to become his hostage for bloody hours, with guys in bullet-proof vests waiting to take a pot-shot at him! I did it because I thought I was going to have my head blown off if I didn't! Sir,' he added, as an afterthought.

Lloyd sighed. 'Oh, what the hell,' he said. 'Yes – let's go for a drink.'

'I don't feel much like celebrating,' said Judy.

'No,' said Finch. 'Neither do I, really. But I thought we could unwind a bit.'

Judy conceded that unwinding might be a very good idea, and they walked from the station to the pub on the corner. Finch walked beside her; Lloyd walked a little way behind them.

'Would you have put Bobbie Chalmers in a line-up?' Finch asked.

Judy had watched Parker, correctly gauged his feelings for Bobbie, and then used them against him. That was enough ruthlessness for one day. She shook her head.

'I would,' said the voice from the rear.

They went into the pub, and Finch tapped Lloyd's elbow, nodding over to the bar, where Gil McDonald sat staring into space, his hand round a glass. He looked up when he felt himself being watched, and made his unsmiling way to where they were claiming a table.

'Fruit juice,' he said, putting the glass of orange down firmly on their table.

Lloyd smiled. 'Good,' he said.

Mac lit a cigarette. 'Are you going to charge me with anything?' he asked.

Lloyd frowned. 'Like what?' he asked.

'I wiped that tape – from the rumours flying round this place, it sounds like it could have been evidence.'

'It could have been,' said Lloyd, sitting down beside Judy. 'But thanks to the inspector, we won't be needing it.' He looked up at Mac. 'I am really very sorry about Mrs Whitworth,' he said.

Mac nodded. 'So am I,' he said. 'But – well, I don't think she would think much of me if I went to pieces now.' He turned to Judy. 'If you're still interested in a test drive, you won't be seeing me,' he said. 'I'm moving on.'

Judy managed a smile. 'Good luck,' she said.

Mac went off; Finch went to get the drinks, and Judy caught Lloyd's hand under the table. 'Sorry,' she whispered.

Lloyd shook his head. 'I just keep thinking what if I'd just gone home? It would have been you that—'

He broke off as Finch came back, a drink in each hand.

'I know you're right about guns, sir,' he said. 'But I just saw his attention wander, and took my chance.'

Lloyd took his drink. 'Let's forget it,' he said.

Finch smiled, and gave Judy her wine. 'You were wrong about one thing, though,' he said.

Lloyd squeezed Judy's hand, then let it go. 'I'm never wrong,' he said, taking a deep draught of beer.

'He's never wrong,' said Judy.

'You were this time,' said Finch, reaching back to the bar to get his own drink, and sitting down. 'I'd *far* sooner have had another lecture on apostrophes.'

Judy didn't know why Lloyd was laughing, but the winding-down process was working. She liked Finch, and she was back at Stansfield, which was what she had wanted ever since the transfer to Malworth. It was the last thing that Lloyd wanted, really; he could have blocked it, and he hadn't. But then he was the unselfish one.

One of them had to be.